REDEEMED

SINS OF OUR ANCESTORS, BOOK THREE

BRIDGET E. BAKER

Purple
Puppy
Publishing

For Isadora Elizabeth, my darling daughter
May you ever be as brave as Ruby and know that you are a
daughter of God.

CHAPTER 1

I watch through thick glass while my biological father's body burns into ash.

No tears well up in my eyes. No sorrow swells in my heart. I didn't cry when my mother shot him, either. It probably means I'm broken inside. Although, to be fair to myself, he was a narcissistic, abusive sociopath whom I didn't know existed until last month.

Even so, his half a million subjects loved him fanatically.

"I hope you've prepared something appropriate to say at his funeral tomorrow," Josephine Solomon says. In spite of being the one who shot him, my mom harbors mixed feelings.

"How's this?" I ask. "David Solomon is dead. I'm really hoping he won't haunt my nightmares any more, now that I've watched the flames incinerate his body into powder. I'm planning to dump the ashes into the sewage processing plant where they'll fit in with the other filth. Succinct enough, you think?"

Josephine frowns. "He was a great man in many ways, you know."

I shake my head. "You keep saying that, but I haven't seen much evidence."

"The point," she says, "is that as the new queen of World Peace Now, you'll need his popularity to transfer to your rule. Things will go much easier for you if the people like you half as much as they loved him."

I snort. "No one needs to like me. They only need to obey."

"Spoken like someone who's never ruled a day in her life."

I grit my teeth. "I don't want to be a queen at all. You wouldn't know this since we just met, but I never played princess growing up. I didn't have make believe crowns, and I freaking hate dresses, with or without princess puffs."

In fact I'd love to walk away from all of this. The only thing I'm dreading more than David Solomon's funeral is my coronation the following morning. I'd gladly run and never return to World Peace Now (usually called WPN), or Galveston ever again.

Unfortunately if I leave, the new leaders of WPN will carry out my biological father's plan to massacre the hundred thousand or so people infected with the Tercera virus. My delightful bio father, the late great monarch, planned to "cleanse" the earth of the plague that almost destroyed humanity more than a decade ago. He believed killing the infected kids, who were struggling to survive on their own, was a small price to pay to ensure the bright future of his half a million subjects.

Actually, he told me killing them was *mercy* on his part. He said God infected people to punish them for their sins. As for the infection of children, well, they were paying for the sins of their parents, and he was dispensing God's mercy by killing them and ending that just suffering.

See? Sociopath.

"If you really can't think of anything to say, I can write something for you," Josephine says.

"Yes," I say. "That's a good plan, but I'm not much of a public speaker. Maybe keep it short."

Behind me, Wesley chokes on a laugh.

I scowl at him over my shoulder. "Why's that funny?"

"I've heard you speak in public, is all," Wesley says.

"I'll keep that in mind," Josephine says. "Since I now have two speeches to prepare, I'd better get started. I do expect you to write your own coronation address." After dropping that bombshell, my mother walks down the hall and turns the corner toward the exit.

I turn to race after her and argue, but I'm met by a tall man with blonde hair and sparkling bright blue eyes. I pull up short, taking in the standard issue gray uniform of the palace guard. Two gold stripes run down each shoulder, which tells me he's near the top of the pecking order. He approaches and salutes.

Once I look at his face, I recognize Adam, the first WPN guard I met when Sam and I were caught looking for the cure. He breezes past the four guards on duty without even acknowledging them, reinforcing my impression that he now holds a reasonably high rank. He stands a few inches taller than Wesley, which puts him about the same height as my boyfriend Sam. His shiny, short hair is combed sideways, not a single strand out of place, and his uniform accentuates his broad shoulders and deep tan. He probably surfs whenever he's off duty. Galveston might have a few things to recommend it when compared to Port Gibson, the perks of beach living among them.

Stuff like that might matter if I were thinking of staying, which I'm not.

He straightens and says, "Your escort's ready, your Highness."

Sam may be the hottest guy I've ever seen, but this guy's face is nearly as pretty. I assume a gaggle of girls probably follow him around too, like they always did Sam back home. "I'm sorry, my escort where?"

"To the bridge, Your Highness."

"Right, an escort intended to keep me safe while I drive a mile out onto a bridge."

Adam frowns. "A bridge currently under attack by infected hostiles."

Hostiles I trust more than my head guard, not that I mention that to him. I glance around. "Uh, where's Sam?"

The tall guard's eyebrows draw together. "Samuel Roth? Your Highness' recently appointed Chief of Military and Strategic Defense?"

I nod my head. "Sure, yep, that's the Sam I mean." I forgot about the title I created so Sam could tell people what to do and come and go as he pleased.

"Your Highness, he has many important tasks to complete. He can't be around to escort you from place to place like a common palace guard. He's in a meeting reviewing security for the coronation at present. My name's Adam Forsythe and you may not recall, but we've met before. I've been voted in as the new Chief of the Palace Guard. Your safety is my number one priority and I assure you I take it very seriously."

I bite my lip before I can swear, since that doesn't seem very queenly. I didn't expect Sam to actually need to do anything with his stupid made-up title. "If you're going to be around a lot, maybe we should review the Your Highness thing. You don't need to call me that. Like at all. Ruby is fine."

Adam's mouth drops open but before he can speak, Wesley throws a hand up and waves it at Adam Forsythe, catching his attention and then shooing him backward. "Hang on a second, pretty boy. Ruby already has a boyfriend, the Sam guy she asked about. And she has a back up boyfriend." He points at himself. "The last thing she needs is another genetically perfect model looking guy following her around all day, flexing, or whatever you're going to do to keep her safe. I'm sure the four guards that already create a tripping hazard whenever we turn around are more than sufficient."

Adam glances from Wesley to me, and back again. "I don't understand."

Wesley rolls his eyes. "I'll enunciate. Go. Get. Sam. And while you're down there at central command, tell them we want the fugliest soldier they have to replace you as Chief of the Palace Guard. Got it?"

"Appearance does not factor into a guard's performance review on any level," says Adam.

I laugh. "You can ignore Wesley. He thinks he's funny."

"You appear to agree."

I roll my eyes. "Most days."

Adam raises one eyebrow. "If you believe my performance to be sub par, I will request the selection of a replacement."

I shake my head. "No, it's fine. We wouldn't dream of interfering with the way you select your positions or evaluate performance. But I do need you to send someone to let Sam know we're ready to go. One of the main reasons we're traveling down to the end of the bridge is so Sam can meet with the Marked leader."

Adam's eyebrows rise. "In his capacity as Chief of Mi—"

"Yes, yes," Wesley says. "As Head Poomba he needs to coordinate with the Marked."

Adam scowls at Wesley, but he walks back to confer with my four guards. One of them sets off down the hall at a trot, presumably to tell Sam we're ready to go when he is.

I glance at the incinerator. My father's body will burn for quite some time yet, but he's surely past the point of resurrection. Hopefully I'll sleep a little easier at night having witnessed that fact myself.

Wesley walks beside me down the hall, and the guards take up positions in front of and behind us, Adam filling in for the one who took off. Having four guards in attendance at all times is super annoying. We walk the half a mile from the Crematorium back to the palace-that-isn't-officially-a-palace in silence, which is strange for Wesley. He generally talks even more than me.

"Are you okay?"

He shrugs. "I'll be glad when this coronation business is past us so we can shut down the Cleansing and actually focus on developing a cure that works."

I only spent a few days in Baton Rouge, the largest Marked community, and I can't stop thinking about baby Rose, the newborn we saved using the antibodies in my blood. The face of her sweet mother springs to mind often as well. Sadly Libby's still Marked, probably because the Tercera virus in her system had already entered the active phase. Antibodies work well to prevent disease, but aren't usually effective once it's entrenched. Unlike me, Wesley lived with the Marked for weeks. He's made friends there and feels even more pressure than I do to save them.

Of course, it's not like his dad engineered the deadly virus, which I know because my dad did. Not the psychopath burning in an oven, but the man who raised me as his own. If David Solomon was right and God punishes children for their parents' sins, I may as well reserve a house down in purgatory. I have quite a list of things for which to atone, coming from both good old dad and my biological father.

"If we're lucky," I say, "maybe Job's already made some progress."

"Except he probably needs more antibodies from you to continue his testing at this point," Wesley says. "We've been gone way longer than we expected."

I bob my head. "I know. I feel bad that I only gave plasma once." And I'm so thin that it wasn't very much. Not nearly enough.

When we reach the palace I sit down on the steps to wait for Sam. I pointedly ignore the gesturing and pointing from my guards and the butler. If I'm really their queen, I can sit where I want, including a pristine porch step made of white marble. I kind of want to lay down and roll around like a puppy, just to see what they'd do.

Wesley puts his hand on my shoulder. "Even if we were still in Baton Rouge, you'd have needed some time to recover before they drew any more blood. Don't feel too bad about a delay in their testing."

I shrug. "But if I were there, I could help Job with inter-preting the data and research."

"You're doing the most good here for right now." Wesley starts to sling his arm around me, but then shifts at the last minute and acts like he was stretching.

I glance around, because that kind of oddball reversal usually means Wesley noticed Sam.

And I'm right. I stand up and my mouth stretches into a smile in spite of myself.

"Hey sunshine." Sam's wearing a navy blue military uniform with four bright yellow stripes on each shoulder.

"Glad you're back, oh great and revered War Chief. The

new Boss Guard says they're ready to take us out on the bridge."

"I'm ready to go." Sam's grin showcases perfectly white teeth. His impossibly handsome face becomes just a little more unbearably beautiful when it's smiling.

"Wow," I say, "I thought you said no uniforms."

He lifts one eyebrow. "I did. Until this girl I know said she had a thing for them."

"She did, huh? Who is this girl? I already dislike her."

Wesley clears his throat. "Those buttons look hard to do and undo. If it means you keep more clothes on, I'm all for a uniform. Not that anyone asked for my opinion."

I roll my eyes at Wesley and then turn toward Sam. "Are you ready to go see Rafe?"

Sam reaches down and takes my hand in his. He squeezes it tighter than he normally would. If meeting Rafe makes my brawny, scientifically enhanced warrior nervous, well, that's about the cutest thing ever. Rafe, also known as Raphael Roth, is the leader of the Marked. He's also Sam's previously lost little brother. They haven't seen one another since before Tercera ravaged North America, a time we usually refer to as Before. Eleven years is a long time between family reunions, even for me.

"Come on." I tug Sam toward the bridge and he lets me pull him along. I know he lets me, because there's no way my ninety-pound self could drag his two-hundred-and-thirty pound brick wall body anywhere he didn't already want to go.

My new captain of the guard strides quickly toward us, falling into step alongside Sam and me. "Samuel Roth, I'm Adam Forsythe, the new Chief of the Palace Guard. Ensuring the safety of Her Royal Highness Ruby Solomon is my top priority. I'll be taking frequent rotations in her personal guard to make sure I stay abreast of everything about her preferences and schedule."

Sam looks Adam up and down and nods. Samuel Roth's a man of few words, but this is terse even for him.

"I appreciate your enthusiasm," I say. "Congratulations on what I assume was a promotion, but out of curiosity, why did the job need to be filled? What happened to your predecessor?"

"He was fired, of course. Under his tenure your father was infected with a deadly virus by a rival and went mad, taking his own life. Peter Richelieu should have taken measures to prevent both occurrences. I assure you, no such harm will come to you on my watch."

Sam releases my hand as we approach the van and opens the door for me. "I'll be with Ruby twenty four seven from here on out. Your services will be superfluous."

"You can't be with her twenty four seven, sir. Everyone sleeps."

Sam raises one eyebrow. "That's true."

"Uh, well." Adam looks from Sam to me and back again. "In any case, when you have meetings or are otherwise occupied, you can rest easy knowing she's in good hands."

Wesley snorts.

"I'm your boss, right?" Sam asks.

The muscles in Adam's jaw tighten and his cornflower blue eyes bulge. "Yes sir." He watches as Sam sits down next to me and puts an arm around my shoulder.

Wesley catches my eye as he climbs into the van and whispers, "This is so awesome."

I roll my eyes. At least neither Adam nor Sam have beat their chests or roared yet. I hope Adam lets it go, because I haven't met anyone who could take Sam out. I'd hate to see Adam take a beating his first day at a new job. Besides, it can't be good for morale.

Adam climbs into the van and tells the driver to go. I told them we didn't need any guards and that the Marked who have gathered are friends, but it was a futile effort. Three other vans full of armed men drive alongside us anyway. I hope Rafe doesn't see this as an act of aggression.

When the Marked come into sight, I lean forward and place a hand on Adam's arm. "I'd like to go by foot from here."

Adam frowns. "It's safer to have vehicles close."

"But it indicates hostility," I say. "I know the Marked who are gathered. I won't scare them or have them thinking this is a show of force. That will only escalate things."

Adam opens his mouth to argue, but Sam cuts him off. "I have six guns on me with enough rounds between them to take out every kid on that bridge. It's fine; you can actually obey the orders from your future queen. If anything comes up, I'll be there to keep her safe."

"That kind of arrogance is dangerous," Adam warns.

"It's not arrogance. It's fact." Sam raises his voice. "Stop the van." The driver stops.

Oh, good grief.

Adam orders the other vans to stop as well with his walkie. I don't wait for anyone to open my door, because I need to escape this puddle of testosterone before I drown in it. I grab the handle, swing it open, and hop out. I've barely gone two paces before Sam falls into step next to me and Adam slides alongside me on the right.

"Don't worry guys," Wesley says, "I've got the rear covered. Nothing back there will make it through me."

I snort. Freaking Wesley.

As soon as the Marked kids see my hair, curly and windblown into my telltale fluffy blonde mop, they start walking toward us. I can't make out the details of his face from here, but I can tell Rafe's at the front because I recognize his hair. No one else has quite the same spiky, russet colored Mohawk.

When we draw near enough to see faces, I notice Rafe and the dozen men with him have guns trained on us. So much for my hopes of a nice, friendly meeting.

"What's going on?" I shout.

"Back away from Ruby slowly," Rafe says, "and no one will be shot. We need her, and we won't leave without her."

I shake my head. "You don't understand Rafe, it's fine. I'm not being held against my will. Put your gun down."

"I will when they do," Rafe says.

"No one's holding a gun on you, you blind idiot." I turn my head toward my people and exhale heavily, because I'm a big, fat liar. Even Sam's pointing a gun at them. "Put. Your. Guns. Down. That's an order."

Everyone but Sam listens.

"How is it that you're giving them orders?" Rafe asks. "And who's the meathead who won't put his gun down?"

"That gorgeous blockhead is your big brother. Sam, stop aiming your gun at Raphael's head. It isn't polite."

"Wait." Rafe squints, his head tilted and his body tense. "That's Sam? Seriously?"

He's wearing a uniform. Duh, I should've thought about that. It's been a weird couple of days. "How about this? Wesley, Sam and I will meet you in the middle. Your people and our people will all walk back forty paces on the count of five. Yes?"

Rafe nods.

I turn to Adam. "Okay?"

Adam says, "Yes, but I'm staying too."

"No, you're going and I'm done arguing. You take orders from me, not the other way around."

Adam scowls, but when I count to five, he walks back

with the others. If he stays a half dozen feet closer to us than the others, well, I'll cut him some slack. It's his first day and his boss is meeting with a bunch of armed soldiers infected with the same deadly disease that he thinks killed the last boss. Of course, no one from WPN knows that I'm immune.

Rafe could lick my face and I wouldn't catch Tercera.

Luckily, I've inoculated Sam and Wesley with the antibodies my dad gave me years ago, so they're also safe. Even so, since WPN doesn't know that, it's best if we maintain our distance. Rafe walks toward us slowly and I take a few hesitant steps toward him too. Sam holsters his gun.

I coo a little, because I can't help needling them. "I am so proud of you boys, both of you sheathing your claws for this little meet and greet. Rafe, meet Samuel Roth, my Chief of Military and Strategic Defense. Sam, this is Raphael Roth, leader of the Marked, and your long lost baby brother."

If I expected them to hug, I'd have been disappointed. I know Sam well enough to have guessed that wasn't going to happen, which will make things easier when we head back to the island anyway. I'd rather not have to explain to my new people that while my blood could certainly immunize them from ever catching Tercera, I'm saving it instead to use in a last ditch attempt to somehow cure the imminently dying.

I'm not sure they'd appreciate my priorities.

"It's actually you." Sam smiles. "I'm glad to see you."

That's it. More than ten years since he saw his brother, and Sam's exclamation of affection is less than ten words. I exhale heavily.

Rafe's grin makes his eyes match the rest of his body for once. He actually looks like a tall twelve-year-old should. "I straight up can't believe you're alive, Sam! You look amazing. Man, I wonder if I'd look like that if I hadn't been on the suppressant for all these years. And Dad?"

Sam shrugs. "He's as big a jerk as ever."

Rafe's grin widens. "I wish I could see him."

Sam raises his eyebrows. "No you don't. Seriously, if you do it's only because you've forgotten what he's like."

"Maybe. Is he really running the Unmarked?"

"Yep," Sam says. "Are you surprised?"

"Not really, no." Rafe glances at me. "So what's with ordering people around? I thought they'd taken you hostage when you didn't come back."

"They did. Long story short, they tossed me and Wesley in prison."

"Yes, and thanks for your great concern over my welfare by the way," Wesley says. "I was thrown in prison, almost shot by ten snipers, shoved into shackles with a gun to my temple, and basically mistreated every way possible. Yet here I am, and no one's even mentioned me." Wesley puts his hand to his heart, and shakes his head. "I'm wounded, honestly."

Rafe shrugs. "You're wheezing and complaining as much as ever, which means you're fine."

"I basically saved the day," Wesley says. "In case that wasn't already obvious."

All joking aside, he's kind of right. Wesley's not tough in the way Sam or Rafe or even Adam are tough, although he's fit and a competent shot, but his knowledge of abused women did bring Josephine over to our side. Without him, we might not be standing here.

I clear my throat. "He's joking as usual, but Wesley did save us in point of fact. He helped me convince my mom to take action against Solomon." I lower my voice. "Josephine shot her husband and now, in the twist of the year, it turns out—"

Wesley bounces up and down like a toddler who needs to pee.

"Fine," I say. "You can tell him."

Wesley beams. "She's his heir! They're crowning her queen day after tomorrow. Crazy, right?"

"That is crazy," Rafe says. "And also, it's not happening. We need you in Baton Rouge now. You can't stay here and be queen of the Bible Belt."

"They're planning to eradicate you and everyone you know," I say. "Maybe I should stay long enough to put the kibosh on that. Or have you decided WPN's well armed and enormous army isn't actually a threat?"

"I worry about the snake that's about to bite me before the one in the tree."

"Triage," I say, "I'm familiar with the concept, but a few days here could eliminate the threat of WPN forever. They'd kill you faster than Tercera, even with the suppressant failing. Besides, there are other reasons it might help you. I can come back next week and bring supplies, including food. Good nutrition will strengthen your people for their fight with the virus, you know."

Rafe scowls. "Why should I believe you'll come back at all?"

Wesley grunts. "Like I told you before, Ruby does the right thing. Always."

Sam growls at nearly the same time. "We'll come to Baton Rouge, I swear it."

"Pardon my lack of faith that you'll come for me big brother, but it's not like history supports your promises. It's doubly hard to believe you when you've gone native." Rafe stares pointedly at Sam's uniform.

"Mom wouldn't take any of Dad's calls, which I don't blame her for, but then the grid shut down. Dad and I had no reason to believe you survived," Sam says, "or any idea of where to look even if we wanted to."

Rafe shrugs. "Where did you *start* looking, then?"

Sam's face falls. "I'm sorry Raphael. I really am. I failed you."

I take Sam's hand. "You most certainly did not. You were eleven, twelve at the most when your mother would've died. There was nothing you could've done. You'd have died if you tried to find him, as Rafe well knows. By the time you were old enough to hunt for him, the suppressant wouldn't have worked on you." I spin around on Rafe. "You were willing to risk the lives of all your people to get your brother back. Stop acting like a spoiled brat and show him some of what you really feel."

Rafe's face collapses and my heart twists in my chest. These poor brothers. So much love, obscured by so much emotional constipation. I decide to throw them a bone.

"Rafe, Sam loves you. I care about you and all the Marked kids who have hovered on the fringe making their own community. Relying on the generosity of others might have kept the hormone suppressants coming, but it hasn't taught you to trust. I know the Unmarked didn't provide much aid. I know they weren't reliably supportive, but I'm not your dad, and I'm not the Unmarked leaders. I won't abandon you like everyone else did."

"Even if I believe you, I need to be able to convince my people. A week is too long after all the time I've already been gone."

Wesley groans. "You've got to be more flexible, man."

I huff. "How about this? I've been thinking that we should establish a care center locally, near WPN. If WPN provides materials in the old Marked maternity ward in Texas City, I can drive out each day and work with Job. Then I could donate plasma as needed and keep order here in Galveston too. That way WPN will be on tap to provide food and any other support the Marked need. WPN's organized and has plenty of grain, meat, and medical supplies." I look at him flatly. "Things the Marked don't have."

Rafe scowls at me. "We have meat and we have grain." He glances back at my guard. "You kind of like the idea of being queen, huh?"

I frown. "Actually, no. I hate it."

"Uh huh," Rafe says. "I just bet you do."

"I'm thinking of what would be best for the Marked, nothing more."

"What's best for us would be you honoring your word. Come back like you said you would before we brought you down here to save your boyfriend and retrieve your daddy's journal. You know, the one that was only lost because you left it." Rafe peers around me to look at the vans. "Where is that journal, by the way?"

"I have it," I say. "Back on the island. I'm reading it now."

"Uh huh, well, how's this for some incentive to do what you already promised?" Rafe asks. "Wesley said the coronation's Friday, which is the day after tomorrow. I'll give you one day after that to get things in order, and one extra day to drive out to Baton Rouge. If you haven't arrived by sunset on Sunday, I'll execute Rhonda. The day after that, I'll execute Job. Before you say I won't, remember that he's no good to me without antibodies to work with."

I clench my hands into fists. What if something comes up? What if a bridge collapses, or a car breaks down?

"You're acting like an insane person."

"No," Rafe says. "I'm acting like your presence is a life and death issue to us. Because it is. Every day you delay means a day we can't work toward a solution. That means more of us die."

"Fine. I don't want to leave WPN until I'm sure things are stable and they won't kill you all, but if you don't mind that possibility, so be it. I told my people that my cousin needs my plasma due to a bleeding disorder. I set up a plasma draw for later today so you can take some of my antibodies back with you. At least stick around for that, so Job can continue the clinical trials while he's waiting for his own execution."

"Fine." Rafe waves at Wesley and Sam, spins on one heel, and starts toward the mainland.

"You know, I told my WPN guards not to worry about me during this meeting. I told them you're a friend and not a threat. I guess that was a lie."

Rafe pivots. "Sam's my brother and Wesley's my friend, but you're not my friend. You're a necessity, nothing more."

I pretend I don't care. "Fine, whatever, but before you leave, at least tell me if you ever heard from my aunt."

"She must've gone back to the Unmarked. She disappeared a few days ago, or so my people tell me. There at night, gone the next morning. When she joined us her husband didn't want her to stay. He kept insisting she could live in quarantine indefinitely. We're assuming she got sick of bad food and bailed."

That doesn't sound like my aunt. She would've wanted to stay where the infection was and truly study the live virus like she couldn't before. Even if it meant she had to eat burned oatmeal every morning.

This time when Rafe turns to leave, I don't stop him.

CHAPTER 2

After dealing with Rafe and his ultimatums, I figured the rest of the day would be a breeze. It's harder than I anticipated to convince Josephine to find me an aphoresis machine to donate plasma for Job's fake bleeding disorder. She plies me with all kinds of questions.

"Why can't someone else donate?" "How long has this been going on?" "Why are you a match, if you're not really related."

"Because I'm O-neg!" I finally yell. "I match everyone."

Maybe I shouldn't have mentioned to her that the last time I gave plasma, I passed out when I upped the amount the machine was set to pull. This time I sit patiently while it pulls half the average amount due to my stupidly small size. Being tiny sucks.

An hour later, thirsty and a little woozy from donating plasma, I sway during yet another fitting for my coronation gown. This time when a clumsy apprentice pokes me with a pin, I don't grit my teeth and bear it. I whimper. Not that anyone notices or cares. And despite Sam's reassurances that I'd never be alone, I'm on my own in here.

After the third poke I throw my hands up in the air. "I'm done with this. Get it off me." I pull at the fabric surrounding me in great swaths. "Now."

"I'm sorry this is taking so long, Your Royal Highness," Melinda says, "but we still have a few more modifications to make. Sewing a gown of this quality in only two days. . . well." My mother's private seamstress clucks. "Some might say it can't be done, but we'll prove them wrong."

I groan. "You'll have to make do with what you've got." I glance at the clock. "I have a meeting in twenty minutes with the Port Heads, and I can't be late. I doubt you want me wearing this to see them."

Melinda's eyes bug satisfyingly. "No indeed. We'll wrap it up."

I've been dreading having to welcome my biological father's cronies, but I'm almost excited for it now. Being poked and prodded with pins while holding absolutely still for the pleasure gives me a new outlook. All my friends in kindergarten who pretended to be princesses should've spent a day being fitted for a ball gown. They'd have changed their minds. From what I can tell, being a princess involves a lot less ordering people around and a lot more being shoved into doing things you'd rather avoid. Every time I blink someone's asking me to do something, and I have no choice about what.

Once Melinda and her cadre of helpers clear out, I change into a button down white shirt and a pair of khaki dress slacks. I'm drinking a glass of water when my mother knocks and walks in, Adam right beside her. Good thing I was dressed.

"The Port Heads are waiting for you in the Garden Room," Josephine says. "I've called for a tea service. I hope you don't mind."

"Not at all. I love tea." I think about my little greenhouse at home. With Job and Rhonda in Baton Rouge and Aunt Anne who knows where, I wonder whether anything's still alive. The downside to a greenhouse is that without someone tending to it, it won't get any water. My poor mint plants have certainly died by now.

I follow Adam down the hall and a few steps from the Garden Room, Sam turns the corner. He's not wearing his uniform anymore. My comment about uniforms was true, I do like them. But on Sam, his typical black shirt, this time with a collar, looks even better. The cotton fabric hugs his pecs and tightens over his biceps and I remind myself not to stare, even if he is my boyfriend. The dark jeans he's wearing fit perfectly and class his shirt up even more.

He grins at me and takes my hand before gesturing toward the door. "Can't let you tumble into the lions' den alone."

I smile. "Nice reference. Mom says these Port Heads are the religious, political, and economic leaders of WPN's Port cities, essentially ruling them like fiefdoms." That's going to have to change, and I doubt they'll like it. Baby steps.

Sam narrows his eyes at Adam, who's standing quietly by the door. "I told you I'd be supervising her private security at all times. You shouldn't have brought her without me."

Adam frowns. "You were still being fitted and she indicated she was ready to go. She's perfectly safe under my supervision."

"Not your call." Sam says.

"Uh, but it is *my* call." I toss my hair and Sam has the decency to look chagrined.

He tugs me along behind him and away from Adam. We walk through the doors and into a room filled with windows and plants. The last time I entered this room I was hoping to see Sam alive. Now I'm walking in with him by my side, and my heart is a thousand pounds lighter for it. Chairs scratch against the floor when Sam and I walk inside, presumably so everyone can stand.

"No, no, please stay seated," I say. "I'm not one for formalities."

Wesley doesn't listen, walking around the table to greet me. He was here the last time I came to the Garden Room, and I'm relieved to see him again, this time sporting a dashing new suit. I guess when you're more patient with interminable fittings and stand still as long as they want, there are some payoffs. Nothing's been finished for Sam or me yet.

My request for informality notwithstanding, Wesley bows when he reaches my side. "Your Royal Highness I'm so glad you're here, although that means I won't have the attention of these amazing women and men all to myself anymore." Wesley widens his eyes at me meaningfully, and I almost pity him. He's so good in crowds that sometimes I forget how exhausting it must be to act gracious and convivial all the time.

The seat my biological father occupied last time I was here is conspicuously empty, as are the seats to its left and right. I walk purposefully to the front of the table and rest my hands on the back of my bio father's chair. Sam and Wesley flank me.

"Thank you Wesley for entertaining these fine men and women until I could be here myself." I smile at each person around the table in turn. Five men and two women, all wearing dark pantsuits, all seated as I asked. I hadn't realized there was some kind of uniform for attendance today. I glance at my white button down shirt and sigh. Too late to change now.

"I'm Ruby Solomon, daughter of David Solomon.

Welcome to Galveston. I'm sure you've all been here many times before, but it's my first chance to welcome you all into my home."

I glance at Josephine, who has taken an empty seat on my left at the far end of the table. Even she should be satisfied by my reference to Solomon as my dad. I hope the reminder's worth the nasty taste in my mouth from saying the words. I force a smile as I sit and gesture for Wesley to take the seat to my left. Sam takes the one on my right.

"You've already met Wesley Fairchild, son of the leader of Port Gibson, and also my dearest friend. This is Samuel Roth, son of the leader of the DeciCouncil of the Unmarked, Jonathan Roth. He's also my new Chief of Military and Strategic Defense. Now if you wouldn't mind, could you please introduce yourselves?"

The man seated next to Sam stands. He has a full head of white hair and deep smile lines crease his weathered face. "My name's Sawyer Blevins, your Royal Highness. I'm Port Head in New Orleans, which also makes me your closest geographic neighbor. Your father was my first cousin, which means we're first cousins once removed." He extends his hand, and I reach forward to clasp it in my own. His smile seems genuine. "We provide more oil and gas than any other port, as well as an abundance of corn, strawberries, and peaches. I'd love to have you out for a visit. You'll adore beignets and gumbo, I just know it." He sits.

I relax a little. My mom's talk of the Port Heads demanding proof of who I am and her claims that my father's enemies killed him had me nervous about meeting them, but it's hard to fear someone who's smiling at me warmly and telling me we're related. Although, blood relation to David Solomon doesn't exactly leave me optimistic about his goodness.

I shift my gaze to the heavy-set woman next to him wearing a floral print blouse under her suit jacket. She stands up and licks her dark pink lips. "I'm Dolores Peabody, and I'm Port Head in Mobile, Alabama. We may not be related by blood, and Mobile isn't the closest to you geographically, but you'll find that we're quite useful to WPN. In fact, we manufacture and process nearly all the coal and most of the chemicals that supply every WPN settlement." She inclines her head, and I'm grateful I don't need to reach across two chairs to shake her hand.

"It's wonderful to meet you. I'm sure we're all grateful for the products you provide." I look around the table, making eye contact with each Port Head. "But of course, I want to make it clear that this isn't a competition."

"Isn't it?" Dolores asks. "You don't know much about the role any of us play in the interconnected web that creates WPN's commerce." She doesn't quite scowl, but her iron gray hair twisted in a tight bun, combined with tightly compressed lips doesn't exactly convey a sense of welcome. "I'm pleased to meet you, happy to educate you, and I look forward to many years of working smoothly together."

Josephine gasps, and I have no idea why. I glance at Wesley. He leans toward me and whispers. "You're queen. She works *for* you, not *with* you."

Good grief. This was exactly the type of pettiness I dreaded. "You're happy to educate me? Well that's fine, but we won't be working together, will we?" I raise one eyebrow and look at her pointedly.

Dolores bows. "Pardon me, your Majesty, I meant working for you. It's been a long trip on short notice. Please excuse my inaccuracy."

I hate word plays, slights, and politics. I want to run back to Baton Rouge now, and let Rafe deal with the

Cleansing if it comes. If I do that, the blood of any Marked kids who die will be on my head. I grit my teeth and wonder whether I'm doing permanent damage to my molars. I glance at the man sitting next to Dolores so he'll realize it's his turn.

There aren't many fat people alive today. In Port Gibson, for example, Dolores would stand out as quite large, and she's only carrying twenty or thirty extra pounds. I vaguely remember people who were much, much, larger Before, and I've even heard that some people had surgery to reduce their stomach's ability to process food. Since the Marking, there simply isn't enough food to go around. Everything we eat requires dedicated work and is carefully divided.

When the man next to Dolores heaves himself upright, I can't keep my eyebrows from rising. He looked a little heavy from where he sat, but when he stands up his belly sticks out far enough that I could set a dinner plate on top and avoid using a table entirely.

"Quentin Clarke," he says. "Pleased to meet you. Port Head for Savannah, Georgia. We provide nearly all the chicken, and much of the pork you'll eat. We also provide all the paper goods."

"Well, I'm sure we're all grateful," I say. "After all, who doesn't like bacon? Pleased to meet you, Quentin."

He bobs his head, his face mottled and red, his hair thinning on top. He collapses back into the chair and breathes a sigh of relief. He seems to dislike this whole business as much as I do, and my heart goes out to him. I imagine it was a long trip on short notice for him too, just as Dolores claimed.

The woman next to him stands, and smiles at me warmly. "My name is Rosa Alvarez, Port Head for Miami, Florida. We provide thousands of tons of citrus and most of your cattle. We also build almost all of WPN's ships. I would love to have you out for a tour anytime, you know. I can show you how to Salsa."

I glance at Wesley. "Isn't salsa a condiment of some kind?"

Rosa's laugh starts in her belly and fills the room. "A condiment? You've never had salsa?"

I shake my head, my cheeks flushing.

"It comes in so many different flavors and varieties that you'll be amazed. It's the most delicious sauce you'll ever taste," Rosa says, "but I was referring to the dance. It's wickedly fun. I'm delighted to meet you and I'm excited to welcome our first female monarch." Her eyes dart quickly to Josephine. "No offense your majesty."

Josephine smiles back. "None taken, Rosa, por supuesto. I understand your meaning."

"I think it's my turn to introduce myself." The tall man with dark brown skin sitting next to Wesley stands up and offers me his hand. No one in Unmarked society would shake hands, not anymore. I wonder whether it's reckless-ness, trust, or pride that prompts them to shake bare-handed. I can't catch Tercera, so I shake the extended hand without fear. "My name's Terry Williams and I'm Port Head for Tampa, Florida."

"Wonderful to meet you," I say.

"Since everyone appears to be playing a game of one up, I'll just mention that Tampa produces more fish-"

Rosa snorts. "If you like catfish, the cockroach of the waterways."

Terry pretends he didn't hear a thing, but he does elab-orate. "We catch substantial quantities of lobster, shrimp, grouper and clams. But we also provide citrus and sugar, as well as the best fertilizer of any port."

I reach forward and take the sugar tongs in my hands,

putting two lumps of sugar in my teacup. "I'm delighted that you make sugar, Terry. Perhaps it's a good time to suggest that everyone enjoy some tea while we continue the introductions. I've been an abominable hostess. Please do pour yourselves something to drink and help yourselves to some snacks."

Two serving maids in grey uniforms, Melinda and Greta I think, walk from the back wall and begin pouring tea into teacups.

A thin man with a shock of bright red hair stands up next to Terry. "My name's Steve Young, and sadly I have no football talent myself."

I glance at Sam to see whether he understands. He shakes his head. Wesley shrugs.

"Never mind," the man says. "I forget how young you all are. It's an old joke from Before. I'm named after a famous football player and everyone used to laugh about it given that I'm so skinny and uncoordinated."

"Ah," I say, "well it's nice to meet you."

"The pleasure's all mine," he says. "I'm Port Head for Jacksonville, Florida, and we manufacture all the automobiles, movies, and electronics for WPN."

"I've been wondering whether the automobiles were made recently or exceptionally well maintained. I'm very impressed that you're still manufacturing them. Nice work."

"Thank you. I'm happy to hear you're pleased with our work. We would love to host you as well, anytime you'd like. And I'd be happy to sit down and take down design notes and ideas for your next shipment. We'd be flattered if you'd place a custom order for whatever car you might want, personally. It's actually my coronation gift to you."

"Thanks," I say. "Maybe I can do a tour and visit each port soon. I'd be happy to see Jacksonville."

Murmurs of agreement come from around the table.

"And I'm the last one to introduce myself," says a man with dark, curly hair and a thick Spanish accent. He stands and opens his hands wide. "Which is fitting because I live the furthest away. I'm Jose Fuerte, Port Head for La Ciudad del Carmen in Tabasco, Mexico. Cars, fish, chemicals?" He scrunches his nose. "Even salsa does not compare with what we bring to you."

He reaches under his chair and Sam tenses beside me. I'm positive he's holding a gun in his hand under the table.

Jose pulls a box out, and places it on the inlaid wood surface of the dining room table. "We manufacture many things, and grow many more, from bananas to sweet potatoes, and even coconut. But we are most appreciated for our chocolate. I've brought you my wife's specialty, a box of chocolate-coconut truffles."

"Tomorrow's the day for tribute," Dolores says. "This is a violation of protocol."

Jose chuckles. "This is not a tribute nor would any truffles be a fit tribute for a monarch. This is merely a gift from a dear family friend." He stands and reaches over Steve and Terry to pass the box to Wesley. "Your father gave me my first job in America many years ago. He supported me and helped me to build a business that was a great success here. It fed my family and I sent much of the money I made back home. I was devastated when you were stolen from him at the hospital. We put pictures of you on boxes of chocolates for years in the hopes someone would have seen you. I'm overjoyed he was at least able to see his beautiful daughter before God called him back home. It is my pleasure to serve you, Your Royal Highness, in anything you may need. Felicidades."

"Wow," Wesley whispers.

I lift the lid on the box and gasp. Gold bars aren't as

rare these days as the beautiful, rich, coconut flake encrusted dark chocolate balls stuffed into this container. I want to eat one now, but then I'd have to share with everyone in the room. I hand them to Sam who tucks them under his chair. "That was a very thoughtful gift Jose, thank you."

He bows his head and shoulders before sitting down.

I might have worried for no reason. Other than Dolores, the Port Heads all seem to be quite welcoming, if a little competitive amongst themselves.

"Thank you all," I say. "After tomorrow's coronation, I'd be delighted to invite you to a dinner to discuss my plans for the future of WPN. You've done a lot with my father's guidance, and I know as God fearing men and women you'll be delighted to hear about the charitable efforts I'd like to undertake to help the Marked population. They're currently struggling mightily. Their hormone suppressants are failing, but they're making great strides with new information they received about a cure. In fact—"

Sam squeezes my hand under the table at the same time as Wesley stomps on my foot.

"Oof."

"Excuse me?" Dolores asks. "Oof? In fact what?"

"I didn't quite understand you either," Terry says.

Sam and Wesley both stopped me from telling them about my role with Tercera and the cure. It might be for the best, but now how do I recover from almost explaining it?

"In fact," I say, "uh, I hope, uh, you'll all agree to join me for dinner tomorrow. I can't wait to elaborate more on my plans then."

I smile and they all smile back. My heart lifts. Perhaps it will really be that easy to prevent the Cleansing and gain the support of WPN's local leaders. I imagine Rafe's shocked face when I show up with a hundred of Quentin's fat chickens or a case of Jose's chocolates. Or better yet, a few of Steve's new cars!

"We're all delighted to accept your invitation," Rosa says. "But for now we feel we better leave you be. After all, your Trial of Faith starts in only five hours. We announced that it will be open to the public and we're expecting quite the turnout. I'm sure you have some last minute preparations to complete."

The smile drops off my face, in spite of my efforts to keep it. "Um, I need to prepare for my what in five hours?"

"Yes," Josephine says, "what are you talking about?"

Dolores tilts her head, "Why the Trial of Faith, my dear. Your husband issued the edict only last week. It stipulates that any heir to the throne of World Peace Now must complete a Trial by Faith to prove their worthiness unto God prior to any coronation. Each of us have done our part and completed our list of questions."

"What questions?" Wesley asks. "We haven't heard a thing about this."

Rosa glances around the table. "I can't speak to the others, but the topic I chose for my scriptural doctrine questions is that of prayer. I'll be asking Her Royal Highness about the proper order of prayer, according to the words of the prophets in the Holy Bible."

Heads bob all around. "Mine focus on the Psalms of God," Sawyer says. "I figured they'd be the easiest thing for you to answer, darling Ruby, since those were David's favorite chapters. Even though you knew him for a short time, I'm positive he set you to read those at least."

"Of course." Josephine's eyes bug out a little, in spite of her forced smile. I know her well enough now to recognize that buggy eyes indicate agitation. Extreme agitation.

"What time did you say it was happening again?" I ask.

"Five hours from now," Rosa says.

"And since we've obviously never heard of this," I ask, "can you tell me? What happens if I don't pass this Test? Who's chosen to rule if I fail?"

"Oh you'll choose, of course," Quentin says. "Through the Divination of Ashes."

"Uh huh," I say, "Well at least now I know. I'll be sure to be ready." I glance at the clock and add five hours. "At seven o'clock sharp."

Wesley makes small talk with the Port Heads. Most of them don't even sip their tea or nibble any of the sandwiches before they leave. Probably because Josephine simply stares at the wall like a crazy person, ignoring anything they say.

I lean back in my chair and close my eyes after the last one has finally gone.

"Ruby, this is bad." Sam swears. "Is there any chance you know anything about the Bible? Have you ever read it? Like, any of it?"

I look him in the eye. "It's long, and it's about a guy named Jesus. That much I know." I shake my head. "But otherwise, nope."

"We're so screwed," Wesley says.

"Maybe there's like a summary I can read or something," I say. "Mom? You're the expert here. Any suggestions?"

When she finally turns around and I can see her face, it's as pale as the cream on the tea service tray.

"Hey, are you okay?" I ask.

"You need to leave right now," she whispers.

"Uh, excuse me?" I glance at Sam and then Wesley. "They said it's not for like hours, still."

Adam clears his throat and looks down his nose at

Josephine. "I believe she's suggesting you leave Galveston. That you run away."

"Why would she suggest that?" I ask. "Even if I fail, I can choose the Port Head I think is most likely to be a good ruler. Maybe I even have time to talk to a few and get a feel for who has sympathy for the Marked."

"No," Adam says, "you won't be choosing one based on your personal preferences. To contain the spreading of disease and utilize limited secure space as well as we can, we cremate all persons who die."

"Uh, weird time to share that," Wesley says. "But duly noted."

Adam frowns. "The Divination of Ashes is the ceremony in which your ashes are scattered on the winds. God will use the wind to direct your ashes toward whichever Port Head He desires for His next monarch."

This time when Sam curses, Josephine doesn't even scowl at him.

CHAPTER 3

Josephine takes my hand. "We have to get you out of here right away."

"You have very little faith in God's plan," Adam says. "Why not stay, study and have faith that God will direct her. She's obviously His chosen."

"Obviously." Wesley turns away from Adam and smirks at me.

"Mock if you'd like, but it's clear to those of us who have been watching. She appeared, alive, after a kidnapping and a plague. She knew nothing of her parents and found them anyway. She went to the headquarters for the Marked, and returned still Unmarked. God protected her at the request of his servant King Solomon, when he failed to protect the King himself. Clearly God was ready to pass the mantle of leadership to you."

"Umm, well, that's all technically true. I am grateful that the work of my *father* kept me safe." I suppress a laugh, since Adam doesn't know it wasn't David Solomon who kept me from being Marked. It was Donovan Behl. Or, er,

Donald Carillon. The whole dad thing's gotten pretty confusing, even to me.

"So," Wesley says. "Mom votes run. Head guard votes stay because God will keep you safe. I'm going to go with, how about we look at this edict dear old dad sent and see what it says. Maybe there's a little wiggle room. A loophole through the ashes that might not require complete abandonment of this plan—" Wesley looks at Adam. "Er, this path that God has set you on."

"Good idea." I stand up and walk toward the door. "I'm going to try and find one of these Port Heads and ask for theirs."

"There should be a copy of all the correspondence that went out in the last month in David's office," Josephine says. "I'll look for that one." She ducks out the door before I can even respond. Copies of all of David Solomon's sordid correspondence are in his desk? I should probably be reviewing all of it. I wonder what's in that pile. An invoice for eye of newt? An edict ordering wives be beaten weekly? Maybe a tax to pay for a larger throne?

"What do you know about the Bible, your Royal Highness?" Adam draws me out of my macabre musings.

I bite my lip. "I wasn't kidding before. Basically nothing."

Adam crosses the room and picks up a large book bound in black leather, with gold edged pages. He carries it across to the room and sets it on the table in front of me. "If you grew up here, you'd have been studying this book at least thirty minutes a day for your entire life. As it is, you may need to rely on God's guidance."

I glance at Wesley, who shrugs unhelpfully, and Sam who shakes his head.

"Umm," I say, "what does that mean? Like, it's an open

book test and God will help my finger find the page with the answer on it?"

Adam points at the Bible. "God's prophets teach that if we listen to God's voice, He will tell us what to do in our mind and heart."

I close my eyes and try not to cry. My insane bio father wants me to be his heir, or ya know, die if I'm not up to speed on the Bible. Being guided by God's word in my heart isn't promising as far as plans go.

"We should still review the main verses on prayer, of course, since Port Head Alvarez indicated that she would ask about them, and also Psalms, in light of Port Head Blevin's comment."

"How's your short term memory?" Wesley asks me.

"It's not bad," I say, "but. . . five hours, guys. There's no way I could even learn enough to get ten percent right in five hours, and I'm guessing that's not a passing score." The heft of the enormous, leather bound tome sinks my hopes of crash-studying it.

"How can you not know anything about the Bible?" Adam asks. "Your kidnapper really was godless, huh?"

"The man who raised me while I was apart from David Solomon," I say, "was busier studying the way the world worked and trying to eliminate disease. If this test was on scientific principles, well, I wouldn't need to cram right now."

"There's room in the world for both kinds of knowledge, you know," Adam says. "Religious and scientific don't have to be at war."

"Maybe we can debate that later, and focus on this test for right now. Prayer I've heard of, but what's this soms thing I'm supposed to study?" I ask.

Adam opens the book and places it on the table,

pointing at the heading on one of the pages. *"Psalms with a Ps* is a book written by a Jewish king named David."

"Oh," I say. "Him I've heard of. He killed Goliath, right?"

He smiles. "I'm glad to find that you do know some things." He points to the page. "He later made some mistakes and had to, hmm. I guess he tried to get God's forgiveness. He wrote Psalms as a request for atonement."

"What did he do?" I ask.

Adam looks down at his feet. "He fell in love with another man's wife." He clears his throat.

I can actually see some similarities between that guy and my bio father. "Go on. To atone for that he wrote some poems?"

Adam swallows. "It got a little worse. Since he was a king, he had the power to send the man into battle."

"Okay." Wow, this David guy was kind of a villain. "And?"

"He sent him to the front lines and the man died. David married the widow he created by his own manipulation."

I'm starting to think maybe my biological father's first name, David, was appropriate. I flip through the pages and pages of Psalms and realize there are a hundred and fifty different chapters. I groan. "I only have five hours." I start to flip through, skimming, and drop my hand in frustration.

"This is a waste of time. If I have to pass this test or die, we should be planning an escape right now, not reading chunks of this gibberish in the hopes some of it will stick. I mean, number 119 has all these little sub-headings. Aleph, Beth, Gimel, and on and on. They could ask about any of this, and I think they will, the sadistic nuts. They have an incentive to make sure I fail, since one of them will rule after I die. Trying to prepare for taking this test is utterly hopeless."

"You don't need to run." Sam's voice drops ominously in volume to a whisper. "If all the Port Heads die, this goes away."

I roll my eyes. "Yes, massacring their leaders sets the perfect tone for how I'll rule my subjects in the new job Solomon foisted off on me. I appreciate the offer Sam, really I do, but I think that's a firm pass on Operation Kill Them All. Rafe wanted me to come straight back and maybe we should do that."

Adam frowns. "I'm sworn to protect you. Knowing nothing of this edict, the Palace Guard has already sworn our vows to you. It'll be difficult to honor those oaths while you sneak you off the island. The Port Heads will be watching, and they'll have brought their own retinues."

Josephine enters the doorway, crosses the room, and places a sheet of paper in front of me on the table.

David Solomon's psychopathic edict.

It is hereby decreed that I have a new Heir, my daughter Ruby Solomon. My beloved wife and I have not raised her, but she is intelligent and resourceful. I believe I can teach her all she will need to know in order to competently rule in my place when I die.

However, it is my wish that should I fail in my attempt to remediate her education, should she not love God and the good word as much as she ought, should she be unable to govern my people under God's direction, should God not desire her to rule in my stead, the rule of my people shall not fall into her hands.

To that end, I entrust you each with a sacred obligation. Test my daughter upon my death by asking her ten questions about the Bible. Ten questions per Port Head, for a total of seventy questions. She must answer more than seventy percent correctly in the standard manner. Failure will prove she doesn't know God. God may then use her to accomplish his Divination of

Ashes so that my predecessor may be chosen by my bloodline, from among my dearest friends, as God wills.

As with all things, I trust this matter into God's hands. He shall decide.

David Solomon

Josephine sighs. "I hate the idea of leaving my home. I would slap David if he were still alive for this insanity, but I don't see another solution. We have to run."

"We?" I ask.

Josephine takes my hand. "I missed the first seventeen years, but that wasn't my decision. I'd have given up everything to have had the chance to raise you and I won't miss another day. I'll come with you wherever you go."

My heart swells. She may be fractured or even downright broken, and she may have failed me over and over, but she does care about me. Late actually is better than never.

"Wait," Sam says. "You're right, this is insanity." He glances quickly at Adam and then back to me. "Could he have already been under the influence of Tercera when he sent this?" He raises his eyebrows.

Wesley shakes his head. "No, look at the date." He glances from me to Sam and back purposefully. "It's a good thing he wasn't, because that would undermine Ruby's right to rule, if when he wrote the very document in which he proclaims her his Heir, he was already mentally unsound."

"Right," Sam says.

"Look, I want to prevent the Cleansing. That's the only reason why I'm even here," I say. "And if I need to pass some quiz Solomon set up with this secret last minute edict, well. I could try, but—"

"No." Sam slams his hand on the table.

"I agree," Wesley says. "The downside should you fail, which you likely will, is far too high."

The tap at the door might have gone unnoticed, but for Sam's hearing. He crosses the room quickly and opens it.

Sawyer Blevins, my dearly departed father's first cousin, pokes his head around the frame. "Ruby, darling, may I come inside?"

Calling me darling reminds me of Solomon and I flinch. "What do you want?"

"Pardon me if I'm speaking out of line, but I've been worried about you." He steps through the door. "You were with your father for such a short time, and he indicated he planned to update your education, but I doubt he had time to do much. And you looked. . . surprised when we mentioned the Trial by Faith."

I narrow my eyes. "Why are you here?"

"I was talking with a few of the other Port Heads, and we don't think it's fair that you had so little notice. We thought you might like a. . . Well, a study guide, so to speak, for the questions we plan to ask."

One of my eyebrows lifts, because this is too good to be true. Dad always taught me that when something seems too easy, it usually is. Sawyer Blevins, loving and considerate first cousin once removed, who has never seen me in my life prior to today, offers me this gift on a silver platter? I don't think so.

"And in return?" I ask.

He grins and I almost cringe when I see David Solomon in it. "Nothing really, a trifle. We only want to guide you and help you recognize God's path, since you've had no real training of your own. When major decisions are made, let us vote on the decision, after careful prayer of course. We have a brief edict of our own that would be your first act as a monarch, turning the burden of certain things over to a vote of a council of Port Heads, which would include you as well."

"So I wouldn't be queen? I'd be part of a council, like the Unmarked?"

He shakes his head. "Not at all. We're only suggesting this council to help you. Governing is hard enough with years of experience and education. I can't imagine how daunting it seems for someone as young as you."

Under his proposal I'd be alive to rule, but I wouldn't really decide anything. It's more than I could achieve on my own with this test, that's for sure. And they'd all be assured a larger slice of the power, instead of taking a risk on having no power at all. Wind's a fickle way to gamble on your new monarch, especially if you don't really believe God's guiding it.

"It's a generous offer and I appreciate your familial concern. You remind me so much of my own *darling* father," I purr. "How I miss him." I force a smile. "Let me confer with my advisors and I'll send one of them to find you in a few moments with my answer."

Sawyer nods his head and ducks out. Sam shoves the door closed behind him.

"Do it," Josephine says. "It's better than running or dying, and those are our other options."

"I'd be a figurehead," I say. "And that's pointless, because the only reason I even wanted to rule was—"

"To stop the Cleansing." Josephine practically spits the words. "I know."

"Rafe was fine with rolling the dice on that earlier. He wanted me to head straight for Baton Rouge. I have what we came for. Sam's safe and Dad's journal's in my room."

Josephine touches my hand. "Why give up so easily? They can't really make you issue an edict after that Trial by

Faith. Why not take their answers, pass the test, and then shred their edict on the spot?"

I shake my head. "They'll be administering the whole thing, Mom. The people know them. They have their own troops. Besides, if I lie and cheat to pass this test, how am I any different than David Solomon?"

"You're different because of why you're doing it," Wesley says. "If you lie, it's not for power or wealth. It's to make things right."

That's probably exactly how David Solomon started out, rationalizing what was and wasn't right. I'm sick of all of this. "All I ever wanted to do was right the horrible wrong that Dad and Solomon set in motion, along with Dad's crappy partner Jack. That one mistake still controls everything, ruining and ending lives every day. But I don't know what to do about it anymore. Right and wrong are getting all confused." I sink onto a chair and drop my face in my hands.

Josephine scoffs. "You're worried about one small thing. Life's about more than Tercera. Young people are so short sighted. You have all these noble ideals and plans, and you want to do one good thing and then race off on a white horse with a javelin. Life doesn't work like that. If you're truly a good person, and I believe you are, you'll do so much more good here running the government that controls the lives of over a half million people. Much more good than you can do working in a scientific lab. Think of how long the good you do here will last. This isn't about a few Marked kids. It's about shaping the world and power structure of humanity for centuries to come, and you can only do that if we take this deal and figure out how to keep you in power."

I bang on the table. "I don't care about the world power structure or my legacy. I have no desire to stay here and mold the future of humanity. I'm here for the people no one cares about. The Marked kids who have nothing because the world took it away when they were too small to matter. I can't help them if I'm the only one who cares and I'm voting against seven selfish jerks just like David Solomon. He made all the rules, set up this entire game, and we're still stuck playing it."

"If you don't want to accept the offer from Port Head Blevins, and you don't feel you can answer the questions on your own," Adam says, "there is another option."

I jump in my seat. I almost forgot he was here. "Yes, I recall your idea that I channel God's voice or something, but Adam you don't know me. There's absolutely no chance that God will speak the answers in my mind. Trust me on this one, okay?"

Adam shakes his head. "I don't mean that. I've gathered your lack of faith in His love for you. I'm referring to an option that has existed with WPN since the beginning."

"What's that?" I ask.

Adam points at the paper on the table. "The edict mentions scoring in the standard manner."

Josephine inhales sharply. "No. She should take Blevin's offer. It's not that bad, and we can work with it."

Wesley leaps up from his chair and picks up the edict. "We need to change the rules of this game, and I think Adam may have an idea of how to do that. What does that mean, the standard manner?"

Adam says, "In trials, King Solomon sat on his throne in the Assembly Hall and heard cases, but when he was sick or couldn't attend Judgment, the Port Heads sometimes filled in. When they did they determined what to do in the standard manner, a set of rules King Solomon set in place to settle things. If one of them disagreed the majority would vote. In the edict, it means they can vote on each answer, determine whether it's right or wrong if they disagree with the answer created by the person who proposed the question. Sometimes the answers aren't as clear as you might think."

I nod. "Okay, but so what?" I glance at Josephine. "Why's my mom freaking out?"

Josephine's nostrils flare. "Adam hasn't gotten to the point yet. All petitioners and accused individuals are offered two sets of options in the standard manner. They may request a hearing to mediate their dispute, or one of the individuals may request a Trial by Fire. It's common when someone has been convicted of a crime, or if one of them disagrees strongly with a ruling."

"I don't like where this is going," Sam says. "I still vote that I should remove the source of the problems one by one."

I roll my eyes. "What does a Trial by Fire involve, exactly?"

"When wicked men forced a king to throw his beloved Daniel into a lion's den," Adam says, "God shut the mouths of the lions and the next morning, Daniel was fine."

"Except, fire version?" Wesley asks. "So we what? Stick Ruby in an incinerator and if she doesn't burn, she's God's chosen?"

Adam shrugs. "The accused may select the method of death, as long as it's something that's inconclusively fatal."

"Game changer." Wesley grins.

I realize what he's thinking. "God may very well choose the next ruler." I smile at Adam. "Your advice has been transformational, thank you. Please deliver a message for me personally. Please go and tell my *darling cousin* Sawyer Blevins that while I appreciate his generous offer, God has directed me not to take it. In fact I feel specifically guided down another, fierier path."

CHAPTER 4

Once I've explained my plan to everyone in the room and sent Wesley off on his errand, it occurs to me. Tricking the Port Heads and all my subjects will probably solve my problem. Which will allow me to be crowned queen and prevent the Cleansing. I can even send aid to the Marked population.

It's also exactly what my biological father would have done if he were in my shoes. I look down at my feet and try to ignore the heartburn that thought produces.

"What's wrong?" Sam takes one of my hands in his.

"This is what *he* would have done in my place," I whisper. "And I'm risking the lives of all those Marked kids on the belief that my plan will work. It's selfish and deceitful." My voice drops even lower. If it were anyone else, I doubt they could hear me, but I know Sam will. "I'm like him whether I like it or not." Bile rises in my throat. I can't do it. I'll have to run after all.

"You're nothing like him." Sam sits down on the chair next to me and pulls me up onto his lap. I should feel like a child, but somehow I don't. I sink back against him, my stress, my fear, and my guilt pouring out of me. "You're doing this for the right reasons, and it's a risk you should take. You're not even worried about your own life. If I'm being honest, that's my only real concern. Instead you're doing this to help people, including my little brother."

"You are doing the right thing," Josephine says quietly, "even if it requires a lie." She sits down on one of the dining chairs, her hand to her mouth. A single tear runs down her face. "For years I've prayed, begging God for your safety and asking him to tell me why. Why He let you be taken from me, why He allowed a madman from my past to steal my darling daughter."

Off the top of my head, if I really believed there was a God sitting up in heaven who was controlling this stuff, I'd think maybe it was to spare me from her abusive piece of crap husband. But I don't mention that aloud. It hardly seems helpful.

"I finally have an answer. In the Bible, Joseph's the youngest, a beloved child of a great man, a prophet renamed Israel by God. Through no fault of his own, Joseph's brothers were jealous of his father's preference for him, and they sold poor Joseph into slavery. He spent many years doing the right thing, but no matter what he did, things became progressively worse and worse for him. He was thrown in jail, tempted and tormented, and no matter who he helped, he was forgotten. Even so Joseph never forgot God, and when the time came, God used Joseph to save his entire family. He was in a position of power in Egypt and he ultimately fed the entire nation of Israel. Without Joseph's ordeal the whole house of Israel would've starved."

Like the Marked kids will die, starving slowly as Tercera shuts down the function of their gastrointestinal tract. "Are we thinking that story's going to be on the test?" I ask.

Josephine takes my hand. "No darling, that's my answer. It's yours too, if you've ever wondered why your mother was taken from you. You don't need to feel guilt about what you're planning. You were taken from me for a reason, so that you'd be prepared to take over and lead our people when the time came. You're a present day Joseph. God wants you to rule, and He always provides a way to accomplish His designs. You and your friend Wesley were smart enough to see it. I still mourn the years with you I lost, but I know this is divine will."

Hmm. Well, that makes one of us.

Once we've worked out the rest of the details I head to my room to change. Adam takes up his position at the door and Sam follows me through the doorway.

"It's inappropriate for you to stay with Her Royal Highness," Adam says. "You'll start rumors."

I roll my eyes. "Sam stays with me at my request. I trust him."

Sam pauses and turns. "It's inappropriate for you to question Her Royal Highness, isn't it?"

Adam lifts one eyebrow. "You don't scare me, sir. My vows are to Her Majesty Ruby Solomon. I speak only out of concern for her well being. You may demote me or challenge me or whatever you choose, but I will speak when I believe it is in her best interest that I do so. Otherwise I would be failing in my duty."

Sam grins. "I can respect that." He shuts the door in Adam's beautiful, self-righteous face.

The second the door closes, Sam snags my hand and pulls me against him. "Say the word and we'll leave right now. My cursed uniform will get us out of here, I promise. You don't need to risk your life on this sunshine. No one would blame you, even your saintly but misguided mother."

"It's fine," I say. "The plan's solid."

Sam leans toward me and brushes his lips against mine, lightly. Too lightly. "It's a good one," he murmurs against me, "but every time we turn around those maniacs have some extra hoop for you to jump through. I'm an inch away from breaking all their prideful necks."

"I'm pretty sure murder's worse than pride."

"Is it?" Sam asks.

I snort. "Actually, that's the problem, right?" I start laughing and for some reason I can't seem to stop. "I have no idea."

Sam smirks. "You're so going to fail this test."

I'm still laughing. "Totally."

He kisses the smiles off my face and I think that's the one thing better than laughter. Kissing Sam.

We're both late by the time we're dressed and ready to go, and I don't even care. Josephine's waiting for me outside, tapping her foot. Her eyes widen when Sam comes out hand in hand with me. I consider explaining that I changed in the bathroom, but she doesn't say a word so I leave it alone. Sam's in his uniform and I'm wearing the deep blue silk ball gown Josephine had made for me. The bright golden embroidery is embellished in places with sparkling rubies.

Josephine's hand flies to her face when she sees me. "Oh, you look striking, Ruby. This color perfectly matches your eyes and your hair, just like I knew it would. I'm so glad I had it commissioned the day after we found you again. They only finished it two days ago you know, on the day your father—" She cuts off and swallows slowly. Watching how sad she gets when she thinks about David Solomon's death hurts me, but I still can't regret it.

I force a smile. My mom cares about these things, so I should try to care too. "It's a great dress Mom, really. Thanks. Now if you'd only thought to sew in a pocket for hiding the answers to Bible trivia, it might be helpful as well as ornamental."

Josephine's hands flutter around my face, finally settling near the crown of my head, smoothing my always twirly and fluffy hair back. "This is the first time most of your subjects here in Galveston will see your face. I wish we'd had time to put your hair up, but this will have to do. At least the curls are unique and lovely. Nearly ten thousand people have come to watch tonight, and many of them are visiting from the far-flung Ports. You father built the Assembly Hall specifically so his people could all come to his Sunday sermons in three simple sessions, but our population has grown so fast that it now takes ten or more sessions to accommodate everyone. He only held the full ten sessions it took for everyone to attend on special holidays."

There's no way I'll ever teach a Sunday sermon. Absolutely no way, but I don't mention that to Mom. Again, what's the point?

Sam holds my hand as we walk down the steps to the front drive. No black van today, not for this. A shiny white limousine waits for us. A guard I don't know holds the door open, and Sam helps me climb inside, arranging my skirts with a half grin.

I hate dresses and the puffier they are, the more I hate them. At least I'm not wearing a blasted tiara. Not yet, anyway.

Sam sits on my right side for the drive to the Assembly Hall and Adam sits on my left. I miss the constant jabber from Wesley and I wonder where he is. He should be back by now. I glance out the window repeatedly, but there's no sign of him yet. My foot taps on the floorboard of the car until Sam rests his hand on my knee.

"He'll do it," Sam whispers.

I breathe in and out. I hope he's right or my ashes will soon be blowing on the wind, dooming all the Marked kids to death.

The limousine pulls around the back of a huge sandstone building. Adam speaks into an earpiece and ushers me out. Sam doesn't hold my hand on the way in because boyfriend Sam is gone. Luckily, I recognize this Sam too. Tactical Sam scans the crowds as we enter the Assembly hall. He monitors the exits and listens to conversations. When I climb the steps and step out onto the raised dais, the crowd falls silent. The seven Port Heads are already seated at two tables, angled out toward the crowd with a podium between. I step away from Sam and toward the podium. When I glance back at Josephine, she's beaming at me.

I wish I had her faith.

Or any faith at all, really.

I think about my dad. I do have faith in two things thanks to him: science and people. I haven't seen Wesley but I believe he'll come. I know exactly what things fire will burn and what it won't. Thanks to Dad's teaching I have faith my plan will work. I glance at the back hall. I meant to simply announce my intention to request a Trial by Fire immediately, but I can't, not yet. I need to buy Wesley more time. As long as I make my request before the completion of the test, it should be fine. I think.

I walk slowly toward the podium in what I hope is a stately manner. Really I'm trying not to trip over my absurdly puffy skirts while walking in the obscenely tall shoes that came with the dress. I reach the podium and rest my hands on the angled, wooden top, which I can reach thanks to the shoes. "I'm happy for the opportunity to meet all of you today, but saddened by the circumstances that brought us here." That's true enough, even if I'm not sad for the reasons they think.

The audience cheers so loudly I grab the podium for support to keep from stumbling. I wasn't sure what to expect. I'm a young girl they've never before seen. In spite of what Josephine said, I worried they'd boo me off the stage.

A throat clears in a microphone and I glance at the tables to the right and left of me, unsure who's drawing attention to themselves and why.

"Welcome, young Ruby Solomon," Sawyer Blevins says. "And welcome to all of you fine citizens who have gathered to witness this Trial of Faith our beloved King asked us to conduct to ensure his daughter was prepared for the grave duty he has entrusted into her care."

"Yes, welcome to all of you," Rosa Alvarez says. "Many of you have traveled from quite a sizable distance to be present on this auspicious day. The Port Heads take the request of our former monarch quite seriously. World Peace Now has thrived in terrifying times because we've hearkened to the counsel of a loving God, a God who was forced to take action because the world had rotted, but He sought to preserve a righteous people. We have been that righteous branch, and now we must ensure our leader is the most virtuous among us and hearkens unto God's will."

I school my face to neutrality to cover my disgust. She's implying that all the people who died from Tercera were *rotten* and deserved to die. Can she possibly believe that's true?

"We've prepared ten questions each," Quentin Clarke says. "We hope you'll all consider during this test whether you can answer these questions yourselves. All of us can stand to spend a little more time learning God's ways. And I'm sure we'll all remember and be conscious of the fact that darling Ruby spent only days with her father before he was taken from her. In light of that, I'll start by asking her the first question. Mine are more questions of faith than of trivia so that we can all see where her heart lies."

My heart swells a little at his words and I wonder whether I might actually pass this test. Wouldn't that be something? Quentin, at least, doesn't seem to be trying to wrest control out of my hands.

"After Port Head Clarke begins, we'll each ask a question in turn, one at a time, circulating ten times, for a total of seventy questions," Sawyer Blevins says. "Per her father's edict she may not miss more than thirty questions, or she will be ineligible to rule. Are you all ready to begin?"

The Port Heads nod and Sawyer turns toward me. "Your Royal Highness?"

I lean toward the microphone. "Yes."

Quentin Clarke shuffles a paper in front of him. "First I'd like to ask you what approach you plan to take when you're inevitably confronted with a difficult decision to make for the people of World Peace Now."

I rock back on my heels. How will anyone decide whether my answer's right? "Um, well, first I'd ask the advisors close to me what they think. Obviously that would include religious advisors like the Port Heads. Then I'd think about it for myself and maybe consult the Bible, if there are applicable parts. Then I'll really ponder it and ask God if he thinks it's right. I'm not expert on that yet but I think He can let me know when I'm on the right path."

Quentin smiles. "I find that to be an acceptable answer.

I beam.

Rosa Alvarez says, "My questions deal with the last part of your reply, Your Royal Highness. Prayer. Specifically, my first question is a simple one. Please recite the Lord's prayer." Rosa smiles, but it doesn't reach her eyes.

The audience boos, and I don't understand why.

"Well, it sounds like the Lord's prayer is a specific prayer, and I'm sorry to say I haven't memorized any prayers in particular. But I imagine if the Lord was praying, he'd pray for his people. So maybe something like "Dear God please help your people to do what's right and be good like you. And thank you for what you've done."

Rosa sighs and shakes her head. "I'm sorry Your Royal Highness, but that's not the Lord's prayer, which is actually more of an instruction for us on how to pray."

The audience boos again, and my hands begin to shake. Where's Wesley? I glance at Sam but he shakes his head.

"My question," Terry Williams says, "is how many days did it take for God to create the earth?"

I lean too close to the microphone and my words boom into the room. "Oh I know this one." I pull back from the microphone. "Sorry about that. I guess I have as much experience with speaking to a lot of people with a microphone as I do governing." The audience chuckles. "But it's seven, I think. It took a week. First light and dark, then water and land and animals and plants, and then stars or something like that. Right?"

Terry frowns. "Almost. It was six days." The audience boos again.

I sigh. The people already hate me because I'm an idiot. "Because he rested on the last day, which is why we have Sunday. Whoops. I'm sorry. I really did know that."

Dolores Peabody asks the next question. "My questions will have to do with the order of the Bible and its creation. What are the two separate books in the Bible called, and how are they different?"

"Oh good," I say. "A two part question. The simple one

part questions were a little too easy for me I thought." The audience laughs and I grin. "Well, I think there's the old bible and the new bible, and the old one is from Jewish people? And the new one is from. . . Jesus? Maybe?"

Dolores presses her lips together. "Old and New Testament, but I'll give it to you." The audience cheers again and I realize they might be supporting me and booing the Port Heads. I did not expect that. "And how do they differ?"

Didn't I already answer that part? "Well, I think the older one is from Jewish people like I said, and it's like their stories of how things sucked before Jesus came. And the new one is about when Jesus came? So the Jews didn't like that one because when he came, they didn't think it was really him or something."

The audience cheers and Dolores shrugs. "I suppose that's close enough."

Steve Young says, "My questions relate to timing. When was Jesus born?"

"He reset the clocks. He was born at zero. That's why BC means Before Christ. I used to think AD meant After Death, but that would leave like thirty years of dead space in between so I found out it's actually it's Latin. It means anno domino, or something like that."

Steve grins. "Anno domini, which literally means 'in the year of the Lord.' I'll give you credit for it." The audience hoots and hollers this time.

Jose Fuerte clears his throat. "Your father gave me a second chance when I didn't have any hope so my questions will be about Christ's lessons on forgiveness."

"Oh good," I say. "Does that mean if I fail this test I'll get another go at it? Maybe in a week or two, after I've had time to study?"

The audience goes wild.

"Uh," Jose looks around. "Well, no. Actually your father made provision only for the one test."

"But he didn't specify a time you had to administer it, did he?" I cock one eyebrow.

Sawyer Blevins leans toward his microphone. "He didn't but we all agreed it needed to take place before the coronation, which I'm sure you can understand."

The audience boos, but I bow my head. "I'd be agreeable to postponing the coronation, but of course I understand that you're only trying to do what's best for the people."

"Exactly. We're doing this for the people."

The crowd boos.

Dolores frowns and taps the microphone. "Please ask your question, Jose."

"My first question is," Jose says, "in Matthew 18, how many times does the Lord tell Peter to forgive?"

I scrunch my nose. "A whole lot?"

Rosa speaks into the microphone. "Unfortunately, that's incorrect. It's a very specific verse. It states Peter must forgive seventy times seven times."

I whistle. "Wow, I only get to miss thirty questions, even though you're supposed to forgive four hundred and ninety times?"

The audience stands up to cheer this time.

Rosa rises to her feet and takes her microphone in her hand. "You're not a supplicant asking for forgiveness, but possibly our new leader. God will forgive the mistakes we make, but that doesn't mean we qualify to manage God's people. I hardly think quips and joke provide evidence that you're prepared and able to lead us in difficult times."

Sawyer Blevins leans forward in his seat. "And yet, a sense of humor can help us through difficult times and can be a real blessing. How about we proceed with the test and see how she does?"

Rosa frowns and sits down. I don't think I'll be scheduling a trip to go dancing with her in Miami any time soon.

"The last question for your first round is this," Sawyer says. "Many of the Psalms are called 'Messianic.' What does that mean?"

Messy? Anic? I raise my eyebrows. "They aren't clean when you read them, or maybe that means they aren't clear? Because I read some this afternoon and I had no idea what they were saying."

Sawyer shakes his head. "I'm sorry but that's not correct. It indicates they relate to Christ and his mission as the Messiah."

The next few questions don't go my way either. Even though Quentin and Steve try to lob me some softballs, it's clear I don't know anything about the Bible. I try not to make jokes, but sometimes the audience laughs anyway. They don't stand and cheer, not since Rosa's reprimand, but it's almost like I know them and they're pulling for me.

Twenty questions later I've only answered two more right, for a total of five correct and twenty-two wrong. I'm definitely doomed.

The fabric around my armpits is darker than the rest of my dress from sweat. Ugh. Not that it will matter when I'm headed for the same incinerator I fed my biological father to this morning. I'm supposed to wait for Wesley, but I can't wait any more. It's time. I'll have to trust that he comes through so I can pull this off.

Sawyer Blevins opens his mouth to ask my next question, but I talk over him. "This all happened too fast for me to prepare for a test like this."

Rosa says, "Your father made no proviso for timing."

"True," I bark, "and you lot jumped at the chance to do it immediately, knowing that the time was up to you.

Knowing that if I fail this test, of which you are the authors, I will die and the scattering of my ashes will name one of you to rule in my place. Regardless, this isn't about my lack of knowledge of Bible trivia or even Bible basics. David Solomon's edict states that the purpose of this test is to determine whether God has chosen me, and whether I will bend to God's direction when it matters."

"That is true." Rosa raises one carefully manicured eyebrow. "And so far I'd say you've indicated you're not very receptive."

Something inside my heart expands and words pour out unchecked. "God doesn't care about trivia. I can't say I know God all that well, and I certainly haven't prayed very often in my life. I've read the Bible even less as you've made abundantly clear. But the night my father died, we discussed the state of affairs in our world. We talked about the future of those children who were Marked, and the ones who had survived by suppressing their bodies' natural processes. Children who were left parentless, resourceless, and without guidance." I turn to face the audience. "Children my father left to starve and die."

I pause and stare into the faces of my people. No one is laughing now. The Port Heads don't say a word either.

Finally I continue. "My father intended for those children to die at WPN's hand. He called his plan a Cleansing. He may have been God's instrument at one point and he may have led you all to where you are now. You're safe, prosperous, and healthy and I'm sure that's a good place to be, comfortable even. I honestly don't know about all of that because I wasn't here. I laud him for saving all of your lives, but King Solomon was dead wrong in his plan to kill a hundred thousand people. If God decided it was time to replace him, that's the reason."

Again, I scan the audience. Every face is solemn. No

one is mocking me, no one is laughing, and no one is booing.

"God very clearly spoke to my heart that night. Those children aren't guilty for their parents' decisions, whether they were right or wrong. They deserve our pity and our help, not our condemnation. After I'm crowned there will be no Cleansing. Instead we will provide help and support to those who have been Marked. The suppressant's failing and they're dying soon. I know it's scary to all of you, like having a rabid dog at your door. Your fear tells you to put the dog down any way possible. Shoot it between the eyes if you have to, but these Marked children, they aren't dogs, they're people just like you and me. If we can find a cure for their illness, and I believe we can with God's help, we'll work to distribute it. If not, we will not put them down. We'll ease their suffering as God wants us to."

Sawyer stands, his face bright red. "The Cleansing was revealed as God's will to all of the Port Heads. We are God's chosen leaders. We are administering this test, and as much as it saddens me to see my own first cousin once removed performing so miserably, I think the results of this test have been clear. You're in over your head and you didn't take the offered lifeline from any of us. You lack the experience, the knowledge, and the humility to lead these people by God's direction."

I toss my head. "Do I? God protected me when I was taken by the Marked recently. My father prayed for my protection, and God listened. I walked among them and as you can see, I am unmarked still. I didn't contract Tercera then, and I can't contract it now because I'm God's chosen. Instead of this test constructed by power-hungry men, I demand a Trial by Fire. And when I survive it, God will tell me which Port Heads are still listening to him so I can replace the ones who aren't."

A gunshot sounds outside the Assembly Hall and all heads turn toward the back doors.

Adam speaks quietly into his walkie. "Yes, bring them inside."

The back doors open. Wesley, bless him, walks through them, perfectly timed.

"Your guards refused to let me inside until I threatened them rather dramatically, but there's a Marked child here who has a message. He claims it's for the ruler of WPN and he claims it's urgent."

I point at Wesley. "Move aside and let him speak."

When Wesley steps aside, I'm surprised to see a young man with hair black as night and skin as pale as bread dough. Where's Rafe?

"Your majesty," a small, high voice yells. "I had a dream last night and an angel told me to come across the bridge and deliver a message to you. He said I was supposed to touch your face, and that God would keep you safe. He said you needed me to help you so you could help all of us."

Josephine walks up the steps and onto the stage. She looks from one end of the Assembly Hall to the other. "I believe my daughter is entitled to a Trial by Fire, and I believe it should be performed by exposing her to Tercera. It may not kill as quickly as fire, but it burns through the body's defenses and kills just as surely as flames. If she remains healthy and uninfected in spite of the contact with someone infected, God's will is clear. Do you agree?"

The audience goes wild.

The young boy walks up the aisle slowly, the people around him bending as far away from him as they possibly can. This young boy is brave, with a stronger heart than the one that beats in my chest. He faces straight forward and walks, step by small step toward me, never looking to the side, never flinching. He walks up the steps at the front of the stage and past the tables. Here on the raised platform though, he turns.

He looks at each Port Head in turn. "Would you stand still while I touched each of you, trusting in God's power to protect you? Would *you* survive a Trial by Fire?"

He reaches his hand toward Sawyer's face, and grand old Port Head Blevins scrambles backward, knocking his chair over. He turns toward Quentin, who holds up both hands and shakes his head. When he reaches for Rosa, she shrieks and claws at the table to shove away from him.

The young boy turns toward the audience. "Remember this, that Ruby Solomon has more faith than any of these educated and polished Port Heads."

I cringe a little when I hear him say my name is Solomon, but I'm sure any onlookers assume I'm nervous about being touched, so maybe it's good. Obviously Wesley told him to call me that, to remind the people whose daughter I supposedly am, to help transfer their inexplicable love for him to me.

He turns and walks the last few steps to reach me. He points at his forehead. "This is my Mark. I've had it for ten years now." He shoves up his sleeves and holds up his arms. "You can see that I've progressed to second year symptoms. I have sores on my arms, my legs and my torso." He turns back toward me and reaches out tentatively. His palm hovers inches from my face, but I don't fear his touch. I may not trust in God, but I trust my father. I lean toward his hand and press my face into it.

The audience lets out a collective sigh.

"How will we know whether she survives this?" Terry Williams asks. "It's not like fire or lions, where tomorrow morning will make her fate clear."

I smile. "It's not, that's correct. If you're all satisfied that this brave young man is Marked, I recommend we release him to return home with gratitude for his willingness to answer God's request."

The Port Heads nod. They can't get rid of him fast enough. Only now, they're looking at me the same way. Like I'm infected, like I'm dangerous, like they might die from breathing the same air as me.

"I'll walk carefully to whatever hospital you'd like to designate and wait until an appropriate amount of time has passed. You may draw my blood and examine it, or scrape my skin cells and examine those, to verify that I am not infected."

"Three days," Sawyer Blevins says. "The Unmarked quarantine people for three days, don't they?"

I nod.

"I'm happy to extend the seven of you the time you didn't offer me before this test." I turn toward the audience. "In three days' time, on Saturday at eight in the evening, you'll have your answer. In the meantime, I'm afraid this means I won't be present for my dear father's memorial tomorrow." I suppress a smile at my cleverness in escaping that torturous event. And I realize with glee, no one will be doing a fitting on me between now and then either. "I look forward with great joy to my coronation, which I'll reschedule for Sunday morning."

The Port Heads nod and the crowd cheers. "See you Sunday," one voice calls out. "Long live Queen Ruby," another yells.

I walk down the steps and back toward the limousine, maintaining careful distance from all of my guards, Sam, and my mom. It's a tight fit in the car with me on my own row. I doubt Sam and Adam will ever want to talk about how close they sat to one another, but we make it work. Wesley rushes toward us before Adam can close the car door.

"Wait, let him inside," I say. "He should likely be quarantined too, with as close as he was to the Marked boy."

Wesley nods, and slides over next to me. "I think that went well."

I smile. "Me too. You had me sweating, though."

Wesley whispers. "When I got there, they were all gone."

"Is that why you didn't bring Rafe?"

Wesley nods. "Cleared out. He's back in Baton Rouge already."

I swear.

"What's wrong?" Sam asks. "You know you're safe." He glances at Adam. "I mean, we have faith that God will protect you again."

I nod. "I believe that, I really do, but without Rafe here . . ."

Sam curses when understanding dawns.

"You'll never make it to Baton Rouge by Saturday," Wesley says. "You won't even be crowned until Sunday."

I managed to outsmart the Port Heads and thwart David Solomon's attempt to reach out and stop me from the grave. I can finally stop the Cleansing and get the Marked the help they need.

But if Rafe doesn't see reason, my cleverness may cost Rhonda her life.

CHAPTER 5

Q uarantine's a nuisance, and the irony of being in quarantine with Wesley this time isn't lost on me. "You know." I play an ace of spades and take his king. "I had to sit in a stupid room like this all by my lonesome last time, reading my dad's boring old journals thanks to you."

Wesley takes my five of diamonds with a six.

"That's just rude."

"I don't make the rules, I only win by following them better than you." Wesley grins. "That feels like years ago, not weeks. I'm sorry you got stuck in quarantine alone. I screwed up a lot back then."

"Not anymore?" I roll my eyes.

"Well, I wasn't going to toot my own horn, but now that you mention it. I went to find Rafe, as ordered, and found a whole lot of nobody. Did I panic? No, I did not. I calmly raced over to the maternity ward, and luckily found a small team scavenging for medical supplies they'd left behind. And I think he handled the story I fed him with aplomb. The kid could be an actor if we get them all healed up."

"I am glad you didn't throw in the towel when you realized Rafe was gone. I'd be a pile of ashes a bunch of power hungry nut jobs were diving for instead of playing spades while skipping David freaking Solmon's memorial service. Thanks for that."

Wesley beats me, again, but this time when he starts shuffling, I stand up. I pace from one end of the room to the other. "I can't play another hand of cards."

"Wow, I never knew you were such a poor loser," Wesley says.

I spin around. "I can't stand it, sitting here while Rhonda's staring at a clock, hoping Rafe doesn't kill her. I'm sure she's wondering where I am. I don't understand why the physicians can't just test our blood and see that we're not infected."

"You know why we haven't pushed for that," Wesley reminds me.

Because if they find the antibodies at ten times the normal level in my blood, that might lead to questions. If they find my dad's journal, which I'm unwilling to destroy, well the whole thing might come out and we'd likely all be shot for deception. Or lack of faith in God. I'm unsure which one they'd consider to be more egregious.

"You need to calm down and be patient," Wesley says.

"I can't be patient. I thought I killed her once before when Rafe's goon Todd captured us. She stayed in my place then, and I can't let her die for me again."

"She didn't die then, and she won't die now. Rafe's an angry guy because he has reason to be, but he's not stupid. He needs you and shooting your sister isn't going to motivate you, not like he wants."

"He's desperate and if he doesn't kill Rhonda, we'll know he won't kill Job. He can't bluff the first hand, Wes." I bite my lip and bang on the wall.

Wesley, unconcerned about my fear, flops back on his twin bed. "Don't be so melodramatic."

We're lucky this time. Our room has actual beds with thick, fluffy mattresses, which is a significant improvement over the cots in Port Gibson. Actually it's much better than what we had in this room only last week when loony David Solomon locked me in with Wesley for being insouciant. It feels strange to be in the very same building where Solomon tried to teach me a lesson about discipline. This one's outfitted differently, with a Plexiglas window we could draw curtains on for seeing people who come to visit, and a tray on the floor that can slide open for the provision of food.

I stomp. "My frustration isn't melodrama Wes, it's an appropriate level of drama for the situation."

He sighs. "We sent a messenger explaining the details and Rafe will be reasonable. Obviously you can't control what WPN decides you have to do before the coronation. He's impatient and he wants to make progress toward a cure, but he's not going to kill Rhonda. You may dislike Todd, but the guy is smart and Rafe listens to him. He used to work for Solomon, actually. He'll talk Rafe out of shooting his leverage."

"He'd still have Job." I continue to pace in the small room, walking from the foot of my twin bed back to Wesley's. They offered us private rooms in case we worried about cross contamination or wanted privacy, but we both wanted company. "Rafe meant what he said. It wasn't a threat."

When I hear tapping coming from the large square

Plexiglas enclosure in the wall, I turn. Sam waves. The low rumble of his voice is muffled, but it penetrates well enough for me to understand him. "I hope my little brother isn't that insane. Rafe's been through a lot, but I really hope Wesley's right this time. You did the right thing, so try to stop fretting about it."

Sam's not pleased that Wesley and I are stuck in quarantine together, but Wesley had to find the Marked kid to be on hand for my Trial by Fire, and that means he had to "save" him when the boy followed him back to the island. Wesley was exposed, according to what they know, and might be Marked.

Sam tried to wait with me in here too, but Wesley appropriately pointed out that we need someone on the outside making sure things are moving ahead properly. Josephine's competency has improved dramatically since shooting her husband, and she seems to genuinely care for me. She's even come around on the subject of the Cleansing, but she's not very decisive or capable in a crisis. As Chief Fancy Pants of the military, or at least interim Chief Fancy Pants, Sam has access to nearly everywhere on the island. Plus he's Sam, so people listen when he talks.

Josephine's head pops up next to Sam's, which tells me the funeral service has ended.

"I hope the proceedings were touching and provided everyone the closure they needed." I don't care actually, but she won't realize that.

Josephine probably means for her smile to be encouraging, but it makes her look a little unhinged. I don't think she spent much time smiling over the past twenty years. Maybe she's forgotten how, or perhaps her jaw's rusty from disuse.

"It was a beautiful service." She wipes away a tear. I'd be

impressed with her acting skill, except I know she's not acting. She really does mourn her late, and very abusive, husband.

"I'm glad you enjoyed it."

Josephine puts her palm to the glass, and I wonder if she imagines I'm going to place mine next to it, like I'm longing to share in some form of mutual grieving over Solomon's passing. If so, she's going to be sadly disappointed. I'm not grieving and I don't need comforting, at least, not over that.

"I'm happy to report that everything's coming along nicely for your coronation," she says. "The extra few days have been a Godsend, honestly. I think you'll absolutely adore the flowers we're having sent from a hothouse in Miami."

I couldn't possibly care less about flowers, or any other coronation details, if I'm being honest. I can't believe she thinks any of this matters. Rhonda may die, but at least I'll have some lovely memories of the time they handed me a crown I didn't care about, to rule a bunch of people I don't know, in a bower of flowers from I don't care where. "Wow, well, that's really . . . wonderful, I guess."

Adam's face edges its way into the corner of my window. His smile looks more natural than Mom's at least. "I'm sorry you missed your father's service. I do hope you're finding your lodgings acceptable."

Adam and I fought yesterday, and he's been super weird ever since. He wanted to prepare rooms for me in the huge white house everyone still insists isn't a palace. I told him a typical quarantine room in the holding facility was fine. I'm tired of them trying to convince me I should be using silk toilet paper. He gave in gracefully enough after I bit his poor, misguided head off. If I close my eyes, I can still see the shocked look on his face when I told him that my poop smells just as bad as his.

"Your Royal Highness," Adam says. "I hate to interrupt your time with your mother, but several Port Heads have requested the opportunity to speak to you."

I raise one eyebrow. "Which ones?"

He sighs. "Sawyer Blevins."

I grimace. David Solomon's cousin is probably my least favorite of all, even worse than the sour-faced Dolores. Every time he calls me darling my skin crawls as though Solomon's actually back.

"Also Rosa Alvarez and Steve Young. Initially all seven requested entrance. I informed them the window into your room only has space for three faces." Adam offers me a half smile. "I think you made them nervous when you threatened to eliminate Port Heads God tells you aren't doing his will. Now that no Mark has appeared, they're nearly frantic. Do you wish to speak with them?"

"Not really," I mutter. "But when has that mattered lately?" I speak loudly enough for Adam, Sam and Josephine to hear me. "Go ahead and send them in."

Sam says, "I'll verify none of them are armed or harboring any ill intent."

Adam narrows his eyes. "I already performed a thorough search."

"Your version of thorough and mine aren't the same." Sam walks out of view with Adam on his heels.

"I've got an appointment with the dressmakers," Josephine says. "Can you believe they're making me fill in for your fittings?"

It makes perfect sense, actually. My mom's almost exactly my size. After she walks off, I stand up and brush off my white button down shirt. I pick a piece of imaginary lint off my jeans and push my hair back behind my shoulders.

Wesley stays flat on his back, staring up at the ceiling. I doubt he'll move when they appear, either. "You don't need to impress them you know. You beat them and now you can fire them all."

I could, but it's more complicated than that. Who would I put in their places? "I have a feeling anything I try to do will lead to a fight. If I were my father, I'd have them all executed and appoint new ones. Or you know, if I was Solomon and I had any interest in doing anything here other than preventing the Cleansing and leaving as soon as possible."

Wesley shrugs. "Firing them all isn't a horrible idea, actually. You can appoint anyone else you like as a new Port Head, and they'll all be terrified of you and simultaneously grateful for their new position. If that's the kind of inspiration he had, maybe there's a reason Solomon ruled for so long."

Adam's face appears at the window. With me stuck in quarantine, like a sitting duck in Adam's words, he's doing double duty as guard and butler. "Your Royal Highness Ruby Solomon, may I present the Port Heads of New Orleans, Miami, and Jacksonville. Sawyer Blevins, Rosa Alvarez, and Steve Young."

Rosa's face appears, her bright red lipstick and perfectly curled hair taking up more than her fair third of the window. Sawyer brushes at her hair with frustration. Steve walks calmly into view, practically ignoring the other two.

"Thanks Adam. Hello Sawyer, Rosa, and Steve. What can I help you with today?"

Sawyer opens his mouth, but before he can speak Rosa says, "We came to help you, actually. It's been almost a full day since your Trial and no Mark has appeared. We first wanted to express our delight that God has protected you. Congratulations on finding His favor. That was a bold move you made."

I sit on the edge of my bed and lift my chin. "Not bold so much as desperate, since I was obviously not going to pass your test."

"In any case," Sawyer says, "we're happy to see how well you're doing."

I exhale. "Are you?"

Steve's jaw drops. "Of course we are, Your Royal Highness. How could we not hope for your success?"

I lift my eyebrows. "Well, seeing as one of you would've taken over for me if I failed, and by failed I mean *died*, I did wonder whether your loyalty to me might have been shake-able."

Wesley whistles.

Sawyer and Rosa narrow their eyes at him. "Why are you whistling?"

Wesley sits up enough that they can see him shrug. "You underestimated my girl, Ruby. She's never been a leader before, but clearly she has more skill and gumption than you expected."

"You've developed entirely the wrong impression," Sawyer says. "We want to help you in any way possible. Clearly God's chosen will be crowned on Sunday, and you'll be leading the largest group of people still living in the Americas. For those unfamiliar with pondering and understanding God's will, it can be . . . complicated."

"As you've mentioned."

Sawyer clamps his mouth shut.

"I do appreciate your willingness to help," I say. "What sorts of things did you want to help me with, exactly?"

Steve says, "King Solomon had to approve each of the trade agreements between the various Ports. This was to ensure fairness and equity, and also to verify we were paying the proper tributes to the crown. I was an accountant Before and sometimes the agreements were hard to understand, even for me. I'd be happy to review the proposals with you, at your convenience of course, and help advise you on what's fair and what isn't."

Sawyer clears his throat. "I'd be happy to help with that as well. Two sets of eyes are nearly always better than one."

"Do you mean three sets are better than two?" I ask. "Or do my eyes not count?"

Sawyer's eyes widen. "Three, yes, that's what I meant. But in addition to helping you navigate the monetary and trade issues, we can help with managing your people and their expectations."

"And I can help you prepare your Sunday sermons," Rosa says. "We women must strike a different tone. The men can bang on the podium and yell, brimstone and whatnot, but the people respond differently to females."

"I'm going to stop you right there," I say. "I won't be giving a Sunday sermon."

All three jaws drop.

Rosa splutters. "Who will administer the word of God on Sunday? It's an excellent time for you to get a feel for your people's wants and needs, and for them to get to know you. And understand your goals and desires too, of course."

Wesley says, "You make the Sunday sermon sound like a political rally."

Steve closes his eyes, exhales and opens them again. "It's not a political rally, but the people need to be reminded of what matters and why. Religion binds us together as a community and reinforces you as their leader. Surely you can see that, Your Royal Highness."

"As you may have noticed yesterday, I lack both religious knowledge and the desire to manage people."

"And yet," Sawyer says, "God chose you, and the people absolutely love you."

I clench my fists. "I'm sure the people will be happy to hear from someone I appoint to share the word of God with them."

Rosa presses her lips together. "Well, I'm sure any of us would be happy to suggest qualified ministers for the role. It's certainly one way to go."

"I really appreciate your good intentions," I say, "but it's nearly dinner time and I'm starving. I'd hate to make you watch me chew and swallow my dinner through a Plexiglas window, so maybe you can wrap things up."

"Absolutely," Steve says.

Rosa glances at him sharply. "Actually, we did have one more thing we wanted to discuss. All the Port Heads were concerned after what you mentioned yesterday."

"Oh?" I ask. "What was that?" This should be good. I'm ready for them to beg me for their jobs.

"You mentioned that your father was *wrong*," Rosa whispers. "Which is a dangerous enough thing to say on its own for reasons we can discuss in greater detail later." She glances sideways as if trying to ensure none of my guards can hear her. "But you also stated quite clearly that the Cleansing was, well, off the table so to speak. You said we should try to *cure* the Marked children, and only if that fails would we ease their suffering."

I nod. "All of that's true. I don't know what precisely about any of that concerns you. Was there a question, or maybe a clarification you wanted?"

Sawyer smacks his lips so loudly I can hear it through the window. "I believe Rosa thought she implied our issue. To contradict royalty, especially someone chosen of God, is problematic. It undermines your authority at a baseline and throws all your future decisions into question, at worst. But even beyond that, to counteract your father's last plan, when your own intentions don't make sense—"

I step toward the window, one hand on my hip. "What part of 'provide aid in seeking a cure, and ease their deaths if necessary' is nonsensical to you people?"

Sawyer throws his hands up in the air. "There is no cure. We've looked, and the Unmarked have looked, and presumably the Marked have looked for over a decade. At this point the final option you mentioned, easing their suffering, that's our only viable solution."

"They aren't dying in a week or two," I say. "It's not like they've been hit with the accelerant."

"Precisely," Rosa says. "But the suppressant is failing. The status quo *has* shifted. If they had been accelerated, that would be more merciful. As it is they will slowly die, and when that happens, their community, such that it is, will break down. They'll begin scavenging and wandering, the ones healthy enough, and that's when they become a real threat to all of your people."

I bob my head. "Because they're just like the rabid dog I mentioned. They're doomed, and we may as well put them down before they can bite us while trying to steal our food."

Rosa's face lights up, but so do Sawyer and Steve's. "Yes, exactly," she says. "You're finally getting it. The thing is, when they aren't ready, before they've gotten desperate, it's the perfect time for us to Cleanse the earth of this wretched disease once and for all."

I lift my eyebrows. "What about providing them with the food and supplies they need?"

"Why should we have to provide for them? We need our resources for our people."

"Right," I say. "So a simple bullet to the head for each of them would be merciful and conserve resources. Is that what I didn't understand?"

Sawyer frowns. "Well, we were thinking to drive them together with a series of controlled fires—"

I slam one hand into the Plexiglas. "We should roast them alive because you greedy tyrants won't share your food? Quentin needs more food, does he? Dolores needs more roast chicken? You, Rosa, you need more salsa? You people are a disease. You'll be lucky to stay alive, much less be Port Heads when I'm crowned. Do you hear me?"

Rosa flinches. "You think we're selfish and greedy. But it's not a bad plan to keep your own people safe from a very real threat, one that can kill us all. It has already killed almost every human on earth. We're all that's left, and we didn't survive by providing for every sick person we could."

I very nearly growl. "As far as I can tell you haven't done a single thing for any of them."

"We never proposed the Cleansing lightly," Steve says.

"Anytime someone suggests taking someone else's life on their own terms and calls it an act of charity or mercy, it's problematic. But you're all missing the point. I think we may be able to save them."

Steve inhales slowly. "Why do you think we'll find the cure now, after we've come up with nothing in eleven years?"

I should tell them, but then they'd know it wasn't God who chose me and I won't stay queen, and these maniacs will kill all the Marked kids. I could tell them about my dad and how he created Tercera, but I'm sure that would come around to bite me in the tush, too.

"Because God told me so. I'm a scientist. Did you know that?"

Rosa and Sawyer and Steve all shake their heads.

"My foster mother among the Unmarked was on the cusp of solving this when I left. As soon as I'm crowned, I'm going to visit her and we'll provide her whatever facilities and resources she needs to reach the finish line. We've allowed this plague to threaten us for too long. It needs to end now, but I won't have my rule as queen begin with a mass slaughter of children. If I haven't been clear enough, let me say it again. There is literally nothing you can say or do to change my mind. We will not *Cleanse* the earth of these children. We will petition for God's aid in saving them. Is that clear?"

Sawyer's lip curls. "And if you can't? If they die anyway?"

"Then they'll die in the nicest beds, with the best food that we can provide for them."

"Why would we do that?" he asks.

"Why indeed, you ask?" I stand up and walk toward the window, my face inches away from theirs. "A man of God is asking me why we should provide charity to children? If I know anything about the Bible, it's that Jesus was humble. He gave and gave and gave. He didn't sleep on ten million thread count sheets. He didn't dine on freshly made chowder. He ate what he needed and shared whatever was left. If I have to grind your face into the ground and take your fancy bed away to make you see that, well. Consider it done. You can thank your lucky stars I'm not my father, because if I was, I'd cut your heads off now."

Rosa and Sawyer exchange a glance before nodding slightly and begging my leave to depart. Steve merely stares at me thoughtfully.

"I believe my dinner of loads of imported and rich food is on its way," I say. "You better leave so I can eat it. But don't get too used to yours."

Adam sees them out and returns with a tray for me. One of the other guards has a second tray. Adam slides the first through, and then on the second, he whispers through the slot. "You need to be careful, Your Royal Highness. You're making some powerful enemies, and you're not in the safest of spots right now."

I sigh. "Sam will keep me safe, Adam."

Adam puffs out his chest. "You mistake me. I'll keep you safe. I'd simply prefer not to have to kill too many people in the process if I can avoid it."

I smile. "Good to know. We're in agreement on that."

Wesley and I set our trays up on our laps since there isn't room for a table and chairs now that the cots have been replaced with beds.

Wesley takes a bite of a crusty roll and sighs. "I'm with you on everything you said. Bravo." He chews and swallows. "But do we really have to give away all the good food, even the chocolate cake?" He stuffs a huge bite of cake with frosting into his mouth and moans.

I roll my eyes, but before I can tell him to shut up, someone bangs on the window.

Sam.

I smile at him. "I wish you could come in to eat with us."

He shakes his head. "There's news."

I set my tray aside and cross the room to the window. "What is it?"

Sam frowns and my chest tightens. He holds up a piece of paper, shoving it flat against the Plexiglas so I can read it.

Your Very Esteemed and Royal High-ney:

I regret to inform you that your request for additional time has cordially been refused. I was quite clear when we spoke not two days ago. I told you that we don't care about WPN or its plans. We are quite capable of protecting ourselves.

The longer you spend dealing with their problems, their tests, and their demands, the longer they will make them. The only way to end the threat of WPN and the Unmarked and everyone else who fears us is to CURE us.

I don't care whether you're the Queen of WPN or the Queen of Sheba. We're running out of time. If you don't report here tomorrow as I initially demanded, I will execute your cousin Rhonda. Or actually, I guess she's not related to you after all. In that case, you may not care.

We'll find out where your priorities are tomorrow I suppose. Stay and get a crown from your daddy's people, or come save your not-cousin.

Either way, the deadline's still sunset tomorrow.

Rafe

My eyes turn toward Sam's so he knows that I've finished reading the letter.

His face reflects the horror in mine.

"I can't leave and go to Baton Rouge, and then simply come back a week or two later to be crowned. The Port Heads are insane, and I just yelled at and threatened them. They'll seize control for sure."

Sam frowns. "Maybe it won't matter. Did they even care about the Cleansing?"

I collapse on my bed, my face in my hands.

Wesley crosses the room. "I take it Rafe declined your request for an extension?"

Sam nods.

Wesley runs his hand through his hair. "Well that really blows, because Stalin and Pol Pot were just telling us how stupid it is to allow the rabid Marked kids to continue foaming at the mouth near enough that the people of WPN might get sick."

"Who are Stalin and Polpot?" I ask.

Wesley shakes his head. "My dad made me read a lot of history texts. Never mind. Look, this really sucks, but we don't have much time to decide what to do." Wesley's voice drops to a whisper. "If Sam's breaking us out of here, he's got to do it tonight or we won't make it in time for Rafe's deadline."

I close my eyes. If I leave tonight and we're successful for the first time ever in actually escaping from somewhere, I can't return. If I walk away from these people, with the seven Port Heads here to spin my actions as a betrayal, well, that's it. If I do leave, Sawyer and Rosa made it quite clear how they feel. They'll eliminate every Marked kid from here to Canada, and I think they have the means to do it, whatever Rafe thinks.

I glance from Sam to Wesley and back again.

"You know her," Sam says.

I do. Blood relative or not, I know Rhonda better than anyone else except maybe Job. I know her well enough to know what she would tell me to do if she was standing right here next to me.

"Ruby." She'd shake her head. "Don't be emotional and don't be an idiot. My life weighed against the certain death of a hundred thousand children? Don't end their extra lease on life before it's begun."

Tears well up in my eyes, and I shake my head to clear the image of ghost Rhonda. I can't handle the thought of her really being gone. I need her sass and her verve and her confidence. I need Rhonda to be alive and well.

"But Job and Uncle Dan and Aunt Anne."

Sam's eyes are sad.

Wesley looks at the floor.

It doesn't matter how often I say their names aloud. It doesn't matter if this decision is agony. It doesn't matter, because if I do this and Rafe doesn't budge, they'll never forgive me. I know that because I'll never forgive myself.

Even so, I'm going to stay right here, and do something I never wanted, something I still don't want. I'm going to be crowned Queen of friggin' Sheba to try and save Rafe's ungrateful and unworthy neck. And if he follows through on his threat, I may have to wring it myself.

CHAPTER 6

F riday and Saturday are both boring. No Port Heads come to yell at me, and none try to assassinate me. I almost wish someone would, if only to give me something to think about other than Rhonda and Rafe's impending deadline.

I suck at cards compared to Wesley, so by Friday afternoon I refuse to play another single hand. Why bother losing at anything else?

Adam tries to help keep me company. It turns out he plays a pretty mean game of Would You Rather. While Sam works with Josephine on last minute details of my coronation, I learn that Wesley would rather be alone for the rest of his life than be surrounded by annoying people. Adam would rather know how he's going to die, instead of when.

"Would you rather," I ask, "have the general public think you're wonderful while your family knows you're a terrible person, or have the general public hate you, but your family be proud, because you treat them right?"

Wesley furrows his brow. "This one's easy. Obviously—"

"Ah, ah, ah," I say. "It's Adam's turn."

Adam bites his lip. "Well, it's not much of a question, really. In one scenario I'm a good person, and in one I'm not, right? I think regardless of who thinks you're good, you should want to be a good person at heart."

I shake my head. "The question doesn't address whether you're actually good or not. You could be good or bad in either scenario. You're you. The question is, which set of people's opinions do you value? The general public? Or your family and close friends?"

Adam shakes his head. "Let's assume I am a good person, then—"

"It's not about truth, Adam. Focus here for a moment. It's about whose opinion matters to you. Which is it? Family or the world at large?"

He shrugs. "I don't have much family. My parents are both dead, and I don't have any friends. I guess the general public."

My heart wilts a little bit. "No family and no friends?"

He shrugs. "My mom and I were really close, but she died of cancer two years ago. I enlisted right after that."

I close my eyes. "I'm sorry, Adam. I haven't known you long but for what it's worth, I consider you a friend."

He beams at me. "Then maybe I'll pick friends instead of the public."

"Oh come on," Wesley says. "This handsome, muscled dude flirts with you all day, but the second I say anything about kissing or relationships—"

Adam splutters. "I would never flirt with Her Royal Highness."

"Woe is me," Wesley says. "I have no friends and no family, which is why I focus on intrinsic goodness, and perfecting my six pack abs. Since I inevitably have time left over, I better work on making my biceps the size of cantaloupes. My perfect hair and Adonis-like facial features can't quite drown out the sorrow of my life." Wesley snorts. "All you need is a puppy and an orphan child you're raising on your own, and you'd be ready to go trolling on the beach."

Adam turns toward me. "I have no idea what he's talking about most of the time. Trolls? There aren't any trolls, and if there were, they'd certainly not be walking anywhere near a beach."

Wesley slaps his forehead. "I was saying that you flirt with Ruby all day long, but if I even so much as think about telling her she looks amazing in those jeans and that t-shirt, which you do by the way, Rubes, then—"

Sam clears his throat.

"See?" Wesley sighs. "Lover Boy shows up to scowl at me and flex his muscles and generally stomp around."

Adam smirks. "I think Lover Boy knows I have no intention of ever wooing Her Royal Highness."

"Wooing?" Sam asks. "And can I just say how happy I am that Wesley's stupid nickname for me is catching on?" He places his hand on the glass, and for Sam I stand up and walk over to place my hand against it.

"I miss you." I whisper, "Especially at night."

Wesley covers his ears. "La, la, la. Come on you two, knock it off."

Adam smirks. "I'll go fetch dinner trays. Do you plan to stay and eat?" he asks Sam.

Sam shakes his head. "I can't. I'm due at the Assembly hall in a few minutes for a last run through on security and protocols. I swung by to make sure Ruby's okay."

"I'm taking good care of her," Adam says. "She's perfectly safe."

Wesley rolls his eyes. "He doesn't mean physically, Mr. Literal."

I think about the time. Dinner. Which means close to sunset. Rafe's deadline on Saturday night. My knees give out and I fall back onto the edge of my bed. Rafe might be shooting Rhonda right this minute.

I could have stopped it and I chose not to.

I close my eyes, but I don't sleep. Not then, not after dinner, not all night. Every time I drift off, Job or Aunt Anne or Uncle Dan take turns pulling guns on me, or roasting me over a spit, or slapping my face.

Wesley's eyes are bright and clear when the physician comes to examine us. At least it's not Dr. Flores. I couldn't deal with her shiny, immaculate beauty, not today. I've already been to the bathroom and seen the terrible dark circles under my eyes, and I'm well aware of the state of my unwashed hair.

Luckily, in spite of my ghastly appearance, the physician pronounces our survival a miracle. I've been cleared.

Sam's already wearing a black tuxedo when he pulls me in for a hug outside the quarantine room door. Adam's standing behind Sam and to the left wearing a fancy uniform, full of stripes and medals. He may not have been a guard for too long, after all he barely looks older than me, but he's earned plenty of accolades. After Sam releases me, I reach over and squeeze Adam's hand. "I hope you'll stand near me for the ceremony."

Adam beams.

"Why do you like that guy?" Sam asks when we walk down the hallway a few paces. "He's a terrible suck up. If I have to hear him call you Your Royal Highness one more time . . ."

"Is it the Royal that bothers you?" I ask, looking at him from more than a foot away, "Or the Highness?" I wink.

He leans down and kisses me quickly. "You look tired."

"Just what every princess wants to hear on her coronation day."

He frowns. "You know what I mean. Couldn't you sleep? Or were you up late talking with Wesley?" Sam glances behind him and Wesley throws him two thumbs up.

"My lack of sleep had nothing to do with Wesley. Does he have rings under his eyes?"

Sam squeezes my hand. "I'm sorry."

When we reach the white non-palace, swarms of ladies descend. Within a few moments, they've shoved me into the shower, dried me off afterward—which was unspeakably awkward— before they applied makeup, and my hair's been twisted up into a complicated, curly mass of tendrils on top of my head. Tiny, sparkly, red beads are threaded throughout next, which takes even longer than I worried it would.

When I hear a knock at the door to my anteroom, they're busy stuffing me into an ivory sheath dress. Again, tiny rubies have been sewn into the bodice, this time into the shapes of delicate flowers. I have almost no curves naturally, but when I glance in the mirror they've suddenly appeared. This dress might have been worth the million and one fittings.

When the door opens, Josephine gasps. "Darling, you look absolutely stunning."

I flinch. "Maybe don't say darling anymore?"

She frowns like she never realized it was creepy. "I'll try to remember, but sometimes I might forget. Like when I see you and you look more beautiful than I ever imagined something could." Her hand flies to her heart and she inhales and exhales slowly.

"It's like you think I'm getting married or something."

Josephine cups my face with her hand. "One day, dar—"

she cuts off, and closes her eyes. When she opens them, she smiles at me. "It's a hard habit to break, but I will."

"Thanks, and I'm in no rush on the marriage thing, you know."

She nods. "I figured, but one day it will happen, and that'll be a happy day for me. For now, you're doing something even bigger in its own way. You're pledging before God to care for His people. You're promising those people that you'll make sure our community stays safe and things will run smoothly. This matters."

I don't bother telling her all people should be God's people, or that I don't want to make any pledges of any kind. I don't say a word about any of it on the ride over to the Assembly Hall. It feels like I never talk to my mom about anything of substance, but we'd hardly have time for a fruitful conversation here.

When the van pulls to a stop, I close my eyes and breathe in and out a few times slowly. The enormous building looks exactly the same on the outside, but when we walk inside it's barely recognizable. Gone are the podium and tables, replaced with baskets and bins of roses. Lilies and birds of paradise spill from vases, and tumbling wisteria flows over the edges of nearly every inch of the formerly bare stage. I thought I wouldn't care about the flowers, but I spent way too many years in charge of our greenhouse not to be a little filled with awe. Some of the flowers I've only ever seen in picture books.

Unfortunately, when I really look around the white lilies remind me of an arrangement that we took with us after my father died. We didn't stay for his funeral, which I now know was because we were on the run, but that arrangement bumped and jounced along in the car with us for hundreds of miles. It makes me wonder whether

Rhonda will need a funeral service. And then I think about whether anyone will bring flowers to that.

My throat closes up, and I can barely breathe.

Luckily the ceremony begins, so I don't need to speak to anyone. For most of the time I stand as still as the hothouse flowers. When my mom walks toward me with a heavy-looking golden tiara resting on a pillow, I start, my eyes blinking, adrenaline pumping through my veins. This is about to happen. I repeat the words they give to me, a pledge to uphold the word of God and establish His order among His people. Then everyone in the room bows and mutters a different oath back to me in unison. To serve, protect and obey.

After they all rise, I'm supposed to walk to the front of the stage and say a few words. Josephine said I'm supposed to reassure them that I'll lead them wisely and under the direction of Providence.

My feet move but when I reach the microphone stand at the front of the stage, all my ideas of what to say have fled. I look slowly from one end of the room to the other. The assembly hall usually holds nearly ten thousand chairs, but for today, the chairs were removed and there are more than twice as many people, all standing. Many of the faces swimming before my eyes are tear streaked. Most of those are female.

A female monarch and a young one at that.

Every face turns toward me with longing and hope. They may not be my people, but they aren't villains, either. These people aren't David Solomon or Sawyer Blevins. These faces in front of me want to do what's right. They need guidance in finding the right path, but they're looking for it. Inexplicably and undeservedly, they're looking to me for that guidance. I won't preach Sunday sermons, but I'd be a fool to miss the chance to tell them the few things I do know.

"Thank you, every one of you, for coming today and honoring me with your presence. Even with the removal of the chairs, it's my understanding that only a small fraction of the residents of Galveston were able to attend. And even if all of the Galveston Island residents could be here, there would be many, many more citizens from seven other Ports and many other settlements who are still unable to attend. I owe the same duty to each of them that I do to you, a duty of care, a duty of equality. A duty of faith. I want you to know that I don't take that duty lightly."

I lift the crown from my head and turn it around until I'm looking at it, the jewels sparkling in my hands from the lights directed at the stage.

"This crown shouldn't be mine. I'm not better than any of you."

The crowd gasps.

"A crown on my head makes it look like I'm somehow more important than you. It makes it seem like you're honoring me for some reason when really, my only job is to keep all of you safe, well fed, happy and healthy. And doesn't each of us have a duty to make the world a better place for ourselves, for our families, for our neighbors and for our children? We should aim to leave them a legacy of which we can be proud. My goal today and every day is to clean up the mess we made, or the mess our parents made. I want to leave something better than this for our children, something cleaner, and something brighter. A world where we don't huddle behind closed walls, where we don't see everyone different from us as a threat to be eliminated. I think if you'll all trust me, if you'll all follow your excellent hearts, we can march toward a more Godly community every day, one small step at a time."

I place the crown back on my head.

"If you happen to run into me on the street, or see me here on Sunday and I'm not wearing this crown or any other, because I hope I never am, I want you to know why. It isn't that I don't respect what you've fought to establish here. It's not that I'm not grateful for the respect and trust you've shown me. It's that I don't want to be different or better than any of you. I want us to all be pulling forward together. Sometimes you need one person in the front, directing the efforts to make that happen. It helps keep everyone going the same way, but it doesn't mean I'm better or that God loves me more. The same is true for our brothers and sisters living in Baton Rouge and in every Marked settlement. It's also true of the people living in Unmarked cities, towns and settlements. We're all human and we're all valuable to God. If you'll help me, we can set things straight again. A few days ago I indicated that I felt my father made a mistake."

I glance behind me at the Port Heads. I make eye contact with Sawyer, and with Rosa, smiling broadly. I turn back to the assembled citizens.

"I want you to know that David Solomon was not perfect. I am not perfect. I'll make mistakes, just like you do. If we didn't make mistakes, we wouldn't need God to forgive us. But we all do need that. The important thing is that when we make mistakes, we own up to them. I promise I'll admit when I'm wrong and I hope you'll all forgive me. If you will, if we all pull the same direction, I doubt there's much we can't do. Together we're stronger. United we're enough. Equal, one and all."

I take the crown back off and hand it back to Josephine. Then I lean toward the microphone.

"I'll have my mom hang on to the crown for me. We don't need riches and fancy flowers, no matter how pretty they may be. I'll do the work if you will. Together, United, Equal."

The crowd cheers wildly, and I walk off stage. Instead of heading for the limousine out back, I slip past Sam and Adam and a few other guards and walk toward the front. People reach out their hands for me, touching my hip, my thigh, my hands, my arms, and my shoulders. Others step back, or bow, or crouch down low.

I lift them up, one at a time. I look them in the eyes.

I spend over an hour meeting the people of Galveston, because I need to see the faces of people I'm using to help the Marked. I need to make sure they're behind me, and right now, while Rhonda may have been sacrificed, I need images in my mind of people who won't load up guns and drive to Baton Rouge. Identities of people who will care and serve instead of hate and kill. I need to believe that if Rhonda did die, as I fear she may have, that death means something.

I'm exhausted after the Coronation, but there's too much to get done for me to take a break. Once we reach Josephine's white-columned home, I walk to the stupid Garden Room, which has become our informal conference room of sorts. Wesley, Sam, Josephine and Adam trail me.

I wave everyone else out of the room, including maids, guards and butlers. Once they're all gone, I take a seat. "Sit everyone, please."

Sam sits to my right and Wesley to my left. Adam and my mom take the seats on either side of them.

"Why are we here?" Wesley asks.

I force a smile. "Funny you should ask, because Wes, I need a favor. A big one."

He points at me. "You want to leave me here, don't you?"

I shrug. "You're the only one who has experience as a ruler. None of the rest of us know what to do."

Wesley barks a laugh. "You're kidding, right? I've never led so much as a book club. Your *mom*, on the other hand, has ruled for over a decade."

Josephine frowns. "I never ruled. David handled everything that mattered, from meetings to ceremonies."

"All of which you've been present for and observed first hand, which means you know a million times more than any of us." Wesley shoves his chair back from the table. "I don't want to stay. There must be a better option. Besides, you need my help managing Rafe, and, for the record, no one here likes me, not like they like you. Speaking of, where in the heck did all that come from? The last time you had to speak in public, you tripped on your shoelace and ate a handful of gravel."

"I guess I needed a topic that mattered to me."

He shakes his head. "You were amazing, but none of those people want me. I'm not their glorious, egalitarian leader."

I place my hand over his. "But you're her best friend."

Wesley exhales heavily.

Adam raises his hand and I suppress a laugh. He's got to be older than me, but I swear he acts like a little boy sometimes and I just want to hug him. "Yes, what Adam?"

"Why are you talking about who's staying? Staying where?"

I sigh. "I brought you in here because I trust all of you."

Sam squeezes my knee, clearly not ready to include Adam, but I brush his hand off. I can't distrust everyone forever.

"No one wants me to trust you Adam, but for some reason I find that I do. People I have faith in are in short supply. What I haven't confessed to anyone here in Galveston yet is that I stumbled across some very promising research. We think it could be used to develop a cure for Tercera. As you know, the suppressant has failed for most of the Marked. Time is of the essence, and sadly only my cousin Job and I know enough to decipher and replicate the research."

Adam bites his lip. "You're saying only a seventeen year old girl knows enough to replicate this research? Pardon me for questioning you, Your Royal Highness, but how is no one else better prepared for this task?"

I shrug. "The man who raised me, who I thought was my father until very recently, was the foremost scientist on viruses in America, Before. It's his work we plan to pursue. His sister, my cousin's Job's mother, would do a better job, but she's gone missing. Wesley's right that we might need his help to find her, or at least his dad's help. Until we do locate her, my cousin and I are all we've got. The Marked kids' only hope, so to speak."

"You're planning to leave now? The same day you were crowned?" Adam's eyes judge me.

Get in line, buddy.

"If Wesley won't stay here in my place, I'll have no choice but to make my mom a regent." I turn toward Josephine and look her in the eyes. "I need you to rule for me until I can get this sorted."

Josephine shakes her head. "They won't listen to me. I've sat along the sidelines for too long. I won't do you any good."

I'm worried she's right. I've seen how the Port Heads look at her. I look up at the ceiling, exasperated. "Wesley, you have to do it. There's no one else."

"What about Sam?" Wesley asks.

Sam cocks his head to the side. "You're going to keep her safe while she travels?"

Wesley fumes. "This is so unfair. I know nothing about WPN, nothing about being a regent, and nothing about the beach."

He's grasping at straws. "You've trained to lead people your entire life. You're smart, you're resourceful, you're funny and you're a natural leader."

He fumes. "I hope my dad's willing to help you find your aunt without me there to encourage it."

I do wish he could come with us, but my mom can't do this alone.

We need someone who understands WPN, the political structure, the major players, and their belief system. Someone who can hold his or her own against the Port Heads. Someone I can trust to make sure the Cleansing doesn't happen. If my position crumbles the second I leave, then I wasted my time here.

Then I risked Rhonda's life for nothing.

Everything around me is a house of cards, one sneeze away from collapse. Sam clears his throat and I glance his way. He tosses his head toward Adam.

He's from here and he knows the players. I trust him. He's sworn vows to me he seems to take seriously. He doesn't know everything, but he knows enough.

"Adam," I say. "What about you? Could you stand in as Regent?" He's good looking. The girls certainly like him.

His jaw drops. "I'm a guard. I couldn't possibly."

"You're the Captain of my guard, voted in by the confidence of your co-workers in spite of your youth. Sworn to protect and obey me."

He shakes his head. "I can't. I won't."

"Why not?" I ask.

Adam looks down at his hands. "I should've told you right away."

My eyebrows draw together. "What should you have

told me right away?" I hate secrets. If anyone ever throws me a surprise party, I might spit on them.

He exhales heavily. "Because I didn't quite rise in the ranks on my own merits, not entirely."

"What does that mean?" I ask.

He frowns. "A long time ago, when my mom was young, she found out she had pancreatic cancer. The doctors couldn't do anything and told her it was terminal. She tried a lot of treatments. She was so young. Ultimately, she met a man who claimed to be a faith healer."

Josephine gasps and something in my stomach feels a little queasy. Where's he going with this?

"He healed her and she was grateful. So grateful, she, well, let's just say he took advantage of her gratitude. She thought they would eventually get married, but a year or two after I was born, he met someone else. Someone from a reputable family. Someone classy, with money and a pedigree."

Adam won't meet my eyes. "What are you saying?"

He looks up, his light blue eyes meeting my own. "My father married your mother instead of mine."

"What?" I ask. "I don't understand. You're saying David Solomon's your dad? And that he healed your mom?"

He shakes his head. "I've looked into it. I think Mom was misdiagnosed and really only had chronic pancreatitis. It improved some when he changed her diet. She credited him with healing her, but she suffered from pain and malnutrition her entire life."

"So, that means . . ."

He nods. "I'm your older brother."

"Instead of admitting you were his son, he did what? He made you a guard?" I ask.

"He didn't even do that, not at first. When Tercera showed up, he called Mom and told her it was a real threat.

He sent her money from time to time. She was one of the first to join his community out here." Adam looks at his hands. "He visited us regularly. When my mother finally passed a few years ago, he made sure I had opportunities to advance."

I turn toward Josephine, searching her face for confirmation. She stares at the window, her eyes glassy.

"Why should I believe you?" Solomon said he had other children, illegitimate ones, but for some reason I assumed they were young. Younger, at least.

"You didn't have much time with him and he wasn't himself, since he was infected. Even so, it was probably enough." Adam meets my gaze, his eyes ice blue, angry, bitter. "David Solomon beat my mother regularly. He came to visit and if everything wasn't perfect, if the tea was too cold, or if Mom said the wrong thing." He shakes his head. "He'd take my mom into another room and close the door. I realized what was happening when I was six. Mother told me not to say a word and never to tell anyone she knew him. I didn't know he was my father until I was older, much older."

Josephine turns toward Adam, her eyes teary. "I'm sorry. I swear I didn't know."

He looks back down at his hands. "I grew nearly a foot in between most of his visits. They weren't frequent and they grew even less common as my mother grew sicker. By the time I was sixteen, mother was bedridden. I met him at the door when he showed up. I told him if he didn't turn around and leave and never come back, I'd tell everyone I knew about his visits. I'd tell them about Mom's bruises, that they weren't from her illness. No one would believe me, but I meant what I said. I would've told them."

He's lucky Solomon didn't kill him.

I look into Adam's eyes and something passes between

us, something I can't describe in words. It's like looking into a mirror that shows the future and the past at once. It's enough to convince me that Adam's telling the truth. I glance at Josephine, and I realize she believes him too.

For the first time it hits me, really hits me. Adam and I have more siblings out there. Siblings I may never even know. I shake my head to clear that train of thought. No time to deal with that yet, but I do send up a small prayer to God that maybe, just maybe, some of them will turn out like Adam and me, and not like their father.

"I hate to say this," Wesley says, "because I like you, Adam, I really do. Even more now that I know you're Ruby's half brother, but Rubes. You can't leave a legitimate heir to the throne behind to rule for you. It's not a good plan."

"Why?" I ask. "Because I have so many other options?"

"Fine," he says. "I could've helped locate Anne or navigated things with the Marked, but I'll stay. Because otherwise, odds are he'll be wearing that crown when you return. The Port Heads aren't fond of you and they'll jump at the chance to replace you."

Adam shakes his head. "I know you don't know me, but—"

I stand up. "I do know you, actually. You grew up just like me, without a dad. And recently, without a mom too. You learned as you grew that your father wasn't who you hoped he was. Instead of caring for you, he broke you a little inside every day. But I also know that those things don't define us. Which is why I'm leaving you to rule in my place. I trust you to prevent the Port Heads from attacking the Marked, and I trust you to serve the people here and prepare to help the Marked, whether we can cure them or not."

Wesley shakes his head. "This is a mistake."

"Then leave us jointly in charge and let Adam help me." Josephine stands up, squares her shoulders and lifts her chin.

"One of you can deal with the Sunday sermons?" I ask. "Those seem to be a big deal."

Josephine smiles. "I've handled one or two before when David was ill."

"I don't like speaking in front of people," Adam says, "but I know the Bible well enough to prepare something."

Josephine puts her hand on my upper arm. "I'll be the official Regent, and Adam can be my Co-Regent so you don't even need to announce your relationship, not until you're ready. How's that? Between the two of us, we'll take care of things."

I shrug. "And Adam, if you turn out to be better at public speaking than you think and you love ruling? Well, I still don't want a crown so maybe we can make this permanent."

He shakes his head. "No thanks. I'd rather no one ever know about my dad. I wish I didn't know about him."

"All I'm saying is, don't massacre anyone and we'll be just fine. If this gig grows on you, we can talk. Deal?" I hold out my hand to shake.

Adam walks around the table and pulls me out of the chair and into his cantaloupe-sized arms. My brother hugs me for a good thirty seconds. For the first time since Rafe's message, I actually feel a flicker of joy.

CHAPTER 7

"We need to leave right now." I stomp.

I want to leave the second everything's settled on Sunday night, but Sam insists driving all night isn't very safe.

"With the state of roads these days, it's an unnecessary risk," he says. "I won't trade your life for Rhonda's."

"Besides," Wesley says. "I hate to point out the grotesque, but if Rafe decided to kill her for missing a deadline it's already done. Tonight or tomorrow won't make a difference."

I go a few rounds, but ultimately my heart isn't in it. They're right. It's already too late. I made my decision and I have to live with it. I spent all afternoon meeting with Port Heads and sending them scurrying out with an earful that was appropriately tailored to their individual brand of nonsense. I swear, each request they made was more idiotic than the last. Now that's done, if I'm not leaving right away, I may as well pack. My mother comes in to help me.

The last time I left Galveston, I didn't make it out with

so much as a stick of gum. This time Josephine wants to load me up with an elephant, six leaping lords, six cars and the trunks to load them all down.

"It's too much stuff, Mom. I don't need any of this." I lift a billowy, blood red ball gown off the bed and shove it at her. "I don't even know where this came from, much less what I might ever do with it."

"You always need at least one ball gown. You never know what event might necessitate its use."

I throw my hands in the air. "Where do you get this stuff? Is there some kind of book? One that's called *A Princess's Guide to Overpacking*? I will never, ever need a ball gown again. Period."

Josephine frowns. "You don't want to be a monarch, I know. You'd rather pretend that you're a nobody with no power, and then you can do as you please. I'm glad you show the insight that this job shouldn't be about perks but about works. But I will share one truth that you're going to disregard at your peril: you never know when you might need a ball gown."

I huff. I puff. My mom does not budge.

I could've packed in fifteen minutes on my own. With Josephine's help it takes me two hours, and even so, the next morning I realize I almost forgot my dad's journal. I shove the messenger bag I took from Solomon's office into my huge duffel at the last second. There's barely room thanks to the stupid ball gown. Sam and Wesley are loading our stuff into a huge white jeep with large, chunky-treaded tires when I notice movement from the corner of my eye.

Adam's walking toward me in full uniform, with twelve more guards behind him. They look like a flock of geese, and I do not want to talk to him because I know exactly what he's going to say.

Everyone always told me siblings were annoying and I thought they were crazy. But now that I know Adam's my brother, he listens to me less and he's far more persistent when I tell him no. As the Chief of the Palace Guard, he insisted on four guards keeping me in their sight at all times. I figured since he was staying in Galveston, I could leave without any uniformed shadows in attendance. I'm tired of tripping over people every time I turn around.

"Adam." I shake my head preemptively. "You better not be about to say what I think you're going to say."

He shrugs. "Have a nice trip?"

I frown. "Why do you have all those guards with you? I already have four here, and I wanted to talk to you about that. I don't need guards where I'm headed. In fact, anything that draws attention to who I am will be bad. It'll make me more unsafe."

Adam acts like he didn't even hear me. "You'll need to take enough that they can take shifts, obviously. I wanted fifty soldiers, but Sam thought that would stand out."

My jaw drops. "You think? Have you lost your mind?"

Wesley clears his throat. "I'm with Ruby. The less people notice us, the better. Especially since we're headed for Marked territory and they know you guys were thinking of wiping them out. A small army of gun toting zealots might be poorly received."

Sam's completely nonplussed, his voice calm, his eyes steady on mine. "I'm glad to hear you two are now experts in security."

I put a hand on my hip. "I was right about Marking our foreheads when we left that church."

Adam's eyes dart from Wesley to Sam, and then over to me. "I don't know what you're talking about. You Marked your forehead? Why?"

I sigh. "I'll catch you up on our long and eventful trip out here later."

"We do have a lot of catching up to do." Adam's mouth turns up into a half grin and I almost lean over to hug him.

I'm not sure why it's so much easier for me to like Adam than Josephine. I want to like her, but it's complicated.

"I did speak to your mother last night," Adam says.

My eyebrows rise. "About?"

He bites his lip and I realize he's nervous for some reason. "I'd like to come with you myself."

I exhale. "We've talked about this."

"I find that I'm more worried about keeping you safe than I am about retaining your power here," Adam says. "And your mother agreed. She feels competent to look after the affairs of state while we're gone."

Sam walks up behind me, his arms wrapping around mine. I smile and lean back against him. "I will be safe," I say. "Sam will be with me."

Adam nods. "I'm relieved to know he will, but no one can be everywhere all the time."

I lean forward until my mouth is only a foot away from Adam's ear. "Not to impugn you guys in any way, but Sam could have taken out your whole base. And he took six gunshots and kept on swinging."

Adam's eyebrow rises. "If lying in a puddle and nearly dying counts as swinging. . ."

"Look," I whisper, "your men make me insane. I trip over Frank every single time I get up to go pee, I'm not kidding."

Adam barks a laugh that sounds almost like a cough. "I'll talk to him or if you insist, I'll replace him, but you can't leave everyone here and sneak off. You're the queen of World Peace Now, whether you like it or not."

"Wait," Wesley says, "she's queen of World Peace Now? Or did you mean to say that now she's the queen of world peace? Because being queen of world peace would be kind of awesome, I'm just saying."

Adam and the other guards standing behind him all frown.

Wesley leans against the side of the jeep and rolls his eyes upward. "Nobody appreciates comedy here. It's a confusing name, that's my point. It would be so much easier if you said WPN, plus it sounds like weapon, which is cool with you guys, right? "

Adam turns toward me. "What's he talking about?"

"I'm trying to point out a few small improvements you could make around here while we're gone," Wesley says. "You'd think people would be grateful. Once you're around it enough, you stop noticing what things sound dumb."

I can barely see it over my shoulder, but Sam's grinning at Adam in a way that unsettles me. It's like Sam genuinely likes him.

"It's good to have someone else around," Sam says, "who gets how annoying Wesley is. Ruby, for some reason, finds him charming."

"Enough distracting me, all of you." I huff. "Quadrupling the guards because I'm leaving makes no sense. We're trying to move quickly."

Adam says, "Two vehicles will arrive just as quickly as one. Like I said, you're queen. You have solid, reliable equipment now."

"Yes, I am queen, and that means I'm the boss, so what I say goes. And I only want Sam, Wesley and I to head for Baton Rouge. Alone."

Adam stomps his black combat boot, almost like a toddler, if toddlers wore uniforms with semi-automatic weapons in their holsters. "I'm the one who has to answer to the Port Heads when they ask for updates on your charitable mission. You're supposed to be determining what aid needs to be rendered to the Marked. Which means I don't care whether you want them along or not. There's no way I can mollify the Port Heads unless I can assure them you're adequately protected." He lowers his voice to a whisper. "Besides, they know you're leaving, and I don't trust them not to try something themselves. I'd send several hundred men, myself included, if you'd let me."

"Oh good grief." I scowl.

Sam lets me go and steps back. "He has a point. I'm good, but I can't do much if one of them sends a small army, and whether you want to be queen or not, you are now. People noticed so acting like it didn't happen isn't realistic."

"So fifty people?" Adam asks.

I open my mouth to argue.

"Twelve is fine," Sam says. "But make sure they're your best."

"Plus the standard four, for a total of sixteen?" Adam purses his lips before saying, "It's my final offer."

"Whatever," I say. "That's fine."

"It's because I care about you." Adam steps closer, and his arms reach out for me. "I just got a sister. I don't want to lose her."

I stiffen when Adam pulls me in for a hug, but he's my brother. The only good thing Solomon ever did for me was give me family. I soften a little and squeeze Adam around his ribs as tightly as I can.

"You be careful here too, okay?" I pull back and look at his face.

He nods. "I'll be fine."

"So will I." I climb into the jeep and close the door, but I poke my head out of the window. "But Frank's not coming right?"

Adam laughs. Why does he laugh? I figure it out when Frank climbs eagerly into the jeep next to me. I glare at Adam and he only smiles back at me. I'm too embarrassed to kick Frank out myself.

Once we start down the road toward Baton Rouge, all the packing and guard negotiation behind us, I wish I could go back and do it all over again. With no one to snarl at or cajole, I have nothing else to think about.

Except Rhonda.

Did Rafe kill her like he said he would? Did he spare her? If he did has she been punished? Rafe likes her and he's basically a good person, right? He wouldn't really. . . I try not to think about it. Wesley knows I'm fretting and Sam must too, because they joke and laugh and tell stories in the front seat, while I mope and stare at the trees out the side window from the back seat.

"Are you hungry or thirsty?" Frank asks.

I grit my teeth. "I'm fine, thanks." Then I feel guilty for being annoyed. I can't even describe what bothers me about him, but he sets me on edge.

The drive itself is uneventful. We navigate around potholes and debris. With eight guards in the van in front of us, we don't even have to clear tree branches or other blockages. We just sit and wait until they've cleared the area. Periodically one of the seven guards in the van behind us waves at me. I roll my eyes and wave back to show them I'm fine.

We stop halfway to eat the sandwiches we brought with us and let everyone stretch their legs. Sam leans against a tree and I lean against him. After I've finished mine, I close my eyes and snuggle into his chest. With his arms wrapped around me and his breath in my hair, I almost forget about Rhonda. Almost.

"Is everyone done eating?" Wesley asks.

When heads start nodding, I hop up to go pee. I've gone ten feet when I notice a guard following me. It's friggin' Frank, of course. "Umm, I'm going to pee. I might want to do that alone."

He salutes and turns back to the group. Being a queen sucks.

Frank won't meet my eyes when I stomp back to the jeep. "Hold on for a moment." I shout so the men will all hear me as they're loading back up into their vans. "We're headed into Marked territory, and while I'm impressed by your bravery, and willingness to risk infection, I want to prepare you as well as possible beforehand."

Sam smiles.

I pull out the set of syringes I made Adam bring me at the last minute when he insisted on sending all these soldiers. "God told me that if I'll share a bit of my . . . uh, my blessed blood with you, he will protect you too."

Wesley chuckles and I ignore him.

Once the sixteen guards have been inoculated, we load up for the rest of the drive to Baton Rouge. I feel like I'm driving to my own execution, watching the miles roll by one at a time, biting my lip and tapping the window in intervals. I wish God did talk to me, or even better, listen to me. Maybe then I'd feel better about Rhonda. As I stare off into the trees flying past, I notice something that's most definitely not a tree. It's a man, waving wildly at us from the underbrush. At first I ignore him. Lone individuals in the wilderness aren't common now, and they almost never carry good news.

Except I recognize him. It's Uncle Dan.

"Stop the car," I say.

Wesley glances behind me and then Sam does too. Their eyes widen.

"How'd I miss him?" Sam asks.

"I imagine he was hiding until he realized who we were."

"How could he know?" Wesley asks.

Sam pulls the Jeep over and twists around in his seat. He reaches back and pulls on one of my ringlets. "Not many people have hair like this."

The van ahead of us slowed when we did, and now it spins in a terrifyingly tight circle to loop back around. The guards pour out of both vehicles when I open my door. Every one of them has a gun drawn, all of them aimed at my uncle. He slows his run toward me and holds up both hands, palms out.

"Calm down." I say. "He's my uncle. He means us no harm."

Uncle Dan walks slowly toward me and one by one, my overzealous guards turned soldiers lower their weapons. Once we're within a few paces of one another, I can tell that his forehead's clear. I breathe a sigh of relief and jog the last few steps. He pulls me into a huge hug and for the first time in weeks, I feel completely safe. Now that he's here, he can take care of everything. Uncle Dan's always been larger than life, or death for that matter. Two time sharp shooting Olympic gold medalist. Owner of a booming security firm Before, and head of Defense in Port Gibson since he arrived. Everyone either loves him, fears him, or respects him. Sometimes all three. If anyone can make things right, it's Uncle Dan.

About ten seconds into my stupidly long hug, I remember that he's going to hate me as soon as I tell him about Rhonda. I pull away, bracing myself against his reaction. I wrack my brain, looking for any way to explain things that he might possibly understand.

Before I can figure out where to begin, he opens his mouth. "I need your help." His voice cracks on the word help and I take a good look at my unbreakable uncle. His lank hair falls in his face. His jacket's torn, his gloves are missing and his nails have been bitten to the quick. His pants are muddy almost up to his knees, and he's got a knapsack slung over his shoulder but it looks almost empty. No wonder my guards freaked out.

My uncle has always been a granite slab: solid, cool and firm. Only, now it's like his slab cracked. Tiny fissures threaten to break him into pieces. I almost can't process his words. My uncle, the superman who raised me in the middle of an apocalypse and never faltered, is begging for my help?

The world doesn't make sense anymore. I want to collapse into a huddle and cry, but I don't. Because that's not who I am, not anymore. I survived the discovery that my dad was a liar and a kidnapper. He created the virus that killed the world. And I powered through the bombshell that he wasn't really my father, and the news that my mother didn't die in childbirth and is in fact still alive today. I survived Marked attacks, an abusive biological father and recently I outsmarted his power hungry political enemies.

I can do whatever my uncle needs too. My voice doesn't waver when I ask, "What's wrong?"

My uncle looks even more pathetic when his shoulders slump, which I hadn't realized was possible. "Your aunt, she was Marked in that attack back in Port Gibson."

I nod my head. "I know. Sam told me."

Uncle Dan reaches out and clasps Sam's gloved hands

in his own bare ones. "Thank you for taking care of her Sam. I can never repay you. Never."

Sam shakes his head.

"What you don't know," my Uncle says, "is that we travelled to the Marked community near Port Gibson."

I nod. "I did know that, actually. You found some anomalies there. The hormonal suppressant was failing, but not in a way that makes any sense."

Uncle Dan's mouth clicks shut. "Yes. How did you—"

"I've been to Baton Rouge," I say, "and we met Rafe. I think Aunt Anne noticed the same thing that Job and I did."

"Wait," Uncle Dan's head swivels wildly. "Where's Job? Is he here?"

I shake my head. "He's still in Baton Rouge. We're headed back there now." A lump rises in my throat and I can't say anything else.

Sam takes my hand in his. He understands.

Wesley clears his throat. "Hello, sir. I was in Baton Rouge too, with Rafe, but never in quite the same place as your wife. I haven't seen her since that night in Port Gibson, but I heard she requested records and samples of the suppressant that stopped working. When last we were in Baton Rouge, Job worried the suppressant wasn't really failing. He suspected that somehow the suppressant was tampered with or replaced prior to delivery. He knew his mother would never do that."

My uncle digs the toe of his black boot into a clod of dirt. "Of course she wouldn't. But she saw the pills, and they weren't the ones she made. Someone switched them for prenatal vitamins for some reason, and she felt there might be time yet for a handful of the children to go back on if we could locate enough of the real suppressant. She rushed back to tell someone in Port Gibson."

The muscles in his jaw tighten and loosen, tighten and loosen. "They charged her with assault with intent to infect when she tried to talk to someone in town. When she begged them to find me, they charged her with a felony. She's already been tried and they found her guilty. No one would even listen to why she returned, and they didn't care that she never touched anyone. She's being executed in five days."

Wesley exhales and rubs his eyes with his hands. "My dad?"

Uncle Dan nods. "And after I never pursued you when you almost Marked Ruby."

Wesley swears.

Uncle Dan says. "Sam, you have to come back with me and talk to your dad for us. He's the only one who can stop this now. Please, I'm begging you. She didn't do anything wrong. She didn't touch anyone. She was only trying to help the Marked kids."

Three days to save Rhonda. Three more to save Job, one of which is already gone. And the reason for Rafe's pressure weighs even heavier. I have no idea how much time we have left before my antibodies won't be able to help these kids. The further they progress, the less my blood can do for them.

I'm needed in Baton Rouge.

But there are only five days until my aunt dies. Sam needs to plead for clemency with his dad. If there is a God, he has a terrible sense of justice and an even worse sense of timing. I'd like to tell him a thing or two.

"We can't go with you." I try to say it loudly, but it comes out as the barest whisper.

"Why not?" Uncle Dan glances around, as if really registering the men surrounding us for the first time.

"Are these soldiers from WPN?"

I sit down on the edge of the road and put my face in

my hands. I need to tell my uncle what's going on, but I can't have these guards listening in. "I need some privacy, guys. Why don't you secure the perimeter for a minute?"

Braden, the broad shouldered, raven-haired guard Adam put in charge, salutes me. He barks out commands, and the men follow, ducking away one at a time.

Uncle Dan watches quietly. "Sixteen WPN guards follow your commands?"

"You never mentioned that WPN's leader was my biological father. Did you know?"

Uncle Dan frowns. "Your dad told us that was a lie."

"You knew his wife was my mother?"

Uncle Dan sinks down next to me. He rubs his hands across the bristle covering his jaw. He clears his throat, but finally he says, "Yes."

Sam walks around us and sits down on my other side.

"You knew she was alive," I ask, "because you saw her on broadcasts?"

He nods.

"You didn't think I might want to know who my mom was and that she survived Tercera?"

He throws his hands in the air. "What a child wants, it's not something you worry about much when you're trying to keep them alive. When you're raising them."

I fume.

"You have a right to be angry with us," Uncle Dan says, "But we concealed the information from you with a purpose. Anne didn't want to tell you about *her* while she was still with *him*. Don told us he was the worst kind of man. Ill-tempered, manipulative, deceitful, and even abusive."

"Dad was right. Although his name was Donald Carillon. You could've been honest with me about that, at least. My own last name?" I shake my head.

Uncle Dan's brow furrows and I feel guilty for being angry. "It all sort of ran together and to maintain the pretense, we had to remember all of it." He runs his hand through his hair. "I don't know if what we did was right. I suppose only you can decide that, but we thought it was right at the time. You've met your mother, I take it?"

"I have and she hasn't had an easy time. Dad was right. David Solomon was. . ." I whistle.

"Was?"

Sam sits close enough that our thighs touch. His support buoys me.

"Josephine shot him," I say.

Uncle Dan's eyebrows rise. "And now the guards are following you around because?"

"Unfortunately because I'm their new queen. Look, the point is—"

Uncle Dan splutters. "I'm sorry, did you say you're the new queen? Of WPN?"

I sigh. "Yep, I am."

He looks from Wesley to Sam and back to me again. "I don't understand."

"It's a whole long story, but the point is, we did find my dad's old study the first time we went, and Dad did have another journal there. The headline news is that Dad injected me with a powerful shot of antibodies which render me immune to Tercera."

Uncle Dan beams. "That's great. You can cure Anne!" He cranes around to look at Wesley. "I assume she already cured you?"

Wesley bobs his head. "She did. Which is why we were attacking, trying to tell you guys. It's why we kept asking for her. I was her first save at the Last Supper, among other firsts." He winks at me, joking about being my first kiss.

Sam's body stiffens next to me, and he scowls at Wesley.

Wes has got to stop poking Sam's buttons.

"I wish we'd listened to you instead of seeing you as a threat."

So many things could have been avoided. So much time could've been saved. If Wesley hadn't Marked me and I hadn't healed him and he hadn't tried to reach me, my aunt wouldn't be Marked. Actually, none of this would have happened. It's horrifying to realize how each of these small events led us to where we are now. Again, I've got some things to talk to the man upstairs about, if he's really up there. And if he really listens, which seems monumentally unlikely given the state of the world.

But I'd never have met my mom or Adam. Solomon would still be terrorizing everyone, and probably eradicating Rafe and all his people in the next few days. Maybe some of it happened for a reason.

"You have five days to save Aunt Anne," I say. "And we want to help you, but I need to tell you something else first, because this isn't our only deadline."

Uncle Dan's eyebrows draw together and his eyes focus, as if he's putting puzzle pieces together finally. "Where are Job and Rhonda again?"

I try to swallow the lump that forms whenever I think about Rhonda, but it's not working.

Sam clears his throat. "The leader of the Marked is a guy named Rafe. Incidentally he's also my younger brother."

Uncle Dan's eyes widen. "Really?"

Sam nods. "That's not relevant, though. Or I don't think it is." Sam goes on to explain how I escaped Galveston the first time and then why I went back. He tells Uncle Dan about Rafe's ultimatum, and why I stayed on the island in spite of it to prevent the Cleansing.

When Sam explains about the Test and David

Solomon's edict, Uncle Dan closes his eyes. "Something happened and it took more than three days."

I nod, but his eyes remain closed so he can't see me. I force the lump down so I can speak. "Yes."

"Rhonda?"

I force the words out. "I sent a messenger to Rafe, asking him for more time."

Uncle Dan opens his eyes. "And?"

I shake my head.

"Surely he wouldn't really kill her?" he asks. "What kind of leader would do that?"

"A leader who thinks he has no other choice." Wesley says. "A leader who started making hard decisions at the age of ten. He's all alone and no one's ever helped them."

"We go to Baton Rouge first," Uncle Dan says. "And then we head back to Port Gibson. Sam, will you help? Your dad will be there for the execution."

Sam wraps one arm around my shoulder and kisses my forehead. "I won't leave Ruby and I doubt Rafe will let her leave Baton Rouge."

Uncle Dan frowns. "Amidst all these details, you didn't mention that the two of you are . . . well, what are you doing?"

"Ruby's my girlfriend."

Uncle Dan glances at Wesley in confusion.

Wesley snorts. "Don't look at me. I was as shocked as you."

"Well, okay." Uncle Dan scratches his head. "I hope we can reason with your brother, Sam. Let's go find out. We haven't had a lick of luck in weeks. I think we're due."

Frank agrees to ride in the rear van so my uncle can ride with us. We reach Baton Rouge an hour before sunset. Armed guards stand near a barricade. Rafe's taking precautions. I'm glad, but I worry about the men Adam insisted I bring. I order them all to stand down and they actually listen. Without Adam around to countermand my every order, they're fairly well behaved.

The Marked guards take their guns, but they don't take Sam's. Then they wave us through. Sam, under Wesley's direction, drives first this time, the Jeeps trailing after.

Marked kids gather to watch us, exactly like the last time. But I recognize some of their faces today, and that almost makes it worse. Even though I see a few I know, I can't read their expressions. If I had to describe their set jaws, their dour brows and their flinty eyes, I'd say they look grim. I hope it means they're mad at me for taking so long. I hope it means they're scared the cure won't work. I hope it means anything but what I fear.

Wesley points and Sam pulls up in front of the same hospital we parked near last time. When I see a reddish brown Mohawk moving toward us in the distance, my stomach ties in knots. It's Monday and I was due back Saturday. Rafe said he wouldn't wait. Was he lying?

He walks straight over to the driver's side window, but he doesn't walk up to Sam. He knocks on the glass separating me from him. I roll my window down.

"Your Royal Highness," he says. "So glad you condescended to come all the way down to Baton Rouge. I can see you brought an honor guard."

I frown. "I'm sorry it took so long, but I came as quickly as I could after ensuring the Cleansing wouldn't be pursued."

Rafe nods. "You did what you felt needed to be done."

I sigh with relief. "Oh good."

"I did what I had to do, too."

He didn't.

Rafe turns on his heel and starts to walk down the main road. He calls out over his shoulder. "Please follow me. I see you have more people with you this time. We can bring some cots for everyone to the plasma center, or we can find them somewhere else to sleep. Up to you."

I open the door and practically run after him. "Don't do this. Don't play games with me Rafe. It's beneath you. Just tell me. Is Rhonda alive?"

Rafe's words are clipped when he says, "I'm not playing *games*, and I won't apologize. This may feel like make-believe to you, but to the rest of us finding this cure is life and death, literally. I don't think you quite comprehend that."

I grab his hand. "Where is Rhonda?"

Sam walks up behind me, and Uncle Dan too.

Rafe lifts one eyebrow. "I don't make hollow threats, and I told you what would happen if you delayed. I executed Rhonda Orien at sunset on Saturday."

CHAPTER 8

I spit at Rafe. "What kind of monster are you?"

Rafe wipes the spit from his face, and turns around to continue on his way as though nothing happened. Todd and the other six armed men walk right alongside him. I force myself to look at them, but I don't recognize anyone other than Todd. I'd feel more betrayed if Sean or some of the guards I met on our trip down to Galveston had been facing off against me.

Sam's voice is low and the words seem to sink into the ground around us as he speaks. "You really are our father's son, aren't you?"

Rafe's shoulders stiffen, but he doesn't turn around, and he doesn't slow down.

Sam's words remind me that I'm not the only person devastated by this news. I turn slowly toward Uncle Dan. I've never seen him cry. I've never even seen him angry. Aunt Anne screeched and squawked when I spilled coffee on her desk. She ranted when I forgot to clean my room or failed to water the garden. She cried when a chicken or a goat died. Uncle Dan only shrugged when Rhonda knocked the glass case off the mantel and it shattered, his Olympic gold medals sliding across the tile floor. Earlier today, when he told me Aunt Anne was being held, he looked fragile, human for the first time. I realized he might actually be susceptible to fear, to pain and to loss.

He collapses to his knees now, hands balled into tight fists, tears streaking his face. His head shakes almost imperceptibly, and I realize he's not fragile anymore, he's not cracked. No, Uncle Dan is shattered. The desperation, exhaustion, and helplessness have travelled deep enough to decimate the core of who he was.

"Why isn't he angry?" I whisper. "I was worried he'd attack Rafe."

Sam pulls me against him. "Rafe still controls Job. And if Dan attacks him, your uncle will be Marked too. Then he can't go back to save Anne. The strongest men know when to fight and when to fold, but it doesn't mean it's easy to do."

Why didn't I inoculate my uncle before we came? I can't even bear to look at him right now. I'm sure he blames me for Rhonda's death, because I blame myself.

Something niggles at the back of my mind. A memory from last week before all the real chaos began. Solomon told me Sam was dead once when he wasn't. Maybe this isn't true either. Maybe Rafe's punishing us with this, making us *think* he killed Rhonda. He's a leader, a tough man, and although it would piss him off, he's not entirely unlike David Solomon.

"Do you think he really did it?" I glance from Sam to Wesley. "Or could he be lying?"

My hope withers on the vine when Wesley won't meet my eyes, but it's not entirely dead. No one knows him better than Wesley, but even he's only known him a few weeks.

I sprint down the path after Rafe, my desperate hope giving wings to my feet. Boots behind me drumming against the pavement tell me Sam, Wesley, and the guards are chasing after me. Good grief. I slow down until they catch up. Uncle Dan forces himself to his feet and hobbles along after us too. He looks ten years older than the man I remember in Port Gibson. At least catching up to me has given him purpose, and he's moving instead of slumped on the ground.

By the time we catch up to Rafe, we're nearly to the plasma center.

"Raphael." I figure using his full given name might remind him that we know him, we know who he is, and his brother's here with us. His answers matter here.

He stops moving, and spins on his booted foot. He raises one eyebrow.

"I came to help you of my own volition," I say. "I've been a friend to you and I offered whatever you needed. I only stayed longer in Galveston because it was the only way to ensure your people would be safe from WPN. I notified you with a messenger of the delay and my reasons for it. I risked my life that day to pass the test so I could end the threat of the Cleansing."

Rafe coughs. "My army protected you when you escaped Galveston. Without our help, you'd have been vulnerable to Solomon's pursuing guards. When you escaped, Sam was shot what? Six times? Without my men, you'd never have survived the day. After which, knowing your blood was our only hope, you still tried to sneak away from our camp. Only your guilt brought you back, and you jumped at the chance to return to Galveston to procure an allegedly valuable journal the following day."

"Allegedly valuable, yes, and I went back with your blessing. To save your brother."

Rafe sighs. "I'm glad Sam's here and relieved he's still alive." He doesn't even glance at Sam and he shouldn't, because Sam loved Rhonda too. Sam's as angry as I am.

"How could you do it?" I ask. "When you knew the reason for the delay? Did your heart stop beating when Tercera kicked into year two?"

Rafe spins around, his eyes flashing. "You want to pretend your time in WPN wasn't the least bit motivated by power or luxury? You stayed for yourself, and you have only yourself to blame."

"I wanted to run from those insane lunatics after they told me I had to pass some Bible Exam. They would've killed me if I failed, which they set me up to do. I only stayed to help your people, you impatient, erratic, egomaniacal lunatic! Your rigid unwillingness to wait is on you."

Rafe steps toward me. "No one ever helps us. No one. They never have, not since the Marking. You aren't the perfect angel you imagine you are."

"We sent you the suppressant for years," I say. "And supplies. I know because my aunt, the mother of the girl you shot, made that suppressant every month."

Rafe snorts. "The suppressant was a Band-Aid. The cure has never been a priority. The worst thing about Tercera is that it kills us *too* slowly. We all know we're dying, but there's never any rush, so the poor Marked kids never, ever come first. You've tossed pills at us from behind your walls for a decade, ignoring the fact that we're barely surviving. When we break an arm, we have to read outdated textbooks that detail how to set it, and bind it and then we have to muddle through the execution on our own. If that arm never works again, well that's too bad. When one of us gets an infection, we guess which antibiotics to take, antibiotics we scrounge from old pharmacies, long since expired. No one cares about us, no one helps us, and that's how it's always been, so don't act like some kind of saint."

"I'm sorry the Unmarked ignored you. I'm sorry no one has helped you, and I don't claim to be a saint, but I've been trying. Basic triage rules require the most pressing issues to be prioritized. That's what I did a few days ago, knowing you might be insane enough to shoot my cousin. I did it because it's what Rhonda would've wanted." I choke up and cough to clear my throat. I wipe my eyes and press on. "I'll continue to do the same now, even though you have clearly lost your mind. We have five days to save my aunt. She's going to be executed for trying to alert the Unmarked about the failure of the suppressants that kept you alive. She thought some of you might still be able to go back on them, if we could figure out where they were exchanged. She was tried for her trouble and is awaiting execution."

Rafe frowns. "We don't want to go back on the suppressants. I'm sorry she's awaiting execution. It's unfortunate, but it's one person. There are a hundred thousand of us."

My mouth drops open. "Unfortunate? It's tragic. And one life may not matter to you in general, but hers should. She may be the one person who could actually take my blood and create the solution I'm beginning to think you don't deserve."

He shakes his head. "You aren't leaving, not for any reason."

"Rafe, I did what I did because we only had a few weeks to prevent the Cleansing, and we have months yet to figure out how to use my blood as a cure. My aunt has days. You must see that there's a difference."

"Wrong," Rafe says. "Your aunt isn't the only person at

risk right now. My people are dying every day. My friend Paul died on Saturday. Morgan died this morning. You don't care about them, but I do. I'm sick of everyone else's emergencies, every other person's problems mattering more than ours. We're your top priority today and every day until we have a solution. I did what I did because you need to understand, all of you. We are done waiting, done being patient. Done with being shoved to the end of the line, and if my actions make me a monster, so be it. If I'm a monster, maybe people will actually listen to me for once."

I glance at Wesley, who looks as confused as me. "You said you 'did what you did'. Are you talking about Rhonda? Did you really shoot her?"

Rafe nods. "My ultimatum got you here, which is what my people need."

Sam says, "We were already coming. Your actions ensured that every single one of us hates you more than anyone else alive."

Rafe flinches. "I did what I had to do."

"Well young man," Uncle Dan says, his voice deep, but still shaky with grief, "you did what you needed to do, and I'll do what I need to do. Tomorrow morning I'm taking my son and my remaining daughter and returning to the Unmarked. I need them to help me halt my wife's execution. We also need Sam to petition his father to hear the appeal of her case, and then we'll all testify on her behalf. Job's testimony is absolutely critical, as is Ruby's. With Sam's petition, we're hoping his dad will reverse the ruling. We will return as quickly as possible."

Rafe laughs. "My dad only cares about himself. He won't reverse anything."

Dan squares his shoulders. "Your father has been a dear friend of mine for many years. He may not be perfect, but he loves Sam and he cares about me. He might reverse the ruling and ask for a new trial because I've asked him, but he certainly will if his son begs."

"I'm his son and he hasn't done a single thing for me, not ever." Rafe walks the last few steps and opens the door to the plasma center. "If you're relying on my dad's help, you're wasting your time." Rafe steps inside.

Uncle Dan calls out loudly. "It is my choice to make, and my time to waste. I'll be gathering my children and taking them with me."

"Well then." Rafe's voice carries from inside the one story, red brick building. "Come on in and see what Job's working on." Todd and three Marked kids I don't know follow him inside.

I look at my surroundings for the first time. The Life Share Blood Center looks the same, down to the armed guards standing on either side of the entrance, but there's far more activity surrounding it. The formerly empty building facing Jasmine Boulevard behind it, and the tall, striped, concrete and columned building to the left of it are both busy, people standing outside and talking, others ducking inside.

"What's going on?" I ask.

"You sent more plasma back," Todd says. "Job found some way to amplify it or replicate it, or something. He's doing some tests using antibodies from his blood too. We've expanded his clinical trials and cleaned up the surrounding buildings to make space."

I walk slowly to the doors and step inside. The last time I came inside, Rhonda stood next to me. My next breath is ragged, but I force myself to keep walking. Sam, Wesley, and eventually Uncle Dan follow me through the door. Frank's on their heels, followed by Stan. I hold out my hand. "My guards will all wait outside."

Frank opens his mouth to argue, and Sam cuts him off. "You'll listen to your queen."

"Queen?" Job's smiling when he stands up. "I thought Rafe was kidding about that. Is that what took so long? I'm glad you sent some extra with Rafe, but we're out of your plasma again. I need more right away. Why didn't you come Saturday?"

Why isn't Job angry, sad, or at least upset? He crosses the room purposefully and pulls me into a quick hug. "Glad you made it." He turns toward Sam, still smiling. "And you! It's amazing to see you standing here. How'd you survive six shots to the chest?" He hugs Sam, too. He does a double take when he sees his dad.

"Dad!" He leaps the two remaining steps that separate them, and pulls his dad into a hug. When he lets go, he looks around expectantly. "Wait, where's mom?"

Uncle Dan sighs. "She went back to Port Gibson to look for information on the suppressant failing, but she didn't get a message to me before she was caught. They tried her for risking Marking the Unmarked on Friday."

Job frowns. "She would never Mark anyone else."

Uncle Dan shrugs. "Fairchild didn't see it that way, probably because of all the Marked attacks. There've been seven people Marked in the last few weeks. He found her guilty. We have five days before the sentence is carried out."

Job turns to Rafe. "The twins can handle the trials for a few days. They're up to speed on all the protocols and requirements."

Rafe shakes his head. "Job, you know I want to help you and you've made it clear your mother would be a real asset, but I can't risk the one person I have who can run these."

Job breathes in once and then back out slowly. "Ruby knows nearly as much as I do."

Rafe says, "She can't leave either because we need you both. I'm sorry."

"You aren't sorry." I cross my arms and scowl at Rafe. "And I don't think you even told Job."

Job's brow furrows. "Told me what?"

Rafe swallows and looks at the ground.

"You've been working in here non-stop," I say. "Right? Day and night?"

Job nods.

"Rafe gave me an ultimatum last week." My hands clench into fists so tightly that my nails score my palms. "He said I had to return to Baton Rouge by Saturday evening."

"And?" Job looks around in a daze, from Wesley to Sam and back to me.

"It's Monday," I say quietly.

Job glances at Rafe. "What did you say you'd do if she was late?"

Rafe's jaw clenches.

Sam grinds out the words. "He executed Rhonda."

Job snorts. "No way. Rafe wouldn't do that."

Rafe looks anywhere but at Job's face. His boots shift, and he shuffles toward the door. "I rule among the leader-less, the cast offs, because my people trust me. I keep every promise I make. I'll let your father leave to try and prevent the death of your mother." Rafe shoulders square. "I'll even let Wesley or Sam go with him to plead with our father if you're delusional enough to think it might help, but I need at least one of them as leverage to make sure Ruby focuses."

"You want me to focus?" I ask. "Say what you mean. You need someone here you can threaten to kill if our results are sub par. Isn't that the truth?"

Rafe doesn't flinch, not this time. "It's non-negotiable."

I've been so caught up with my own anger that I didn't watch Job or notice his reaction to the news about Rhonda. A small whimper catches my attention. Job has collapsed to the floor, his knees folded against his chest, and he's rocking back and forth. Tears flow freely down his cheeks. Uncle Dan walks over to him and pulls Job against his chest. He pats his back, finding some hidden reserve of strength left with which to comfort his child, Rhonda's twin.

I almost hope Job's useless now. I hope Rafe broke his mind, temporarily at least, and has to watch as all his people die because of his own rash, unfeeling, sociopathic actions. He deserves that. Besides, the Marked don't deserve to live if this is how they operate.

Libby's sweet face looking down at little Rose rises in my mind. Sean's scarred face, always smiling, flashes through it next. The twins, one brusque and rude, and the other helpful and grateful remind me that people are complicated, but we're still people. All of us have value.

The Marked aren't all like Rafe and I can't blame them for his actions. Even so, anger fills nearly every inch of my body to bursting and despair fills in the cracks, all directed at Rafe. How could he kill Rhonda? I think about her beautiful face telling me my Path doesn't make me who I am. I think about her brushing my hair and braiding it for me. I remember when she taught me to set snares, and in the same moment I recall when she sacrificed herself for me, being Marked in my place. I think about how she liked Sam, but she didn't begrudge me my good luck when he liked me instead. How she comforted me when I thought he died, and how she supported me when I left to save him.

The more I think about Rhonda, the greater my hatred for Rafe grows. He needs to pay, and I'm the only person here they can't shoot. I'm safe while others pay for my decisions, because of my stupid blood. I leap at Rafe, hands clenched in painfully tight fists. When my right fist connects with Rafe's nose, I hear a crunch and my heart accelerates. For the first time, I understand this side of Sam, the desire to control someone around me, to defeat them. Rafe deserves to pay, and I'll make him do it.

Blood pours down Rafe's face, his nose bent at an angle. My right hand screams at me, so I swing with my left hand next, arcing toward his jaw this time. Rafe's right hand catches my left fist before it can connect and he twists. My entire arm screams from my wrist to my shoulder, and he presses harder until I sink to my knees in front of him. "Your anger with me is a defense mechanism, you know."

"What?" I ask.

"You're angry to keep from feeling guilty. Rhonda's death is your fault. You could have prevented it, if you weren't such a power hungry little—"

Sam's fist slams into Rafe's jaw in a way mine never could have, and Rafe flies across the room like a rag doll. I scramble away to avoid being kicked in the head.

Todd and Rafe's three men stood still when I attacked him, but they move now. Suddenly Sam's fighting five people, not just his little brother.

I've never stood idly and watched Sam fight and I find that I'm transfixed. Todd's the biggest man here, excluding my uncle and Sam. He trained with WPN before being Marked, so when he rushes Sam from the front, I actually worry. The three other Marked guards who followed Todd inside try to sneak around behind Sam while he's focused on Todd. Rafe's on the floor with Sam's boot on his chest. Todd tries to put Sam in a headlock, but Sam ducks and slams his elbow into Todd's chest. When Todd stumbles back, Sam steps closer to Todd and snags two guns from his holsters. He slams Todd in the face with the butt of one of them.

Two of the Marked guys have guns aimed at Sam from several feet away, their backs to the wall. Sam fires from each gun, his shots hitting both of them in their gun holding hands. They each drop their firearm and clutch their hands. One of the dropped weapons fires when it hits the ground, and the bullet flies past Wesley to hit the wall behind him. I sneak around the back of the room toward the discarded guns. I'd like to remove them from play before someone gets injured or one of Rafe's men picks one of them up.

A banging comes from the front door. Apparently someone locked it.

Sam swears. He tucks one of his guns into the back of his pants, leaps across the room, and kicks the third guy's gun away. It flies across the room and into the cart for the aphoresis machine with a clang. Sam punches the third guy rapid fire. The man drops into a heap when Sam stops.

Rafe climbs back to his feet. He wheezes when he calls for reinforcements. "Doug, call for Marco. We need support in here. Now."

Sam shakes his head. "You're done issuing orders, Raphael. You suck at it." Sam grabs Rafe by one shoulder and shakes him like a dog with a rat. "We're all leaving. Ruby, me, Dan, Job, and Wesley. We're going to Port Gibson and you'll wait to hear from us. If Ruby decides to return, which she probably will because she is the saint you think she isn't, we'll return. If not, I won't force her to take one step this direction. Is that clear?"

Rafe's eyes flash. "You aren't in charge here Sam. You're nobody. Even you can't defeat thousands of us."

Sam snorts. "I've got their leader right here. That'll be enough."

"You won't hurt me. You can't. You've never been able to harm anyone you love. Even if you think I'm evil, even if you're angry, you still care about me so you won't do a thing." Rafe pulls a gun from his holster and places it against his own temple. He stares at Sam. "Do it. Take this from my hand and pull the trigger. If you do that, my men will let you all walk away, including Ruby." Rafe glances at Todd and Todd nods.

"Do it." Rafe stares at Sam. "Or stop acting tough and defending your girl and join me instead."

Sam takes the gun and shoves it against his brother's head. The veins in his arm pop out and his arm shakes.

"He deserves it," I say. "He shot Rhonda."

If I had that gun, I'd pull the trigger. I wouldn't even feel guilty, but it is his brother. I can't ask him to do that. I know Sam well enough to know he'd never forgive himself. "But I don't expect you to," I say. "It's okay, Sam. I love you no matter what."

Sam holds steady, his arms taut, his jaw working, his hand on a gun pressed against his little brother's temple. After a full ten seconds he drops his hand and his brother.

Rafe smiles. "I knew you couldn't do it. We're family, you and me. That's stronger than any feelings you might have for some girl."

Sam shakes his head. "Don't mistake my inability to shoot my mother's son in the head for something it isn't. You shot Rhonda who I consider to be like a sister. I sincerely hope that's the girl you mean. If I had to choose between the two of you, if shooting you would save her, we wouldn't be having this discussion. But you didn't give me that chance and I don't think two wrongs make things right. They only make bad into worse. But if you meant Ruby when you said our connection is stronger than me and some girl? I'll choose Ruby over you a million times and not regret it."

Rafe flinches.

Sam shakes his head. "I'm sorry you've been alone all these years, more sorry than you can possibly know. I'd go back and change that if I could, but I love Ruby and I'll always love her."

Boots pound on the pavement outside the building. A lot of boots. I hear yelling. Frank and my other unarmed guards are shouting outside. I want to tell them not to risk themselves. I want to make sure they're safe but I can't, not right now because I see something in Rafe's face that holds all my attention. He wants to hurt Sam, but more than that, he wants to hurt me, and I realize he has the means to do it.

Rafe scowls at his brother. "Why would you pick her over me? She was kissing another guy a few days after she thought you died. She doesn't deserve your protection or your devotion. If her insane dad hadn't injected her with some kind of supercharged antibodies, I'd shoot her right now and not regret it."

Sam rolls his eyes. "You're trying to drive a wedge between us, but it won't work. She told me already. She kissed Wesley to keep from being discovered when she was trying to escape your camp. She did it because she wanted to try and save me."

Wesley's eyes meet mine until I close my eyes. Why didn't I tell Sam then? I should have come clean that first night.

Rafe barks a laugh. "Is that what she told you? I didn't even know she kissed Wesley that day. She's even worse than I thought. But brother, I assure you there was no thought of you running through her head when I caught her and Wesley kissing alone, leaning against a big tree at night, right by the bridge over to Galveston. I have no idea what happened inside the tent they shared that night, but she didn't kiss him to save you, that's for sure."

Sam's eyes widen and cut to mine.

More than a dozen men pour through the doors a second later, and I'm almost relieved to put my hands up in the air and surrender.

CHAPTER 9

"I'm glad to hear the twins have things well in hand here," Rafe says. "That way I don't feel bad about securing the rest of you."

Rafe tells his men to take us to a holding facility a few blocks away. He points out the machines they'll need to transport in order to draw plasma from me regularly. Rafe may be evil, but his people don't seem to mind and they jump when he gives orders. Sean, a Marked kid I first met on the way to Galveston, enters on Rafe's command. His hair falls in his face when he reaches my side, and he swipes it back with one hand, a gesture that reminds me of Wesley.

"I'm sorry to do this." When Sean frowns, the scar crossing his face from temple to chin pulls tight. I wonder whether it still hurts. "Orders, though." I don't struggle when he zip ties my hands.

More notably, my uncle, Wesley and Sam don't struggle either.

Thunder booms outside. A rainstorm complicates any travel we might try to make. Five days. "What about Aunt

Anne? Are you still going to release my uncle and either Sam or Wesley at least? You said you would."

Rafe smiles. "I imagine Sam will be happy to leave."

Sam shakes his head, lips pursed, eyes downcast. "I'm staying with Ruby."

Rafe snorts. "You're like a dog whose owner died, but he just keeps waiting. Stupidly loyal. She's not worth it."

"You know nothing about me and even less about her," Sam says. "So shut your mouth."

Rafe walks to the door. "Fine. Release Wesley Fairchild and Daniel Orien. Provide them with transportation and supplies to reach Port Gibson. They have business there, and they'd like to get out ahead of the storm."

Sean cuts the zip ties from Wesley's hands, and Wesley knocks his hands away. "I can't believe you're here Sean, taking orders like a soldier." Wesley crosses the room to stand near my side. "I don't want to leave either. Not now, not with all this up in the air. I'm not even sure what I could do to help. It's in Roth's hands at this point. I feel bad about my dad's role in it, but you still need me." He whispers. "Maybe more than ever."

I feel Sam's eyes on me, and I know he can hear every word.

"Go," I whisper. "Just go, okay? Save her for me if you can. She needs you much more than I do."

"You're my top priority, always," Wesley says. "And that was messed up, how that went down back there. Rafe had no context, and he sat on that like it was a bomb or something, using it to hurt you when it would do the most damage."

I close my eyes. It's my fault it even could go down the way it did. I lied when I didn't tell Sam the whole truth and I deserve his anger now. "I caused this Wes, and I'll get myself out of it."

"I was there too, you know. It wasn't all your fault." Wesley touches my arm.

I shake his fingers off like they burn me, but I'm not prepared for the hurt in his eyes. I want to reach up and brush his hair back. I want to keep him with me, but I can't. Not if I want to fix this, and I do. Every part of me wants to fix things with Sam.

"It's okay Wes. Please go help Uncle Dan save my aunt. No matter what it takes." My voice drops so low I can barely hear it myself. "I can't lose anyone else. I can't."

Wesley closes his eyes and nods slightly. "Fine. But if you get hurt—" He glances at Sam.

Sam growls. "Whatever happens, I'll always keep her safe better than you ever could."

"Rude." Wesley shakes his head. "And moody. There's more than physical safety, you know?" He keeps shaking his head, but he walks toward the door and waits there quietly. Uncle Dan says something softly into Job's ear that I can't hear, and then he stands up and crosses the room to where I'm standing.

I'm afraid to look into his face, worried that anger lurks there, or reprimand. Or worst of all, blame. I deserve all that and more.

"Before you leave, please let me give you some blood. A few drops, even." I turn to Rafe. "If you have any regret over what you've done, let me set this right. Uncle Dan's been exposed today. If he winds up Marked, they won't let him inside and my aunt's dead for sure. If you're going to let him head back, let me do this."

Rafe frowns at me, but he nods.

After the blood draw, I breathe a huge sigh of relief. At least I've made Uncle Dan as safe as I can. He leans toward me and presses a kiss to my forehead. "It wasn't your fault. You need to listen to me about that and be safe, as safe as you can anyway." He glances at Rafe. "I know we never talk about God and we don't really believe in all that, but if you don't think it sounds too stupid, maybe say a prayer for me and Wesley. It can't hurt, right?"

I don't tell him that I'm not sure I believe in prayer, and I have no idea how to pray. Instead, I nod and choke back tears when Uncle Dan and Wesley walk out the door.

Flashes of lightning, followed by crashes of thunder, punctuate the sky when Job, Sam and I leave the plasma center bound for our new holding cell. I'm getting sick of being locked in rooms. I'm tired of people being stupid. I'm sick and tired of death and viruses and all the rest. But mostly, I'm exhausted from dealing with the results of my own stupidity coming back to bite me.

Sean keeps one hand on my upper arm while I stumble along, tripping over rocks and rubble as we walk down a wide road. Signs say we're on the Acadian Thruway, not that I care where we're going. Thunder sounds all around me, but no rain falls yet. Every new flash draws my eye. The six men guarding Sam start and jump right along with me, which makes me nervous since they have their guns drawn. Job only has two guards assigned to him. I wonder where my WPN guards are. Maybe they'll go with Uncle Dan and Wesley.

Wesley.

Why did I kiss him that night? Only a few hours stood between me and my walk down the bridge to Galveston to save Sam. I'm such an idiot. I'm sure that Sam's angry, but worse, I bet he's hurt. I should've told him about this days ago when I had the chance. I should've talked it out with him, but instead he hears it from his brother in front of a crowd of people, including my family. Rafe used the knowledge like a weapon to attack Sam, to make him look stupid, and to undermine Sam's faith in us.

Sam's hurt and Rhonda's dead, and one is way worse than the other, but they both hurt and they're both my fault. Not a good week for Ruby.

I don't resist when Sean leads me through the front door of a small, rundown, flat-roofed building with peeling white siding. The glass in the front door frame is split by a long crack, the paint someone slapped on over the siding curls away along the sides of the panels, and the sign squatting above the front door reads "Cash America Pawn."

"A pawn shop?" I ask. "Really?"

Sean shrugs. "It's got two secured sections, bars on the windows, and cages around each section. What can I say? I guess pawn shops had to protect their stuff, so it was an easy place to secure."

The six men escorting Sam argue over how to enter, but eventually two of them duck inside first. Two of them shove through sideways, each with a hand on Sam's arm. The other two shoot through afterward. If Sam really wanted to leave, none of them would stop him. Job follows with his two guards right after.

"Two sections?" Sam asks Sean after we're inside.

"You can share with Job," I say. "I get it."

Sam shakes his head. "I'd rather be with you."

My heart lifts until I try to look into his eyes. He won't meet my gaze.

"I told Wesley I'd keep you safe and I will."

I want to curl into a ball but I don't, because that's not me anymore. You can't fix anything when you're huddled and scared. You only fix things by forging ahead. Of course, it's hard to forge in leg irons, literal or figurative.

Sean leads me past a fairly large front room filled with glass cases. Most of the displays have been smashed, jagged glass edges forming a macabre decoration around the frames. At least someone cleaned up all the glass shards. Clearly this place has been used before. Job walks in a trance, eyes straight ahead, each step small. He doesn't even react to the thunder, which has me worried. Flinching at those loud crashes should be an automatic response.

I'm stepping through the doorway into the back of the building when a large whamming sound, followed by cursing comes from the doorway. My head pivots like an owl's to see what's going on.

A girl and two boys struggle with the aphoresis machine. I know two of them. Amir and Riyah, the twins who are helping run the experiments. I guess they'll be running them alone for a while, at least as long as Rafe keeps Job and me locked up in here.

"Hey Ruby," Amir says. "I'm so sorry about Rhonda. I wish I could have done something." He lifts the back end and pulls the cart fully inside.

Riyah doesn't meet my eyes, which is strange for her. Usually she'd be glaring and hissing at me.

Not ten seconds pass after they enter before another loud crash of thunder sounds, and the sky opens up and begins dumping buckets of water outside. Riyah hops over to the door and yanks it shut. "We made it just in time."

"I wish we could have said that," I mutter.

Amir's shoulders slump. At least someone here realizes how wrong Rafe was.

A moaning sound comes from Job and his two guards shove him through the doorway into the back room. When I walk through with Sean, they're already shoving Job into a five by five cubicle. Shelves line three sides and large iron bars close off the front. No bathroom, no bed, no chair. Filthy concrete floor. The two boys don't cut the ties on Job's hands, so he sinks to the floor, hands bound behind him, pulls his knees up against his chest and drops his face against his thighs. He looks like a broken puppet with its strings cut, discarded in the corner of the room.

Sean guides me into a cubby on the other side. It's larger than Job's makeshift cell. Ten by five feet, give or take. Shelves line the walls on three sides with bars across the front, the same as the other side. Sam's guards zip tied his hands behind his back before we started out of the plasma center too, but I guess they decided that wasn't enough. Somewhere they found handcuffs. A particularly eager kid clips them around Sam's wrists over the zip ties.

Still not satisfied, they lash his feet together. Finally, they shove him into the same cell as me and slam the door shut. I hear the lock catch. All of the guards other than Sean move into the front room. I wonder how many will stay at the Pawn Shop to keep an eye on us. Probably most of them, since we're Rafe's prize possession.

Now they're gone, there's enough room to breathe. Amir drags the machine through the narrow doorway and into the three-foot aisle between Job's cell and mine. He rolls it alongside where I'm sitting with my arms still bound behind my back.

"If you promise to behave yourself, we'll cut your zip ties," Amir says.

"You'll cut them either way," I say flatly, "because you need my plasma."

He smiles. "True. We do." He pulls a knife from his boot and holds his hand out. I scoot around and push my hands over to the bars. "I am truly sorry for all this nastiness. You have always tried to help, and this hardly seems the best way to repay you."

I turn away because even though I like Amir, I don't want to make polite conversation. Not now, not with anyone here.

If I thought giving plasma the last two times was uncomfortable, I had no idea what discomfort really meant. My arm goes to sleep while I reach through the bars of the cell and let them hook a wide bore needle to the vein inside my elbow. My butt goes numb on the concrete floor. Around and around, I watch the blood flow out, the machine circulate it, and the red blood cells flow back inside.

On the third rotation, something louder than rain happens in the front room. I can't tell what's happening, and when I shift to try and look, the needle jabs painfully into the crook of my elbow. I don't want to blow my vein.

"Don't hurt yourself, princess. It's just your bags. Rafe ordered they send them over." Sean jingles the keys. "Of course, they've gone through them to make sure there's nothing dangerous in there."

Riyah ducks through the door, and comes back with a black backpack. Sean opens the lock on Job's cell first, and tosses it through the cell door. Job doesn't move.

"He's not even shifting. Even if your scientific background focused on cows, you should recognize the signs of shock," I say. "He needs medical attention."

Amir shakes his head from where he's standing against the doorway. "We've all lost family. He'll survive it."

"You idiot, I don't mean he's surprised by his sister's death or even sad about it. Sometimes cases of extreme grief, like the loss of a twin," I glare pointedly at Riyah, because Amir should understand this, "can cause physical symptoms. Medically speaking, shock means there isn't enough blood flow in the body. Having his hands bound behind his back while sitting in a heap on a concrete floor certainly isn't helping. With insufficient blood flow, organs can die. The heart tries to overcompensate for the lower volume, and it makes things worse. One in five patients die of shock."

Technically that's true. I don't explain that statistic applies to medical shock and Job isn't suffering from that, because I want them to undo his zip ties. He doesn't deserve this. He's worked tirelessly to help save them, so they shoot his sister, tie him up, and lock him in a cage? I clench my hands and the blood flows out even faster. My machine begins beeping when it over collects and Amir glares at me.

Sean's opening Job's cage and cutting his ties when someone else I know walks through the door. I always called her Beefy in my head, and I'm embarrassed not to recall her real name. She's a large, heavy set, ruddy-faced girl who had a crush on Sam. She was with Sean when they almost caught me on my way to Galveston the first time. As much as she liked Sam, that's how much she disliked me. She sucks on her teeth and lifts my large black duffel bag. It looks much lighter than it was before. I wonder what they removed and why.

"Rafe thought you might need something in here. He didn't figure you'd need that fancy crown with the sparkly gemstones." She lifts one eyebrow and spits on the floor.

Good riddance.

"But he left you that fancy red dress. Figured you might wanna put it on for his brother to try and win him back." She chortles, and I glance at Sam.

He pays her no attention at all, and it's the kind of behavior he wouldn't have tolerated two hours ago. I want to curl up like Job and pretend nothing matters. Old Ruby would have done it.

Sean closes Job's cell door again and I glance over, hopeful. In spite of the removal of his restraints, Job hasn't even shifted, his hands still clasped behind his back. I offer up a silent prayer. Please God, if you're there, keep him alive and safe.

Sean walks over to the far end of my cubby where Sam sits on the ground, knees up, hands bound behind him. "I'm going to open this door, alright?"

Beefy points a gun at my head. "I'll shoot her if you try anything Sam. You hear me?"

Sam's face doesn't show a single emotion when he responds. "You wouldn't shoot her if I sliced your friend up into a dozen pieces. You need Ruby too much."

"Fine." Sean grunts. "We'll shoot that one. Briggs." Beefy, apparently also known as Briggs, swings her gun toward Job.

Sam rolls his eyes. "You need him too, but if the threat makes you feel better."

Sean opens the door and tosses my bag into the space between Sam and me, then he slams the door shut again. "Hey Briggs, where's his stuff?"

She shakes her head, the corners of her mouth turning up in admiration. "Rafe said his bag was full of weapons. Nothing we could bring to him."

I smile. That's my Sam alright.

A puddle is forming around my bag. Clearly they didn't get it here before the deluge began. I hope the rain didn't ruin any of my stuff. The clothing should all be fine, except maybe that stupid red ballgown. I roll my eyes. Now that I actually have one, I realize parents are ridiculous.

Oh man, my Dad's journal!

I use my toe to pull the bag closer to me, cursing the stupid needle in my arm. Once I finally pull it close enough, I unzip the bag and rummage around with my right arm. I finally find the messenger bag and open it. The journal's gone. I throw the messenger bag against the wall with a shout, and swear loudly.

Sam's eyes follow my actions, but he doesn't speak. Why doesn't he say anything? I want to talk to him about it, but I don't know what to say or even how to broach the topic.

Eventually, Riyah crosses to where I'm sitting, crouches down and disconnects the needle from my arm. She binds the entry wound carefully. Before she stands up, she passes me a bottle of water. "Stay hydrated. We'll have food sent over soon." She meets my eyes and for once, hers aren't angry. They aren't full of hate. At first I can't figure out what I'm seeing. She pulls something from her pocket and passes it to me.

"One of my friends loves to take pictures. She had this on her wall and I thought you might want it."

It's a Polaroid photograph of Rhonda from our first day in Baton Rouge.

My eyes well with tears. "Why would she take this?"

"She took several of you on the day you arrived." She rolls her eyes. "She took that one as a contrast, the savior we thought and the one we really got."

I bite my lip. Everyone would be better off if only Rhonda and I could've traded places. She'd have made the right decisions and she'd have been stronger, faster and better at making them. Why couldn't I have died instead?

I stare at the image, Rhonda's high cheekbone clear because her face is turned toward the sun. Such a gorgeous face and I'll never see it again. "Thank you." The words come out in a whisper. When I meet Riyah's eyes, I recognize what I couldn't before. Now that Rhonda's gone, Riyah doesn't hate me anymore.

She pities me instead.

Riyah and Amir gather up the plasma machine and accoutrements and push them through the door. Sean looks from me to Sam and back again. He clears his throat.

"If I loved someone and I lived in a world where there was no guarantee of tomorrow. And if that person always tried to do what was right, well I might forgive them for most anything."

Sam raises one eyebrow and tilts his head.

Sean stretches and yawns. "Not that any of that has to do with either of you. But I think I'm just going to rest my eyes for a minute on the other side of this doorway. I'll be able to hear anything louder than say, a strong cough. So don't try anything, okay?"

I would hug Sean if I could. But part of me also wants to yank him back in here. Clearly I don't know what I want. Except once he's gone I have no idea what to say, so I sit helplessly on the concrete floor and stare at Job's still form.

Seconds pass, or maybe they're minutes. I don't know. I can't count them because my mind spins like a top, like the bottle from that fateful night at the Last Supper. The night when all I thought about was Wesley and our first kiss. Only now I don't want to kiss Wesley. I only want to kiss Sam. I realize what I need to say, and I'm not sure why it took me so long to find the right words. They're so simple, so universal, and so necessary.

I whisper the words, but I know he can hear me. "I'm sorry, Sam."

No response.

I scoot across the floor until I'm only a foot away from him. "Are you ever going to talk to me again?"

"Why?" Sam's eyes are closed.

At first I think he's asking why he'd talk to me again, but then I realize what he's really asking. He wants to know why I did it. Why did I kiss Wesley? Or maybe he's asking why I didn't tell him.

I look at his face, his breathtaking face. Large square

jaw covered in blonde stubble, and full, thick golden hair, a few strands falling forward over his cheekbones. Flawless golden skin. Full lips, barely parted to show large, straight white teeth. And his eyes are closed, so I don't know whether they look greener or more gold in this moment. I'm not even sure which one I prefer.

He's everything I want, and everything I've lost by my stupid indecision.

"I don't know why. I think I kissed him that night because, well, maybe I felt like I didn't deserve you. I left you on that bridge to die, but you lived through it. I gave up on us when I never should have. You suffered because of me, and I felt guilty about it. You're so much better than me, stronger, faster." I shake my head. "I didn't deserve you then and I definitely don't now. I guess I knew that already and I figured—"

Sam's eyes open and he shakes his head. "I don't care about that. You hoped I was alive, but you thought I wasn't. I get it and I don't really care that you kissed him." His jaw clenches. "Or I'm trying not to anyway. Either way, I get it because I know you, Ruby. I knew you'd feel guilty about leaving me." He chokes. "I can get over that. What hurt me most was that you lied to me. Why you didn't *tell* me when I asked you that night? Why lie about it?" He leans his head back against the shelf and closes his eyes. "There's only one reason I can think of and it's not a good one."

My stomach sinks. I want to cry but I can't hide behind that, so I blink back the tears. Sam isn't even upset I kissed Wesley? I should've told him that first night. I take a deep breath to tell him I lied because I was afraid to lose him, because I need him to survive. I'm still a big fat coward, even now, even after everything else. My mouth opens to confess the words, but then it closes again. He says there's only one reason he can think of, and it's not that. Sam doesn't think I'm a coward, and if I'm being honest I don't either. Not anymore.

I can't lie to him now, which means I can't lie to myself anymore. The only other reason I'd have kissed Wesley right before discovering whether Sam was alive was if I wasn't sure Sam was the one for me. If I wasn't positive, and I wasn't ready to commit to being Sam's girlfriend, maybe I'd want to preserve another option. If I wasn't ready to end any possibility with Wesley, then I couldn't admit to its existence in the first place.

My voice sounds small, even to my own ears. "I don't know."

Sam grunts. "I do."

"What does that mean?" I ask.

"It means I know why, and you know too, and you don't have to say the words."

"Then does that mean you'll forgive me? What can I do?"

Sam shakes his head. "I don't need to forgive you, Ruby. You haven't done anything wrong."

I scoot closer, and lean against his arm. "What are you saying? I don't understand."

His greenish-gold eyes stare into mine. "You're still so naive sometimes. You think everything is black and white, but black and white don't exist in real life. The entire world's drawn in shades of grey. I love you and that means I choose you every minute of every day. With everything I say and everything I do, I choose you again and again. It's a conscious choice. People think love is like a gift, or a one-time decision, but it's not. It's something you do over and over and over, like Sisyphus rolling the rock up the hill. As soon as you stop, the rock rolls away, and you either keep pushing or walk away. If you really love some-one, it takes work and you make the choice to do it every single day. You have to choose to be whatever that person needs."

"Who's sissy fuss?"

Sam sighs. "It's a Greek thing. Never mind. I'm hurt Ruby, not angry. If you're kissing Wesley and keeping things from me, that means you aren't choosing me back. It means you aren't sure yet, and that's not something you need to apologize for, it just means we aren't in the same place like I thought we were."

I take his hand in mine. "I do choose you. We *are* in the same place."

His mouth smiles, but his eyes are still sad. "When you're forced to choose, you pick me. But when no one's asking, you're not sure. The thing is, you're still so young. You're supposed to have time to make these decisions. I don't want you to take this the wrong way, because it's really a gift."

"What is? I don't want to take anything the wrong way, because that sounds ominous. With the day we've both had, let's not do anything we'll regret."

"Ruby, I'm dumping you. We're through."

I thought my heart was already as broken as it could be after Rhonda. I didn't think it could hurt more, but it does. When I hear Sam say we're through, my heart splinters into a million pieces, and they burrow down into my chest cavity. I scoot away, pull my legs up into my nose, and wrap my arms around them. Tears leak down my cheeks. "Don't, don't do it. You said you aren't even mad. You don't mean it."

Sam sighs. "I'm not breaking up with you because I'm hurt. I kept things from you before, like Wesley's message, and I've regretted that decision every day since. I'll never do that again because you're my one constant. But it's not enough for me to be sure."

I gasp. "I choose you too. I said that."

Sam sighs. "You don't, not yet anyway, and that's okay. I shouldn't have pushed you before. It was wrong. We've been under a lot of pressure and you don't need more, not right now, so I won't push you again."

I bump him with my shoulder. "I want you to pressure me. I do, because I need us to be okay. The world's upside down, and we're locked up again, and I need us to be alright. Something in my life has to be good."

Sam strains his arms, muscles bulging, veins popping. A small pop followed by a larger one. He rotates his shoulders and brings his arms around to the front. "I can't be with you because you need something good, like a lifeline for someone who's drowning. You need to be okay on your own before we can ever be okay together. We all live in prisons of our own making." He reaches toward me and I gasp. His wrists are bleeding.

"Sam."

He puts one finger on my mouth. "Shhh, it's fine. They'll heal in the next few minutes. I didn't want to break them because it'll make them even more nervous around me, but you need to know this, Ruby. I'm all in. You aren't sure what you want yet, and that's okay. If you love Wesley, and I know you do." Sam swallows and his hands shake, but he stills them. "If you do love that wise-cracking idiot more than you love me, well, I'll be alright. I'll always do my best to keep you safe, even if I get frustrated or annoyed. My support for you isn't contingent on your picking me."

"Things are almost okay," I say. "The world's so close, if people will just stop being stupid long enough that we can fix it."

Sam pulls my head against his chest. "Oh, Ruby. You're so absurdly hopeful sometimes. We can't ever 'fix' the world, because Tercera isn't what broke it. Humans broke it, and they won't stop even if we fix this problem, and the one after this. And the one after that."

I exhale and shift, turning toward Sam, trying to savor this moment and the knowledge he isn't mad. I may not be sure yet why I kissed Wesley, or exactly how I feel, but I know I love Sam. I know I do.

"I don't want us to be broken up," I say.

Sam presses a kiss to my forehead. "When you can tell me why you kissed Wesley and promise me it will never happen again. When you can tell me you don't need me, but you want me, then we can be together. Until then, I'm not going anywhere. I'll still keep you safe, and I'll try my best not to bash Wesley's idiotic head in every time he touches you. And if you want to kiss him." His arms tense and a vein pops in his temple. "If you kiss him I'll turn the other way. You're free and you have time. That's why I'm dumping you."

I don't know if I'll ever see Wesley again. My gaze lowers to the messenger bag, slumped on the bottom shelf. At least the journal didn't get wet if Rafe took it out before bringing the bag to me. I notice something white poking out from the edge of the bag and squint at it. What is that?

I push forward and crawl across the floor toward the white paper poking out. I open the biggest pocket in the bag and shake it. A packet of letters slides out. I forgot those were on top of the journal. I shoved them into the bag that night back in Solomon's office, right after my mom shot him.

Sam says, "What is it?"

I crawl back over and lean against him again. "Some letters were bound up next to my dad's last journal. They weren't in the safe, so I guess Solomon got them from somewhere else. I forgot I even had them. Rafe took the journal, but he missed these."

They're letters from Anne Orien, my aunt, to her twin brother, my dad. Most of them are about their kids. The last one, though, it's not to my dad, and it's not a letter, not a traditional one anyway. It's an email that's been printed off, and it's short.

Michelle:

I will mail you the amount of your final paycheck as promised, but I need something from you first. The police will lock the home and office down in the next few hours. I need the financials, all the journals from my brother, and any other documents you can find. A lot of them are probably in Don's briefcase. Send me everything to this PO Box. I'll arrange to have it collected in a way that won't lead anyone to us. Delete this as soon as you receive it and empty your cache.

Best,

Anne Orien

I sit up and gasp. "We're trying to use my blood to do something my dad never intended. He knew it would only work as a preventative, not a cure. But he had a cure, and it wasn't my antibodies. His cure was the hacker virus. Only, that was a dead end."

"I know," Sam says.

"But what if it's not a dead end? What if we could identify the partner of my dad's, the one who might have set him on fire, the one who must have stolen the final two strains of the hacker virus?"

Sam tilts his head.

"My Aunt has the financial files, like the partnership agreement. She must have them because this email says so. I've read the journals, but I wasn't sure where the hacker virus went until I saw my dad's last journal, the one from his safe. It said the last two samples were in his lab, which means his partner stole them after killing him."

"We need to go and get it," Sam says. "Rafe will have to agree. We need to get to Port Gibson right away."

"If we can find this partner and locate the hacker virus," I say. "Then—"

Sam interrupts. "We could finally cure every single Marked kid on the planet, including Rafe."

Yes we could. We could even save Sam's horrible little brother.

CHAPTER 10

S am uses the handcuffs on his wrists to bang on the bars. After Sean runs through the door, his eyes widen. "Why are your cuffs off? What's going on?"

Sam's dealing with Sean, which gives me time to watch Job. He doesn't move a hair, not even an involuntary flinch in response to the banging Sam's doing and Sean's reactionary yelling. I'm going to insist on medical treatment when Amir shows up.

"Technically, my cuffs aren't off." Sam shakes his hands, and the cuffs spin around his wrists. He only snapped the chain connecting them.

"It's not what you think, okay?" I hold up a letter. "I read some old correspondence and discovered something Rafe's going to want to hear."

Amir shakes his head and leaves. Sean presses his lips together before exhaling heavily and ducking back out of our holding room.

A few moments later, Rafe's signature Mohawk bobs through the door. "What's so important that you need to see me?" he asks.

"First, Job is not alright. After murdering his sister, you could at least take precautionary measures to ensure that he doesn't die too." I point at where he's still as a statue, arms no longer bound behind him but still held together near his lower back. His head's down and no part of him moves. "He's in shock and I'm worried about him. His blood flow is bad. Look how pale he is. If he dies of grief I'll kill myself, I swear I will. I'll find some way to do it, and every last one of your people will die."

Rafe snorts. "Stupid melodrama. I should've known." He shakes his head. "I'm leaving."

Sam speaks softly. "We called for you because we know where to find the hacker virus. It's an actual cure, not a shot in the dark. Not kids trying to conduct science experiments that are way over their heads."

Rafe snorts. "How stupid do you think I am? You've found a pie in the sky and you want me to what? Let you chase after it? Oh I know, the information you need is back home in Port Gibson? The very place you recently asked me to let you go?"

Sam frowns. "I don't think you want me to answer that question."

"You aren't going anywhere to search for some miracle cure I hadn't heard of before I threw you into a cell," Rafe says.

"I told you about it before," I say, "or if you read through the journal you stole from me, you'll read where my dad talks about it. It's a virus that consumes other viruses, but isn't harmful to the human body. My father had been testing it with no negative side effects on animals, and was requesting human trials. He was confident enough in it that he injected himself with it when he caught the virus he called Triptych. We now call that virus

Tercera. And the hacker virus ate Triptych up and spit it out. It healed him."

"It took you two forty-five minutes to come up with that story?" Rafe rolls his eyes. "Or was that just how long it took for my pathetic big brother to forgive you?"

I slam one hand into the bar on my cage. "You deserve to die Rafe, but your people don't. I'm trying to help them and I'm not lying about this. Read the journal. We're not making it up."

Rafe grins. "Let's say this is true and there may be evidence of some other cure somewhere. What are the odds it survived ten years without anyone realizing it? If it's a virus, it's long since dead. I'm not going to sit back and watch as the best lead we've found in ten years walks away from our camp."

"I am your best bet," I say. "But not because of my blood or my plasma. I'm your best bet because for the first time in a decade, I'm digging up answers to what really happened back then. Answers that explain how we can fix the nightmare that started when my dad's greedy partner killed him. Sticking me in a cell is like anchoring Christopher Columbus to the ocean floor a hundred miles from the Americas. Or not letting him sail beyond Puerto Rico."

"What exactly do you want me to do, your royal whatsnot?"

"First and foremost, I want a medical kit for Job and the chance to treat him. Sean cut the ties on his hands and he didn't even move. He's not a threat to anyone but himself right now, and you know it."

"Correction," Rafe says. "He wasn't a threat before you told him about Rhonda. Now he's a wild card who, for all I know you concocted this plan with as a way to attempt to break out."

"You are so bad at reading people," I say. "But in any

case, Job's no good to you dead. He's also your head scientist unless my uncle frees my aunt and they're crazy enough to come back and try to help you after what you've done."

"You want me to take care of Job? That's it?"

"It's a start," I say. "We also need something to eat and maybe some blankets. Potty breaks would be nice, too."

"Potty? Like the training of a two year old?" Rafe leans against the doorway. "And if I give you food, and *potty* breaks, and take care of Job, you'll sit here contently and let my people draw blood whenever they want?"

I nod. "Yes, I will. But you're moronic if you don't follow this lead." I hold the letter up so he can see it. "This is an electronic message from my aunt to the lady who managed my dad's business affairs. Aunt Anne asked her to send every piece of information from my dad's office and computer to her home. The woman wanted to be paid, so she did it."

"So what?" Rafe asks.

"That paperwork must be with Ruby's aunt in Port Gibson," Sam says. "Donovan's journals make it clear his partner stole Tercera, but we're virtually certain he also stole the hacker virus. If we can find paperwork saying who he is, we can track down where it went."

"What are the odds the partner's even alive?" Rafe asks.

"Good," I say. "If he stole the cure. I don't know why he didn't sell it, but I want to find out."

Rafe sighs. "I was young when Mom died and I hadn't gone to much school, but she taught me things in her final year, as much as she could. And she made me read. Just last week I read this phrase: a bird in the hand is worth two in the bush. It means if you caught a bird, you shouldn't trade it for two that are loose, because they'll probably just fly away and leave you with nothing. This magical virus you're talking about, even if what you're saying is true, could be gone. Or it could not be effective against Tercera, or it could have been initially but not in the long run. The partner could be dead already, and any cure he had long lost. Who knows whether this will amount to anything at all, even if you follow it to the end of the line."

"You'd rather not know?" I ask.

Rafe grins. "I think I'll hang on to my two swallows, thanks. You aren't going anywhere, not for a very long time." He walks toward the door, but turns back with a smile. "I'll think about those potty breaks, but I imagine things will get pretty uncomfortable for you two if I refuse. And with the way I feel about you, Ruby, I like that idea."

I want to slap the grin off his face.

Food shows up an hour later. Job doesn't touch his because he still isn't moving. An hour after that, Sean brings a bucket and drops it in front of our cell.

"It finally stopped raining," Sean says. "Boss said to take you outside."

"What's the bucket for?" I ask.

Sean opens the door and waves me out. He tosses the bucket inside the cell. "Bucket's for the one we think might break free. You get that potty break you wanted." Sean walks me outside to squat in the bushes in front of a crumbly apartment building, but at least he turns away while I go. The sun's setting on the horizon, and between that and the rain, the temperature's dropping. I wish he'd stand more than five feet away, but it's better than a bucket twelve inches from Sam.

"This sucks," I say.

Sean frowns. "I know and I'm sorry."

"Help me," I say. "We've got a chance to find an actual cure, but Rafe's too blinded by anger to listen."

Sean shakes his head. "I think the way he's treating you

is unfair. My guess is that he's jealous of how much his brother cares about you and that's clouding his judgment. Even so, I don't disagree with him about the virus. We've got something right now that's treating Tercera. Why chase after some unicorn?"

WHOMP.

Sean and I both turn toward the noise like a muted explosion that came from far west of the city. We run under a tree to take cover. Whomp, whomp, whomp. Objects slam into the ground around us, the closest only a few feet away. Hundreds of tiny objects fly across the sky in front of us, illuminated by the setting rays of the sun.

"What's going on?" I ask.

Sean shrugs. "I have no idea, but it looks like we're under some kind of attack."

The tin can looking object that landed on the ground nearby hisses, and orange gas seeps out alarmingly fast, spilling out around us and mushrooming to fill the space around our ankles in a twenty-foot radius. Sean drags me toward the pawnshop and pulls me inside. Neither of us talks and I assume that like me, he's holding his breath. Of course, with a broken window in the front room and a cracked door, being indoors doesn't help much. Orange smoke slowly filters into the interior of the building. Sean unlocks the cell and shoves me inside.

Sam pulls his shirt up over his face, and reaches over to pull mine up, too. "Don't breathe any more than absolutely necessary." He steps up on a shelf. "Get up as high as you can. The gas is sinking down toward the floor."

I nod and do as he says. Sean does the same, climbing up on a stool outside the bars. I notice Job still hasn't moved.

"Sean, open his cell. I'll bring him into ours, but we've got to get him off the floor!"

I hop down from the chair and walk toward the door.

Sam lifts me from behind and sets my feet back up on the shelf. He shakes his head at me and then turns to Sean. "Move."

Sean's eyes bulge with fear, but he hops down and unlocks Sam's door. Sam slams Sean in the face with his elbow and Sean crumples.

I scamper to follow Sam, orange smoke swirling around my legs. Sam lifts Sean up as easily as I'd lift a sack of potatoes, and sets him on the top shelf of the large built in bookcase in our cell. He lifts the hunting knife out of Sean's belt sheath and closes the door, locking Sean inside.

Sam opens Job's cell and tosses him over his shoulder. Sam inclines his head toward the back of the room. I grab my duffel in case I need that email or anything else, and throw it over my shoulder.

I shake my head. "We can't get out there. There's not even a door."

Sam grins, and when we reach the back of the room, he kicks the wall repeatedly until it crumbles away amid a chorus of chirps and squeaks. "Rat nest. I could smell it and I knew they'd weaken the wall."

I shudder, but I shove my duffel through first, widening the gap. Then I hunker down and climb through the hole Sam kicked out. The smoke's actually clearing already outside, and I hope we didn't doom Sean to a miserable death by locking him inside. Sam pushes Job's arms toward me, and I drag him through slowly, a few inches at a time, heaving and yanking.

Once I finally get him through, I prop him up against the wall of the building and pat his cheeks. "You've got to snap out of it Job. I need you."

Job's eyes rise to mine. "What do you need?"

"We need to go now. Rafe's trapped us here, but we

need to help your mom. She's in trouble. Do you understand?"

Job nods and stands up.

Sam crawls through, tossing a squirming rat aside when he stands.

I gag. "Let's hope that orange gas isn't toxic and that we don't catch leprosy or something from those rats."

"Any idea what it is?" Sam asks Job.

Job inhales deeply, and I thump his chest. "Don't try to breathe it, idiot!"

He shakes his head. "It doesn't smell. That's a good sign. Mustard gas is sweet and spicy, according to victims of World War One. They smelled it when it evaporated. That's where it got its name. Most blister agents smell good." He stands up. "Other gases, blood agents, almost all smell bad like rotten eggs, apples or garlic."

"Carbon monoxide doesn't have a smell," I say.

"It wouldn't hurt anyone like this, where it can quickly diffuse." Job shakes his head. "No, the real risk here is a nerve agent. Most of them are odorless, but we'd also have started twitching already with all the ones I've heard of. I don't know what it is."

"I do." Rafe steps out around the front of the building. "It's an air-borne accelerant. Looks like Ruby's extra days didn't stop WPN after all. We've all got about a week left, I'd say."

"How could you possibly know it's accelerant?" I ask.

Rafe walks around the corner, and I follow. He picks up the can Sean and I fled from. He tosses it at me.

I miss, but Sam's fast. He reaches down low and snags it. Sam rotates the can to show me the side of it, which reads: Dying slowly is a curse the accelerant will free you from.

"You got what you wanted," Rafe says. "You can leave. Look for the hacker virus, or don't. We're dead either way."

I shake my head. "This is not what I wanted, none of this is. But we will find my dad's partner, and once we do, I'm hoping we'll find that virus. If we do, we'll race back with it. Not to save you, but for your people. That's a promise."

"Who do you think did this?" Sam asks.

Rafe shrugs, his eyes lifeless, his countenance devoid of any emotion. My heart orders me to hug or comfort him in some way, but my mind refuses. He killed Rhonda. He deserves this and more.

I shouldn't say it, but I can't help myself. "I might have left WPN too soon."

Rafe meets my eye and nods. "Maybe you did, and if so that's on me. Either way this is my fault."

The admission doesn't satisfy me. Actually, it feels like I imagine it would feel to kick a baby goat.

"I hope this didn't come from WPN," Sam says.

Because if it did, it means Adam and Josephine aren't managing very well. I only just met my brother and mom. "I hope everyone is okay back in Galveston."

Sam nods. "Me, too. Losing family sucks." He may mourn the loss of family and Rafe's impending doom, but he doesn't extend comfort to Rafe either. After a long, awkward pause, Rafe turns around and walks away.

CHAPTER 11

Not everyone in camp takes the news as calmly or quietly as Rafe. The shouts and crying don't drive me out of town, but if I weren't already leaving they might. One person we pass isn't crying. She isn't shouting, or pulling her hair out, either.

"Ruby," Libby says.

My heart expands. Libby's holding baby Rose, the first baby my blood ever cured. Her sweet face is unmarked, clear. Her tiny pink hand is in her mouth, drool covering her fingers and running down her arm. It sounds disgusting, but the rightness of it fills a hole in my chest.

"Libby and Rose. I'm so sorry about all this." I reach out and touch Rose's strawberry blonde head, stroking her tiny curls.

Libby shakes her head. "It's not your fault. In fact, I didn't think I'd last a week after Rose's birth. I'd been off the suppressants a long time and here I am, a few sores but otherwise okay. Your blood might not have cured me, but it saved my baby, and it knocked Tercera back on its butt. I'm forever grateful." A tear runs down her cheek. "You gave me the one thing I had lost any hope for. Time with my daughter."

"May I?" I ask.

Libby passes Rose to me and I worry she'll cry. Rose squirms a little and her face turns red, but then she toots and her face returns to newborn pink. I laugh. "She seems to be doing well."

"I've been able to nurse her, even," Libby says. "I was worried at first, but she loves it and so do I."

I thought holding her would feel like holding a football, or a bag of beans. She weighs about the same, but the difference is indescribable. Rose is warm and she coos, and holding her wraps a bandage around my battered heart. This is the reason I waited, for Rose. I need to help her and her mother and the other Marked kids. Rafe was wrong to shoot Rhonda, but I'm right to keep helping the Marked anyway. My biological father and his minions wanted to wipe them all out, but we still need to give them the best shot we can at a good life. Even now, reeling from Rhonda's loss, I'll race after any chance we have at a cure as fast as I can.

"We aren't running away." For some reason, I feel the need to clarify.

Libby smiles. "Of course you aren't. I was very, very sorry to hear about Rafe's threats, and even sorrier to hear he shot your cousin. I know people were scared and angry, but I begged him not to do it. Rhonda didn't do anything wrong, and neither did you. I'm so sorry."

I lean down and kiss Rose's perfect forehead. The smell of her hair fills me with hope.

"We're looking for a virus," I say, "one that might consume Tercera. If we can find it, we hope the accelerant won't matter anymore. It's a long shot, but don't give up, okay?"

When I pass baby Rose back to her mother, Libby catches my hand. "Ruby, even if you fail, you gave me more time. If this doesn't work, remember it's not your fault."

I nod my head, but I can't speak another word as I watch Libby walk back toward central Baton Rouge. Typically we'd wait until morning to leave on any sort of trip, but we don't even discuss a delay, not after seeing Libby, not after the accelerant bombs. We're literally the last hope for tens of thousands and seconds matter right now. Rafe gave Uncle Dan and Wesley an old broken down truck, so all three of our vehicles are waiting for us, along with my stressed out and overwrought guards. Frank's so relieved to see me safe and sound that he races toward me, spins me around, and pulls me close for a hug. I stiffen involuntarily and then he won't meet my eyes.

"I'm so sorry Your Royal Highness, but I'm just so relieved that you're okay." Frank's eyebrows pull together and his hands close and open, close and open.

I'm lucky to have people who care whether I'm alive or dead. I hug Frank and this time I don't stiffen when his arms squeeze me. I don't think he even notices the tear I wipe away when I finally let go. Sometimes you need a hug, even when you don't think you do.

When we load up into the vehicles, I don't argue about Frank sitting in the jeep with Job, Sam and me. I do finally understand why Sam never wants to drive in the dark. He insists on taking point this time and the guards, too shell shocked from our time in Baton Rouge and the recent attack, don't argue. The shiny, new jeep from WPN jounces and jolts over potholes, logs and other debris that even Sam can't spot quickly enough to entirely avoid. We wouldn't have risked this at all, except that we've got brand new cars, but I hope we don't bust a drive chain. The vans struggle a bit more than we do, but they don't slow us down too much. And every time Sam needs to stop, the guards pour out quickly to lend a hand.

It's nice to have their help, but I miss our drive down from Port Gibson, when it was only Sam and me. Rhonda was alive, and I thought she and Job were safely back at home. Things seemed so much simpler then. I wanted the cure to help Wesley, but no one I knew was imminently dying if I didn't find it. None of the bad things were my fault yet. My dad's fault and his partner's fault yes, but I was simply Donovan Behl's child, daughter of a scientist who got confused and was killed for his efforts. I'm still his daughter, I remind myself. And we do have a chance to fix things, even if the grains of sand are slipping through an hourglass too quickly while we crawl along this road in the dark.

It should only take about three and a half hours to Port Gibson, according to Sam's estimates. It'll take another few hours to search my old home. If we locate the documents, and they name the partner, then we'll have to develop a time estimate on finding this Jack. I'm assuming that if he's alive, he can probably be tracked from Galveston, since most of the survivors started out there and spread to the other Port Cities slowly. That's another full day, or a day and a half's drive, but at least I have a little pull with them. I'm sure if he's alive and still with WPN, we can locate him.

I close my eyes and attempt my first ever prayer. I think if there really is a God, he doesn't need fancy churches or impressive words. He's got to care mostly about what's in my heart, right? Surely? I whisper the words as softly as I possibly can.

"Please God, if there is a God, let Dad's partner be alive, and maybe in Galveston so I can do something about finding him. Too many people have already died. I can't handle more."

If God exists, he doesn't bother answering me, but I feel a little calmer. Maybe that's the point.

Once I've mapped out a mental timeline for finding the hacker virus before the Marked die, I fret about my mom and Adam. "The accelerant couldn't have come from anywhere else? Or could it?"

Sam sighs. "We know WPN has the accelerant. We don't know whether others have it too."

"Could the Unmarked have done it? Do you have any reason to believe your dad might have meant the Marked kids harm?"

Sam shrugs. "He certainly would take that kind of action if there was a purpose to it, if that's what you're asking. He wouldn't have qualms about killing them, but I can't think of a way it benefits him. My dad does nothing without a reason."

I bite my lip. "Would Adam have done it? Did I misread him entirely? Maybe he was in the Port Heads' pocket all along."

"I genuinely doubt it," Sam says. "But we don't know him very well. I suppose anything is possible."

Or there could have been a coup already. Or one of the Port Heads could have simply taken action themselves. I close my eyes and massage my temples. I wish I had a spy network or something.

"Your mother didn't oppose the Cleansing when David Solomon was alive," Sam says.

"No, she didn't. Do you think Adam could've convinced her to reverse positions when it was the one thing I told them not to do? I don't know what's worse. Having my mom and brother betray me like that, or thinking the Port Heads have seized control and they're in danger."

"I think the most likely answer is that one of the Port Heads acted unilaterally," Sam says. "Technically it wasn't an attack. They didn't take a single life. If one of them had a cache of accelerant, he or she might've decided to fix things on their own."

"Which means I let Rhonda die for nothing."

I glance back at Job. He's still staring out of the window, with no sign he's even hearing anything we say. His eyes are glazed, his hands tapping the glass rhythmically. Because I'm looking back at him, I notice a small campfire off the side of the road. It wasn't visible from our northern route, but looking backward the flames shine brightly.

"We should check that out," I say.

Sam glances over. "A single campfire?" He shakes his head. "Absolutely not. Too dangerous to stop at night."

"It can't be more than one person. They could need help, and I'm sure they're cold if they've risked a fire."

Sam shakes his head again and panic inexplicably floods my body. We should press on but for some reason, I need to stop. We may be unable to save anyone else, but we have to help him or her.

I put one hand on his arm. "Please Sam. I can't explain it, but I feel like we should."

He groans and pulls the jeep over. I reach for the door, but he slides over and yanks me back. "I'm doing what you asked, but you do not get out, do you hear me?"

I want to argue, but I don't waste my breath. Sam climbs out of his side and signals the guards to follow. I count slowly to ten. Sam and the guards have circled the campfire, but they don't seem to have found anyone. I can't see what's happening from here. Sam's going to be annoyed, but I gave him a head start.

"I'm following them," I say to Job.

No response. Job's still staring out the window despondently. Apparently unless I need him imminently, Job has checked out.

I bite my lip. I've waited and waited. Sam knows me well enough by now to expect this. I hop out and run up behind them. A brand new sleeping bag lays near the campfire, but it's conspicuously empty. He must've heard us coming. I glance around, hoping the traveller will come out, whoever he is.

"Gone," Sam says.

Frank nods. "Ran off. Probably hiding from something or someone. If they don't want to be found, it's for the best we leave them be."

Sam orders the guards back to the cars. "Time to go, sunshine. Can't help someone who doesn't want it." He takes my arm and I let him lead me back to the jeep.

Something catches the corner of my eye, a flash of gold. I turn back and my breath catches when I see the red knit cap, poking out of the top of a nondescript black backpack. A gold puffball adorns the top. It's absolutely hideous, but my heart surges in my chest when I see it. Because I made that cap.

"Rhonda!" I scream and spin in a circle. "Rhonda, it's Ruby! Come out!"

Sam covers my mouth with his hand. "Stop that right now. You'll alert anyone within miles to our presence. After that accelerant attack, the Marked are volatile. Plus their attacker could be out here, waiting to see how they react."

I point at the red cap poking out of the open pocket of the backpack and Sam lets me go, his eyes scanning the darkness with newly found excitement. "Maybe someone took if after," Sam says. "Don't get your hopes up."

A stick cracks behind us, somewhere deep in the pitch-blackness of the woods and my heart races.

"Ruby?"

Rhonda emerges from the woods, her boots crunching

twigs and dry foliage underfoot. I barrel toward her as fast as my legs can propel me. I want to spin her around and throw her up in the air, but I'm not strong enough. I settle instead for clinging to her like a baby koala. Tears stream freely down my face. "You're supposed to be dead."

Rhonda pats my back. "Rafe had to execute me. His people were losing faith. They were talking about choosing a new leader, about storming the Unmarked towns or attacking Galveston in real numbers. He had to show them he was taking action and would soon be making progress."

I shake my head, and swipe at my wet cheeks. "But you're alive."

"He insisted on doing it himself," Rhonda says. "He took me out past the old Baton Rouge Zoo and held the gun to my temple. He shook his head back and forth, clearly agitated." She sighs. "I actually felt sorry for him. Or, you know, I would have if I hadn't been tied up and defenseless, waiting for my brains to be blown out."

"And?" I ask.

"A wild hog burst through the underbrush, barreling straight toward us. Rafe shot it, and then he got a strange look on his face. He yanked his belt knife off and sliced it open. He wiped blood on his arms and cut my ropes. He made me swear never to come back to Marked territory, and then he made me run. He said I couldn't stop until I ran past Baker. Ten or fifteen miles, I'm not sure. I don't know what he would have done if that pig hadn't surprised us, and I don't know what he did after that, but I'm guessing he didn't tell another soul exactly who or what he killed that day."

I close my eyes. The things I said to him, the fight between Sam and his brother. I can't take any of it back and he didn't even do it.

Sam smiles. "I'm glad you're okay." He pats Rhonda's

arm, and she pulls him against her for a hug, all of us laughing at his awkwardness.

Job never left the car, apparently not even recognizing Rhonda's name amid our shouting. When I realize that, I sprint back to the jeep. "Job." I tap on the glass.

He stares at me blankly.

Last time he only focused when I needed him. "Help me, Job. I have a problem."

His eyes orient and meet mine. "What's wrong?"

"Get out of the car right now."

Job opens the door and looks around frantically. "Why'd we stop? What's wrong?"

I point behind him and Job's eyes follow my finger. When he sees Rhonda, his jaw drops, his eyes widen and his hands shake. Rhonda jogs toward him, and when she slams into him, she looks so much like a golden retriever puppy that I'm surprised when she doesn't lick his face. Even with the time constraints we're under, the minutes ticking by while I watch Job with his twin don't make me anxious or impatient. They're entitled to take a breath to recover, especially Job.

I catch Rhonda up on what's happened while we drive toward Port Gibson. By the time 33 dumps onto 61, she's up to speed. Of course, that's when my nerves kick into overdrive. I haven't seen Port Gibson in weeks, and the previously familiar surrounding areas look alien to me now.

When we pull up to the checkpoint, I recognize the guard.

"Hey Barrett," Sam says.

Barrett's chocolate brown eyes widen as they take us all in.

"Will you let us through?" Sam asks. "The vans back

there are with us. They're from WPN, but they answer to me. I'll vouch for all of them."

Barrett coughs. "I doubt you can really vouch for anyone. You're in a lot of trouble, Sam. Mayor Fairchild isn't pleased you left when you did."

"My departure ended the Marked attacks though, didn't it?"

Barrett runs one hand through his short, dark brown hair, leaving it sticking up all over. "There was one more, but then yeah, they stopped. How'd you know?"

Sam sighs. "Let me past."

Barrett's fingers fidget on his clipboard.

"It's me here in the back, Bar," Rhonda says. "I'm sure you saw my dad pass through not long ago with Fairchild's son. His no-longer-Marked-son."

Barrett nods.

Rhonda smiles. "You aren't sure what to do because that already caused a lot of unrest."

Barrett nods again.

"Trust me, okay. Sam was your boss, but I'm a friend. We're here for a good reason and we're all healthy. You can let us in."

Barrett takes a deep breath. "Okay, you can pass." He points behind us. "But they have to wait outside."

Frank is not going to like this.

Sam agrees to Barrett's terms, and he and I walk back to ask them to wait outside the city wall. I worry Paul's head is going to explode, but ultimately none of them can take Sam in official rank, or physically if it came to that. Eventually, they agree to set up camp just past the southern barricade. It's a good thing we brought some supplies from WPN and that Rafe left their food and tents in the vans.

"I think we should head straight for your house," Sam

says after we climb back into the jeep. "I'm guessing Dan and Wesley have at least been there."

We all agree. When we pass the Claiborne County Medical Center, it looks smaller somehow, less impressive now that I've seen bigger facilities. When we turn on Greenwood Street, my hands begin to shake. I expect our house to look different too, smaller or shabbier, but when we turn onto College Street and it comes into view, it looks exactly the same. Partially enclosed front porch, freshly painted light blue siding that probably needs to be replaced soon. Two stories tall with a tiny window at the very top that looks out from my bedroom. My greenhouse looks the same from the outside, but I'm sure all my precious little plants are already dead.

No vehicles are parked out front. Rafe said he gave Wesley and Uncle Dan a red pickup truck. Shouldn't it be parked here? When I glance at Sam, he shrugs. I hold out my hand for him when we walk up to the front door, but he doesn't take it. Rhonda frowns at me and lifts one eyebrow.

I shake my head. I'll have to explain later. I wish being dumped didn't hurt so much.

I grab the knob, but the door's locked. Job grabs the hide-a-key from under a family of stone owls that live in our front flowerbed and unlocks the door. When it swings open freely, I wonder who repaired the damage Sam did the day we left. The day he handed in my Path for me, and I fled my home of almost nine years.

"Uncle Dan?" I call. "Are you home?"

Silence.

"Wesley?" Job yells as he walks up the stairs. "You here?"

Nothing.

My heart rate accelerates when I jog toward my aunt's office, but not because of the exertion. Job's feet clomp back down the stairs, and he and Rhonda follow behind me, eager to help. I start with the office drawers, while Job begins with a bookcase, and Rhonda opens boxes that are stacked in the corners.

"Where should I look?" Sam asks.

"Maybe you should find Uncle Dan," I say. "I'm sure he'd love to know Rhonda's with us."

Sam shakes his head. "We aren't splitting up. I have no idea what reception your uncle found." He doesn't mention that it's not promising that Uncle Dan isn't home. He doesn't have to. We all know.

Sam dives into the second box next to Rhonda.

Two hours later, minutes until midnight, we've searched every piece of paper in the office and checked my aunt and uncle's closet. We even rummaged around in the garage without success.

"No one has seen a single thing that could've been Donovan Behl's?" I ask. "Or Donald Carillon's?" My dad assumed a fake name when he stole me from my mom and ran, which makes me wonder how many of his papers I might have seen without even knowing they were his.

Rhonda and Job shake their heads.

"How can that be?" I groan. "It was all sent to Aunt Anne, I'm sure of it." I rock back on my heels, deflated, borderline depressed.

"It's possible they left it in Nebraska, isn't it?" Job asks. "Didn't Mom say they only looked through the boxes right before they left? Maybe they didn't think financial paperwork was important enough to bring."

Aunt Anne's words rise up in my memory. "She found boxes of journals and his briefcase." I look around the room despondently. "No briefcase. I bet they left it."

I want to curl up and sob. All those kids. I was counting

on finding the name of Dad's partner with time to track him down.

"Mom and Dad had to travel with me and Job, you, and Sam. That's four kids for just three adults, the two of them and Sam's dad. I would've left boring financial paperwork behind too," Rhonda says. "If I was headed into the unknown. Especially if I was already hauling a box of cumbersome old journals."

"We're wasting our time here." Uncle Dan hasn't come home by midnight, and I need to know why. "Your dad might remember whether they left that stuff."

Job and Rhonda look at each other and nod. "Fairchild's our best bet for finding Dad."

I sigh. Wesley's house isn't too far. Wesley came with Uncle Dan, and his dad's the one controlling Aunt Anne's fate.

As quickly as we arrived, we load back up in the jeep headed for Wesley's house. It's almost midnight, which isn't exactly an ideal time to be knocking on the Mayor's door. During the drive, I wonder whether Mr. Fairchild has seen Wesley yet. I wonder whether he's amazed and excited, or just relieved. I hope he's in a better mood. Maybe he'll be pleased enough about his son's return to release my aunt. I hope my blood helps her, or if not, that we can find this hacker virus. My foot taps a staccato rhythm on the floorboard.

Rhonda lays a hand on my arm. "Everything's going to be okay."

I wish I believed her, but too much is piling up. Too many problems, too many fears and too many people I love in danger. A red pickup truck is parked in front of Wesley's house, as well as a large white Range Rover. Sam pulls up behind it and cuts the engine.

"Mayor Fairchild got a new car?" I point at the white Range Rover.

"Maybe." Sam's voice wobbles. I've never heard his voice sound like that, almost nervous. What could make Sam nervous?

"Who else could it be?" I narrow my eyes, because I suspect he knows.

Sam shrugs. "Anyone, I guess."

We all sit still for a moment, as though none of us really want to go knocking on Mr. Fairchild's door. He's nice enough I guess, but kind of scary too. Light streams out of the glass in the front door, and the windows in the front room, but it's not bright, and I don't see any shadows so there's no indication of movement. Maybe they left a candle burning. It's a violation of rule 23, but who's going to turn in the Mayor?

I grab the jeep's door handle and force it open. I've known Mr. Fairchild for a long time. I don't mind waking him up, not when my aunt's life hangs in the balance. Rhonda and Job stride up, one on either side of me. I feel Sam more than hear him behind me. The three of us up front all lean forward and pound on the wood together, electing not to use the huge metal knocker.

There's no pause before boot steps clomp toward the door, which means at least someone was awake. The solid oak door swings open with a creak. I expect to see Mr. Fairchild, a tall, thin man with a black, grey-streaked beard. I wouldn't have been surprised to see Wesley's mom, an equally thin, and nearly as tall woman with a kind face. Her shiny, dark brown hair is always swept up into a high ponytail, like she never quite gave up on the style after high school cheerleading ended.

The man standing behind the door looks nothing like Mr. or Mrs. Fairchild, except perhaps for his prodigious height. He stands several inches taller than Rhonda, and maybe only an inch or two shorter than Sam. His golden eyes stare into mine, then shift slowly to Job, then Rhonda, and finally lift over our heads to Sam. He's as old as Mayor Fairchild, but better looking, much better.

"Hello son. I've been wondering when you'd turn up."

"Can't say I'm glad to see you," Sam says. "You'd know that was a lie."

My eyes widen and my eyebrows rise. I don't remember Sam disliking his dad this much. At least, they never fought back in the cabin I don't think.

Job says, "Well I'm glad to see you, sir. We're sorry to knock at such a late hour Mr. Roth, but have you seen our father?"

John Roth leans against the doorframe. "Hey Job. I'm glad you came. Your dad said you were being held by a group of insane Marked kids. He's inside."

Rhonda smiles in relief. We don't know Mr. Fairchild well, and Sam may not like his dad, but at least we know him. "May we come in, sir?"

John smiles warmly. "Rhonda." His eyes crinkle when and he exhales deeply. "Dan thought. . . well, he's going to be ecstatic to see you."

"We all thought she was dead," I say. "The Marked leader told us he executed her."

John steps back and gestures for us to walk past. Job and Rhonda run ahead, but John's hand shoots out and his fingers circle my wrist. "Little Ruby isn't quite as little anymore. I've heard a lot about you lately, and even more about your late father. I'm glad to see that you're healthy and whole. Last I heard you were being held by the Marked kids too, as a lab rat."

"We bring some news about that actually," I say.

Sam walks past his father and keeps walking into the

family room. He ducks behind Job and Rhonda and out of my view.

"What news?" John Roth asks.

"Someone hit Baton Rouge with accelerant in tin can bombs. The Marked have been gathering there since the suppressant started failing. There were ten thousand or so who hadn't arrived yet, but the majority of them had reached the city. Everyone present now has less than a week to live unless we can find the cure."

"I thought *you* were the cure," John Roth says.

Wesley's voice comes from the stairs. "I told you she wasn't. Her blood is more of a preventative." He runs down the stairs, a smile on his face when he looks at me.

"Worked well enough for you," John Roth says. "But you did mention it wasn't effective for those in advanced stages."

Wesley starts down the stairs. "It worked for me because I ingested Ruby's blood around the same time my Mark showed up."

"Yes, I heard the story on that. You two kissed at the Last Supper if my sources got it right." John Roth lifts his eyebrows. "And now I hear you're dating my son."

Sam glances back at me sharply. He shakes his head.

"Uh, no sir," I say. "We aren't together. Not anymore."

John Roth frowns. "Not anymore? My, my, I can't keep up with you young people."

"You're not the only one." Wesley smirks from the bottom step.

Shouts from the family room draw my eye. Uncle Dan's arms wrap around Rhonda and my heart lifts as he spins her in a circle like I wanted to do. Now we just need Aunt Anne back. John Roth walks into the family room, but before I can follow him, Wesley steps off the stairs and jogs over to where I'm standing in the foyer. He reaches out and pulls me into a hug.

He's standing so close to me that his words ruffle my hair. "I heard about the accelerant from upstairs. I'm so sorry, but I'm glad that maniac let you go."

"I actually almost felt sorry for him after the attack, and I still thought he'd killed Rhonda at the time." I shake my head, but there's too much to deal with to waste much time on relief. "Wes, they're all dying. Every single one of them." I pull away and look up into his dark blue eyes. "Speaking of. Have you guys talked about Aunt Anne yet?"

His brows draw together. "I better let my dad explain."

I follow him into the family room, but everyone's already moving toward the kitchen by the time I get there. Mr. Fairchild stands next to Job by the wooden table, gesturing at a document.

"What's going on?" I ask.

Job meets my eye. "Dad said Mom was charged with assault on an Unmarked person, and initially she was. Fairchild convicted her, just like Dad said, but after she was convicted and before Mayor Fairchild could reconsider, she confessed."

I shake my head. "That's not legal. She could've been under duress. And anyway, why would she do that?"

"Not to the assault," Rhonda says. "She confessed to something else, something entirely different."

I stalk toward the table, noting the slump of Uncle Dan's shoulders, and the downward cast of Rhonda's eyes. I glance down at the paper.

I, Anne Carillon Orien, hereby swear that the following statement is a true and faithful representation of the facts as I know them. In early June I discovered some of the Marked children had voluntarily ceased taking the hormone suppressant. Failure to take it allowed their bodies to develop. Several of them became pregnant. I grew concerned with this change and notified the proper authorities. I believed then, as I do now, that such action would result in a perpetuation of the Marked threat, with no indication of a cure in sight.

When the leadership chose not to take action, I took the problem into my own hands. I substituted the hormone suppressant for sugar pills with the intention that the Marked children would die out naturally as they should have years go. This would finally terminate the ongoing risk that they pose to all the Unmarked, including my own children.

I attest this is a true statement, and it was written in my own hand.

Anne Carillon

It's in her handwriting, but I don't believe a word of it. My aunt would never have done that, any of it. Besides, the suppressant wasn't replaced with sugar pills. It was replaced with prenatal vitamins. My aunt would know that, since she investigated it firsthand. Even so, it's hard to petition for an appeal when you're staring at a signed confession for a more egregious crime.

"If she weren't already slated for execution on the grounds of criminal assault," John Roth says, "I'd be forced to sentence Anne Orien to death on the grounds of treason."

CHAPTER 12

"This paper is a lie. The suppressant wasn't changed for sugar pills, for one thing. I demand to see her." I slam my hand down on the paper. "Aunt Anne would never write that. If she caused the suppressant failure like this says, why would she freak out when she found out about it? And why come rushing back to try and save them? It's clearly fabricated and it makes no sense."

"Guilt does strange things to people," Mr. Fairchild says. "She told me she exchanged the suppressant because the Marked kids were slowly starving. That's exactly the reason my Wesley got Marked, you know. His big heart saw a starving girl and tried to help. But when your aunt saw those starving children, and realized some were having babies, babies that would perpetuate this horrifying cycle, she felt guilty. Or she fled because she was overcome with shame and used that fictitious purpose as a pretense."

I shake my head. "She wouldn't have changed the suppressant without telling anyone. She's not devious. She would have explained her reasons to the Council."

"Not devious? She held on to her brother's journals all

these years without sharing that she even had them," John Roth says. "She never told you the truth about your father or your mother."

I frown. He's right. Uncle Dan pulls out a chair and sits down, his face downcast. Something doesn't add up, but I can't think what.

John Roth pats my shoulder. "Sometimes we least understand the people we love the most." He glances at his son.

I shy away from his hand because he's wrong. I know my aunt, and she didn't do this.

"I'm not trying to hurt you," John Roth says. "I love your aunt too. She's a good person. These are terrible times we live in. I heard from your uncle that you survived quite an ordeal down in Galveston, and then to be captured by the Marked and locked up again? You must be exhausted."

I pull out a chair and plonk down in it, my eyes still transfixed by the alleged confession. He's right though, I am exhausted. Maybe I'm not as rational as I should be.

"You should be back there now," John Roth says. "In Galveston, where you can actually do some good. My son can go with you and keep you safe as I hear he's done several times in the past few weeks."

"You want me to take Sam and go back to WPN? Actually go back down to rule as their queen?"

John Roth shrugs. "They have resources, tools, and advanced tech that we've lost the capability to reproduce and maintain. It could be quite the positive partnership, to work with them instead of against them. Cooperation between us could change an awful lot of lives among the Unmarked for the better."

A month ago I had no idea what Path to choose. I was literally collecting garbage and cleaning toilets in Sanitation. Now it's like I'm a prize mare, or even worse, a character from an insipid Jane Austen novel. I hate everything about it.

"I have no intention of ever ruling in Galveston, just so you know. I met my half brother while I was there. He's older than me, he's lived there all his life, he actually believes in God and he doesn't mind giving the people the preachy sermons they want. I left him to run things temporarily, but I'm planning to make it permanent as soon as I possibly can."

John Roth frowns. "As you know, I try to maintain open communication with as many of the WPN leaders as possible. Multiple lines of contact help keep them honest, and they help us assess the possible benefits to trade and other cooperation, versus the threat of violence or attack. I recently received a letter from a Port Head indicating you survived a Trial by Fire and were crowned queen."

I exhale. "That's technically true." I scrunch my nose. "Which Port Head wrote you? Sawyer?"

John Roth shakes his head.

"Rosa? No, wait, I know. Dolores."

John Roth smiles. "You're a persistent little thing, I'll give you that. And it was a stroke of brilliance to demand a Trial by Fire and request the method of death be infection by Tercera. It only worked because you rather prudently failed to share that you're immune, but whatever works with lunatics like them. I admire that you didn't run when threatened with death, but changed the rubric instead."

John Roth never spoke to me when I was a kid and we lived for years in the same cabin. It was like he didn't even see me back then. I wish I could revert to that. "Um, thanks. The thing is, I think we have more pressing issues right now than who's wearing a crown down in Galveston."

"Like what?" he asks.

"My dad's old journals mention that in addition to the antibodies, there's a virus Dad was working on. He called it the hacker virus because it gobbled up other viruses and made them into more of itself. He worried his partner would sell Tercera, which obviously he did, and he said there were two more doses of this hacker virus."

"But there's no way the virus could have survived this long, right?" Mayor Fairchild asks.

I shake my head. "No, but if the partner stole the cure too, and we can find financial documents that show who my father's business partner was, then we can find him. If he has the cure, we can use it to save the Marked kids."

Mayor Fairchild whistles. "You're hoping to save all those poor kids? Ninety or a hundred thousand kids are dying this week, and you think you really might find the key to saving them all? After eleven years of this horrible virus stumping every scientist in America?"

I scowl. "We know it's a long shot, but if we can find the paperwork, at least we can try. No one ever solved a problem by giving up."

"Don't you think if this partner had the cure he'd have done something with it?" John Roth asks. "He could've sold it at any point for an astronomical price, I imagine."

"We don't know any details, and only he can answer that," I say. "What if he did have it and sold it to another country?"

"Then finding him would hardly help," John Roth says. "In that case, it would be beyond our reach."

I shake my head. "WPN has boats. We might not get it in time to save the ninety-thousand who were accelerated, but what about the other ten?"

"Without locating the partner, we'll never know," Wesley says. "It's knowledge we undeniably need. For instance, if the partner planned to wait until things were desperate to drive up the price and he waited too long, perhaps he missed his window. By the time the government was wiped out, traditional money had no meaning. The whole world shifted."

Mayor Fairchild beams. "We're so happy to have you home. You're developing quite a fine head for this sort of reasoning."

Uncle Dan rolls his eyes. "Or maybe he didn't know what he had. The point is, until we know who the partner is, we can't track down the answer. That's the point."

"We thought the records would be at the house," I say. "An email from Aunt Anne indicates they were in some kind of briefcase. Do you remember anything like that?"

Uncle Dan shakes his head. "No, but we focused on bringing all the supplies we could carry. Other than obviously practical things, all we made room for were your dad's journals. We still hadn't read them at that point. If I'm being honest, Anne and I have worried several times that we might have left a journal or two behind."

"We have to go back," I say. "If there's any chance we might find out something we can use, we have to go to Republican City."

John Roth laughs. "That's twenty hours away by car, if the roads are even passable anymore. I can't imagine that cabin survived eight years without upkeep. No, the better bet is to search the documents and materials down in Galveston. You've got total control there. You can turn your dad's office, home and lab upside down, not to mention combing through any police and government evidence. David Solomon was a canny man. I imagine he saved everything related to Donovan Behl and his work."

"We need to focus on saving my mom first," Rhonda says. "When can we talk to her?"

Mr. Fairchild sighs. "She's already been sent to Nashville. All executions take place there."

Uncle Dan puts his head in his hands.

"If you need someone other than her husband, I'll formally petition for an appeal," I say. "I don't believe this confession one little bit, and I demand you rehear her case and question her about why she's falsely confessed. Try her on both charges if you insist, because I'll bet she can clear herself of both. Besides, what's the downside for her? She still dies?"

John Roth's voice is low, and reminds me of both his sons. "I'm sorry little Ruby, but I already explained this to your Uncle. I walked in at the end of Anne's interrogation and I watched her write the confession myself. It's real, as much as I wish it wasn't. I have to deny the appeal. We must keep order and I can't pardon people because they're my friends."

"Why not?" Sam asks. "It's not like it would set a bad precedent. You don't have many."

"We'll talk later," John Roth says. "We have a lot of things to discuss, but I'm not changing my mind about the appeal. I can't afford a vote of no confidence right now, with the Marked threat and a regime change in Galveston. It would be catastrophic, especially with Counselor Quinn questioning everything I say and do."

I don't even bother asking who Quinn is. John's reasons for having a weak spine don't interest me. We never had a chance to appeal my aunt's sentence. We were doomed from the start, just like we were in Baton Rouge. Like every attempt I make to fix things, I've failed again.

"One thing I'll never understand," I say, "is Unmarked society's rush to expedite the death of people already on death row."

Mayor Fairchild coughs. "Excuse me." He clears his

throat. "I do want to apologize for how the entire thing happened. It was a terrible business for all of us. I'm sorry for my role in it. But Ruby, if you don't plan to return to WPN and search for documents, we'd love to coordinate with you on preparing something to inoculate the Unmarked here in Port Gibson. You and Wesley could work on the protocols together, with Job's supervision of course. I'm happy to offer Job his mother's position, er, once it's officially available that is."

Which will happen when Job's mother is executed. Because of Mayor Fairchild's ruling. At least he has the decency to recognize what an awkward place his eagerness to use my immunity has shoved him into. "But for now, I'm sure we all need to sleep. My brain is so foggy I can barely string two words together."

"I agree with you. We all need sleep," John Roth says. "But it's something to consider, Ruby. If you decide not to return to Galveston, I'm sure all the communities of the Unmarked would do whatever you might need to facilitate the development of an inoculation. It may be too late for all those children, but we can at least ensure this dreadful plague dies with them."

Everywhere I go, people want to pen me in, tie me up and pump blood out of my body. I'm like the dopey virgin teen with perfume smelling blood in one of those bad vampire movies everyone loved Before.

I think about Adam and Josephine back in Galveston. I hope the Port Heads haven't taken over, but at a baseline I fear one of them has gone rogue. I need to go back and find out who. If I can't help Rafe, Lily, and Rose, at least I can make their murderers pay.

"I'll go back to WPN," I say. "That doesn't mean I don't want to help, but I need to resolve some things there, stuff I left without addressing fully."

"My son will accompany you," John Roth says. "I can smooth things over here on his behalf. It won't hurt for me to report that he's been placed in a key position there. Chief of the Army, or some such, huh?"

"I'd dearly like to know who you're talking to," I say.

John Roth's only answer is a non-committal shrug.

"Did your contact mention anything about my regent?"

John's eyes rise. "Your mother, I believe."

I nod. "Nothing else?" Like whether there's been a coup.

John Roth shakes his head. "No other details, but I'm sure if there is any unrest, my son can take care of that for you." He pats Sam's shoulder and I notice that big, brawny Sam flinches.

I want Sam to come with me, of course I do, but being told he's coming with me by his smug father and that Sam will fix all my problems for me, well it pisses me off.

"I wouldn't dare impose on any part of your family any further. Sam's risked his life for me over and over and apparently it's landed him in some trouble with you. The good news is that I brought a substantial number of guards. They're waiting for me just outside of Port Gibson, and they're more than adequate to safely escort me back to Galveston where my mother's waiting for me."

Sam's eyes are pained when they meet mine, before he looks away.

"We can talk about the rest of any details back at home," Uncle Dan says. "We've imposed long enough."

"Indeed." Job's eyes flash. "Don't let us keep you awake any longer with our vain pleas that you consider saving our innocent mother's life."

Job, Rhonda, and Uncle Dan stand up and walk toward the door. I glance at Wesley, who shrugs, so I stand up too. He squeezes my hand before I can leave. "I'll be over as soon as I can."

I don't acknowledge that I heard him. I square my shoulders and walk to the door. After my family has walked through the doorway, I turn back. "Mr. Roth, something to consider. I'm returning to WPN imminently. I haven't decided whether to rule, or pass my rule off to someone more capable, but either way it won't help the Unmarked if they recently killed my aunt, who I love like a mother. It might even make me hang on to the position, out of a desire for revenge."

John Roth's mouth turns up, but the smile doesn't reach his eyes. "You've caught on quickly, haven't you Ruby?"

I shrug. "Just an observation. I might be persuaded into a friendly trade position with the Unmarked one way or another, but once my aunt is dead, any hope of that dies with her. You'll have made an enemy. And one more humble observation if you don't mind. WPN outnumbers the Unmarked by at least two to one, and we've got far, far superior firepower. Even if you can't pardon your *friends*, you might consider what you could conceivably do in exchange for a political alliance, or if things got really ugly like they might with falsified confessions, to prevent a war." I turn on my heel and walk out.

"She's a real fireball, isn't she?" I hear John Roth asking as I slam the door.

Rhonda and Job are sitting in the red truck with Uncle Dan, which I don't fault them for. Even with the news about Aunt Anne, it's got to be exciting to Uncle Dan to have Rhonda back.

I climb into the jeep alone and pull the keys out of the glove box where Sam left them. Uncle Dan starts the truck and heads home, but I wait on the street for at least five minutes for Sam to emerge. Finally, I see movement from behind a bush on the side of the house. A dark figure runs toward me. I turn the key in the ignition. The figure opens the car door and my heart flutters with excitement.

My heart plummets when I realize it's Wesley.

"Oh," I say. "Hi."

"You look surprised, and maybe even disappointed. I'll pretend that doesn't sting. You were hoping for Sam, I take it?"

"Forget it." I pull out onto the road and turn toward home.

Wesley sighs. "What happened? Sam broke up with you because of what Rafe said?"

I nod.

"You know what they say. Big genetically enhanced pecs . . .tiny brain. I was jealous for a while, I'll admit. But I'm actually grateful right now that I can't melt metal objects with my laser beam vision."

I roll my eyes. "He snapped his handcuffs earlier with nothing more than a simple flex and pull movement."

Wesley groans. "Fine, I lied. I am still jealous."

I snort. "It's okay. I am too. I can barely pop the top off of cans." I pull up in front of my house and park the car on the road.

"Look, if you go and apologize really soundly, I bet he'll forgive you," Wesley says. "He's obviously still gaga for you. You were busy fighting with his dad, but Sam alternated between brooding and staring at you longingly the entire time you were at my house. He was basically Heathcliff in *Wuthering Heights*. Wealthy Heathcliff, not the young insecure one."

"Of course." I open the car door and climb out.

Wesley closes his door and walks alongside me.

"The thing is," I say, "Sam's waiting on me, I guess. To be completely sure. He wants me to be totally ready to commit to him."

"Ready to commit for what?" Wesley shakes his head. "To bear him beefy boys?"

"Gross, Wes. Eww."

"I'm kidding, but I swear that guy isn't making my job easy."

"What does that mean?" I ask.

"He's not leaving any socks on the floor. That's what I mean. If he'd be a little more annoying or a little less noble." Wesley opens the front door for me. When I walk through, he drops his voice. "If I'm being totally honest, I actually like him, Rubes. I wanted to hate him, but he treats you really well and he makes you happy. When he's not dumping you over principles. Stupid, noble, kind of gentlemanly principles." He runs one hand through his hair. "I can't believe I'm saying this to you, but as your best friend and not a jealous wannabe boyfriend, I'm duty bound to admit that you could do worse, like way worse. He's not as great as me, but he's not horrible either. I guess that's the gist of what I'm saying."

Wesley's candor and his obvious care for me remind me why I liked him for so many years.

We walk in the door quietly.

"You're back. Finally." Uncle Dan paces. When he notices Wesley, he says, "I didn't expect you here."

"My parents think I'm asleep."

Uncle Dan shakes his head. "Maybe you should be."

Wesley says, "Not if Rubes needs me, and I'm pretty good with making plans. We were slow coming home because Ruby took it upon herself to threaten the big man himself. She told our Chancellor that WPN has more weapons, and more people and he oughtn't get off on the wrong foot by executing the new queen's aunt who she loves like a mother."

Uncle Dan's eyes widen. "What did he say?"

"He didn't respond other than to say he was impressed with my initiative," I say. "But I'm not letting it go so easily. I have no idea what's going on down in Galveston, but maybe with a formal request from WPN I can pry her free. I've decided to head back tomorrow. Roth's right. My best hope for finding the paperwork that lists Dad's partner is in Galveston. Besides, I'm worried about Josephine and Adam. That accelerant never should've hit Baton Rouge."

"Are you sure it came from WPN?" Rhonda asks.

"No," I say, "I'm not, but I know Solomon had it, and who else had motive?"

Rhonda throws her hands up in the air. "My mom had no motive at all to trade out the suppressant, but for some reason everyone believes she did that."

Wesley sits down in our big blue armchair. "I don't think she did it at all. Rafe said she was upset, like genuinely upset when she discovered the pills weren't the same. She rushed back here to investigate knowing she'd have difficulty communicating with anyone. Why would she do that if she had substituted them herself?"

"But who else could've done it?" Job asks. "That's been my hang up all along. My mom was my first suspect too, and would be still if I didn't know her so well."

The beginnings of an idea form in my head. Tiny clues, so small I can't trust them. "I wonder whether, and bear with me here, could Rafe have done it?"

Job snorts. "Why in the world would he?"

I perch on the edge of the sofa. "Think about it. His people were going off it voluntarily, at least some of them. They were sick of side effects, sick of their lives being on pause. And some of them wanted children. Libby told me she wanted to be a mother and she wasn't even sure if she could be thanks to ten years of hormone treatments. Their own parents left them, and they knew they'd be doomed to leave their own kids, and they did it anyway. That sounds like despair, or maybe just garden-variety depression. I don't know which, but Rafe was already captaining a sinking ship."

"Side effects are better than dying," Uncle Dan says. "So what if a few kids voluntarily stopped taking it?"

I shake my head. "Something he said struck me as super odd. He said 'that was why he did what he did.' I assumed he meant with Rhonda, but it felt strange at the time. Knowing he didn't even shoot Rhonda, I wonder whether he meant something else entirely. Like swapping the suppressant to get them some attention."

"No one ever prioritizes them," Wesley says. "That's what he was talking about when he said he 'did something about it.' I remember you looking at me and I knew you heard it too."

I nod. "Could he have meant that he did something about them being ignored? He eliminated the permanent time out? Forcing us to deal with their impending death instead of throwing pills at them indefinitely?" I bite my lip. "After the accelerant hit, when we were leaving, Sam said it was Rafe's fault for making us leave WPN too soon. Rafe said either way it was all his fault or something like that. I wonder if he blames himself because without going off the suppressant. . ."

"The accelerant wouldn't have done a thing," Job says.

"Monumentally stupid move if it was him," Uncle Dan says. "I actually feel bad for him. I know what it feels like to ruin everything while trying to help."

So do I.

"The other option is someone set Mom up," Rhonda says. "Someone within the Unmarked."

"Sam and Rafe both hate their dad," I say. "Could John Roth have forced Aunt Anne to sign that confession?

Could he have changed out the suppressants for some reason? Maybe he saw a chance to pin it on someone else and took it."

Uncle Dan shakes his head. "He's a tough enough guy to do that, even to a friend. He's done some things that were hard, but I don't think John would do that to *us*. We aren't really just friends. We're more like family. We've been best friends for twenty years, since we were in the Olympics together. And we lived with him through the end of the world."

Maybe, but there's something about John Roth I do not trust. "He's been ruling the Unmarked for a while, and you don't see him much anymore."

Uncle Dan collapses on the sofa. "We don't see him as often, it's true. But he has no motive. Why would he swap the suppressants? And if he did, who would ever hold him accountable for it? He's not a dictator, but no one's truly challenged his leadership in . . . well, ever. So why set up a dear friend to take the fall for something that no one would blame him for?"

"Except for this Quinn," I mutter.

"What?" Uncle Dan asks.

"Never mind," I say. "But I don't trust him."

Uncle Dan leans on his arm. "I do like him and I do trust him. If you give him a solid reason he can use, I think he'll pardon her. He's canny enough he might actually have refused to help her and made up some crap about a political rival so he could come back and argue for concessions from WPN. In fact, the more I think about it, I think he was probably angling toward this all along."

I grit my teeth. "Your dear friend would allow you to suffer psychological pain of unknown quantity in order to negotiate with me?"

Uncle Dan shrugs. "Maybe. In his mind it's not real harm."

Some friend.

Wesley nods. "I was wondering the same thing. He knew an awful lot about Ruby's new position, and she's new, like really, really new. I doubt everyone living in a WPN city or settlement even knows her name yet. I bet Roth's been planning to spare Anne, but figured he might as well get something out of it."

"Would he really bait me that way?" I ask. "What if I didn't think of threatening him?"

Uncle Dan snorts. "He would have led you there if he had to."

"I told you I didn't like him." I fold my arms and lean back in the sofa, breathing deeply of the smell of home.

"I think the WPN angle's our best bet to save her," Wesley says. "Plus, John Roth is right about one thing. If there's evidence of your father's partner anywhere, there's probably some kind of copy in Galveston. Maybe we can even fire up some old computers or something."

A dark thought occurs to me that I can't even mention to Job, or Rhonda, or my uncle. But what if there isn't any evidence of the partner. . . because my aunt already destroyed it? I sit up and prop my chin into my hands. What if *Aunt Anne* was my dad's partner? She had money as a physician and also from my uncle's endorsements. She could've invested in her brother, and if things went south she might've needed cash badly. Would she have threatened to release a virus? Could she have pulled the trigger?

Dad calls his partner Jack, and always says 'he', but what if he promised he'd keep no records of her involvement or what if Jack was a nickname, or a code word for Anne? I wouldn't recall ever meeting "Jack" since when I saw Dad's partner, I'd really have been seeing someone I knew already as my aunt.

Except she's Marked now. If she was the partner, she should have the hacker virus and be immune, right?

Unless it didn't work or she lost it. Or sold it. Or any of a million other bizarre answers that might explain how this partner let the world burn. I know she knew a lot she didn't share, about Tercera, about my dad. About my mom.

I sink back down into the couch and stuff my face into a pillow. We don't know enough and it all happened too long ago. I'm grasping at straws at this point. Tomorrow I'll be thinking maybe a dragon incinerated the partner and ate the hacker virus.

Wesley sits next to me. "You're exhausted. You need to sleep."

I sit up straight. "You're all as tired as I am, and we're still planning because we're running out of time. Any hope of saving Rafe and his people disappears if we can't figure out who my dad's partner was soon. And we need to save Aunt Anne somehow too. With those as our goals, let's talk options."

Job nods. "Yes goal one is to save Mom. Goal two, save a hundred thousand Marked kids. Options as I see it, if we save Mom right away, we can talk to her about your blood. Maybe there's something I'm missing, a way to boost the antibodies immediately. You'd have to book it down to Galveston and send an official edict to John Roth and the Unmarked demanding her release."

"Assuming Ruby's not walking into a coup," Rhonda says. "In which case Ruby might die and WPN won't be sending any kind of statement to the Unmarked."

Job curses. "How did everything get this bad this quickly?"

I shake my head. "I don't know. But option two is going

to Nebraska on the off chance that briefcase was left there and hoping it contains the financial info we need. Once we know who Dad's partner was, and assuming he's still alive, we can try and track him or her down and maybe get the virus or try and trace it back to the origins."

"I lied earlier," Uncle Dan says quietly. "I remember a briefcase, but I didn't want to go into it in front of Mayor Fairchild. I'm sorry Wesley, but I'm struggling with how he could convict my wife and sentence her to death for doing exactly what you did to my daughter. I don't trust him."

"No offense taken. I'd be way less calm than you are if it were Ruby in Nashville. Do you remember what was in the case by chance?" Wesley asks.

Uncle Dan shrugs. "Papers? I didn't pay attention to any of it. I'm sorry. The police were handling the murder investigation, or you know, mishandling it, I guess. They didn't find a single lead. Which is actually criminal, when you think about it. Donovan stole a baby! Anne and I worked hard to cover that one up, but you'd think the police could have uncovered it when they started digging around to find his murderer. And beyond that, he had enemies from his last job. Plus how could they not have realized the partner was a villain?"

"Well, to be fair to the investigators," I say, "you had the journals that outlined the partner's flaws. Without that, maybe they didn't realize the partner had a motive. Actually, they may not have even known there *was* a partner at all."

"I guess," Uncle Dan says.

"As I see it," I say, "option three is to stay here while I try to broker a deal for Aunt Anne with John Roth directly. He obviously knows it may not hold if there's been some kind of revolution back in Galveston, but he might release one person on the chance of promising trade channels or tech. And if you're right and he's looking for a reason to save her. . ."

Uncle Dan shakes his head. "It probably would've worked, but you told him about the accelerant and he'll think that through. An attack by a Port Head means you're not in control, at least not fully. I doubt he'll broker a deal unless he knows whether you have the authority to authorize it."

I mutter under my breath.

"Galveston's closer and easier to reach than Nebraska," Wesley says. "And the people will recognize you. They love you already. Maybe if Adam and your mom are in trouble, we can help them."

"Or maybe we split up," Rhonda says. "I don't like the idea, but it makes the most sense. If we have two options, we should try both. Dad, Job and I go to Nebraska. Ruby, you and Wesley take your guards and head for Galveston. Our goal in Nebraska would be saving the Marked kids, even though we want to focus on Mom, because we can do it while you head for WPN. Your goal is to save Mom, because that's the best way to negotiate for her release."

My stomach sinks at the thought of splitting up again. The last time we did that Aunt Anne got Marked and I went all the way to Galveston where Sam almost died. And this time, I'm not at all sure Sam's even coming. I told John Roth that Adam's assigned guards were just as good, but I don't feel nearly as safe about the thought of going without him.

"What about Sam?" I ask.

"He's in trouble," Uncle Dan says. "He left his post without permission. There's going to be a hearing tomorrow. That's why he didn't follow you tonight. Unless he left at his father's bidding with you, and you said you declined the offer, he won't be free to leave."

My heart sinks. He told me this would happen back in the truck that first morning. I forgot all about that conversation, our first fight. He said his dad wouldn't let it go that he took me to Galveston. I thought he was giving me space but really, Sam's in trouble. And it's my fault.

"We had no choice when we left. The Marked kids caught us out in the open and we had to escape. I need to go tell John Roth."

"You're going to tell him that you and his son had to flee. . . all the way down to Galveston?" Rhonda raises one eyebrow. "They had every other path blocked?"

"If leaving was so wrong, why didn't John Roth hold me for a hearing?" I ask.

Uncle Dan sighs. "First of all, you were a minor when you left so you aren't accountable. Secondly, the real decision fell to Sam. But beyond that, you're the Queen of World Peace Now, and he wants to maintain a good relationship with you if he can. Charging you or trying you for leaving could start a war at this point. He'll take his pound of flesh from Sam."

I stand up and walk to the door. "Well, Sam's my Chief of Defense and Guards or whatever. He can't be charged without causing a fight either. I'll go tell his dad that right now."

"I'd suggest you leave it alone. This particular hearing is more between a father and a son than a leader and subordinate," Uncle Dan says. "John won't let them kill Sam, but he's going to make things miserable for him. And maybe he should."

"Excuse me?" I ask.

"Sam shouldn't have taken you down there alone. I told him to keep you safe here."

I snort. "Nothing is safe, not anymore. Aunt Anne got Marked right here in town, remember?"

Uncle Dan stands up and shakes his finger. For the first time since I saw him on the side of the road, he looks like himself. "Sam disobeyed my direct order, and your aunt and I were worried we'd never see you again. He must be held accountable."

Wow, I hit a nerve.

"Fine," I say. "Then I guess it's settled. Wesley and I head back to Galveston with my sixteen tweedle dees and dums, and you three make the trek to Republican City."

Uncle Dan sighs. "I'd like to go to Nashville and try to see my wife. But if she were here, she'd tell me to do anything I could to find Don's partner and save those kids."

"Wait," Wesley says. "You read the journals way back when, or at least your wife did. You knew the partner was pressuring Don. Wouldn't you have seen him as a risk for releasing Tercera and murdering Donovan? Wouldn't you have looked over the financials in that briefcase before you left to figure out who he was?"

Uncle Dan shakes his head. "You're confusing the time-line. When Don died we assumed it was Solomon who killed him. Don told Anne he was worried about being found. We hadn't taken the time to read through all the journals, so the thought of a partner hadn't entered our heads."

"It was David Solomon who shot him," I say. "He never even denied it. Solomon said Dad shouldn't have died from it, but I don't know whether I believe that."

"Your aunt and I assumed David Solomon shot Don, so we didn't worry about other leads. We couldn't pursue that one without being sure, because testifying about his motive exposed that you weren't our niece. Or that you might not be."

"Which is why you ran."

Uncle Dan nods. "The partner has to be someone he

knew from Pfizer or through his connections there I'd think. Someone who knew how brilliant he was and had enough money to take a gamble on it. By the time we read the journals, years had passed since the Marking. It didn't much matter then who released Tercera, only that we escaped infection. We were way past trying to pin this on someone, not that we'd have been able to do anything about it if we had been able to prove blame."

"Why didn't you want to locate the hacker virus?" I ask.

Uncle Dan tilts his head. "You're tired Ruby and you need some sleep. We didn't know the partner stole it. You found that information in the journal you recovered in Galveston."

Duh.

He's right. I'm tired, probably too tired to be making any big decisions, but we don't have time for a siesta.

"We all need a few hours sleep," I say. "But I don't want to sleep until we're on our way. Then we can take shifts. Uncle Dan, can you draw me a map to get to the cabin in Nebraska? Mark the route you're taking for me. I hate the idea of splitting up, but this way if anything comes up, at least we know where you're headed."

Dan nods. "Good plan. Rhonda and Job and I will leave now and drive in shifts. John Roth may not let us leave if we wait for morning. He's wrong about the twenty hours. It's a fifteen-hour drive with good roads, but I imagine it'll take us much longer. Probably even more than the twenty John mentioned."

"Yeah the roads are going to suck this time of year," Wesley says.

"I'll have the guards drive Wesley and I in the vans," I say. "You can take the jeep since it's in way better shape than that crappy truck, and it's still got three full gas tanks in the back. That should be enough, or at least close to enough."

Uncle Dan nods. "I've got another tank or two for emergencies. Combined it'll be fine. Please be safe."

I smile. "I'll be okay. I outmaneuvered the Port Heads last time, and I'll do it again. I hope we can find something useful. Solomon mentioned he had the police file. Maybe it'll say who Dad's partner was." Could it be that simple? Was the answer at my fingertips down there and I didn't even think to look?

Wesley and I have to hike down south of the city, but Uncle Dan tells us exactly where to walk to avoid detection. It's nice to be leaving with his blessing for once.

"Your dad's going to be mad," I say. "Do you feel a little guilty about leaving so soon?"

Wesley shakes his head. "My dad's a good person, but he gets confused a lot. He should never have convicted Anne. I think he was upset because I got Marked and you didn't. He took it out on her unfairly. He told me he wished he could take it back, but it was too late."

"But still, he's going to be upset you left. He may have done some dumb things, but we all do. At the end of the day, he's still your dad."

"If they'd do what needed to be done instead of hiding back here." Wesley frowns. "We wouldn't have to do this if he would listen to me. Or if any of them actually cared about the Marked kids. But they haven't met them or seen what we've seen, so it doesn't feel real to them." He squares his shoulders. "The answer is, I do feel bad about leaving my mom, but this is important."

"It's going to wreck her when she realizes you're gone again."

"At least this time I'll be coming back." Wesley walks in the dark without stumbling or tripping. "What about you?"

"What about me?" I ask. "I'm headed back to see my mom."

"I mean, how do you feel about Sam?"

I stop moving. "I think I should do something to try and help him, but if I do the wrong thing, it could make everything worse. I should probably let him give me space like he said."

"What does that even mean?" Wesley asks. "Space, like you want a restraining order?"

"I think it means he's trying to put no pressure on me. Life has been boxing us in, and he doesn't want me to be with him just because I don't feel like I have any other choices."

"Um lady, I think you know what your options are." Wesley grins. "But his suggestion doesn't make sense. Deciding things in a floating cloud of no pressure and no hard calls is a precious idea, but we don't show who we really are until we're being crunched."

"True, but you can't make the best decision if someone's rushing you either."

Wesley kicks a rock. "Nah, those are the decisions that matter. Think about it. Let's say there's some guy and he seems pretty nice. He wants people to like him, so he says please and thank you, and drags his neighbor's trash out to the road. Only, the neighbor has a nicer house, a motorcycle, and an amazing book collection. One day Guy Smiley finds his neighbor on the edge of a cliff, dangling by one hand. He can save him or shove him off. Or even less sinister, he can simply watch while the neighbor's fingers slowly loosen and he falls over the side. He didn't do anything *wrong*, but he didn't save him. Now Guy Smiley can take the fancy house, the book collection, and the motorcycle. Or he could save this fantastically blessed guy who makes him jealous. What does Guy Smiley do? That decision tells you more about who he is than you'd learn from a year of Sunday dinners and hand holding and slow kisses on the porch."

"Wow, I'm glad I don't have a motorcycle or a fancy book collection," I say.

"Yeah, all you've got is a pile of tiaras and ball gowns laced with rubies." Wesley bumps my shoulder with his. "My point is, when there's pressure you know what you want and your desires define you. When you thought Sam died, you left the island and completely ignored me. You were devastated. Once you realized he might have survived, all you wanted was to return to him. When Sam caught you running away, he should have hauled you back by the ear. Even after the Marked attacked, he should've turned right around and tossed you back into your house like your uncle told him, like his boss ordered. Instead, he drove you down to Galveston. He saved you on the way, and then rescued you when your attempted rescue failed."

"What's your point exactly?" I ask. "Because that's a lot of jabbering."

Wesley grabs my hips, one hand on either side, and pulls me toward him until our bodies are flush from my thighs to my shoulder. He leans down slowly, his eyes meeting mine, calm and sure. He closes the gap between our heights, his lips moving toward mine, his eyes flashing. "No matter what, no matter the pressure, you're all I want." He lowers his head further. "And this is my point." His mouth closes over mine, his lips warm in the cool night air.

My heart lurches, but not in a good way. I can't be doing this, and I don't want this. I love Wesley, but not like this, not anymore. I shove him back. "Wes I'm sorry, but I can't. It's wrong."

Wesley smiles, but his eyes are sad in the moonlight. "I know you can't. It kind of pisses me off, but it's so obvious.

You don't need space. You just need to accept that you need Sam. It's scary to need someone, and if you'd lost a lot of people and had no one to rely on, you might struggle with doing that. But it doesn't mean you should give up."

"Then I can't leave him here," I say. "I can't let him be tried as a criminal for helping me out."

"You can't waltz in and save him either," Wesley says. "He'd resent you for thinking he needs to be saved. You spend all your time saving everyone else, but you can't go save him. Not this time."

"That's stupid," I say.

"Boys are stupid."

I swear.

"Besides, we've got to get to Galveston and make sure Adam and Josephine are okay. And then figure out how to apply pressure to save your aunt. And dig up the police file so we can see who your dad's partner might have been. Wow, we have a lot to do."

It hits me then, a thought I would likely have had earlier if I'd been less exhausted. "The police file won't help us."

"Huh?" Wesley runs his hand through his hair.

"Think about it. The police investigation turned up nothing because Dad's dumb secretary sent everything to Aunt Anne. They would've pursued any leads on a partner, at the very least apprising Aunt Anne that they interviewed him. Uncle Dan said they did nothing, which means they knew nothing, which means. . ."

Wesley stops dead in his tracks. "The police file's useless. Solomon would've told us the partner's name if he knew, and he'd have known if it was in the file."

I nod my head. "If our main goal is saving those kids, we're going the wrong way."

"What about your aunt?"

I smile. "We send my guards back to deliver a message to Mom and Adam telling them about Aunt Anne. If they don't know about the accelerant, my message will alert them to the possible problem. If there's been a coup, well my sixteen guards wouldn't have made much of a difference, and at least I won't die down in Galveston before we can try and help the Marked kids and my aunt. But if everything there is fine and the accelerant came from somewhere else. . ."

"Then what?" Wesley asks.

"I'm going to order Adam to send a formal message to the Unmarked. Release Anne Orien into the custody of their queen and negotiate a trade agreement, or WPN declares war."

Wesley's eyes widen. "Are you sure?"

I smile grimly. "Only because it would be so very lopsided that I know what John Roth will say. The Unmarked can't withstand a fight with WPN and they know it. They'll hand her over. No one is worth that possible threat."

"And after we dispatch your guards?"

"John can't know I didn't head for Galveston with them."

Wesley frowns. "How's that going to work?"

"I'm going to need a little favor."

"What exactly did you have in mind now?"

I try to smile my prettiest smile, but I'm afraid I might look like a deranged beauty pageant contestant. "Your dad is on cloud nine right now. He'd forgive you of most anything, right?"

Wesley huffs. "I don't like where this is going."

"How do you feel about breaking Sam out of your house and stealing his dad's Range Rover?"

CHAPTER 13

"Not very good," Wesley says. "Actually, I'd say I feel terrible about that idea. It's got to be the worst suggestion I've heard in weeks. And things have been whack, so you're being compared to like, replacing hormone suppressants with prenatal vitamins. It's a high bar, but you've managed to clear it."

"What's your brilliant plan then?" I ask. "We've got to help Sam without letting his dad know I'm not en route to Galveston. Plus, somehow we need to get up north to Nebraska. My jeep's already gone, and the guards need the vans... so."

Wesley mumbles the entire walk south of Port Gibson. He grumbles while I convince Frank, Paul, Greg and Demetrius, the four commanders, to sign off on my plan to send them back to Galveston while I travel on without them. To Nebraska. Wesley mutters while we sneak back to College Street, where of course the jeep is already gone.

I lean on the old red truck. "Sam's already in hot water. How much worse can it be?"

"Stealing the car that belongs to the head of the

Unmarked's DeciCouncil won't help him. Plus, they might actually hunt us down like dogs and shoot us."

"Fine, then we take this." I kick the tire of the truck Rafe gave Uncle Dan. "It runs fine, mostly. And really we only need to catch up to Job and Rhonda. After that, we'll all fit in the jeep."

"So we aren't taking Sam?" Wesley asks.

I swear. "Only five seats in the jeep."

Wesley nods.

I sigh. "Okay, we take this the whole way. It's a good idea to have two cars anyway, in case something happens."

"How are you planning on breaking Sam out?" he asks.

"I have no idea. Think he's still at your place?"

Wesley shrugs. "There or in a cell."

I really hope his dad didn't lock him up.

"I guess we'll go to your house, see if he's there, and kind of go from there. I figured he'd be there, and we'd tell him the plan, and we'd all hop in his dad's car and go."

"Yeah, I'm not going to be an accessory to presidential grand theft auto, but we could take this old rust bucket. Let's say we do find him, and he can Sam his way out. What about gas?" he asks. "Rafe gave Dan and I a full tank, which got us here, but it's half gone. It won't go fifteen hours up and another fifteen back."

Wesley's turning into a real pain.

Not that any of this is his fault. I'm just so tired that I don't want to deal with anything. I want to go inside, curl up, and take a nap. But we can't. In one week, every kid in Baton Rouge will be dead, including Sam's little brother. I don't even know whether Sam told his dad about Rafe. Would that change John's mind? Possibly?

I have no idea.

I flog my tired brain. My problems are gas for the truck, and finding Sam, because I need him. I've got to tell him how I feel and convince him I don't need space. I only want him.

Solutions. Come on, brain. Work. Frank and Paul had extra gas in the vans, but it won't help us now. They've already left. My uncle had some extra, but he took it. Even if we find Sam, he won't know where the Defense trucks are anymore.

"We'll steal some gas," Wesley says. "My dad has some in his garage, I think. I'll risk that even, but again, we are not taking John Roth's car."

One problem solved! I smile and lean against Wesley. "Fine." He wraps one arm around me to keep me from falling over. It's good to have a best friend, but I wish I was leaning on Sam instead. I need to open my eyes so we can get moving, but it feels so good to close them. Just for a moment, to pretend nothing is wrong. My body relaxes and I'm almost asleep.

"Looks like you're enjoying your space," Sam says.

I shove away from Wesley, stumble over the curb and fall flat on my bottom. In a mud puddle. Sam leans down and offers me a hand, but I wave him off. He looks far too put together in jeans, a black shirt and a dark jacket, with a backpack slung over his shoulders. I've been imagining him suffering in a cell, when he was clearly taking a shower and freshening up. Me on the other hand, I'm wearing the same clothes I've had on for days, now coated in mud.

I refuse both of the offered hands and stand up without help.

"Actually," Wesley says. "We were brainstorming how to come break you out of a cell. We aren't quite the brain trust of tactical maneuvers you might have hoped for, as it turns out. It appears you took that one off our plate before we could swoop in to save you."

"What were your ideas?" Sam asks.

"Well, Ruby thought we should threaten your dad," Wesley says. "Tell him WPN demands the release of its head of Defense."

"And your idea?" Sam asks.

"Actually, I hadn't had one yet. But she had a fall back. I was going to sneak back into my own house and do some recon on where you were being kept. Then Ruby thought she could pelt the window with pebbles until you broke yourself free. Which is sort of what happened, minus the recon and the pebbles."

I wipe my muddy hands on the red truck. It makes a mess on the truck and my hands don't look any cleaner. So basically, it was as good an idea as I've had tonight.

Sam says, "Good plans. I'm impressed."

"Oh, shut up Mr. Perfect," I say. "We've been focused on other stuff, like figuring out where to go next."

"And where are we headed?" Sam asks. "Galveston? Or Republican City?"

I want to throw my arms around him as tightly as I can and never let go. I want to tell him I don't want any space between us now or ever, but Wesley's a foot away, and it doesn't seem like the right time. Also, I need to change my pants. A shower wouldn't be the worst thing.

"Neither," Wesley says. "Nebraska."

Sam rolls his eyes.

"Republican City's the town in Nebraska where we lived," I explain to Wesley.

Sam grins. "I think that's the right call. If there was any information in Galveston, you'd have heard it from Solomon or seen it yourself. I don't think you'd find any answers there."

I don't point out that it took me an hour to come to the same conclusion he just reached in three seconds.

"I'm going to go change," I say, "but we need gas if we're taking this truck that far."

Sam shakes his head. "We're not taking my brother's junker. I have a much better idea."

I raise one eyebrow. "Wesley won't steal your dad's Range Rover. I already asked."

Sam whistles. "Wow, that's a monumentally bad idea sunshine. Besides, Range Rovers break down regularly and parts are impossible to find. My dad's an idiot for driving it. No, I thought we'd take Port Gibson's tactical ops vehicle."

"The Land Cruiser?" Wesley asks. "It's hidden and you can't possibly know where."

Sam shakes his head. "Can't possibly? I spent the last few hours in the Mayor's house. I bit my tongue while my dad alternated between yelling at me and interrogating me. I swallowed my pride and apologized to him every time I could see he wanted me to. When he finally went to bed, I broke into your dad's safe. Pathetic security measures, by the way. I stole the location, and it's close enough that we can hike to it easily."

This time I do hug Sam. "I'm so glad you're back."

His whispered words tug at my heart. "You weren't going to leave without me, were you?"

"I didn't know what to do. I'm so tired." I lean my head against his chest.

"Go change and we'll go get the Land Cruiser. Then you can sleep."

"Aren't you tired?"

"I'll be fine." Sam pulls back and I reluctantly walk back to the house to change.

"Do I have time for a shower?" I ask.

"Wesley can catch me up while we wait," Sam says.

One cold shower and a pair of dry pants later, I'm much

more awake as I run down the stairs. Wesley and I follow Sam out of town, leaving via the same blind spot Uncle Dan showed us before.

"If you know about these, why not deal with them?" I ask.

"For exactly this reason," Sam says.

Wesley says, "Ah yes. You leave the weaknesses in our defenses so people can steal town resources to attempt a rash cross country trip in the vain hope of locating evidence that will lead us to the man who stole a hacker virus that might save your long lost little brother. That makes a lot of sense."

"Have I told you lately," Sam says, "how much I enjoy your company, Wesley?"

"I don't think you have." Wesley grins. "But it's always good to have a fan."

At least the sarcasm's better than the sniping. It keeps me awake until we reach the Land Cruiser, which is right where Sam said it would be. Wesley climbs into the backseat without comment, and I open the door on the passenger side.

I stay awake long enough to hand Sam the map, take off my coat, and ball it up by Sam's thigh. Sam stretches his jacket out over me, and buckles my seatbelt.

When I finally wake up to the sound of a chainsaw, the sun's already high in the sky.

I rub my eyes. "How long did I sleep?" Once I look around, I realize no one's in the car to hear my question, much less answer it. I smooth out my jacket and slide my arms into it, because it's gotten much chillier. I stretch and look around.

Sam's moving a tree trunk, the muscles rippling in his back as he drags Wesley along with it. I've been there, dragged along and feeling useless. I open the car door and the cold air hits me like a wall, stabbing my lungs as I take a deep breath. I grab Sam's coat and jog over to take it to him.

"Where are we?" I ask.

Wesley grins at me. "You're awake."

Sam scowls. "I told you the chain saw would wake her up."

"And I told you the truth. We weren't going to move this trunk without cutting it."

"I feel great." I hand Sam his coat. "I want to help."

"Tell him to sleep, then," Wesley says. "Or he's going to pass out and kill us all."

I snort. "Sam, even you need to sleep sometime."

Sam nods. "I told them I would when you woke up."

"Wait, who's them? Or is Wesley finally acknowledging his other personalities?"

I turn around to see Rhonda waving at me from behind the wheel of our WPN jeep. I breathe a sigh of relief. We met up with them, and the sun is high. It's been at least seven hours. Now if one of our cars dies or gets stuck, we can still get back.

Sam jogs around the car to the passenger side, since he's not driving anymore, and I follow him over. He reaches for the handle, and I step even closer. Mere inches separate us.

Sam says, "You're driving, right?"

I nod.

"Great, but Dan and Job are going to take point."

His breath warms my face, and I struggle to think clearly. "Why? You think I can't navigate?"

"You can't clear most of these limbs and trees, even with Wesley's help."

"Oh," I say.

Sam whispers. "I'm trying to give you space sunshine, but you're making it hard."

"What if I don't want space?"

Sam's eyes search mine slowly, almost in a daze, and I realize just how tired he is. This isn't the time, not yet. "You need to sleep. We can talk later."

He grins at me. "We will. And as soon as we hit snow, you wake me up."

I pull the car door open and slide inside. He follows behind me as I scoot over to the driver's side. "We haven't hit any yet?"

Wesley's already sitting in the back seat. "We've been lucky, or so Sam says. I slept through a few hours of it."

I look around us, but I don't see anything that identifies our road. "You never answered. Where are we? How long did I sleep?"

"We're on Interstate 40, almost to Fort Smith in Arkansas. We've been driving for nearly ten hours, which is pretty good considering we had to stop about a dozen times in the last hour."

But we have at least another ten hours to go, and the roads are only going to worsen. As far as we know, no one really lives up here. In spite of the weather and disuse of the roads, the drive passes uneventfully. Sometimes we go fifty miles without needing to stop. Sometimes we stop a dozen times in a mile. Since I'm not clearing the road, I do a lot of sitting.

A few hours in, I glance back and realize Wesley's asleep, too. Probably for the best.

It's sleeting when we reach Wichita, and I shake Sam.

He sits upright immediately, eyes alert.

"Sorry," I say. "I didn't want to wake you up, but it's sleeting. I figured you'd count that as snow."

Sam's eyes look more green than golden when they first

meet mine. His dad's are such a bright golden color, and Rafe's are pure green. I wonder what his mother's looked like.

He yawns. "I'm glad you did."

I pull over on the side of the road and Sam jumps out of the car. He doesn't even shiver when he jogs up to talk to Uncle Dan, his breath puffing out in a big white cloud as he speaks.

Wesley stretches and yawns as well. "Sorry I fell asleep again."

I shake my head. "I was fine and I'm glad you did. It's not quite the same in the car as it is in a bed. It's been a long few days, and I doubt it's going to get easier. We should all sleep whenever we can."

When Sam comes back, he jogs around to the driver's side. I slide over so he can get back in.

"We're taking point again," Sam says. "Hope you brought a rain coat, Wes. It's cold out there."

We're still at least an hour away when the sun begins to set. "It's a miracle we haven't hit any real weather yet," I say. "Right?"

Sam sighs. "Coincidence, luck, whatever you want to call it. Sure, it's a practically a miracle."

Thirty minutes later, we turn off 81 onto 24 and our luck runs out. It's not snowing, but piles of snow lie in drifts all over. The jeep gets stuck just before the turn onto 36. It takes Sam, Dan, Wesley and Job nearly an hour to get it out. When the boys climb back in the car, they're shivering and Wesley's lips are blue.

"Maybe we should take one car," I say. "If this one's better, we can all pile up?"

"It was plain bad luck they got stuck," Sam says. "I think these cars are evenly matched, so we're better off if we keep going with two in case one of them suffers any real damage."

I nod. "Okay."

When we reroute to avoid crossing the dam on county road 1815, the jeep gets stuck twice, and our Land Cruiser gets stuck once, too. Finally, when the Land Cruiser lodges high center on a drift right before West Road, on the 706 past Naponee, even all four boys together can't get us out again.

"It's only a few miles from here," Uncle Dan says. "Let's take the Jeep."

"I'll go in the back," I say. "I don't mind."

We move most of the remaining gas and supplies from the Jeep into the beached Land Cruiser. "Maybe we can get it on the way back out," Sam says. "But you don't need to breathe all those fumes back there."

The last few miles take us past fields and roads I vaguely remember. When we finally turn down Cedar Point Road, I try to recall the visits I made here with my dad. I think about why he bought this place, the real reason. To hide me away from my birth parents. We may finally find out what kind of awful person would sell Tercera to a foreign government just to make a buck, and possibly the identity of my dad's true murderer.

My heart races and my hands tingle.

Uncle Dan's driving with Job sitting shotgun. Sam, Rhonda and Wesley all sit on the back seat.

Sam turns and takes my hand. "Are you cold?"

I shake my head.

"You're shivering."

I can barely talk past the lump in my throat. "Nervous."

Sam reaches his whole arm over the seat and wraps it around my shoulders. "You're okay."

I want to talk to Sam about us so at least one thing in

my life is solid, but I can't. Not with Wesley and Rhonda ten inches away, and Job pretending not to notice, but periodically glancing back at us.

Job finally says, "Are you two broken up or not? I can't keep up, and frankly you're acting super weird right now."

Wesley smirks. "You aren't the only one who's confused, but I'm thinking they may be waiting to DTR when we aren't all in the car staring at them."

"DTR?" Rhonda asks.

"You know, define their relationship. It'll go something like this." Wesley adopts a falsetto. "Oh, Samuel, your arms are so big and so strong and I need them in my life. I just love to rub them."

Sam frowns, but my heart lifts a little.

Wesley continues, this time sticking his lips out and talking gruffly. "But my love muffin, buff arms are not enough. You need to want me for my brains, too. How else will I trust you won't leave me for that guy with the amazing hair who makes you laugh?"

Sam's shoulder stiffens. "This is—"

Wesley cuts him off in his falsetto. "Because, my big hunk of a meathead. Even with his fabulous hair and hilarious mannerisms, all I can think about is you. Just kiss me already and we can make up."

I giggle, my stress and anxiety melting away. I can't help it, and I notice Sam's grinning too. Wesley's so stupid, but we needed something stupid. Some kind of distraction from the anxiety.

I smack Wes on the shoulder as Uncle Dan pulls into the driveway. The headlights on the Jeep cast eerie shadows across the red log cabin and the big white barn, but they both appear intact. I wait for everyone else to climb out, and slide over the seat. We all scramble over dirty piles of snow, and scraggly, dead vegetation to reach the front door.

Uncle Dan tries the knob, but it's locked.

Sam shoulders his way past my uncle and rams the door twice without success. Thankfully it gives way on the third slam.

"I guess I know who to thank for the shattered hinges at home," Uncle Dan mutters.

Sam shrugs. "It's already fixed."

"You owe Mr. Nyugen a favor," Uncle Dan says.

I can't help my snort. "Told you he was going to be pissed."

Job hands me a flashlight as I near the front door. "There will be animals inside, Ruby. Every building with a roof that hasn't collapsed will house a plethora of wild residents."

Sam says, "I can clear them out first, but it might take a while."

The wind gusts cut through my jacket like a thousand frozen needles. "I'll take my chances. I might freeze solid if I wait."

Sam checks the basement, Uncle Dan takes the bedrooms, and Rhonda and Job look in the family room and kitchen. Wesley shines his flashlight on my face. "I'm the only one who hasn't ever been here. Where should we look that they aren't already checking?"

"It's not a very big place. The barn and garage are the only places left, and paperwork wouldn't be in the barn. We only kept animals in there."

"Lead me to the garage, then." He waves his flashlight at me and bows with flourishy hands.

An opossum lives in the garage. I don't scream, but the bones in Wesley's hand grind a little when I squeeze them.

"Sorry." I shine my light at Wesley's face. "That scared me, but I didn't mean to grab you so hard. Are you okay?"

Wesley grimaces. "It's a good thing your boy has super healing powers."

I roll my eyes, not that he can see it. We displace another furry something, but at least there aren't cockroaches this far north. Or I don't remember seeing any when we lived here.

"Here's a box." Wesley pulls a rectangular shape out from under a pile of cans.

I shine my light inside it eagerly, but it sadly contains years and years of tax returns.

"Who's Russell Charzewski?" Wesley asks.

"Look at the address," I say. "It's for this house and those are super old. I'm guessing they've been here since before my dad bought it."

He sighs. "Yeah, probably so."

I knock over a box of screws, trip on an extension cord, and search through a bin full of snow boots, displacing a nest of mice.

"I think we either need to wait until morning," Wesley says, "or call it good in here."

I sigh. "I'm glad some living things are thriving, but if I'm being honest, I'm sick to death of finding critters all over."

"It's dry in here and warmer away from the wind. I can't really blame them."

I walk toward the stairs back up to the door into the house, and stumble on something. I shine my light down hopefully.

"An air pump." Wesley says.

I roll my eyes toward the ceiling, and that's when I see it thanks to Wesley's bobbing flashlight. Wedged between the top shelf of a metal storage rack and a light fixture rests a black leather briefcase.

"Look there!" I hop down from the steps and shove my way past some fishing poles and a mop.

Wesley boosts me up and steadies the wire shelving while I climb. I cling to the gaps in the rack with my left hand and the fingers on my right hand close around the briefcase handle. I tug, but it doesn't budge.

"It's stuck."

"Of course it is." Wesley grunts.

I let go of the shelving and grab the handle with both hands. I yank it as hard as I can and the handle flies off. I tumble to the floor, landing squarely on Wesley. It reminds me of the last time we were in a cell together, right after I saw Sam alive for the first time since he got shot. I was so happy he was alive that day. This time when I collapse on top of Wes, my stomach's churning. If we can ever get it down, the key to all of this might be hiding inside that little rectangle of dead animal skin.

Wesley and I brush ourselves off, and I tuck a screwdriver I found on the floor into my waistband before climbing up again. The entire rack shakes and shivers each time we move up a shelf. Once I'm within arm's reach of the briefcase again, I wedge the screwdriver between the ceiling and the black leather. I pull it toward me and it pops the briefcase loose. It falls to the floor with a thump. I almost wish we could collapse in a pile again, but this time we climb back down as slowly as we scaled it. One wobbly shelf at a time.

My heart races, my pulse hammers in my throat, and my fingers stiffen, making my fingers even fumblier than usual.

Wesley and I both cross to where the black briefcase

lays on the filthy concrete floor. Wesley holds his flashlight on the latch, and I try to open the case.

"The handle's so rotten it flies right off, but the lock's completely functional." I roll my eyes. "Of course it is."

My hands shake, and my breath puffs in front of me as I key in my dad's birthday. It doesn't work. I try my birthday. No dice.

I swear. "Why won't this open? What other number would he use?"

Wesley hands me the flashlight. "Maybe it's the right number, but it's sticky. It has been in this nasty garage for more than ten years."

Wesley picks up the briefcase and whams it against the concrete floor once and then twice. He pushes on the release buttons.

The latch clicks open.

I reach for the documents inside with stiff fingers. The first page is a letter to a Xander Smith. I lift it up. The next page is an invoice for supplies. The next is an equipment rental statement, then a lease document. Both of them list the partnership name, Jack-of-All-Trades. Cute. My dad signed for each one as Donovan Behl. My hands shake as I lift page after page, but every single one lists either Jack-of-All-Trades, or Donovan Behl on the recipient line.

Wesley puts one arm around me and uses his other hand to wipe away a tear I didn't realize had leaked out. "It was always a long shot."

I shake my head. "No, we have to know. The answer has got to be in here somewhere. I wish I knew more about businesses." I look through the papers again with no luck. I slam the briefcase with my hand, and my frozen fingers cry out in pain. A yellow paper slides out from somewhere. An invoice for mice.

I poke at the interior and realize there's an inside

pocket that adhered to the lining of the briefcase. I reach inside and pull out a thick, stapled bunch of papers. A yellow post-it note still clings to the front with the words, "Chuck, let me know what my options are to get out of this" scrawled on it. The handwriting is my dad's.

The first page says "Jack of All Trades Partnership Agreement" in bold letters. I can't breathe. My shaky, numb-with-cold fingers flip too many pages and I have to flip them back slowly, painstakingly.

Wesley runs his hand through his hair. "I think this is it, Ruby."

Thank you, Captain Obvious.

I finally reach the second page. My eyes scan the legal language. *This Partnership Agreement, dated blah blah.* I skip ahead to the names of the parties.

Donald Carillon, and Jonathan Roth.

Wait, Sam's dad was my dad's partner? My mind spins. How could it be John Roth? The partner's name is Jack, not John. No one ever called him Jack.

"It can't be right," I say. "We've known John for years and years. If he had the cure, he'd have done something about it, obviously."

Wesley's jaw drops. "I never even thought of this, but Jack's a nickname for John sometimes."

"When?" I ask. "That makes no sense. They're the same length, Jack and John. Nicknames are shorter. Besides, we've always known him. I'd have recognized John Roth if he was Dad's partner."

Wesley shakes his head. "No you wouldn't. I mean, you'd know who he was, but that explains why you don't remember seeing your dad's partner come over. You didn't see a partner. You saw an old family friend, someone who your dad knew. And you'd have seen him so many times before and since, in totally different capacities, that if you did ever think of him as a partner for your dad, any memory of that evaporated because he had other, more important labels in your mind."

I can't stop staring at the paper. It can't be right.

"This is good news, actually. It means we know who has the hacker virus. We can reach him, and maybe we can even save Rafe. Obviously he'll want to save his own son."

I don't think anything is obvious with Jack Roth. My dad's partner would have known what Tercera was. If the hacker virus worked, he'd have known how to cure all those people. He didn't say anything, and that's the bajillion dollar question.

Why didn't he do or say anything?

He could have saved his wife and his other son. He could have saved the world. He should've come clean. Why didn't he?

I recall Sam's story, that his mom's brother was one of the first infected. The first person I've heard of being Marked was a man Jonathan Roth knew and actively disliked. A man he didn't approve of. A perfect test subject, in a limited contact environment. An inmate in a prison.

After the Marking, it would've been safe for John to travel, but he hid in a cabin in Nebraska with us instead. Somehow, between then and now, he's taken over leadership of the Unmarked. I shake my head. We've vastly underestimated my dad's partner for years and years.

My breathing becomes choppy and too frequent when I realize we told him where we planned to go. I need to warn the others right away. My knees wobble, but I force myself to my feet, paper clamped between clumsy fingers. "I have to be the one to tell Sam."

"Okay," Wesley says, "but I don't think he's going to be that upset. He doesn't like his dad much anyway."

I race up the stairs with Wesley only a step behind me. I

fling the door open and my stomach drops when I stare right into familiar golden eyes.

"Well, well, little Ruby Behl. Or should I say Carillon? You're supposed to be in Galveston. Someone needs to teach you to obey." Black boots, black pants, and a black coat seem fitting for John Roth, now that I know who he really is.

I shove the paper behind my back as I glance around. Three men with guns pointed at my head stand behind him, but I don't see Sam, my uncle, Rhonda or Job.

John tsks, and leans toward me. Faster than anyone I've seen except maybe Sam, his hand shoots out and snatches the papers out of my hands. Another man holds a lantern up so he can read. "It looks like that moronic secretary did send our partnership agreement to your aunt after all. I couldn't really ask about it, not without alerting them to its importance."

I can barely force the words out of my lips. "You stole Tercera. You killed billions of people."

John frowns. "I didn't kill them, and I didn't kill your father either, no matter what story Solomon concocted to ease his conscience."

"You have the hacker virus," I say. "Why didn't you share it? Why not release it?"

John Roth lifts his chin. "It's kind of cute that you think you have any standing to be asking questions."

"Where's Sam?"

Jonathan Roth's laughter is the last thing I hear before his fist knocks me on the temple and everything goes black.

CHAPTER 14

Someone slaps my face. Whap, on the right. Whap on the left.

I moan and mumble, "Stop."

The slaps let up and I open my eyes, but it's so dark I can't see my attacker, or anything else for that matter. My hands are tied, but at least they're in front of me this time. I reach out, but my fingers touch only frosty air. I'm sitting on icy concrete, my legs extended out in front of me, and a rushing sound fills my ears. My ankles aren't tied, so I shift one knee up and rest my face against it. I pull back immediately, because the right side of my face throbs when I touch it, like I took a beating. The last thing I remember is.

. .

Jonathan Roth is Jack. He stole Tercera and sold it, laying waste to the world.

Sleet laced wind lashes my face and hands. I struggle against the rope, but it doesn't make a difference. I blink repeatedly, trying to adjust to the pitch black.

"Ruby?" I can barely make out Sam's voice over the

sound of roaring water, but I think he's only a few feet away.

I shift myself one icy, bum-bruising hop at a time toward the sound of his voice. "I'm here. Are you okay? Where are we?"

"I'm not sure," he says.

I bump into something solid. My eyes have adjusted enough that I can see Sam's coat. I reach my hands out, and he takes mine in his huge paws.

"I found the partnership agreement," I say. "It was in the garage."

"It was my dad." Sam's voice cracks. "I should've known. How did I not see it?"

"No one did." I squeeze his hands. "Can you undo the rope?"

Sam shakes his hands and I hear a faint jingle. I shift my fingers up to his wrists and feel handcuffs. He broke those before. I shift my hands further. A second set of cuffs. I slide my hands up a little further. A third.

"Your dad knows what you can do."

Sam grunts. "He's the reason I can do it, so yes, he knows."

"You should be thanking me." John Roth's boots step into view next to my thigh. There's a whumping sound, and then a humming noise as a bright light floods the area.

I close my eyes and blinding, circular, retinal burns cover my line of sight. I blink, even though I know that doesn't clear them any faster.

John says, "If I hadn't enrolled you in those clinical trials, you'd be as average as your mother. I've made you spectacular. I'm the only reason little Ruby likes you in the first place. You think she'd have liked boring, shy, unimpressive Sam?"

When I reopen my eyes, I can actually see the asphalt beneath us. Sam's booted feet stick out in front of him, tied together with the same type of rope as my hands. His shackled hands still rest over mine, thawing my fingers slightly. His father stares at us pensively.

"Where are we?" I ask.

"Not far from the old cabin. Harlan County Dam," John says. "I made sure when the grid went down that two spillways were left open. For a while, your uncle and I pulled electricity from the flow and kept the area clear of debris. It's held up pretty well, thanks to the extensive remodel that took place a few years before the Marking. We're standing above the open spillways now, and they're still running. I'm delighted with how well it's weathered the apocalypse, actually. I thought it would've become backed up with sediment and overflowed by now. If it had, we couldn't be sitting right here. I didn't even imagine this road might still be passable. Remarkable feat of engineering, really. It's quite lovely during the day I imagine. I'm thinking of sending some Unmarked here, re-settling it. It's a shame to let this free electricity go to waste."

"Where's everyone else?" I ask. "Wesley? Rhonda? Job? My uncle?"

John smiles. "Just arriving. I'm not usually one to make a big production out of things, but you don't just shoot your oldest friend and his family in the head and leave them to be eaten by wild animals. Besides, the dam was so close it was practically begging me to bring you here."

"You're shooting my aunt in the head when you get back home," I say.

John snorts, which I can see but can't really hear. "Not at all. Her mind, like your dad's, is far too fine to waste. It's more complicated to keep her around now that she's

Marked, but as you've figured out, she can't infect me. I'll receive a formal request from the Queen of WPN and pardon her, and then I'll tuck her away in my private research facility in Nashville. Who knows what she might come up with in the next few years."

"You killed my dad, even though he was producing."

Several men in camouflage coats and pants walk along the bridge, pulling Rhonda and Job. I presume Wesley and Uncle Dan are behind them, but I can't make them out yet.

John Roth's face contorts in anger. "I most certainly did not kill Donald Carillon, and I'm sick of being accused. I would never have done that." When John Roth paces, he looks exactly like his son.

"David Solomon told me that he shot him, but that his gunshot wound wouldn't have killed Dad. He said you came after he did, and you set him on fire—"

John's eyes flash. "That's ridiculous. I found your father laying in a pool of blood, and I couldn't feel a pulse. I should never have called your real father in the first place, but I was trying to motivate Donald. If I'd had any idea how that would play out, I never would have—" John shakes his head. "The point is that from the moment Solomon showed up on the scene, everything that could go wrong did. He shot your dad, instead of threatening him or calling the police, the two logical actions I prepared contingencies for. When I showed up and checked his pulse, your father was already dead. I'd left fingerprints on him, and a neighbor had alerted the police, so I didn't have time to clean things up rationally. I searched the office for any paperwork implicating me, grabbed other essentials, and cleaned up my tracks by setting the papers on fire underneath a fire alarm. I wiped his body with alcohol, to clean off my fingerprints, and I guess that caught fire somehow. I never intended to set his body on fire, but I guess it happened. Trust me when I say, he was not alive. I'd have called 911 immediately if there had been any hope of saving him."

"You released Tercera," Sam says. "Almost wiping out the human race."

Two men in camouflage walk toward us, each carrying people over their shoulders. The first one dumps the body next to Sam, and blonde hair spills from a red cap. Rhonda.

I gasp. "Is she okay?"

"They're fine for now," John says. "We knocked them out, same as you. It took me a good five minutes to wake you up, and I only completed that onerous task so my son would stop badgering me."

The next guard dumps another body. I crane my neck until I can make out Job's nose and mouth.

Two more men walk Wesley and Uncle Dan past me and toss them to the concrete like bags of rice. Wesley shifts with a groan, and then collapses face down a foot and a half away from me. Uncle Dan slowly sits up, his arms flexing and releasing, like he's testing the strength of his ropes. His feet are lashed like Sam's. The four guards line up behind John Roth, guns in hand, eyes on us.

"Should we wait for them to wake up?" I ask. "Wouldn't want them to miss the show."

John rolls his eyes. "I doubt they'll miss much."

"I don't know," I say. "You were just going to tell me why you released Tercera and destroyed the world. I've wanted to know the answer to that for a long time."

John crouches down on the concrete so we're on eye level. "I'd like to blame the terrorists, but I suppose technically it was me. I found a motivated buyer who was willing to pay, but he wanted a demonstration."

Sam's voice is flat, almost emotionless. "You demonstrated on Uncle Chaz."

John smiles. "A stroke of brilliance, really. Did your mother ever tell you why he went to prison?"

Sam frowns.

"She called him to complain any time our marriage hit a snag, no matter how small. One night she called him about steps I'd taken to curtail her frivolous spending. Chaz turned up drunk on my doorstep after that call and tried to kill me. He had a knife, which I easily divested him of, but his attempted assault crossed the line. I couldn't simply let that go. What if I'd been sleeping? No, I pressed charges and he pled guilty. Any regret I felt evaporated when he swore in the courtroom to kill me in vivid and imaginative ways. He told me he'd make contacts in prison that you can't buy on the outside, and thanked me for the networking opportunity. Releasing Tercera in a prison provided the demonstration I needed, ensured I infected people who deserved to die, and eliminated a threat all at once. An elegant decision, don't you think?"

"You deemed any visitors, guards, and other personnel to be acceptable collateral damage, I suppose?" I ask.

"I warned Jaclyn not to visit him," John Roth says. "I told her he was dangerous and begged her to stop on multiple occasions. She ignored me, and she and Rafe came home Marked that day. Her process server had handed me divorce papers an hour before she returned home, so I let her go."

Uncle Dan coughs and coughs, and then he wipes his mouth. "Why didn't you sell the hacker virus? You could've made a fortune. Or even if you didn't feel good about selling it, how could you let everyone die? I don't understand."

John laughs bitterly and crouches down in front of me

and Sam. "That's the question everyone wants answered, I'm sure. I can only say that Donald Carillon was as magnificent a liar as David Solomon. I stole the two remaining syringes from Don's lab, along with the sheath of papers and notes he kept with them. I knew he'd been working on a cure. He told me all that remained was perfecting the delivery mechanism. He said it was nearly ready, and the only difference was, it needed to be injected so it could bind to the recipient's blood at present, and wouldn't pass via touch."

"And?" I ask. "You refused to sell it because it wasn't easy to manufacture?"

John glares at me. "Yes. I've always been a sadistic mass murderer. All my initial attempts at wiping out humanity were foiled, but this one... this one finally succeeded."

My eyes widen.

"Of course not." He shakes his head in disgust. "I'm sure it's easier to believe that someone planned the apocalypse. But I injected myself with one of the doses I stole before dosing Chaz with Triptych, and kept the other to replicate and sell. When the virus spread as indicated, I dosed some prisoners with the accelerant, which Don developed to allow quicker lab testing on the progression of the virus. After all, if we had to wait years on each round of trials, we'd have died of old age before we could take it to market."

"And your buyer found the death toll satisfactory?" Uncle Dan shakes his head.

"Yes, they did. They paid me a significant sum of money, which I used to pay off my debts with plenty left over. I knew I'd make even more on the back end with my cure. I meant to put some into a trust for little Ruby, actually."

"But you got so caught up twirling your mustache and counting your money that what? You forgot?"

"Your dad lied to me. He didn't formulate a cure. I took the papers that accompanied the doses I stole to another virologist, a qualified one, Don's former boss. He told me that what I thought was a cure only worked on me because I was healthy when dosed. What I stole was some kind of reverse engineered antibodies that self-replicate. Not a cure at all. There was no way to ever spin what I stole into a cure, thanks to the makeup of the Triptych virus. It would only ever work as a preventative. Don's boastful lie killed the world, not me."

I can't speak, because I can't even think. We found the partner, but there's still no hacker virus? What was my dad writing about then? It doesn't make sense. I slump where I'm sitting. Aunt Anne will die. All the Marked will die. Our hope was false all along. Why would my dad lie about something like that? Especially in his own journals?

Unless his partner stole the wrong syringes? Surely John couldn't be that stupid, but I don't believe my dad would lie about having a cure when he didn't.

"You may call him boastful, but my dad never wanted Triptych released," I say. "He died because you insisted on selling it, literally over his dead body."

John leans toward me. "Your dad was such a pathetic guy, so laser focused on his work to the exclusion of all else that he lost your mother to an abusive sociopath. He went crazy after that and stole you from your rightful parents, which I didn't discover until years later. He lied to me about the progress of the project I financed, which I discovered he was secretly planning to give away instead of sell if it ever actually worked. He robbed Josephine of her child, and he planned to rob me, and he deserved everything he got. He's the one who doomed the world, and he's the one who led us all where we are. It's his fault I'm forced to do another horrible thing in a long sequence of actions I never wanted to take."

"Then don't do it," Uncle Dan says. "You're right that this wasn't your fault. We're dear friends, and we've been through a lot. You can still fix this, John. Do the best you can with the information we have, and let us go. We may not be able to save the Marked children, but we can ease their suffering."

John stands up. "Ease their suffering? They've got less than a week before it's permanently concluded."

I assumed David Solomon somehow developed the accelerant, and I never suspected my dad or his partner. But John said he had the accelerant, which means it might not have been a Port Head at all.

My eyes widen. "You accelerated the Marked settlement. But why did you want them all dead?"

"They're a threat to my people," John says. "Same as they were to Solomon's. We've discussed it for years, going back and forth on whether they help us by creating fear that unites our people, or endanger us by their very presence. That kind of ongoing threat undermines our rule if it continues too long. Leadership is a balancing act, and they've been teetering between helpful and damaging for years. Ultimately, now that the suppressant's failing, they're a wild card. That shoves them over into the liability column."

"They're humans, not the bottom line on a financial statement," Uncle Dan says.

"Those humans keep the possibility of another outbreak alive, and we've feared the virus would mutate for years. If Tercera goes airborne." John shudders. "They've already survived far longer than they should have."

Longer than they should have?

"Wait, did *you* change out the suppressant?" I ask. "And set up my aunt to take the fall?"

John stands back up. "If I'd changed out the suppressant, no one would've been able to tell the pills looked different. Using prenatal vitamins was sloppy. I don't know who botched that, but it certainly wasn't me."

"But the accelerant," Sam says. "That really was you?"

John rolls his shoulders. "This is tedious now. Of course that was me. The Marked were getting restless, rebellious even. It was time to knock their numbers back. We only hit Baton Rouge where most of them had gathered thanks to the bungled leak of Solomon's plan to Cleanse them. They ran to Baton Rouge like rats huddling together. Safety in numbers isn't a bad idea, except you're also an easier target."

"Dad," Sam says, "the leader who consolidated the Marked, the one who made them dangerous." Sam closes his eyes. "It's Raphael."

John shakes his head. "That's impossible."

Sam turns away. "You abandoned him once, and now you've killed him outright."

John swallows once and his eyebrows draw together. "Your little brother died with his mother. I couldn't locate them."

Sam says, "Which means nothing. He survived, which I know because I saw him. I hugged him, and punched him in the face a time or two when he did something stupid. The Marked call him Rafe, but it's my brother, without a doubt."

John glances at me, and then turns to Uncle Dan. "You would've said so earlier. You're lying."

"You're the only one here who lies," I say.

John kicks me, his boot connecting with my hip. Pain shoots up my side.

Sam's jaw muscles tighten and he strains against his restraints. "Don't touch her again."

John tilts his head. "Or what, Samuel? You'll make up more ridiculous stories I won't believe?"

"You'll believe what you want Dad, but I didn't tell you earlier because you were too busy yelling and threatening me. I assume the others didn't tell you because they didn't want to intrude on our family news as a courtesy. I was trying to decide whether I should tell you, if we couldn't find a way to save him. Ironically, I didn't want false hope to cause you any pain."

"I already dealt with that pain." John Roth swallows and I see uncertainty in his eyes.

"It isn't a story. Real life is more unbelievable in this case. Your brilliant son, the born leader, the one who was exactly like you?" Sam leans forward, spitting out each word. "He is alive. You still sure you don't have that cure? Because it would really come in handy right now to clean up your mess."

"I've been cleaning up messes my entire life. Speaking of." John holds out his hand to one of his guards. "Firearms, please."

The tallest guard, the one to the right of him, hands him a large black gun. I'm sure Sam would know what kind it is, and how loud, and how powerful.

"The thing about cleaning up messes. If you aren't careful, they leave a stain." John turns to the other men. "You three, step back."

They step back.

"Put the safeties on your guns and toss them to the ground."

The three of them look at one another, and then glance at the tall guard. He shrugs.

"Don't listen to him," I say. "You're the stain he's about to clean."

John sighs. "Yes, listen to the captive instead of your leader." He rolls his yes. "It's a demonstration, boys. And Jeremy, come back here by us. You can help me with this part."

Jeremy walks back to where they're standing, and the other three toss their guns to the ground. Because they're well trained.

Well-trained morons.

I exhale heavily and close my eyes, because I don't want to see this.

Bam. Bam. Bam. Bam. Four shots. Four bodies. John drags them over and pushes them off the lake side of the dam one by one. I can't even hear their bodies hit the water, it's so far down.

"If you train your men well, messes are easy to clean up. I can't risk them telling anyone what happened here, or what they heard. Unfortunately," John says, "I trust you lot to keep quiet even less than I trusted them. You're not as well trained and you have scruples. Far too many scruples."

Uncle Dan whistles, and I can barely make it out over the water cascading behind us. "You've gone over the edge like those boys you just shot. What's the plan for us? Six more bullets? Six more deaths on your head? I suppose once you've killed billions, ten more seems insignificant."

John says, "Nothing so inelegant as bullets, my melodramatic friend. I don't really want to do this, you know. I wish there was some other way."

"Let us go," Uncle Dan says. "If there's no cure, there's nothing we can do. You haven't done anything wrong, other than shooting those guards, and Rhonda, Wesley and Job didn't even see that."

John kicks Wesley's still form where he lies next to me. "Poor little Ruby, couldn't choose between this pathetic wretch and my son?" He shakes his head. "Embarrassing, really."

Wesley moans and sits up. He glances at me, blinking repeatedly, blood running down the right side of his face.

I put my fingers to my mouth.

John tucks his gun in his waistband like Sam does when he has no holster handy. "You've noticed it's cold, I'm sure. I've kept you all bundled up, so 35 degrees doesn't feel too deadly yet. You're shivering, sure, but you can stop the physical reaction if you want. The shaking hasn't become involuntary."

I'm shivering like he says, but when I try, I can still my body, which means hypothermia hasn't set in. I'm not mumbling, and my thoughts still track. I stretch upward as far as I can and look over the edge. There's nothing but inky blackness outside of the pool of white from the floodlight.

"That water's barely above 32 degrees. Warm enough it's not frozen, but cold enough to kill you quickly. You won't last more than ten minutes in there, fifteen if you're really lucky, and you'll be too numb to move, much less swim effectively. When you add to that the bindings on your hands, well. You get the point. Zero percent chance of survival, but it's not a bad way to go."

"Wait, are you saying we'll die from drowning or hypothermia? I need to know which one to prepare for," Wesley says.

I snort, and somehow his joke makes me sadder this time. I'm so sorry I let him come. I turn my head his direction. "I'm so sorry Wes. I should've made you stay with your mom."

"Oh come on," John says. "With his mom?"

I turn toward John Roth. "You are the worst person I know, and I killed David Solomon, so that's saying something."

John shakes his head. "That reminds me. With you and Solomon both tragically killed in such close proximity, I imagine your mother will be dreadfully depressed. She might need some consoling. I've heard she's still a lovely woman, and accustomed to doing as she's told. A visit to WPN to take your regent the news of your death might be in order."

I struggle to my feet. "You will not touch my mother. Not ever."

"Little Ruby struggles to her feet, making her our first volunteer," John says. "Maybe you can let us know which option's better. Wesley's apparently dying to find out."

"You disgust me," I say.

"You bore me," John says simply.

Sam jumps up behind me, wobbling slightly from the tight bindings on his ankles. "You will not kill her, father."

"Why not?" John pulls his gun out and trains it on his son. "I don't want to shoot any of you, but if you force my hand, I will."

Sam steps around me. "Shooting, drowning, hypothermia. No matter how you do it, it's still murder."

John sighs. "I have to kill them. We've been through this."

"Them? What about me? You'll really kill your own son in cold blood?"

"Actually," John says, "you're the one person I'd risk keeping alive. Promise me that you'll keep your mouth shut, promise me you'll do as I say when we return home, and I'll spare you."

"What about Ruby?" Sam shakes his head. "I won't let her die."

He couldn't possibly be willing to go along with his dad in exchange for sparing my life.

John sighs. "So noble and so stupidly in love. Ruby can't survive. She's too uncompromising. She won't lie for me. I'm not even sure she believes most of what I told her tonight, and I have no reason to lie. Besides, she's technically queen of WPN, and my contact tells me the people love her more than they loved her lunatic father."

"Think of the possibilities, with her and I ruling together in Galveston."

John frowns. "You've gotten cleverer. I'd have loved that yesterday, but now I can't allow it. In fact, the only way I can trust you is if you push her off. Shove her over the edge, and you come back home with me. We'll never speak of any of this again."

Sam's hands fly forward to strike his father. If it were anyone else, I'd bet on Sam. But John won two Olympic Gold Medals in boxing. He may not be genetically enhanced, but he's fast, well trained and accurate. Sam's hands are triple cuffed and his feet are hogtied.

John ducks and Sam sprawls forward, barely raising his hands in time to avoid face planting into the icy concrete. The momentum of his fall carries him across the slippery ground quickly, until he rams into the safety rail on the edge of the dam.

"Pathetic attempt. You can't even see straight with her around. Perhaps she's not a good test of your loyalty." John leans over and grabs the back of my coat, bunching up the fabric behind my neck in his hand. When he lifts me into the air, I flail around, hands swinging, legs kicking. Sam slips and slides, trying vainly to get to his feet, but John's angry and Sam's winded, numb with cold, and bound. John strides purposefully to the edge of the bridge and shoves my shoulders out past the guardrail, my feet hooking on it. I don't dare thrash anymore, unsure whether I'd free myself only to fall to my death.

Sam scrabbles over to John's feet, and grabs my ankle.

"Let her go, son. I'm doing you a favor. She's an anvil around your neck. You can't see it like I can, because you're too close."

Sam's hands encircle my leg above my shoe, but John lifts up his booted foot to kick them away. I claw at the zipper of my coat, trying to take it off so I can slip out, but my fingers are so numb they won't comply.

As John's boot comes down on Sam, a figure flies past me in a blur, slamming into John and knocking John and the blurry person both into the guardrail. In his shock, John releases me and I collapse in a heap on the ground. Without my weight to keep him balanced, John loses his footing and he and his attacker topple over the railing. The floodlight points the other direction, and my eyes strain to see through the metal mesh of the guardrail. Someone dangles from the icy concrete, holding on by the fingertips of two closely placed hands.

Who is it? Is it John? Do we even consider saving him? I try to slide my fingers under the space on the railing, but with the rope binding my wrists, my hands won't fit through.

When I stand up to look over the edge, my heart leaps into my throat. The hands belong to Wesley.

"Wes!" I swing my left leg over the rail, determined to get to him. Sam's hands circle my right ankle before I can cross over. I shake and shake my leg, but he holds on just as tightly as he did a moment ago.

"Sam!" I shriek. "Let me go."

Wesley's eyes widen. "Don't, it's too icy. You'll fall. Ruby, I love you, remember that."

"Stop it, Wes. You're not dying." I kick at Sam's hands until he loses his grip and I swing my right leg over, balancing on the icy edge of the bridge.

Wesley says, "You idiot. You can't help me without falling yourself. Don't feel guilty. This was my choice. You've always been my choice."

He lets go and falls into the darkness.

CHAPTER 15

My feet slip and I almost follow Wesley over the edge. My fingertips on the rail are the only things keeping me on the bridge, and I consider letting go. Maybe if I fall, I can help Wesley swim to the edge. Sam's hands yank me back over to the top of the bridge, and I land hard on the unforgiving cement.

I bite at the rope on my hands. "Maybe we can drop a line to Wesley. We've got loads of rope between all of us, and your feet, too."

Sam hops to his feet and leans over the rail. "That's more than a hundred feet down."

"So?" I tug on the rope with my teeth, working it loose as quickly as I can.

"You probably have ten feet of rope there. If I have ten on my feet, and your uncle has twenty, and Job and Rhonda each have ten, by the time we tie them together, we're only looking at fifty some-odd feet." He shakes his head. "It's not enough, Ruby."

Fear, anger and frustration flood my body and carve their way out through my throat as I scream at the top of my lungs. "No! There must be something we can do." I jog down the road into the darkness. The sleet stopped, but wind whips at my jacket and freezes my face. Maybe if I reach the shore, and if Wesley survived the fall, and somehow swims to the edge of the lake, maybe then. How far is it? I close my eyes and force my brain to work.

A long way.

We lived on the bend near the Cedar Point ATV trail. It's at least a mile from the bridge to the trail, and at least twice as far to cross the bridge. The bridge follows the line Wesley would have to swim to reach the shore, and he'd be swimming against the current flowing from the dam gates to reach it. After surviving a hundred foot fall into thirty-two degree water with his hands tied. And he doesn't know the area at all.

My boot strikes a pile of rubble and I stumble forward. My hands, still bound and numb with cold, come up to break my fall, but not fast enough. My wrist wrenches sideways and the right side of my face, the side where John knocked me out, the side that already hurt, collides with the ground. I skid along the icy rubble of the path face first. I lie on the ground for a moment, dazed. When I push upward, my injured wrist howls at me in agony, but my face doesn't even sting, which isn't a great sign. I may be colder than I thought.

I turn on my side, and curl my legs up against my body to think. A fall into water at 100 feet. A human can't survive a fall to the ground above fifty feet. To survive a fall of 100 feet into water, he'd have to fall just right. Even so, he'd likely break his ankle, maybe more. But if he didn't break anything, and if he can untie his hands while kicking with his feet, maybe he could swim for shore.

I sit up on my side and scream. "Wesley! Wesley, if you

can hear me, swim toward my voice. Wesley!" I scream until my throat is raw, and then I keep screaming.

I wonder if he can hear me. And if he can hear me, should I worry about John Roth? His hands aren't bound, he's a former Olympic athlete, and he wasn't injured. If he can make a one-mile swim in freezing water while fully dressed, he could pull up on shore, wet and freezing. I'm calling him to me like a beacon.

I think about the logistics of swimming a mile and run the math in my head. No one can swim a mile in less than fifteen minutes, especially not fully dressed, and factoring in time to remove his clothing, he'd be way over fifteen minutes. John Roth, healthy, unbound and whole, will be dead from the cold long before he could reach this shore. He can't possibly survive to reach me, even if he survived the fall uninjured.

Which means Wesley can't survive either, even if every single thing goes right.

I collapse back down to the cracked cement path, my face resting on chunks of ice and rocks while heaving sobs wrack my body and tears leak down my face. Why couldn't Wesley have shoved that maniac over without falling himself? Why did it have to be Wesley? It should've been me, to set right the wrongs my dad and biological father started. Or maybe even Sam, to fix what his dad did. But not Wesley, who only came along to keep me safe.

Which is exactly what he did, but the price was far too steep.

"I wish it was me and not him, too." Sam sits down next to me. "It should've been me. My dad caused all this, and I should have stopped him, but Wesley did what I couldn't. Don't cheapen his choice by refusing to accept it."

When I process Sam's words, I realize he's right. Wesley chose to save me, and he knew what he was doing. He only let go because he was worried I'd fall, too. "If I hadn't tried to climb over, or if I'd untied my hands instead, maybe I could've used that rope." I close my eyes and replay the scene over in my mind. How could I have saved him?

The ground beneath me is hard, bumpy, and cold, but Sam's arms are warm and strong when he gathers me close to him. He unzips his coat and pulls me next to his chest. The heat radiates outward and I sink against him.

"It took me several minutes to get your Uncle's ropes off," Sam says, "and several more for him to use pieces from the floodlight rack to pry my handcuffs loose."

My hands feel for his wrists, and when I find them I gasp. The skin all around both wrists is torn and bleeding.

"You couldn't have done anything in time," Sam says. "If you had leaned forward, you'd have lost your balance. Besides, his fingers were already slipping when he let go. The edge of that bridge is icy and wet. It's a miracle he held on with bound hands for the few seconds he did. It went the only way it could've gone, the best way any of us could have planned. If my dad had thrown you over the edge, I'd have killed him, probably by dragging him down, and you've done the math on that equation. No one could survive the combination of the fall, the ice water, and the distance. We'd all have died."

Someone clears his or her throat, which startles me. My eyes search and find Uncle Dan standing a few feet away. I hadn't even realized he was near. "We may not be able to save the Marked kids without the hacker virus we all hoped for, but we can still save Anne."

Rhonda stumbles along behind Uncle Dan, with Job trailing a few feet further yet, slowed by the weight of the floodlight he's dragging.

"How much further to the cabin?" Rhonda asks. "I should remember, but I'm too tired to spell my own name, and my head feels like it's been stuffed with cotton batting."

I mumble, "Maybe a mile?"

Uncle Dan shakes his head. "Closer to two, and we better hurry. We've been out in the cold for too long, and thanks to the sleet we're all soaked. We need dry clothes, food and sleep."

"I'm not leaving until we've swept the shoreline for Wesley," I say. "We have three days for Aunt Anne still."

Uncle Dan doesn't argue, and neither does anyone else.

We trudge home and dry off. I chew and swallow the jerky and dried biscuits Sam hands me, but it all tastes the same. I finally collapse on our dusty old family room sofa, my back to Sam's chest. I offer up a prayer of thanks that we survived, in case God really exists and listens to us. Then I ask God to tell Wesley I miss him. Stupid and superstitious, but what could it hurt? As Sam's breathing evens out, my mind shuts off and I drop off to sleep.

I wake up at first light, pull my damp boots and soggy coat back on, and trudge outside. Sam and Job are no more than two steps behind me, and Sam's carrying a gun. We walk the shoreline for more than two hours with no luck. We could've shot a thousand different kinds of birds, but we don't see a single person until we reach the trail off the lakeshore toward our cabin. A flurry of birds fight and dive and squawk a hundred yards down the shoreline, and Sam runs toward them. I sprint to try and keep up, which I only manage because it's so near. Sam stops abruptly and holsters his gun, and when I realize why, I have to turn away.

The birds are shredding a ration pack lying alongside a single black boot.

"We should go," Job says. "I really don't want to see a bloated corpse."

I can't block the image of Wesley, his body swollen and stuck underwater somewhere, being eaten by fish, or birds. I bend in half and vomit chunks of jerky into the silty dirt of the shoreline.

"His parents would want his body." I wipe my mouth on the sleeve of my jacket, stand up and keep walking.

Three hours later, Uncle Dan finds us and begs me to stop looking.

I can't meet his eyes.

"Ruby, it was a fifteen hour drive to Nashville Before. It'll take us twenty if we're lucky. Anne's execution, without John Roth to halt it, will not wait for us."

I know it's childish, but I don't want to stop thinking about Wesley and start trying to save Aunt Anne yet. It feels wrong somehow, like I didn't care about him.

I shake my head. "Not even two days ago I told him I didn't love him, not like he wanted. He's been my best friend for years. We did everything together, and now he dropped a hundred feet into freezing water to save me. I can't abandon the search for him less than twenty-four hours later."

I can't.

Except Aunt Anne's still alive, and she can't wait either. It's like I told Rafe a few days ago. Triage rules apply. I have to mentally block the pain from Wesley's death until we've done what needs to be done. If Aunt Anne dies from my childishness, I'll never forgive myself for that either. Uncle Dan doesn't argue with me. Rhonda and Job don't beg me to let it go. Which is how I know that I need to.

"Fine. We head for Nashville." I clench my mittened hands into fists and begin walking toward the cabin.

"What's the plan when we get there?" Job asks.

"John Roth didn't grant a stay of execution, and they have a signed confession," Rhonda says.

"Which is clearly a lie John either forged or made her write," I say.

Sam nods. "My dad won't be coming back, which no one in Nashville will know. We can file an appeal with the CentiCouncil, and if we can find a few supporters, it'll buy us some time. We'll need to identify where the new charges related to the suppressant issues originated, and make sure they don't resurface. Shouldn't be too hard, since they weren't formally filed."

"Do we tell them what happened with your dad or go into his involvement in . . . Well, in everything?" I ask. "They know about my dad's journals. If we show them the partnership paperwork, they'd probably believe us."

Uncle Dan holds the papers up. "I grabbed them, but it's Sam's decision. It's his dad."

The toe of my boot catches on a rock and I stumble forward.

Sam's arms catch me and swing me up against his chest, his arms cradling my back and underside of my knees. "I need to think about it."

Sam's dad died, and Wesley was his friend too. I shouldn't be relying on him so much, but I can't help it. I tuck my face against his collarbone and close my eyes. He carries me inside and sets me on a sofa while the others prepare to leave. We load up in the jeep again and drive to the Land Cruiser.

I hop out to try and help free it, but after wringing my hands uselessly for ten minutes, I climb back in the jeep. At least being inside cuts the wind.

Sam, Uncle Dan, Rhonda and Job eventually free the back tires on the Land Cruiser, and Sam and I switch into that again. After we've divvied up the remaining gas, Rhonda, Job and Uncle Dan pile into the Jeep. I don't remember much about the first ten hours in the car, except how depressing Kansas City is with no one living there. Deer bound across the freeway, birds swoop from the tops of buildings and the few remaining upright power poles. Weeds and spindly trees grow everywhere, transforming normal sights into alien ones. I should be grateful the roads are mostly clear, but I'm too numb to recognize any emotions other than desperation and sorrow.

The temperature's risen by almost ten degrees, and everything around us melts. That's probably why we don't get stuck in ice or snow. When we stop for blockages and downed trees, Job and Sam clear the roads quickly. Sam doesn't ask me any questions along the way or try to initiate a conversation. He holds my hand when I want reassurance, and leaves me alone when I can't bear the guilt of being comforted. We drive, we ponder, and we grieve.

It's enough.

St. Louis takes longer to navigate past because it's an active Unmarked settlement. We stop a few miles out to coordinate our stories. Uncle Dan explains that we went on a mission for John Roth up north to recover some data. He tells the guards we're headed to Nashville to make sure the Council gets the data it wanted, and to ensure the execution of Anne Orien is halted. As close to the truth as we can manage.

They ask us all a lot of questions, and I try my hardest not to sound like a zombie. They let us pass and even refill our gas tanks, so I must've succeeded.

We drive past the Arch, a tall, metal structure that bends up, up, up into the sky, and then bows and comes back down. I marvel that such a thing exists, and that it somehow survived the decimation of the world. I'm still peering out of the window when we drive past a street marked Rose Street. The next road down is Liberty.

Libby and Rose. I wonder who'll care for Rose when Libby dies. We can't save the Marked, but we need to get down there and make sure the babies I inoculated don't die too.

How could there not have been a cure? My dad was infected, and he used it on himself. Was that false? Did he die infected? I think about that night, about his face, but it was clear, no rash.

My mind whirls furiously trying to recall everything I've read between the original journals, the journal we found in the safe, and the letters I've seen since. I think about dad's entries, as many as I can remember, one by one. They included a lot of technical information focused on his conclusions and interspersed with personal notes, introspection and reflection. The journal we recovered in Galveston was different. It came from his lab, and consisted almost entirely of dense scientific notations. Rafe stole it, but when we left in pursuit of this Hail Mary play, he gave it back.

I scramble over the seat and dig it out of my bag.

"Everything okay?" Sam asks.

"Yeah, I'm just thinking about what your dad said. I can't make sense of why my dad would lie about having a possible cure in his personal account. He wrote in his journal that he injected himself with the hacker virus after exposure and the injection worked. It doesn't make sense for that to all be a lie. Wouldn't he be scared, at least of infecting me or others?"

I flip through the pages of the one I have and like before, I can't really digest a lot of the notations. Hopefully my aunt will be able to. Maybe she can figure out how to boost my antibodies into a cure. Maybe. But not in two days. Even Aunt Anne can't turn water into wine on a moment's notice.

If only John Roth had stolen the hacker virus. A weight presses on my chest when I think about his monumental stupidity in stealing a virus and unleashing it on the world when a cure wasn't yet prepared and verified. I keep coming back to the same question over and over.

Why lie in his own records?

Dad might've lied to Jack because he was freaking out about money. Maybe Dad wanted to convince John not to rush into anything or do anything hasty. But there's no reason for him to lie to himself. Unless he thought Jack might steal his journals? But even then, what would be the point? He'd have had to lie about a lot. About injecting himself when he was infected, about his hopes. It's too convoluted. When all other things are equal, the simplest solution is usually the correct one. What simple explanation can there be?

I close my eyes and think about the last journal I read, the one I finished in the last few moments of quarantine. It revealed that I could reach the place where important things were kept. 'Ruby can always find what she needs,' or something like that. I always assumed it was the safe, but maybe he meant because he injected it into my blood?

Either way, that wasn't actually the end of Dad's entry. A chunk of pages were torn out after that statement. I assumed my dad wrote more about the virus, or details about the cure. I wondered at the time whether maybe he explained more about me or my mom, and Aunt Anne didn't want me to see it. She insisted she never saw the pages, and if that's true, who would have removed them? His office manager? Maybe David Solomon, or John Roth if they found something they wanted to keep a secret. But if they'd seen it, they'd know I housed the antibodies, and neither of them knew. What else could've happened?

Maybe none of them tore them out. Maybe Dad did.

If Dad had the epiphany about reverse engineering the antibodies at home, and scrabbled the parameters of the solution out there in his personal journal, and if he read the article about stimulating the CpG oligonucleotides in our condo and realized he could apply the same principle, he could've written down the process on whatever paper he had handy. But he'd need the sophisticated equipment at his lab to implement the idea. Dad might have ripped the pages out himself, carried them to his own lab in the black briefcase, and possibly even shoved them into the bio safe to make sure no one else saw them.

Until John Roth found the notes lying on top of the syringes he stole.

What if John assumed the notes documented the contents of the syringes? Maybe the notes had nothing to do with the contents of the syringes. Maybe the syringes contained the hacker virus, and John really had it all along without knowing it? What if he only shared the notes with Dad's old boss?

It's an awful lot of maybes.

I bite my lip. I wish I could go back in time and ask my dad. And I'd really like to hug him, too.

"What's wrong?" Sam asks. "Did you think of something?"

"I'm not sure. I'm sad and tired and I might be grasping at straws. Crazy, crazy straws."

"Want to walk me through it?" he asks.

"It might help to go through it out loud. Last night your dad said he didn't have the cure. He said he took the notes about what he stole to an expert, and what he took was really just a roadmap for how to reverse engineer antibodies. That's essentially what my dad dosed me with."

Sam grunts.

"That's what you heard John say, right?"

Sam says, "Yeah something like that."

"You know your dad better than I do by a long shot. Let's say he dosed himself with one of the doses like he said and then he administered Tercera. He didn't contract it, so he knew it worked. Then he wanted to replicate the cure so he could be ready to sell it. He has one dose left to use, and some notes. Would he have taken notes *and* the one remaining dose for testing? Or would he show up at the meeting with only notes?"

Sam frowns. "He would definitely have started with just the notes. He'd want to meet the guy, take his measure, and figure out whether he could trust him. He wouldn't work with anyone unless he had some kind of leverage. He called it necessary collateral, knowing something damaging that he could use to force partners to comply."

"Which is exactly what he had on my dad—knowledge that Dad stole me from someone. I wonder how he found out about that to begin with."

Sam says, "He paid a lot of people to investigate any possible partners. He said digging up dirt was his due diligence, which I didn't realize was a business joke until I was much older."

Poor Sam. "What if he didn't trust the scientist, but he was too paranoid to take the actual syringe? Might he have only ever taken the notes?"

"He would've been nervous to tell someone what was really going on. They could've reported him. Tercera would already have been out at that point, even if no one knew how bad it was yet."

"What if the paperwork he had, the notes, were from my dad's journal, but they weren't reflective of what was in the syringes?"

Sam glances back at me. "What are you saying, Ruby?"

"My dad's journal mentions he had three doses of the hacker virus, but he took one himself, so he should've had two left, just as your dad described. According to my aunt, the police didn't find anything like that in my dad's lab or home office. No viruses in cold storage, no syringes. I assumed Jack stole the last two doses of the hacker virus before Dad died."

"But my dad says it didn't exist."

"What if your dad didn't know what it was? Maybe he only knew it stopped Tercera. If I'm right, and Dad put the notes he had from home in the same place as his remaining two samples, maybe your dad took the notes he found with it, which were actually detailed instructions explaining how Dad made what he injected me with. Your dad thought they diagrammed what he stole, but what if they didn't? What if John Roth really did steal the hacker virus, but he never knew it because he didn't have the last dose itself examined?"

Sam whistles. "Either way, he would've been safe."

I climb back over the seat. "I think he might have had the cure all along and never realized it."

"Would the remaining dose still be alive after all these years?" Sam asks. "I know where my dad keeps stuff that he values. Or at least, where he did last time I was in Nashville. I could probably get into his safe."

I think about our trip from Nebraska to Port Gibson the first time. I shake my head. "No, he didn't have any items he carried in an unusual way." A live virus couldn't have survived without special measures.

Sam curses. "Dad's dead now, so even if his body did contain the hacker virus, it's gone too. He's done nothing but ruin things from start to finish, including dying when we might actually have gotten something of value from him. No redemption of any kind, not from Dad."

I bite my lip. "One thing I will say for John Roth that I can't say for David Solomon is this. He loved his child."

Sam scowls. "You're wrong. He detested me."

"I'm frequently wrong, but not this time. This time I'm right." I place my hand on his. "He wanted to save you, to take you home with him, against his better judgment. He took care of you all these years and made sure you were safe. He sucked at expressing it, but he did love you."

"He manipulated me constantly, enrolled me in clinical trials, and kept me aware at all times of my many failures."

"Things he thought would make you stronger and better. In his twisted way, I think he loved you deeply."

Sam says, "What's your point?"

"There were two hacker virus syringes if I'm right, and he thought they were antibodies that would prevent infection from Tercera, a virus that was running unchecked throughout the world. That left one dose of preventative, and not something that he could easily sell without questions. Or maybe he could have, but it wasn't as valuable as he thought. Maybe it wasn't worth the risk that news of the identity of who released Tercera in the first place might get out."

"You think he dosed me?"

I shake my head. "I don't know if any of this is true. It's all a complete hypothetical, even if I'm right about the hacker virus existing and your dad not knowing. Even if that's true, he still could've sold it to someone who was really wealthy." I think about the years I spent with Sam growing up. "Your dad was never sick. Never caught a cold. Never had the flu."

"So?"

"Neither were you, Sam. When was the last time you puked or ran a fever?"

Sam's eyebrows draw together. "I don't remember, maybe two years ago."

"What was it?" I ask. "Cough, temperature, body aches?"

Sam shakes his head. "Sore throat. Doctor in Nashville said it was strep."

"A bacterial issue. Bacteria are much larger than viruses, and they operate differently. Viruses need a host, and they steal other cells to live. According to my dad, the hacker virus attacks and consumes all viruses that enter the human body immediately. If I'm right, your body shouldn't have ever suffered from the effects of a virus."

"And if you are?"

"I need to ask you something. I think it's something you don't like to talk about, because you've never mentioned it to me. We've had an insane past few weeks, but even so, after spending hours on end in the car, you've never mentioned it once."

"Just ask, Ruby."

"What exactly happened in the genetic modification trials your dad signed you up for?"

Sam's hands grip the steering wheel tightly enough that his fingers turn white. "What do you mean?"

"Let's start with the basics. How many patients were there?"

"Twelve."

"And what did they do to you? Injections? Radiation? Chemical therapy? Gene sequencing? What?"

His jaw muscles clench. "They put us in machines a lot, but whether it was a treatment or to run a test, I don't know. It was loud. There were injections, and a lot of pain followed each one. They did some kind of light therapy. It lasted months, round after round, and then after that, multiple blood draws a day, combined with physical fitness and abilities tests. Run a mile as fast as you can. Run as far as you can without breathing. Run blindfolded. Listen to and identify sounds, attacks, and smells. Jump over a hedge, a fence, and then over razor wire topped enclosures. Lift your maximum weights."

"It sounds miserable."

"Some of it was fun, like a contest. Some of it wasn't. They cut us and monitored our healing. They exposed us to cold, to heat, to light, and to dark. They tested our reflexes."

I nod. "You're faster and stronger than you should be. Your senses are heightened, and you're better able to heal."

He bobs his head.

"How about the others? Did you all have the same benefits? I heard one of them was exposed to Tercera."

Sam grits his teeth, and I wait.

"Some of them improved in some areas, and some didn't. One or two of them healed quicker. A few were fast, but not as fast as me. No one else had the same outcome, especially not in multiple categories. In the end, I was the only success in the trial."

"How did they define success?"

Sam stares straight ahead, eyes blank, but his hands are still white on the steering wheel. "I survived."

My jaw drops. "Wait, are you saying?"

"Only one died from Tercera. The others—" He shakes his head. "Clayton died after the light therapy. Greg didn't survive the third round of injections. Lydia contracted Tercera, and before you ask, I don't know whether they intended her to be exposed."

"Were you close to them?"

He shakes his head. "I wasn't close to anyone other than your family, and they didn't encourage us to befriend one another. They fostered competition so we'd try our hardest. But even so, we shared something miserable and that bonded us. After the sixth round of injections, the remaining eight participants became sick, really sick. Fevers, coughing, diarrhea, and cramps that left them folded over for hours, moaning incoherently. Within a few days of the last shot, they all passed."

I take his hand with mine. "I'm so sorry."

"I had zero symptoms. I didn't suffer at all."

"It's hard to be the one who survives, especially if you're the only one." I close my eyes and think about my dad's death and how often I wished I'd died with him. And now Wesley. Fresh tears stream down my face.

Sam squeezes my hand. "I guess you understand."

"I think you survived because of the hacker virus, Sam. Do you recall your dad injecting you with anything, after your mom left?"

Sam's eyebrows furrow.

"He wouldn't have told anyone else, so it would have had to be your dad injecting you. That might have seemed strange."

After a moment, Sam shakes his head. "Not that I recall."

I bite my lip. "Even so, I think we may have had the cure all along. You'd think we'd have thought of that, after what we discovered in Galveston about me."

"How will we know?" Sam's eyebrows furrow. "Can you see it in my blood?"

"Well, not exactly, but if we can find a scanning electron microscope, we can sort of see it, maybe. We could also test your reaction to other viruses. Our fastest way to test my theory would be to dose Aunt Anne with your blood and see what happens to the Tercera cells. The microscope kills the samples, but we could see the viruses at varying levels."

Sam grunts.

"The extensive testing they did is my biggest reservation."

"Why?" he asks. "Could they have killed it?"

"I suppose so."

"But that's not what has you worried."

I shake my head. "No it's not. If my aunt did all that testing on you, and you had a viral cure in your body, how could she have missed it?"

"They did say they couldn't figure out how I survived."

"Maybe they weren't looking small enough. Viruses are much smaller than bacteria."

I hope for the sake of Libby, Rose, Rafe and all the others that I'm right. And if I am, I hope there's enough time to do something about it.

CHAPTER 16

We don't make very good time once the sun finally sets. Sam sleeps for short breaks after I insist on driving, jolting upright without cause. The night drags on and on, and it feels like we'll never reach our destination. Finally though, a few hours after the sun rises, we see signs for the city. Fifty miles outside of Nashville, we stop to coordinate our plan.

"I don't think we should tell the Council about John Roth's involvement," Sam says. "Not yet, and not because I want to preserve his good name."

Sam's never cared much about that kind of thing. "Then why?" I ask.

Sam sighs. "If we tell them what happened up there, I'll go under review and they'll lock me down. But beyond that, have you interacted with the DeciCouncil? They don't move fast. They'll take days and days to work through everything, including hearings and nominations for the new Chancellor. My dad was their leader, but they're almost the opposite of WPN where there's one leader and the people love him. In some ways, the average person is way more invested with WPN. Most normal Unmarked citizens have no idea what's going on, and this handful of rulers run things. If you want to pursue your hunch, we need to focus this so it's only about your aunt."

"What, what hunch?" Uncle Dan asks.

"I think the hacker virus still might exist."

I explain the details as quickly as possible.

"It makes sense to me," Job says. "When you told me what Roth said, it sat wrong. I couldn't put my finger on why, but I didn't like it. I should've thought of this possibility myself, but I never read Uncle Don's journals back home."

"If we want to figure out whether I'm right and reach Baton Rouge with any time to administer a possible cure," Sam says, "we can't give them any reason to detain us."

"Which means we need to keep things as simple as possible, and leave your dad out of it if we can." I nod my head. "Should you wait outside then? I don't see how we can avoid the topic of your father if you come into the city with us."

Sam frowns. "I don't like the idea of you going in without me, but you might be right. Everyone in Nashville knows who I am."

"Even if we leave Sam to wait on us," I say, "we still need to discuss our approach. Do we ask for an appeal of her sentence, knowing John Roth isn't there to grant one, or should I request a diplomatic pardon as queen of WPN?"

Sam and I both look toward Uncle Dan. She's his wife, so these are ultimately all his decisions to make.

He scratches his head. "There are too many variables to know how this will play out. Sam's always an asset in a bad situation. If they ask about your dad, we tell them the truth. There's been enough lying, but if we can avoid getting into all that, we will. Let's start by filing a simple appeal. If that doesn't go well, Ruby can make a formal request as Queen."

"Will slinking in under the radar undercut the likelihood of them believing I really am the new Queen of WPN?" I ask. "Maybe we should lead with that?"

Uncle Dan shakes his head. "You're not going to slink in. Job and I will go in first to file an appeal. Job can attest to the need the Marked have of Anne's very targeted knowledge. I have a friend who will notify Rhonda at the edge of town if there's a problem, and she'll come for you. Sam will keep you safe, and he'll come with you if we end up needing to threaten them."

"And then I'll what? Waltz in wearing ratty jeans and a t-shirt, and tell them I'm a queen?"

"It won't look ideal," Uncle Dan says. "But we'll make do with what we have. You have that huge bag in the car. Maybe change into something cleaner. But ultimately, John Roth won't be the only one with connections to WPN. Someone on the Council will be able to verify your claim, I'm sure of it."

Something hits me then. I glance back at the huge duffel bag my mom foisted off on me.

"This might be a good time to show up in a ball gown with a tiara."

Uncle Dan's jaw drops. "You have a tiara and a ball-gown in there?"

I close my eyes momentarily. "My mom insisted I bring them. She said I never knew when I might need it."

"Seems your mom might've been right. Let's hope it doesn't come to that," Uncle Dan says.

Uncle Dan and Job head for the center of Nashville to make their formal appeal, and I pull my stupid ball gown out of the duffel bag we've been dragging around. It's pretty rumpled. "I can't believe I may have to wear this."

Sam's half smile breaks my heart. "If it frees your aunt, you'll have to thank Josephine for making you bring it."

I shake my head. "This was a stupid idea. If I put this on, I'll look worse than I do now. I'll look like a little girl playing dress up."

"You'll look beautiful." Sam leans over and picks up a rock the size of the end of his thumb. He tosses it once in the air. "How many of these could we hide in the sash of that dress?"

"Excuse me?" I ask.

He shrugs. "If we have to talk to the Council, they won't let me take any weapons."

He rummages through his bag and pulls out an extra pair of socks. He slides one into each pocket.

"What are those for?" I ask.

He shrugs again. "You never know what might come up."

Uh, okay. Sam's acting super weird.

"You might want to get your dress on," Sam says. "If Rhonda comes to get us, she's going to be in a hurry. She won't want to stand around while you get that on."

I eye the fluffy pile of red silk and sigh heavily. May as well get it over with. Sam takes the sash from the dress and begins tucking rocks into it at intervals. While he's turned away from me doing that, I struggle into the dress. Except I can't quite get the back of it laced up. The icy air whips at my skin and goose bumps ripple up my arms.

I clear my voice.

Sam turns around. "Need help?"

I nod.

He reaches me quickly and his huge fingers deftly lace up the back of my dress. Then he ties the sash around my back, tucking another stone or two into the place where he ties the bow.

"What's up with the rocks?" I ask.

He smiles but doesn't answer. Now that he's done, I expect him to step away. Between his father and Wesley, it just hasn't been the right time to talk about us. It still isn't. But Sam doesn't step away. He opens up his coat and pulls me against his chest, the warmth from his body enveloping me.

I tuck my head below his chin and breathe in the smell of him. I've missed this, his strength and his touch. "I need you, Sam."

He presses a kiss to the top of my head. "I need you too, sunshine. More than ever."

I turn my face toward his and open my mouth to tell him I don't want space, or time or anything else. All I want is him. But before I can say the words, the Jeep careens into the clearing behind us, nearly crashing into the Land Rover. Sam's arms tighten around me.

Rhonda leaps from the driver's side. "We need you right now, Ruby."

Apparently things are not going well with the appeal.

Sam and I jump apart, and icy air traps me again. Sam tosses me my coat, the one Wesley gave me. My heart trembles, but we race over to the jeep. I snatch the old, dilapidated black briefcase of my dad's and climb inside. I open the back door, and Sam circles around and climbs in next to me, leaving the front passenger seat empty. Rhonda glances at me meaningfully but doesn't say a word, mercifully.

"What happened?" I ask.

Rhonda shakes her head and throws the car into gear. "Apparently Mayor Fairchild showed up yesterday, furious that Wesley was gone. He demanded John Roth explain his departure and his son's disappearance, assuming John took Wesley with him and Sam. He told them everything, from your antibodies to the coronation. He even told them about the acceleration of the Marked."

I whistle. "Which means all the council doesn't know is that John is Jack, and that Wesley's—" I choke up.

"Yes, that's right. And since John's not in Nashville to explain himself, or the disappearance of Wesley, Sam, and the rest of us, the CentiCouncil was at odds with the Deci-Council. Dad burst in there, telling them he couldn't wait days to be heard since Mom's scheduled for execution tomorrow."

"Surely they offered him a continuation," Sam says.

Rhonda nods. "We need her now if there's any hope for Rafe. He declined."

Now he's created a mess and wants us to wade in there and reinforce his story. The Council thinks Aunt Anne switched the suppressant, effectively murdering a hundred thousand innocents, when in fact we need her to save them. What a tangled heap.

If I'm right and Sam might have the hacker virus, we don't have time to argue over my aunt's release. It would be way easier to figure this out with her, but the hacker virus should attack Tercera on its own. If Sam really does have the virus, delaying could mean that everyone dies pointlessly. If we go without my aunt, we may only save a fraction of the people we could with her help.

I suck at making these decisions. Why do they keep getting thrust upon me?

"Stop the car," I say quietly.

Rhonda slows down. "Why?"

"Maybe we leave your dad to fend for himself. Surely they'll delay Aunt Anne's execution and talk this into the ground. I can give you the paperwork proving John Roth is the Jack my dad mentions. They have Dad's early journals already. I'd love Aunt Anne's help with the Marked, but if we go in there, we risk never getting down to Baton Rouge with Sam. If the hacker virus really is inside him and we go south now, maybe we can save a lot of them with rudimentary injections. It's better than nothing."

Rhonda punches the gas. "No. Mom will help tremendously once we free her. Besides, I'm not willing to risk her again."

Having just lost Wesley, I understand her point. I don't argue any further. A tall, white-haired man in a suit waits by the guardhouse. He nods at Rhonda and the gate opens. She barely even slows down before flying through the gap.

"That's Dad's friend," Rhonda says. "I wish Dad had connections outside of Security, though. Other than Mayor Fairchild, he doesn't know anyone on the Council."

And if Uncle Dan told him what happened with his son, he'll be out for blood.

Heads turn toward us on every street as Rhonda shoots down them like a pinball, bouncing unchecked through town. She finally skids to a halt on a red curb in front of a stately old building. The Unmarked set up their administrative offices in the former Tennessee State Office building, an imposing structure of limestone that rises five or six stories high. I'm nervous to enter a place that, as far as I can tell, will be full of arguing Port Heads. Sam's face looks like it always does, perfectly beautiful and completely calm. I reach for his hand and he doesn't hesitate to take mine.

It's such a simple connection, palm-to-palm, fingers interlaced. It shouldn't ground me. It shouldn't center me. It shouldn't give wings to my heart. After all, I'm strong, I'm capable and I don't need Sam to save me. I'm a queen for heaven's sake.

But knowing Sam sees me, that he loves me for the good and accepts the bad, well. It gives me the energy to hold my exhausted, Medusa-haired head high as we climb the steps into the State Office building. I don't need Sam, but there's no one I want to be with more.

Rhonda marches in front of us, her booted feet pounding up the stairs straight for the entrance, like a missile headed for an unsuspecting grain silo. We're stopped at the entrance by two armed guards.

The tallest one, his dark hair slicked back, scowls at Rhonda. "You can't park there. You'll have to move that car."

Sam steps around Rhonda. "I'm Samuel Roth."

The black haired guard's eyes widen. "My apologies, sir. Please go ahead."

I hear him speak into his walkie as we move past them.

"I just admitted Samuel Roth. He has two women with him, both blonde, one in a fluffy red dress, over."

Static, followed by a loud voice. "Detain him. Over."

I expect Sam to knock the guards out in half a second. He surprises me by splaying his boots on the ground and holding his hands up.

The guards won't meet our eyes. They take Sam's weapons: twelve handguns, four knives and a throwing star. The shorter guard pulls a sock from Sam's pocket.

"Uh, what do I do with this?"

"You're confiscating spare pairs of socks now?" Sam chuckles. "I haven't been gone that long, have I?"

The black haired guard shakes his head and the shorter man hands Sam his sock back. The taller guard reaches over to pat me down, while the shorter man with light brown hair searches Rhonda.

Before the guard's hand touches me, Sam grunts. "Mike, don't tell me you're going to do a body search on the Queen of World Peace Now, because that's a terrible idea."

"Uh, I have to. Sir."

Sam shakes his head slowly. "Touching her is a capital offense with WPN. They believe she's God's chosen."

Where's he going with this? Maybe he's worried they'll notice his rocks.

Mike glances from me to Sam and back again. "I've been ordered to detain you," he says to me. "I need to search you as a part of that order."

I hold out my dad's old briefcase. "You're welcome to look at this." I lift one eyebrow. "But touching me is considered by World Peace Now to be an act of war. I offer you my assurances that I do not have a single knife, gun, bullet or throwing star on my body."

Mike searches the briefcase, which he can barely pry open. Then he turns toward me. "Uh, I don't know—"

A deep voice interrupts the uncertain Mike. "You disarmed Samuel?"

I turn toward the voice. A tall man with flinty eyes wearing a dark brown uniform faces us, flanked on either side by half a dozen soldiers. All of them have guns trained on Sam.

"I did, sir."

"That's sufficient, thank you Private Collins. I'll take custody of them from here."

"I'm sorry," Sam says, "why am I being taken into custody?"

The man in uniform smiles. "Significant charges were recently leveled against your father."

Sam's eyebrow lifts. "I'll ask again. Why am *I* being taken into custody, Drake?"

"Commander Drake," the flinty-eyed man says with a smile. "You're being taken into custody because I deem you dangerous and you'll stay there until the Council tells me to do otherwise."

I expect Sam to argue. He shrugs his shoulders and

nods, looking for all the world like he's chosen to walk alongside fourteen armed guards, rather than being taken into custody by them.

As we walk down the hall, my dad's old briefcase safely clutched in my arms again, my mind races. Uncle Dan surely caught them all up. Which means they know John Roth is Jack. They know the Marked are dying en masse, and soon. Rhonda says they know I'm queen of WPN.

Do they know Sam may be able to save the Marked? Do they even care?

"Where are we being taken?" I look around me. We've nearly reached the far left side of the entry hall a hallway opens up to the left and to the right. To the right the building opens up and a set of large, heavy double doors are shut. To the left, sunlight shines from a glass door. To the outside.

"You're all going to holding cells," Commander Drake says. "Offsite. Until the Council decides what to do with you."

"I'm about done with holding cells," I mutter so only Sam can hear me. "I've been stuffed into one like every few days for the past few weeks."

Sam nods at me, and I know he's ready.

Commander Drake turns left ahead of us, but if we turn right, we could walk right down the hall to those double doors. I'm pretty sure that's where the Council is meeting. I hear raised voices coming from that direction and I strain to hear what they're saying. I narrow my eyes at the Commander and slow my pace. "Where exactly is the Council making these decisions?"

Commander Drake turns toward me, but before he or I can say anything else, Sam trips me. There's no doubt in my mind he did it on purpose. Sam's far too coordinated to trip me accidentally. I stumble forward, dropping dad's briefcase, and fall on my face, cursing loudly.

Before any of the soldiers can help me, Mike shouts, "Don't touch her. It's a violation of WPN protocol. It could start a war."

While the guards scramble backward, one of them retrieving the black briefcase, Sam ducks toward me, his hands wrapping around my waist. He lifts me up, and sets me upright. I notice that my sash is lighter now. Several rocks lighter than it was before.

Commander Drake scoffs. "Where did you get that idiotic idea?"

Mike's eyes widen. "From her! She's the queen of WPN, that's what they said."

"This little girl?" Commander Drake snorts. "Why do you think that? Because she's wearing a tiara?" He shakes his head. "Could you be any more idiotic?"

Sam grunts. "Actually, Ruby is the queen of World Peace Now. Also, I don't like your tone."

The next part happens so fast I'm not entirely certain how it goes down. It looks like Sam swings a sock full of rocks in a circle, slamming Commander Drake and four other guards in their heads and knocking them to the ground. Rhonda disarms Mike in the upheaval, while Sam kicks another guard's weapon away.

The guard right behind me tries to put me in a head-lock, but I'm learning. I elbow him in the stomach and then I duck. While he's groaning, I snatch his gun and point it at his head. "Uh, uh. I'm not going to any more cells."

By the time I turn around, Sam's holding two guns with who knows how many more tucked away, and fourteen guards are clutching their heads on the ground. The walkie closest to me on the ground crackles.

"Wade? Where are you guys? Shouldn't you be outside with Samuel Roth by now? Over."

Sam kicks it away and turns to me. "I think you've got something to talk to the Council about," Sam says.

Rhonda bobs her head toward the door. "I don't think we have much time before someone checks on good old Wade."

I hear loud shouts coming from inside the double doors, and I start toward them. It's time the Unmarked hear WPN's demands.

CHAPTER 17

I retrieve my dad's briefcase, pull the partnership paperwork out of it, and walk toward the double doors, Sam and Rhonda on my heels. I shove the doors open a little too hard and they fly back and clang against the wall loudly. I gulp when more than one hundred sets of eyes turn my way. I square my shoulders and straighten my head, the weight of the crown my mother insisted I bring resting heavily on it.

"I am Ruby Carillon Behl Solomon, only biological daughter of the now deceased David Solomon, Queen of World Peace Now. I've come to demand the release of my aunt, Anne Orien."

I notice out of the corner of my eye that Uncle Dan and Job are standing, hands behind their backs, at the edge of a raised dais at the front of the large room. Rows of tables with high backed chairs, a wide column between them, lead up to the front. A man with a thick shock of white hair tilts his head and purses his lips.

"If you're planning to try and detain my uncle, Daniel Orien and his son Job, I'll be clear right now. They're all coming with me. We will leave in the next few hours, because your former leader John Roth sent a strike team to Baton Rouge, accelerating the death of almost all of the Marked kids who are still alive."

The man with all the white hair frowns. "Welcome to the CentiCouncil of the Unmarked, Ruby Carillon Behl Solomon. I'm sure we're all pleased to welcome an Unmarked citizen, one whom I understand recently turned seventeen and became an adult."

I don't repeat that I'm queen of WPN. I also don't ask who he is. Doing either thing would weaken my position, but I do offer this man a half smile. "I brought evidence with me, evidence that your Chancellor John Roth, worked with my father more than a decade back and was ultimately the man responsible for the release of Tercera." I hold up the partnership document.

I take a step forward, and the man at the podium inclines his head to the side.

Before I realize what's going on, Sam fires a dozen shots. Men all around the room fall to the ground, clutching their legs. Rhonda jogs around the room, collecting firearms from injured guards. Shouts fill the room, as well as the sound of chairs scraping on tile. The squawks and beeps from walkies, and groans of injured men surround me, but Sam steps up to my side. "Counselor Quinn. As Queen Solomon's Chief of Military and Strategic Defense, I obviously couldn't allow you to harm her."

"This girl walks in here threatening war. Does that mean you're a one man army now Samuel?" Counselor Quinn sneers. "Will you shoot us all? If this girl and her raving uncle are to be believed, your father caused the death of millions upon millions. I suppose you're primed to follow in his footsteps, starting with the murder of everyone in this room if we oppose you?"

My eyes flash. "Sam merely shot the men you planned to have take me out. We aren't killing anyone."

One voice rings out over the cacophony of the room. "But you killed my son, didn't you, *Queen Ruby*?"

I turn slowly to face Wesley's dad. His red-rimmed eyes meet mine and his mouth twists. "You and your insane uncle killed John Roth and my son when he wouldn't go along with your plan. You were desperate to free your aunt, and no story was too absurd, no action off limits."

I shake my head, no longer worried about anyone else in the room. "A few weeks ago, I'd take that blame you're laying at my feet. I'd wallow in it and punish myself for it. You know I didn't kill Wesley, and you know that because you raised your son. He's a hero and he was my best friend and he died to save me. Saying I killed him lessens his decision. When a bad man, John Roth, tried to do a bad thing, killing all of us because we'd discovered his long-buried secret—" I choke up and take a big breath so I can continue. The room has fallen utterly silent. "When John Roth tried to kill me, and Sam couldn't save me, Wesley dove over the side of a bridge, taking John with him. In that moment, with no time to think, Wesley Fairchild showed his true colors, proving himself a hero and saving my life."

Mayor Fairchild's face falls, his eyes locked on mine. He shakes his head, very slightly.

A single tear runs down my face. "Wesley has been my best friend for years, sir. I would do anything to bring him back to you. I wish he hadn't sacrificed himself for me, but he did." I look around the room at the men and women gathered here today, deciding the fate of Rafe and all the other Marked kids. Deciding how the world will look in a week, a month, and a year. "I am leaving with my aunt and uncle and their two brave children, and we're going to try and set things right. We believe we may have found a cure to Tercera. We won't know until we have time to run some tests, but if we have even the slightest chance to cure the Marked kids who are on death's door, we need to take it."

"We can't free a confessed criminal." Counselor Quinn bangs his hand on the podium. "In the absence of our Chancellor, and in light of the charges laid against him, I call for a vote of no confidence."

"Let me be very clear," I say. "Your first vote will be with regard to my aunt. And if you vote against freeing her and try to hold me here, you will be declaring open war with World Peace Now. They have tanks, they have jets with missiles, and they have a standing army that will consume the Unmarked government whole. Don't worry though. After we've wiped you all out, I'll be happy to step in and clean up the mess."

A tremendously large sound, one unlike any I've ever heard, starts from the south and grows, culminating with a whooshing sound overhead. The chairs shake, the floors vibrating beneath me. I hunch down while all around me Counselors duck and huddle under the tables.

"What was that?" I ask Sam.

He shakes his head. "I don't know, but it's not something the Unmarked ordered."

Banging at the double doors startles me.

"Answer that," Counselor Quinn orders.

The man closest to the door turns toward me.

"Don't look at her," Counselor Quinn shouts. "She's nothing to you."

"Respectfully sir, her Chief of Defense is holding the only active firearm in the room."

"You can open it," I say.

I brace myself for hundreds of armed Unmarked soldiers to pour into the room. Sam turns and aims his guns at the door, his hands steady and his eyes flashing.

When the man opens the door, and I catch my first glimpse of the soldiers on the other side, I almost stumble back. "Frank?"

Frank's face lights up when he sees me. "Your Majesty!" He bows deeply and then straightens. "Your mother and brother sent us to relay your message. I'm so glad to find you here."

A tight little knot I didn't even realize existed in my chest eases. Josephine and Adam are okay. I breathe in and out once, then twice. Frank bows deeply and the men standing behind him do the same. I cross the few steps that separate us and hiss. "Stand up." More loudly, so the rest of the room can hear, I ask, "How many of you are there?"

Frank glances around the room. "Only fifteen hundred soldiers came, Your Highness. Adam didn't want to frighten the Unmarked, but we wanted to make sure you were safe. Also, he sent two fighter jets. They're flying above the city now, waiting to see whether you require an airstrike."

I turn toward the front of the room and put my hands on my hips. "How about it, Counselor Quinn?" I spin around, making eye contact with men and women across the room. "CentiCouncil? I have evidence." I wave the partnership paperwork at them. "I've got witnesses." I point at Frank, Sam, Rhonda, my uncle and Job. "And I have an army. All I'm asking for is that you release my wrongfully accused aunt. Do we need that airstrike, or can you see reason?"

CHAPTER 18

The CentiCouncil unanimously votes to release Anne Orien and remand her into my care. They also readily offer the supplies I need and access to the equipment I want, but only on condition that I send the army directly back to Galveston. Do not pass go, do not collect two hundred dollars.

Frank and Paul don't like it, but they reverse direction and head back, making plenty of threats to return immediately if I don't quickly follow. I tell them to have Adam send me aid in Baton Rouge as soon as he can.

Counselor Quinn releases Dan and Job and signs Anne Orien's pardon, and we're ready to depart. I spin on my heel and almost slam right into Mayor Fairchild.

I pull up abruptly, Sam's hands bracing me on either side.

Mayor Fairchild's eyes follow the motion and I feel guilty about Sam. I shouldn't because I had Wesley's blessing, but I do. Maybe I always will in my heart of hearts.

"I don't think I can ever really convey how sorry I am. About Wesley." My eyes well with tears again and my hands clench into fists, my nails digging into my palms. "It shouldn't have been him."

"Wesley always said you reminded him of a gale force wind stuffed into a teakettle," Mayor Fairchild says. "I never saw it. You were so timid around me, so soft-spoken and unsure."

I look down at the ground, my feet not even visible in this stupid ball gown.

"I saw it today, Ruby. I saw what Wesley always saw in you, from the very beginning. And you're right." Mayor Fairchild's lips compress and his hands shake. "I dealt with losing Wesley last month when I heard he was Marked. It felt like a knife sliced up my insides that day. Horror, sorrow, and an underlying feeling of guilt, because I knew he had Marked someone else. You."

I shake my head. "It was an accident, a misunderstanding. And I'm fine."

Mayor Fairchild shakes his head. "He told me when I saw him again that it was the worst mistake he ever made, not going to quarantine, his greatest regret. He told me you were the miracle that redeemed him from it. He told me that about you, right before he snuck out and left with you."

Tears stream silently down my face, and Sam's arms wrap around me from behind.

"Wesley loved you, and I'm not surprised he did as you say. He was a hero, and I'm free to be proud of him again. Unreservedly proud. He wouldn't want me to blame you or be angry with you, and I don't want to lessen his decision." He nods stiffly. "I need some time to be as gracious as I should, but I'm going to try not to be angry at you. Now go save as many of those kids as you can." He whispers this last part. "And tell those kids about my son and his sacrifice when you do it."

"I will," I promise.

We leave the Jeep behind so that Uncle Dan's friend can load it up with the supplies we need. Rubbing alcohol, syringes, fluids, and bandages. Rhonda explains where he should go to retrieve the Land Rover, too.

Pardon in hand, we all jog past the old Tennessee State Senate building and the Musician's Hall of Fame, its front doors now wide open, all the artifacts long since looted. By the time we cross the James Robertson Parkway, my hands are shaking. I'm sick of wearing this ball gown, especially now that it makes it even harder for my short legs to keep up with everyone else's long ones.

"We should've insisted on taking the car," I mutter.

When we finally walk up the steps to the white brick holding facility, I bite my lip. I can't wait to see my aunt again. Since I last saw her she's been Marked, and I found out she lied not only about my dad's involvement with Tercera, but also about who I really am. How different could my experience in Galveston have been if I'd known who I was before I crossed that bridge?

How different would my life have been if I'd known she wasn't really my aunt all along? Would I have felt more left out and unloved? Or would I have known each and every day that even though we weren't biologically linked, she had chosen me? Would I have grown up happier, knowing my dad gave up everything to keep me, instead of being stuck having to raise me alone after my mom died? Would the truth have broken me or given me wings?

I'll never know, which in the end is why I have to forgive her.

When we walk through the door, a short guard with thinning black hair sits behind a desk playing solitaire. Sam isn't the most patient guy to begin with, but today we're all impatient.

"I'm Samuel Roth. Your name is?"

The guard's eyes bulge, and he stammers. "St-St-Stuart."

"Nice to meet you Stuart." Sam leans on the desk and his jacket falls open, displaying the gun resting on his hip. The balding man shoves his chair back. I knew Sam was a legend at the games, but I didn't realize people were scared of him here.

Sam slams the pardon down on the desk and grunts. "This pardon for my girlfriend's aunt, Anne Orien, is pretty clear and quite simple. We're here to collect her."

Stuart's eyes widen and he points at the elevator bay. We all start for it when Stuart clears his voice. "I meant to say that, ah, the, well."

"Spit it out, Stu," Uncle Dan says.

We're all a little crabby, too, it seems.

"The elevators are broken."

Sam rolls his eyes, which may be the first time I've seen him do that, and pivots on his heel. I follow him to the stairwell and when we turn toward it, Sam reaches for my hand again. Grouchy, threatening Sam is gone in a blink. My heart rate slows, and my shaking abates.

It doesn't take long to locate my aunt on the second floor in one of the locked quarantine rooms.

"Anne." Uncle Dan rushes to the window and presses his hand to the glass.

She places her hand on the opposite side and I sigh. I was lucky people as good as them raised me instead of David Solomon. I learned love instead of torture. I followed their example to a healthy, strong guy who supports me in making hard decisions. I shudder to think how I would have turned out if I'd followed Josephine and David's example instead.

The guard monitoring the halls of the second floor unlocks the door for us after one glance at the pardon.

Sam and I linger in the hallway to let Dan and her kids greet Aunt Anne first. Uncle Dan swings her around and kisses her full on the mouth while the guard looks on, horrified.

"He's immune," I say.

The guard practically chokes.

Uncle Dan catches her up, telling her how Dad injected me with antibodies. He explains that now they've all been inoculated, so she can touch them without fear.

"Where's Ruby? Didn't I see her?" Aunt Anne's voice drifts toward me.

"I'm here," I say. "I thought I'd give you a minute with your family first."

Aunt Anne's been Marked, joined the Marked community, investigated suppressant failures, attempted to notify Port Gibson, suffered through a trial, and then been stuffed into a cell to await her own death with no real hope for a reprieve. In spite of all that, she looks exactly the same as the last time I saw her. Her clothes are neat and tidy, a light brown pants suit, and her hair is pulled back, not a strand out of place.

Her heels clack on the tile floor when she walks toward me and pulls me against her chest.

"Nonsense. Ruby, you are my family. I should've told you the truth before, but I didn't want you to ever think—"

"It's okay," I say. "I'm pretty sure I understand."

As we explain the rest of what happened, she wastes no time reaching the right conclusions. "You don't want to try and cure me with your blood, even if it's not too late, because we need my blood to test Sam's on."

I nod. "If I'm wrong, Sam's blood won't help. If I'm right. . ."

Aunt Anne calls out to the guard who unlocked her door. "Randall, I'm going to need access to some of the testing equipment. You guys have it all in storage on the third floor, don't you?"

"Yes ma'am, we do," he says. "I can take you upstairs, or we can bring it down."

Aunt Anne works out the details with Randall, who treats her more like a friend than a detainee. Sam and I follow her upstairs, Uncle Dan, Job and Rhonda close on our heels.

"Missed me, I take it?" Aunt Anne laughs. "Why don't you three see if you can gather up all my things so we can leave as soon as possible? I promise not to disappear in a poof this time, okay?"

Uncle Dan frowns, but they head back downstairs.

Once we reach the largest room on the third floor, Aunt Anne croons. "What a beauty. Look at this! The doc who owned this practice didn't scrimp. You're lucky the Nashville quarantine rooms were set up in a Pathology lab. Otherwise we'd need to go hunt one of these down."

"See this?" She waves at a desk looking thing with a huge box beginning on the floor and extending nearly to the ceiling on the left. The largest part has a sequence of white boxes and cylinders over the main mechanism with an interconnecting series of containers. It's the column for electron beam generation, the specimen chamber, and the vacuum pump of a scanning electron microscope. I know because I've used one before as part of an experiment in Science.

"Does it still work?"

She nods. "I used it last year after I came here for a presentation. It hasn't been perfectly maintained, but it's been rehabbed well enough."

Aunt Anne sets me to cleaning off the electronic console and display monitors.

"I need a few options for a negative stain." She glances

at Sam. "Viruses are small, and Ruby says Don described this one as quite small. I'll need a special stain to see it. Which is probably why we never saw it, if it existed during your clinical trials."

Sam nods.

Once we're ready, Aunt Anne draws her own blood, and then hands me the other syringe.

"You want me to draw his blood?" I ask.

She says, "Sam would probably prefer that I never draw his blood again."

The corner of Sam's mouth turns up. "She's not wrong."

I draw it, marveling at his big, easy to find veins. We mix up several samples to test various stains.

My aunt puts the first two samples under the microscope, and turns it on. Once the image finally comes up, she uses the tracking ball to shift it until one of the samples comes into view. She magnifies and shifts, magnifies and shifts. She shakes her head over both. When she replaces them with two other options, I close my eyes and say a little prayer. If there's something to see, please God let us find it so we can figure out how best to replicate it fast enough to save these poor kids. A few minutes later, the image appears, and Aunt Anne magnifies and shifts, magnifies and shifts. Then she exhales loudly, and her hand waves me over.

I squint at the monitor, not sure what I'm seeing.

"These viruses are dead now, killed by the electron blasts, but look here Ruby." Aunt Anne points at several tiny puffy spots, frozen in time. "I think that's Sam's virus."

My heart speeds. "You think there is one, then?"

She nods. "Look right there." She points.

Sam peers over my shoulder, which makes me smile.

"This is where Tercera has invaded my cells." There's a big blob with what appear to be short noodles clustered around it. Her cell, invaded by Tercera. The squid-like shapes surround her cell, their largish heads attaching to the cell wall, and long tentacles spreading away, hijacking it. "Tercera resembles Ebola sort of, but look here." She points at the edge, where the tiny puffy spots converge on the end of the tentacles. "I think your virus is eating Tercera, just like Don said it would."

Once we've found a successful stain, we wait and scan more images, giving Sam's virus more time to work. At two hours out from the combination of Aunt Anne's blood with Sam's, the Tercera virus has been entirely replaced by the hacker virus. "It outnumbers Tercera four to one once it's consumed the larger virus. What an efficient little bug."

"Can we start creating more while we travel to Baton Rouge?" I ask. "We're running out of time."

Aunt Anne shakes her head. "It's harder than that. Viruses can't be grown in a nutrient broth like bacteria can. They require living cells. I need to run more tests to determine exactly how large a dose of virus we'll need to give each patient."

"Can we run those numbers while we drive?" Sam asks. "Because those kids are out of hope. I worry what they might do, or even once we reach them, how much time we have."

I call Job up from below, and he helps his mom and I for about three more hours. Aunt Anne runs tests and does calculations, and Job and I direct Sam, Rhonda and Uncle Dan on which things to load up in the cars. Aunt Anne injects herself with five ccs of Sam's blood before we leave.

"Are you worried about blood types?" I ask.

Anne shrugs. "Sam's O positive, so I'll be fine. It's not really a universal donor, not like you Ruby with your O neg, but it's awfully close."

"You're A, right?" I ask.

Aunt Anne nods. "I am, so O positive is fine for me. And if my numbers are right, I should be entirely cured and ready to donate hacker virus riddled blood to the cause myself by the time we arrive."

"I'm happy to be injected as well," I say. "Then we'll have more people ready to donate."

Sam shakes his head. "I've had quite enough of you getting your blood drawn, thanks."

I roll my eyes.

"Don had concerns about mixing the hacker virus with your super shot of antibodies. I'd rather test that under a microscope before we try it on you."

"Ruby gave me her blood already, for what it's worth," Sam says. "And I felt fine."

Anne shrugs. "Still, better safe than sorry. I'd expect any issues to show in the reverse. Have any of you not been given antibodies?"

Uncle Dan shakes his head.

"Very well." Aunt Anne sighs. "I hope there's a microscope there I can use in Baton Rouge."

Job smiles. "I'm sure we can find one. It's a big town. I have a pretty decent microscope at my lab, but it's not an electron microscope. Once we get there I'll talk to my team, whoever's still functioning, and we'll find what you're looking for. You're bringing the sodium silico-tungstate, right? I doubt we'll find a lot of negative stains there. Not readily in any case."

Aunt Anne smiles and pats his cheek. "I was born at night, but not last night. I've got it packed to take. I'm also bringing some of the neutral phosphotungstic acid, just in case. I didn't have time to check it, but it does quite well with viruses that dissociate at low pH, even if the contrast isn't quite as good."

We leave for Baton Rouge at sunset, routing away from

New Orleans, because there's no way I want to bump into my dear cousin Sawyer. Not yet anyway.

Luckily the roads are fairly well maintained, and we make good time even though we're driving at night. We stop briefly in Birmingham to deliver a message for the leadership there from Interim Chancellor Quinn, who appears eager to drop the 'Interim' from his title. I don't really care who leads the Unmarked, as long as I don't have to get involved. And anyway, this Quinn guy can't be worse than John Roth.

We don't take the time to check the cars or their gauges, but we should have. I'm asleep while we're driving past Meridian, Mississippi, but a few miles past the town, Sam's swearing wakes me up.

"What's wrong?" I rub my eyes.

Job bangs his fist on the dash. "Stupid car died. Electronics went out."

"Could be the alternator, maybe." I climb out of the warm spot I've made on the backseat bench, and circle around the car to aim my flashlight under the hood. "Yep, I think it is."

I look around us. Nothing for miles.

"We need to find a compatible alternator." I read the specifications and repeat them a few times in my mind. "We can't fit all the junk in the back, plus you, me, and Job in the jeep with Rhonda, Aunt Anne and Uncle Dan. We need all that stuff, right Job?"

He nods.

"Well," I say. "I'm going to start hiking. An alternator we salvage shouldn't be ruined from ten years of disuse, necessarily. I'll look for one, or maybe we'll get lucky and see a parts store."

I'm about a hundred and fifty yards from the Land Cruiser before Sam reaches me in the Jeep.

"Where's everyone else?" I climb into the passenger side.

He reaches for my hand. "Thanks for getting me out of my funk. It just seems like everything is going wrong."

"We had good weather for the most part between here and Nebraska," I say. "WPN showed up just in time, and you do have the hacker virus inside you."

Sam sighs. "You're right. Some things are working. The others are gonna try to sleep for a little bit until we find something. It didn't make sense to split up, and no reason to go hiking on foot, since we still have one functioning car."

We don't find a parts store, but we do locate a Toyota truck with an alternator that works ten miles or so away. I'm feeling pretty good about my resourcefulness, right up until I try to help replace the alternator and it pinches the meaty part of my thumb.

"Ouch," I complain.

"Okay that's it, you're done." Sam takes the screwdriver from me and hands me the flashlight. "You hold this."

Once he loosens the bolts and yanks on the alternator to remove it from the mounting bracket, his hand slams into the hinge. He exhales and I glance down. Blood covers his knuckles.

"What a waste," I say.

He frowns. "So now I'm the walking blood bag, huh?"

"I hated it, too."

Sam shrugs. "I don't mind, actually. If this works to save some of them, I won't mind at all."

I know what he means.

We finally reach Baton Rouge right before noon on Friday. Almost four full days after the accelerant bombs exploded. Rafe doesn't meet us at the barricades. In fact, no one does. The once busy streets are empty: no work noise, no laughter, no shouts, and no peering faces.

I hate the silence.

We drive up to the main hospital where Wesley parked almost two weeks ago, and a wave of sorrow crashes over me. Please let us not be too late for all of them. By the time Sam and I open the car doors, Aunt Anne has already climbed out, bag in hand. She prepared more than a hundred doses on her way here, ready to begin immediately.

We walk toward the entrance, my heart beating a staccato rhythm. Where is everyone? Are they already dead? All of them? I think about baby Rose and Libby and bite back a sob.

When a short kid with blonde hair meets us at the door of the hospital, I almost clap with glee. "Oh, you're alive. Where is everyone else?"

The boy looks up at me from under the fullest eyelashes I've ever seen. "Rafe called for all of us, everyone who wasn't accelerated, to come here and take care of them that was."

"And you all came?" Aunt Anne asks. "How wonderful."

The boy shakes his head. "Not everyone, but some. We've been trying to feed them that would eat, and make sure they have water."

"We need to see Rafe right away," I say. "Can you take us to him?"

The boy nods.

"What's your name, son?" Aunt Anne asks.

"Brayden, ma'am."

"Thank you Brayden. Before we go inside, I need to ask one more favor. I've got something here that will help you. Something we need to inject you with. Will you allow it?"

Brayden steps backward, his eyes darting from my aunt

to me and back. "Who are you? Does that mean poke me with a needle? Why do you need to do that?"

Aunt Anne hesitates and glances my way. I'm sure she doesn't want to say it's a cure, lest it create some kind of frenzied panic.

"You know Rafe was working on a solution," I say. "Well, we were part of his plan. We left to get something we needed and we're back. This medicine should make you stronger, and you can help take care of the rest of them more effectively."

He looks at each one of us in turn. "You people ain't Marked, but you're standing here with no fear?"

"Yes Brayden, we want to help," I say. "No weapons, no threats. Just medicine. Will you allow it?"

He lets us inject him and becomes our first patient. We follow him to Rafe's room, almost at the end of the long hallway.

"Why inject him now?" I whisper. "Shouldn't we save the doses we have for the worst cases?"

"We need to inject as many healthy-ish ones as we can on the front end," Aunt Anne says. "Hopefully within a day we'll be able to use their blood to treat others. The weak ones will probably be useless for treating others."

I'm glad Aunt Anne's here to think about these things. I hated being Job's backup. Now I'm not the B team, I'm a far distant C team.

I'm even happier when we walk into Rafe's room. I would've punched him in the nose and never looked back on Monday night. Today I can barely handle the sight of him lying on a hospital bed, his face so pale it almost blends with the bed sheet, his arms limp at his sides, and sores on his cheek near his right temple and on his hand. I look away.

"Rafe," Sam says. "You're still alive."

Rafe shifts and tries to sit up. "You came back." His words state a fact, but his eyes shine with hope.

"We did," Sam says. "And we think we have a cure."

Aunt Anne crosses the room purposefully and injects Rafe with one of her prepared syringes. "This should help. Quickly, I hope."

"How much do you have?" Rafe mumbles.

"We have ninety-eight more doses right now," I say, "with more to come."

"Ninety eight?" The corners of his mouth droop and his hands shake. "That's all?"

"We're preparing as much as we can, as quickly as it's safe," Aunt Anne says. "We'll treat the healthiest patients first in order to culture more of the cure. Then we'll triage everyone and prioritize the sickest patients."

He nods. "It *is* a cure, then?"

Aunt Anne says, "As soon as we locate the proper equipment, we'll confirm that Tercera's gone from my system, replaced by my brother's hacker virus. We do believe it is, yes."

Rafe collapses back against the bed, his eyes closed, but a smile on his lips.

Aunt Anne turns to me. "We have a lot to do. First and foremost, we need to find someplace that has a scanning electron microscope. If I can see how quickly the hacker virus takes over Tercera at the volume I'm injecting, it will tell me what doses to plan. Then we can prepare the doses, test the children for their blood type and isolate which doses to give to each child."

I lay my hand on Aunt Anne's arm. "These kids are going into total organ failure *right now*. We don't have time to refine this. We need to take our cues from the patients, not the microscope. And if someone gets a few ccs of the wrong blood type, what's the worst that happens? Because if we have to blood type the kids before we can treat them." I shake my head.

Aunt Anne's nostrils flare. "I hate that we have so little time, but you're right. I've grown so used to research that I'm running this like an experiment, and it more closely resembles a trauma code. A few ccs of blood that's the wrong type might not be good, and it varies widely by person and blood compatibility, but it shouldn't do more than make them ill. When you compare it to death. . ."

She spins on her heel and marches into the hall. "You there." She points at Brayden. "Bring me nineteen of your friends who aren't accelerated. Immediately."

"How much blood can we take from Sam, maximum?" I ask. "It's ten percent of blood volume, right?"

Aunt Anne shakes her head. "Sam, are you okay with being weak and maybe even sleeping for a while?"

He glances at me and I nod. "But I'm not alright with him being at risk of dying himself."

Aunt Anne says, "What's your weight and height? Two-twenty, and six-four, right?"

Sam says, "Two-thirty, close enough."

Aunt Anne closes her eyes, her lips moving silently. "That's around six and a half liters, total volume, right Job? Check my math."

Job's lips move, and his fingers tap his thumbs on both hands. He nods. "Yeah, six point seven five, I think."

"That means ten percent is a little more than half a liter," I say.

"He'll survive higher, like twenty or thirty percent at least," Aunt Anne says.

"No, he lost half his blood volume two weeks ago. We can't risk that, not again."

"It's me," Sam says. "I'm fine."

"We already drew a quarter unit for testing and those

initial doses." Aunt Anne taps her lip with her finger. "We can draw another liter probably, without doing any permanent damage, maybe a liter and a half."

Job frowns. "That's enough for what? Eight hundred doses."

She nods. "Twelve hundred if we draw a liter and a half. It's what we can do right now."

"Draw more," Sam says.

"No." I take his arm, visions of him lying in a pool of expanding blood flooding my brain. "Stop being heroic and be smart. This is triple the typical maximum draw. It's enough."

Brayden arrives with more Marked kids and I count. Twenty-four.

"She said nineteen," I say.

He shrugs. "I asked for some volunteers and this is who came."

Aunt Anne nods. "You did great, son. Job can you please administer the doses to them immediately and keep them all here? Brayden, how many Marked patients do we have?"

He looks down at his boot. "We aren't sure, honestly, but we think close to eighty-thousand were accelerated." His voice drops to a whisper. "A few thousand have already died."

My aunt's face remains impassive, but her shoulders droop and her hands shake. No matter what we do, we can't save that many. Not even close.

John Roth will have a lot to atone for if there's an afterlife.

"Brayden, I need your friends to come with me so we can test you near Job's lab. We're dosing all of you first so that you can help us grow a cure for everyone else. The accelerated kids won't be able to donate, not while their organs are recovering. Only those of you who answered Rafe's call and weren't accelerated have a hope of saving them now." Aunt Anne turns to me. "We'll need to give every other dose of the initial rounds to the unaccelerated volunteers. The bigger the volunteers are the better, because the blood volume will be higher, which means greater blood draw capacity later." She turns back toward the Marked kids who answered the first call. "Go and call as many of the friends who came with you as you can, but don't tell them why. We can't risk a panic. Can you do that?"

When Brayden nods, she turns toward Job. "Please take your father and Rhonda and find me supplies. We have syringes by the truckload, but we need more bandages and rubbing alcohol. We really need to find a functioning electron microscope too, so I can determine when their blood can be used to treat others." Aunt Anne wrings her hands. "It's like I'm doing this blind. If only I could test my progress. I'm twelve hours ahead of them, so we could get a read on the twelve hour mark immediately."

Over the next two hours, Aunt Anne sets up camp in the Life Share Blood Center and teaches me to prepare doses. We draw a liter and a half from Sam, and I convert them all into doses of the hacker virus. Brayden brings round after round of volunteers, and I inject them one at a time. We instruct them to report back in twelve hours. We dose the first hundred and fifty quickly, but then twenty minutes pass before we see Brayden again.

"What's taking so long?" I ask.

He frowns. "I found all the volunteers that are close, but now I'm having to walk further and further away to find them."

"I'll get you some keys to one of our cars and you can use it to bring people faster."

"I don't know how to drive," he says.

I roll my eyes heavenward. "Alright, then wait here until my cousins come back. I'll have one of them ferry you around."

In the meantime, I run more numbers.

"Aunt Anne, check me on these figures," I say. "If these kids are roughly half Sam's size, we can draw approximately half as much blood, so half to three quarters a liter each."

Anne nods. "That might be a little aggressive, but we can shift that down a bit. Go on."

"If we use the same ratio as we did with Sam's blood, and we won't know until we check the blood whether that's viable, we would have enough for sixty-thousand doses from the hundred and fifty we've already dosed. Hopefully within twelve hours."

Aunt Anne looks over my numbers and sighs. "It's rough, but you're not far off. We're close. Perhaps we should start dosing the roughest looking of those who are accelerated with the rest of Sam's donation. That will start to give us an idea of what sort of recovery to expect."

The door slams open. Job pants and leans over, resting his hands on his knees.

"Are you okay?" I ask.

He holds up one hand. "I'm fine, just excited. I found a microscope, and the room that housed it was interior. It wasn't exposed to anything other than dust and even that's minimal. I think it still works!"

CHAPTER 19

Sam's asleep, so I jot down a quick note telling him where we've gone. I tell Brayden to hold off on finding new recruits for the time being, and I take a sample of his blood to test. Once we have everything ready, Aunt Anne and I race out to the car. She checks the back to make sure she has her negative stains and specimen containers, and then we drive toward Job's find.

He pulls up in front of a dark stone office building more than five miles away from the blood center.

"How'd you find this?" I ask.

He shrugs. "I found the address on a brochure advertising to pay for subjects for a research study. We got lucky, I hope."

"What are we going to do about power?" I ask.

"I sent Rhonda to find a portable generator," he says. "Rafe has some and I told her where he kept them."

We race upstairs to the fourth floor and sure enough, there it is. My aunt sighs.

By the time Rhonda arrives, we've cleaned up the microscope and prepared the samples. We boot it up after the generator goes online, and the console lights up. I whoop with joy, and so does Job. Aunt Anne smiles calmly. She places the samples of her blood, and the sample from Brayden's blood, inside the specimen chamber. The three minutes it takes to process the scan creep by, feeling more like an hour. My eyelids drift closed. I haven't slept well in days, and it's catching up to me in a big way.

The noise of my aunt's hands moving on the tracking ball jolts me awake and I focus on the screen, blinking my eyes to clear them. I don't see any tentacles poking out of the cell. Fluff balls float all around it, though.

For the first time in my life, I hear Aunt Anne whoop for joy.

It's probably best she doesn't repeat that, but Job and I drown her out with our cheers. We check Brayden's blood next, at the three-hour mark.

The sample includes fourteen cells, and only four of them still have Tercera tentacles remaining. The sample shows dozens of hacker viruses floating around, and on two cells they're already actively attacking one of the tentacle viruses.

"Fourteen hours out and no sign of Tercera, three hours out and it's on the run." Aunt Anne's eyes well up. "My brother found the cure. Now let's go treat as many kids as we can and hope their organs can recover from whatever damage was already sustained."

The time between our discovery and sunset passes too quickly. Job doses the patients closest to us with the rest of Sam's samples and the samples I make from Aunt Anne's blood. We segregate those treated with my aunt's blood for signs of an allergic reaction. Rhonda and Uncle Dan bring in a steady stream of syringes. My wrists ache, my back throbs and my head pounds, but I keep going.

Poor Aunt Anne rests after her blood donation for all of

half an hour, sipping water quickly, before she climbs off of the cot and begins to check on each patient one at a time, assessing organ damage and watching them for reactions to her donation.

We push on into the night, notifying the infected and identifying and locating as many as we can. When the alarm sounds at ten a.m. signaling the twelve hour mark from first injection team, a cheer goes up in the blood lab. Brayden reports to have his blood drawn, and we test it on the microscope as quickly as possible. It looks just as good as my aunt's did. Aunt Anne and I work as quickly as we can to convert his blood into new doses. I slap my face every twenty or thirty minutes to keep awake, and try and avoid making any mistakes. Even so, a few of the doses are doubled, wasting precious resources.

Just after one a.m. Sam puts his arms around me and pulls me back. "You need to take a break."

I shake my head. "I can't." My voice drops to a whisper. "Job told me they've found five hundred more dead since we arrived. I literally kill people if I sleep."

"I heard that. He also told me it was to be expected. Eighty-five thousand kids in varying stages of the viral progression were accelerated. Some of them weren't going to make it no matter what you did from day two on." He kisses my forehead. "You can and should sleep, at least a few hours. This process needs to be handled right and quickly, and to do that you need a two hour nap. Your aunt does too."

I open my mouth to protest, but Sam scoops me up and carries me over to a cot. "Ten years ago, I threatened to force feed you. This time I'm threatening to sit on you until you pass out if you won't go to sleep of your own volition."

I nod and close my eyes. "Two hours, Sam. Not a minute more."

His hand strokes my hair once, and I don't recall anything else until his hands gently shake my shoulders to wake me up.

I roll over and bat at him. "Go away. Too tired."

"You made me promise," Sam's voice says. "Two hours. It's been almost three, because you wouldn't even open your eyes at two."

When I force my eyelids up, my eyeballs feel like they've been scrubbed with steel wool. I smash my face with the heels of my hands until my eyes start processing light again, and shove up into a seated position. My neck screams, my back shouts and I want to take some acetaminophen and lay back down. Until I think about Liberty and Rose, who we still hadn't located when I went to sleep. They can't be dead already. They can't, and I need to keep working so we can save all the Libbys and Roses out there.

"I'm up, I'm up, I promise."

Aunt Anne's already drawing blood from one of the Marked kids, a small, dark-skinned little girl, who can't possibly weigh eighty pounds.

"Don't take too much," I say.

Anne snorts. "Thanks for the helpful advice, Rip Van Winkle. I looked up the right amount. I'm too tired to estimate properly."

She and I prepare more doses while Job, Rhonda and Uncle Dan administer them. I almost drop the syringe I'm filling when the shouting outside begins.

I stumble out the front door, Sam at my heels.

The last thing I expect to see in the hours before dawn is Adam's handsome face. "Ruby!" He runs toward me and pulls me into a big hug.

"Adam, what are you doing here?"

Four huge, military looking trucks are stopped so that their headlights blind us. The dull roar of their engines running in the street behind him would've alerted us to their presence before the shouting if only we'd been awake enough to notice it. When I pull away from Adam and squint in their direction, I make out men with guns drawn peering out from the windows of every truck.

"We left as soon as I got the message from Frank and Paul." Adam sounds annoyed.

"I'm so glad you're here, but I figured you'd send aid, not come yourself."

He shakes his head. "I'd have been here before you if the idiots had sent the jets ahead with a message. As it was, the jets arrived and told us they weren't needed. No one told me you were headed here instead of back to us or that you needed supplies until Frank returned."

I hug Adam again, happier than I expected to see him alive. I hardly know him, but I trust him already. And now he's come through for me twice. "You really saved me back there in Nashville."

"Your guards arrived explaining what you went to Nebraska to find." He shakes his head reprovingly. "They also said you sent them all out of concern for my safety. That's sweet, but if I really were in danger, I'd have wanted you to keep as many of them with you as possible."

I shrug. "I've got Sam."

Sam reaches down and takes my hand in his.

"You didn't need to worry. Everything's safe and well in Galveston, but I figured if you were coming back to Baton Rouge, you might have located the one in a million cure you hoped for. I'll admit." Adam ducks his head sheepishly. "I wanted to see for myself."

"We did find the cure, and not a minute too soon." Even through my bone deep exhaustion, a smile tugs at the corner of my mouth.

"If that's true, why do you look so awful?" He wrinkles his nose. "And not to be rude, but you stink pretty bad."

I snort. "Minutes matter right now. In fact, I shouldn't have stopped even to talk to you. To say we're understaffed would be the understatement of the week."

"Good thing I'm here with reinforcements, then." He waves at the trucks, and the men drop their guns and climb out. Frank and Paul are some of the first men who reach us, and I grin at them both. They salute me, and thankfully this time they don't bow. They're learning.

Once the men are out, they begin unloading the backs of the trucks. Food, IV fluids, IV kits and bags, boxes and boxes of medicine, and case upon case upon case of liquids. Water, juice, and soda.

"I brought a half dozen nurses, and two physicians as well. I thought you might need some people with medical training."

"Adam, if you weren't my brother and I didn't love Sam so much, I'd kiss you right now."

"I'll settle for one more solid hug," he says. "We have a few hundred of those to catch up on. I've only had a sister for a few weeks, but I missed you a lot when you left. More than I thought I would."

I wrap my arms around him as tightly as I can, but when my eyes begin to drift closed, I straighten up and pull away. "Well, we better get them started."

Dr. Claudia Flores exits the truck in the very back, surveying her surroundings with a scrunched nose and a glare.

"Oh good grief," I say. "Did you have to bring her?"

Adam's eyebrows rise. "You don't like her? She's the best physician we have. The staff calls her Mílagro trabajadora or something like that. It means miracle worker—"

"I know what it means." I exhale heavily and turn

toward the lab. "Better tell them all to come in. We don't have any time to spare."

We inject the new recruits who I didn't formerly dose with antibodies with the hacker virus immediately, and start a timer for them. Another three-dozen donors might come in handy. Since they'll be exposed to Tercera non-stop for the first while, the hacker virus should replicate almost as quickly in their blood as it has in the Marked kids.

Aunt Anne places Dr. Flores in charge of treatment of the recovering patients and focuses herself on identifying which patients to dose next.

"You should sleep a few more hours," Sam says, "now that help is here."

I shake my head. "We're on day five since the acceleration. If we want any hope of saving the remaining infected patients, it has to be now, before the damage to their organs is irreversible. For many of them, it already is. The next ten hours are the most critical. I'll sleep after that."

He sighs. "Fine, but I can't stand around doing nothing any more. I'll ask Dan put me to work bringing patients in."

I grab his wrist. "You can't do that. You're not standing around like a bum. You're supposed to be recovering like all of them." I point at Brayden and the other early volunteers, all convalescing with IVs now that we have fluids. "You had almost three times as much blood drawn as you should have and even you will take time to recover from that loss."

Sam smiles. "I love that you're worried, but it's me. I'm completely fine."

I shake my head. "Samuel Roth, you push too hard. It's one of the things I love about you, but I want to keep loving it so. Go. Lay. Down. Right now!"

"I didn't want it to be this way, you know," Sam says.

I set the measuring tools down and turn to face him. "What way? What are you talking about?"

He sighs. "We can talk later. I don't want to distract you when you can't even take a shower." The sorrow in his eyes when he stands twists something in my heart.

"I can spare a few minutes. Please sit."

He glances at the nurses and another physician, Dr. Blackwell, who Aunt Anne's training.

"None of them will pay us any attention," I say.

"I believe you love me, but I know you were trying to decide between what you felt for me, and what you felt for Wesley." He sits on the stool again and runs his hands through his hair, pulling it out of its ponytail. It falls around his face like the hair of a Spartan warrior. "I didn't want to be chosen by default. I genuinely liked Wesley, and I'm sorry about what happened." He looks down at the ground. "It should've been me that died, not Wesley. I promised to protect you and I failed."

I take Sam's hand and wait until he meets my eyes. "Sam, you have never failed me in your life. You're tremendous and amazing, and—" I choke up. "If we'd had time, I would've talked to you before we reached Nebraska. You gave me space and I appreciate that, but I didn't need it, not really. I only needed to see that even though I do rash things and miscalculate, and even though I'm wrong sometimes, I'm good enough for you."

"You're better than me in almost every way," Sam says. "You always have been."

I snort. "Not even close, but I appreciate the sentiment."

"If Wesley hadn't died—"

I shake my head. "Wesley loved me, and I cared for him a great deal. Before I learned more about who I am and what I wanted, I thought he and I would be perfect. I had this lovely dream, this image of a fanciful future featuring domestic bliss in sleepy little Port Gibson. Life happened, though. Dreams don't withstand reality, but love survives and thrives among the real."

"If I could knit, I'd knit that into a pillow." Sam grins. "Love survives and thrives among the real."

I laugh out loud. "You can't knit something into a pillow."

"You can't?" Sam lifts one eyebrow. "You mean you don't know how? Or that it can't be done? Because I'm pretty sure it can."

I roll my eyes. "Knitting is for like sweaters. Look, the point is that Wesley knew, ever since you and I made that trip down to Galveston, that there's only been one man for me."

Sam's eyes are greener than ever before. He squeezes my hand.

"Wesley regretted almost Marking me from the very second he did it. He wished he was more of a warrior, more like you I think. He finally realized after we reached Port Gibson again that none of those things, not your healing abilities, or your fighting skills, or even your impossible-to-handle good looks were the reason I loved you more than him. You're still here with me, in spite of being shot six times. In spite of attacks, journeys, imprisonment, and my confusion about who I am and what I want."

"You picked me because I'm hard to kill?" Sam squints at me. "That's not very flattering. Cockroaches are hard to kill."

I swat his arm. "No, just listen. You're still here in spite of it all. Your brother told you I kissed Wesley and you didn't freak out. You were calm, so calm. You're my rock in a stormy sea. I love you because you're the other half that makes me whole, and because you get me, even when I don't get myself. I might have been happy with Wesley, if I'd never woken up and seen the real Sam, but I did. And from that moment when I sat next to you on the night of the Marked attack." I look down at my hands, and then up into his eyes. Eyes I wish I could never look away from. Eyes I trust, eyes that draw me in every single time I glance at them. "From that moment on, there's only been you for me."

Sam leans down and his lips brush mine. My heart pounds and the butterflies swoop and swirl in my chest.

I whisper, "I chose you, Samuel Roth, long before Wesley saved us all on that bridge. His choice may haunt me, actually it may haunt us both, but it doesn't change how I feel about you. It doesn't shift my feelings about us. We belong together, not apart, now and forever. That's my choice, and I'm ready to choose it over and over, every day, no matter what comes."

Sam's lips cover mine, and my arms reach up to circle his neck. He scoops me onto his lap and deepens the kiss. My hands run over the muscles in his shoulders and then his chest.

"Excuse me," a shrill voice says. "Anne Orien told me you could show me the syringes."

Sam shifts and I see Dr. Flores, toe tapping, eyes sparking, staring down her nose at us.

"I thought you were managing the patients who've been dosed already?"

She exhales heavily. "I am, but I need to know the basics of the process, so that I know what stage they're at and how the underlying method works."

"You don't know what a syringe is?" And she's WPN's best physician? I stifle a giggle. I want to tell her to shove off, but I think about sweet baby Rose and her mother. I lean my forehead against Sam's chest and breathe in and out once, and then I sit up and slide off his lap. Sam swats my backside before he goes looking for Uncle Dan to be put to work.

I walk through the process of how we prepare the doses with Dr. Flores, but she doesn't seem to care much. As I suspected, she just didn't want to watch Sam and I making out. My distaste for Dr. Flores aside, Adam's people are expediting things exponentially. If that means I need to suffer through tense interactions with Claudia Fancy Pants Flores, well, so be it.

After I've prepared the doses for the current blood draws, I decide to check on Rafe. It's been more than twelve hours since we dosed him, closer to eighteen actually, but we haven't seen him. I hope he's improved dramatically.

I wind my way down the street, watching the flurry of activity that had all but died off before we arrived. I hope it only increases over the next twelve hours. When I reach the hospital entrance, a sullen looking Marked girl in all black stops me. "State your purpose."

"I'm an aid worker, same as everyone. I need to talk to Rafe."

"Rafe's in a meeting with his chief security officer at present." The girl tosses her hair over her shoulder and rests her hand on a gun at her hip.

"He's meeting with Todd?"

Her eyes widen.

"I'm Ruby Behl, and I brought the cure here. I think he'll want to talk to me."

Sean turns a corner down the hall. I wave to catch his attention, and the sullen girl pulls her gun on me.

"Stop that Pam," Sean says. "Let Ruby through. I'll take her to see Rafe."

I roll my eyes at the overeager gate attendant. "I'm glad to see you up and walking. When were you dosed?"

Sean smiles, and it pulls at the skin of the enormous scar that covers his gaunt cheek. "Not quite ten hours ago. I felt good enough to eat a few hours later, and now I'm ready to dance."

I almost laugh until I realize he's not kidding. Compared to how he felt before, he's energized enough to dance a jig or something, which is exciting. I smile at him. "I'm so glad, Sean. Hopefully you'll be Mark and Tercera free in another day. It looks like your organs didn't suffer any permanent damage."

He nods. "I'm one of the lucky ones, I know."

I follow him down the hall and around a corner. Then we head up an elevator, and down another hallway.

"How many doses will you be able to make?" Sean stops in front of a door, his eyes cast downward, his boots shuffling when he asks.

"We plan to dose every single Marked patient in the next twelve hours. It's simply a matter of locating them all. There weren't a lot of protocols placed on where people chose to live."

He shrugs. "We did what we could."

I put a hand on his shoulder. "I know you did. You did really well. We're going to save every single person we can."

Sean meets my eyes. "I know you are. I'm sorry we locked you up. I should've let you go, and I'm sorry I didn't."

"For what it's worth, Sam's sorry he knocked you unconscious," I say.

"No he isn't." Sean smiles.

I shake my head. "No, he isn't."

Sean says, "Dax still hates him for that gunshot, but

Sam does what needs to be done and doesn't feel guilty about it. It's necessary right now, impressive actually. I admire him for it, because guilt eats at me all the time."

"Me too."

Sean pushes the door open. "Rafe, Ruby wanted to check on you."

Rafe and Todd sit across from each other, intently focused on some papers on the round table in front of them. "Ruby. Come in."

Rafe's hair isn't spiked and it looks inexplicably bizarre falling softly around his face, like he's a normal person now and not a punk rock cartoon. He's dressed in fresh clothes and he's taken a shower, which is more than I can say for myself. Todd looks almost exactly the same as he did the last time I saw him.

"How do you feel?" I ask. "Both of you. When did you get dosed, Todd?"

Todd looks pointedly at Sean. "Thanks for bringing her to us, but if you're up to it, you should resume your post."

Sean ducks out and closes the door behind him.

"I was dosed an hour or two after Sean," Todd says. "I feel amazing too. I hadn't progressed as far as most because I was in my first year. No second year symptoms yet when the accelerant hit."

"How did you get Marked?" I ask. "I don't think I ever heard."

Todd grimaces. "I was the leader of one of David Solomon's border guards, tasked with keeping the area near Galveston clear of Marked individuals. When a Marked kid jumped from a tree and landed on my back, my entire unit turned on me. They were going to shoot me like they shot my attacker. The honorable thing would've been to let them."

"Are you saying you aren't honorable?" I ask.

He tilts his head. "I'm saying that when my circumstances changed, my allegiance shifted."

"I'm glad you joined us," Rafe says. "Your training and guidance was invaluable in getting us through some difficult months."

I bob my head. "Well, I'm happy to see you both feel better. Have you eaten anything yet?"

Rafe nods. "Soup and crackers. Juice. It was nice of you to have WPN bring us supplies."

I want to growl at him and say I told you so, but I don't. "My brother did that. I asked for aid with no way of knowing whether it was coming. It's called faith."

"Interesting concept," Rafe says. "Maybe it's one I'll come to understand in the coming months. Thank him for me, please."

I nod. "Since you're both doing so well, I'll head back to work on preparing more doses."

"I'm glad you saved your aunt," Rafe says. "I hear she's been instrumental in administering this."

"She has." Am I imagining things, or does Rafe look guilty? "Do you know what the charges against her were?"

Rafe's brows draw together. "Wasn't it assaulting the Unmarked when she went to ask them about the suppressant?"

I watch his face for any sign that he might have been involved. "Yes, that was one of them."

"There was more than one?" Rafe asks.

"The other charge was that my aunt, who has devoted her life to trying to fix her brother's mistake, after a decade of making and ensuring delivery of the hormone suppressants to the Marked, suddenly decided it was time for all of you to die. Someone forged her confession stating that she substituted the pills she made for the last few years with sugar pills. And we know they were actually substituted for pre-natal vitamins, which is quite odd. Of all things." I shake my head. "Why would she be stupid enough to use pills that don't even resemble the ones she made? And if she was, why would she confess to the wrong kind of pill? Or ask you about the pills everyone was taking when the suppressant failed, if she made them herself?"

Rafe frowns. "Why would she?"

"Why indeed." I step toward Rafe, my eyes locked on his. "It made me wonder, since I knew she would never have done any of that. I knew she'd been working on a cure to Tercera for years. I thought, who else might have swapped the suppressant? It wasn't David Solomon, because he would have confessed proudly. No, he only planned the Cleansing because of the failure, not the other way around."

Rafe shoves back in his chair. "What are you saying, Ruby? We may not always have gotten along, but you've always been straight forward, which I appreciated."

My blood boils. I'm glad Rafe's fine, but he needs to know it's in spite of his stupidity, not because of it. "Fine. You want me to be clear? Did you get sick of waiting for someone to help your people? Were you tired of watching all your friends lose faith and go off the suppressant voluntarily? Maybe your girlfriend went off of it. Maybe she died and you freaked out. I don't know what precipitated it, but I think you swapped the suppressant yourself, because you were sick of waiting and you're a gambling man. With a timeline, maybe the Marked would finally be a priority."

Rafe's eyes flash. "I would never gamble with the lives of my people. Never." He sits back, his mouth open. "But—"

I glance to the right at Todd who's holding a gun on Rafe.

"What's going on?" I ask.

"They weren't really my people, were they?" Todd asks. "All of you kids could live indefinitely. A miserable existence it's true, but you had time. An adult who contracts Tercera doesn't have years and years to wait on a cure. And no one cares about the fate of one single person, especially if he's a former WPN guard. But an entire community of children dying imminently? That would attract attention. Giving you all a timeline that matched mine was my only play."

"You're cured now," I say. "Put the gun down."

Todd shakes his head. "I'm cured, but now that you know I did it, every single death in this entire city will be laid at my feet. Thousands if not tens of thousands. No one will acknowledge that the cure only got found when I applied pressure. No one will thank me, which they should. No, I think I'll kill you two and take my chances."

Bam, something crashes to the floor and clatters against it.

We all turn toward the doorway where the sound originated. Sean stands, both hands on a black firearm, his nostrils flaring, and he pulls the trigger. Inside the hospital, the report from the gunshot reverberates loudly. I cover my ears a moment too late.

Todd drops his gun and stumbles back while a red circle blooms on his chest. "What?" Blood dribbles from the corner of his mouth. He falls back, and lands on the chair, his hands on his chest. His breath is ragged.

Sean says, "Pam sent me back up with some food. She thought you'd be ready for it, Rafe. I reached the doorway, and heard Todd threatening you."

"You did the right thing," Rafe says.

"I can call Aunt Anne," I say. "She might be able to stop the bleeding and maybe even repair the damage."

Rafe shakes his head. "We will do nothing for him. He's right. Every death in Baton Rouge is on his head, and when he realized I'd connect the dots to the truth, he was ready to kill all of us to keep his secret." Rafe walks around the table and stares Todd in the face. "I hope there really is a miserable burning rock somewhere in the afterlife, so you can go where you belong. Tell my dad and Ruby's we don't say hello."

Todd's eyes close.

Rafe walks to the doorway where Sean dropped the plastic tray and picks a sandwich up off the ground. He takes a bite. "You can go back to work, Ruby. You don't need to worry about me. We're all healing as well as we can."

I nod and walk through the door, but when I reach the lab, I send a nurse to make sure Rafe isn't suffering from shock. I want to tell Sam what happened, but he's out hunting for Marked people we've missed. I settle for doing as much as I can to distract myself. I'm flying through the preparation of doses and helping direct triage for the patients Adam's men locate when the door swings open with a bang so loud that we all jump.

Sam's carrying a prone figure, and Uncle Dan enters behind him holding something small. I take a few steps toward them before I recognize the woman he's carrying, her blonde hair dirty and stringy.

Libby. Which means Uncle Dan must be clutching baby Rose.

A single tear escapes and slides down my cheek. "Is she?"

Sam shakes his head. "I can't find a pulse." He lays her down on a cot. "They were in a house alone and no one realized they were there. Not enough volunteers to find everyone. I only found her because I heard the baby."

Aunt Anne rushes to Libby's side and presses a stethoscope to her chest to search for a heartbeat. After a moment, she turns away.

Sobs wrack my body, and I slump onto my chair. We risked everything. Wesley died. We convinced the Unmarked and freed my aunt and still, so many people are dying. We can't save them all, and every new death is like a dagger to my soul. If there is a God, he's not very good at his job. I ball my hands into fists, anger replacing sorrow, my nails digging into the flesh of my hands. The pain helps me withstand my guilt, but I stop when I hear it.

A tiny mew, barely recognizable.

Baby Rose. I leap to my feet and cross the room. I peer down at her tiny, unmarked face. Her hand shifts, and her eyes open. If baby Rose can survive this, maybe God hasn't totally forsaken us. "Someone find a bottle."

One of the nurses darts out the door, and a few minutes later he returns with a bottle. Little Rose latches on with zeal and I sit down to feed her, her fuzzy head nestled in the crook of my arm.

Milk sprays her face as she greedily sucks, and I coo. "Not so fast. We're here now, and you'll never be alone again. Ruby's got you, and I'll take care of you forever, I promise."

CHAPTER 20

S even long days later, the Unmarked send a dozen truckloads of supplies. I guess they were waiting to see whether we survived long enough to need them. I wish I could go back and order that airstrike, but I guess done is done.

Adrien Kang is the Unmarked delegate who's directing disbursal of the supplies. He looks up from checking numbers on his clipboard, his black hair blowing down flat against his head in the wind. "How many Marked children have been treated?"

"What's the final count?" I shiver as a gust cuts through my coat.

A bone weary Dr. Flores stands in attendance so that the Unmarked will take note that WPN provided personnel and supplies far before they did. She looks down at her paperwork and purses her lips. "We dosed sixty-two thousand, four hundred and nineteen people during the thirty-six hours following Samuel Roth and Ruby Solomon's arrival. Another fourteen thousand, one hundred and four were dosed in the next twenty-four hours."

"And how many have survived the week?" Aunt Anne asks.

Dr. Flores glances down again. "Seventy-one thousand, eight hundred and twelve."

I sit down and close my eyes, my mind choking on the number that wasn't listed. That of those we lost. Sam places his hands on my shoulders. So many died that we could have saved, if only we'd known the location of the hacker virus sooner. Every time I think about it, I see Libby's face while she's holding tiny Rose, squeezing her tightly swaddled form with a smile on her lips.

Rafe clears his throat. "We have more Marked people to treat, but thanks to WPN's support we are well on our way to a protocol. By our estimates, all individuals infected with Tercera should be cured within the next thirty days." He grins at his brother. "They provided the miracle we had given up on."

Adrien smiles and I can't help stare at his big, shiny white teeth. "We're glad to hear that our expedited pardon and release of Anne Orien, as well as our willingness to free you all from further questioning allowed this phenomenal success. I've brought a list of supplies we have here, and Interim Chancellor Quinn has provided a checklist of items we are able to provide upon your request, Mister, uh, Rafe, is that right?"

Rafe lifts one eyebrow. "Raphael Roth. Rafe to my friends."

Adrien's eyes widen. "Roth? As in—"

"My brother," Sam says, "and John Roth's youngest son, yes."

Adrien says, "That is a strange coincidence indeed. I also have a proposal from the Unmarked CentiCouncil

offering a plan of integration for all of you into our settlements. A few of you originated in an Unmarked community, and some of our citizens are hopeful that they might
find and reunite with lost relatives. We have had a pattern
of cooperation over the years."

"If you call chucking meds at us from over the river
cooperation. Now that we're healed you're hopeful, but
before you wrote us off as a lost cause." Rafe folds his arms
and glares.

This isn't super helpful. I decide to throw Adrien a
bone. "I'll show you to a place you can stay the night, Mr.
Kang. Once you've gotten settled, you can come back and
review the lists with Raphael."

Adrien bobs his head in agreement, but pauses. "May I
have a moment to speak with you first, Sam?"

"I'll walk with you and Ruby," Sam says. "You can say
anything you have to say to me in front of her, I assure
you."

Adrien frowns, but follows us when we start walking
down North Boulevard. Once we've made it more than a
dozen yards away from everyone else, he says, "You met
Interim Chancellor Quinn briefly in Nashville last week."

Sam nods. "Ruby did. I, unfortunately, have known him
for years."

"He plans to attempt to take over the leadership of the
Unmarked now that your father's gone."

Sam shrugs. "I don't know him very well. I know my
dad disliked his ambition and the moves he made to take
control of the Unmarked, but my dad's disapproval isn't
really a mark against him, is it?"

Adrien glances my way.

"I don't mind if you two talk without me, Sam," I say.
"You can show him to his room, and I'll go check on Aunt
Anne."

"It's fine." He glares at Adrien. "Please continue."

"When Quinn announced I'd be bringing the supplies to you, more than a dozen members of the CentiCouncil approached me. They don't trust Interim Chancellor Quinn, and they worry his ties to your father. . . Well, they'd rather not have a repeat of the same problems as before."

Sam stops walking and turns to face Adrien directly. "I am John Roth's son." He lifts one eyebrow. "Are you suggesting these Council members want me to replace my father because Counselor Quinn has *closer* ties to him than I do?"

Adrien stumbles backward. Sam's full attention will do that to you. He swallows and says, "Yes, they did suggest I talk to you about replacing Interim Chancellor in a permanent capacity. I think you'd find the support you need to be voted in. The Council trusts you, in large part due to your heroic actions, your tremendous success here, and the safety it brought to our world. Beyond that, they also appreciated your honesty and bravery at the recent hearing. And of course you're hugely popular with the people because of your wins at the Games and well—"

I suppress a giggle. Adrien doesn't want to say it, but everyone loves Sam's gorgeous face. I can't blame them.

Sam closes his eyes and shakes his head. He opens them again and says, "How could they possibly want to replace my dad with his son?"

"The son who hates politics, you mean?" Adrien smiles. "The son who swept every event at the games for several years, becoming an Unmarked icon? The son who deposed his own father and then risked his life to cure a hundred thousand Marked kids because it was the right thing to do? Is that the son you mean?"

Sam rolls his eyes. "For precisely all of those reasons,

that son has zero interest in being involved in anything relating to the governance of the CentiCouncil."

"We need a strong leader to help integrate the Marked, who, coincidentally are led by your brother." Adrien looks at Sam purposefully.

I giggle and Adrien looks at me. "You're the queen of World Peace Now, and we've heard that you're Samuel Roth's . . . girlfriend?"

Sam's face looks pained for some reason.

"Uh yes," I say. "Technically, both those things are true. Although, to be perfectly honest, I've talked to my brother Adam. I'm going to transition my rule to him and he's going to dissolve the monarchy slowly. Once they know the truth about David Solomon, I think the people will understand and support our reasons for transitioning WPN to a democracy."

I stop myself from telling this delegate of the Unmarked every single thought in my head. "My point is that my control of WPN will be quite short-lived. If there was a word that meant the opposite of ambition, that would describe how I feel about ruling in Galveston."

Adrien shrugs. "Desire to rule and obligation based on circumstances aren't the same. You two have a lot to think about, but the vote for the new Chancellor happens in thirteen days. We can nominate new candidates for the next eleven. Think about how much good you could do in that position, and how much harm the wrong person could inflict."

I force a smile. "We will definitely think about it."

By the time we're done showing Adrien around, I'm eager to get back to the blood center, which has become our home base. Aunt Anne hands Rose off to me the second I walk through the door.

"She's been crying for the past two hours." The bags

under Aunt Anne's eyes and the halo of fuzz around her head back up her claim.

"Come here, Rose. What's wrong?" The second I take her in my arms, she quiets. Her big blue eyes blink and she sighs and burbles.

"She's too young to have a preference for you already," Aunt Anne says. "It's ridiculous."

Sam leans over my shoulder and beams at Rose. "Yeah, ridiculously cute."

"If you've got her, I'm going to take a nap," Aunt Anne says.

I nod. "We've got her. Dr. Flores said she'll take care of the kids who are still on medication until six tonight, so you're fine. Go sleep."

Aunt Anne walks down the hall and ducks into my little room, pulling the door closed.

Sam swivels a chair around next to me, and once Rose finishes her bottle, he takes her and puts her up on his shoulder to pat her back. He's a whiz at burping babies, as it turns out.

"You've gotten pretty good at that," I say. "Impressive, for someone with hands like a ham hock."

"I love pork, so I'm taking that as a compliment." Sam coos when Rose burps loudly. "Good job tiny girl. Making me proud."

I laugh. "In my wildest dreams and fantasies, I never imagined you taking care of a baby."

"So you're saying you fantasize about me." Sam finishes burping Rose and hands her back to me. "We need to talk more about that later."

I'm surprised when he passes her back so soon. "You don't want to hold her any more?"

He kneels down in front of me. "It's not that I don't want to hold her. It's that I do."

"Huh?"

"This is not how or when I meant to do this," Sam says, "because I know you're still really young. But I think you know I'll do anything and everything that you need me to do, no matter when it comes or what it is. If that means raising a baby with you, or ruling WPN, or leading the Unmarked, or completely abandoning all leadership and building a cabin in Wyoming, I'll do it. As long as you're doing it with me."

I realize Sam's not kneeling. He's kneeling down on one knee.

I gasp. "Uh, what are you saying right now?"

"It's what I'm asking. Ruby Carillon, er Solomon, or Behl, whether you're a scientist, a janitor, an adoptive mother or a queen, I love you. Every inch of you, every variation of you. Will you marry me and save us all the name confusion by changing your last name to Roth?"

I swallow. "Uh."

"Or I'll change mine if you prefer," he says. "But you'd have to pick one. Either way. Or since it's a brave new world, maybe we should make up a name. Your dads didn't seem to mind doing that."

I lean forward and kiss him lightly, making sure not to squish little Rose in the process. "Sam, I would love to marry you, but we're both suuuuuper young."

"If I'm going to help with Rose, it'll be way easier if we're living together, and I think. . ."

The door from the back room opens and Aunt Anne walks in, hands on her hips. "Sam I love you, but that's a horrible reason to propose. You don't need to worry about the baby. Ruby may not know this, but I always wanted a house full of children. There were complications when I had the twins, and I couldn't have any more. I should've called David Solomon and told him I had his daughter when Don died, but I couldn't give you up. You were my daughter from that very first minute, and now I feel the same way about little Rose, even if she cries more with me right now. Let me raise her, and then you don't need to feel such pressure. You're young. *Be* young."

"And in love," Sam says. "I don't care if we're not engaged, as long as we're still in love."

I kiss his nose, and then his lips. "I most definitely love you, you big goofball." I lean down by his ear. "And if my aunt hadn't intervened," I whisper, "I would've said yes, in case it comes up again in, I don't know, maybe a year."

A knock at the front door startles Rose and she starts to cry.

"Here, let me try," Aunt Anne says. "I couldn't really take a nap anyway. Too much running through my brain."

Sam crosses the room and opens the door. It may be the first time anyone's knocked. Frank stands at the door, official guard uniform on, hair covered by a stupid looking grey hat with a little black brim.

I stand up. "What are you doing here? I thought you went back with Adam two days ago."

Frank bows, and straightens. "Your Royal Highness is correct. I did return with him, but he sent me back with a message." He reaches his hand into the inside of his uniform, pulls a white envelope out, and extends it to me.

I sigh and take it.

Dearest sister,

I hate to bother you, as I'm sure you're quite busy setting things right in Baton Rouge. However, it's my duty to inform you that disturbing rumors have arrived regarding our beloved first cousin in New Orleans. He isn't pleased the Marked are healed, and means to block any attempt we make at integrating them here in Galveston or other port cities.

I will do my best, but I feel your presence could eliminate the need for violent conflict. The people like you even more than they liked our father, if that's possible. Please let Frank know what you plan to do, and whether you'll be returning any time soon. If you do not plan to return, please direct Josephine and I so that we can carry out your wishes to the best of our abilities.

Yours truly,

Adam

I hand the letter to Sam. He scans it and meets my eye. "Well sunshine, we cured Tercera. That's what we set out to do, but like I told you before, humans were the real problem all along. At least life around you won't ever be boring."

"I could use a little boring, honestly," I say.

Sam grins. "Maybe someday. But for tomorrow, what's the plan?"

I don't have one yet, but together we'll figure it out. Sawyer Blevins might have scared little Ruby Behl, but now I know the truth. I've accepted parts of what I learned and overcome the rest. He doesn't scare me, not anymore.

"Tomorrow's the memorial for Wesley, but after that I think Rafe, Uncle Dan and Aunt Anne can manage without us for a few days."

I grab a piece of paper and scribble a message for Frank to take to Adam.

Don't worry about Sawyer Blevins, big brother. I'll see you in two days. I'll head that way to help you clean up this latest mess, and then we need to talk transition. Cuz I'm done with people calling me Your Highness.

Love, Ruby

Sam pulls me into his arms and kisses me until my toes curl and my heart sprouts wings and flies. When he finally lets me go, he whispers against my mouth. "You'll always be my queen."

I roll my eyes. "That's the only title I ever wanted in the

first place." I lean my head against Sam's chest. "How do you feel about taking a little trip down to the beach?"

Sam groans. "Do I have a choice?"

"Not really. Now that we've fixed our parents' mistakes, mostly, we'll just have to make sure we don't make too many of our own."

Sam pulls me close and I realize, no matter what comes, we've got this.

THE END

* * *

IF YOU ENJOYED the Sins of Our Ancestors series and want more, don't worry! I just finished a new book, Already Gone. It's YA romantic suspense. You can read a preview of the first chapter next.

Please sign up for my newsletter! I'll send you bonus content, updates on upcoming releases, and promotions from my friends.
Visit: www.BridgetEBakerwrites.com to sign up!

Finally, if you enjoyed reading *Redeemed* (or Marked, or Suppressed!), please, please, please leave me a review on Amazon!!!! It makes a tremendous difference when you do. Thanks in advance!

CHAPTER 21

Lacy

Time's a fickle trickster.

If I'd been born a few weeks earlier, I'm pretty sure it wouldn't have happened. If my vivacious little sister had been born a few weeks later, it might not have taken place. If Mason had shown up just one day after he did, it probably could've been avoided. If the principal had waited a few minutes that day, well, I don't know. Sometimes I think if I could've scraped together a handful of leftover seconds, we could've saved her.

She might still be alive.

* * *

It's Hope's fault that I'm here, but I can't focus on that, not right now.

I'm supposed to sign in when I arrive at the shrink's office. The little white sheet with blank spaces stares at me accusingly, like it knows what I've done. I want to sign in with a beautiful curly script, as if somehow that will make things better. I can't do it though, because there isn't a pen or pencil in sight. What kind of crappy, rundown office doesn't have a pen by the sign in sheet?

When I lean over to pull one out of my backpack, I unzip the front pocket too far. Pens and pencils scatter all over the faux-wood, scuffed laminate floors.

I want to swear, but I bite my tongue instead. Who knows what this secretary might tell the doctor? I really need him to write a positive evaluation for the court. Pens and pencils scattered all over the place, one shiny yellow number two pencil broke about a third of the way down. I stare at it dumbly, transfixed.

I broke it. Like I break everything.

The secretary walks around the counter to help me, and I notice she's wearing the exact same orthopedic sandals as my grandma. I wish Granny could still work in an office, instead of just laying in bed in a nursing home.

"Oh dear," the secretary mutters. "I do this kind of thing all the time. Here, let me help."

My conscience kicks me when she crouches down and starts gathering my clumsily scattered pens and pencils. I don't deserve her help. I don't deserve anyone's help.

I lean over to pick them up myself. "It's your fault this happened. Who doesn't have a pen out for the sign in sheet?"

She straightens up and glares at me. "Excuse me for helping."

I sigh. I should be thanking her, not yelling at her. My hands shake as I gather up the rest of my writing utensils, but I can't force out an apology. It's a good thing my mom's not here. She'd be furious.

I pick up the broken pencil and scrawl my name on the

white sheet with it, scrunching my fingers to make the little nub work.

"I am sorry I didn't have a pen out." The secretary holds out a blue ink pen and when I reach for it, she smiles. I notice she has lipstick on her teeth. I tap meaningfully on my tooth with the pathetic shard of my yellow pencil while she's looking at me. She inhales quickly and rubs on her tooth. "Did I get it?"

I shake my head.

"I'll just duck into the bathroom for a second."

I raise my eyebrows at her leaving me here unsupervised but don't stop her. After all, I know I'm not really a lunatic.

While she's cleaning the lipstick off, I glance around. The larger, shattered end of my pencil lies on the floor alone. I ought to pick it up and stick it in my bag. With a little sharpening, it'll be fine.

I wish people could be repaired as easily as writing utensils. Resharpened when we get dull, a little pink cap slapped on our heads when our factory erasers run down. I could use a little sharpening, too. In their own way, humans are more fragile than a pencil, and when we break, you can't just sharpen the shards and keep on writing.

The desk plaque for the younger-than-Granny secretary reads: Melinda. There's a stack of office supply order forms in front of her and I think about checking a box for some new pens as a joke. When I lean over it, something beneath it catches my eye. It pokes out from under the order forms, and I can barely make out the font at first. When I tilt my head, I realize it's a rèsumè, Melinda Brackenridge's résumé. I know why I want to escape this tiny office, since my butt was court-ordered to come in the first place, but why does she want to leave?

I hear the bathroom door and jump, straightening guiltily.

"How long have you worked for Dr. Brasher?" I ask to distract her from the guilty trembling of my hands.

"Oh, years and years now. First we were at a group practice, but they made him take a lot of patients he wasn't too happy with. He likes helping kids and teens. He started his own practice so he can do what he wants. You'll like him. Everyone does."

Somehow I doubt if he left a group practice to be a do-gooder. I bet he got fired or something and tells people he left to help kids. Sounds a lot better. "So he's what? A saintly shrink?"

Melinda's eyebrows draw together and her lips compress. "Dr. Brasher is the best child psychiatrist in the state."

"Then why do you want to leave him?"

Her jaw drops.

I point at the résumé.

Her face blanches. "I don't want to leave, I swear. Please don't say anything. He's such a good guy, and an amazing doctor."

I raise my eyebrows.

"I haven't had a pay raise in years and my son, well, I need a raise." She gulps.

If she meant to say that out loud, I'll eat my broken pencil, but I kind of like her more now. "Family should always come first."

She nods.

Family is complicated.

If it weren't for my little sister Hope, I doubt I'd be in this fusty old office, waiting on a shrink whose evaluation will determine whether I'm capable of being released into the world as an adult. And yet, the thought doesn't make me nearly as angry as it would have last week. I don't think I realized how much time I wasted being angry with Hope.

So many seconds thrown away. I wish I could gather them up and hug them close. I wish I realized then that you can't hug people forever.

Melinda snags the clipboard and reads my name. Or she tries to, I think. So much for making a good first impression. "Angelique Vincent?"

I clear my throat. "Umm, I should be on the schedule. Lacy Shelton? I have a three-thirty appointment."

She squints at the tiny words on her paperwork. "Shelton. Yes, there you are. Let me see if he's ready." She ducks through the doorway that I assume leads to Dr. Brasher. When she opens the paneled wooden door again, she waves me over.

Melinda looks frazzled and guilty when I walk past, which is one emotion I recognize easily. It's obvious she doesn't want to quit, and I'm guessing she can't bring herself to ask for more money either. I wish I could help, but I don't have time to worry about her problems. Mine are about to slap me between the eyes.

For a moment Dr. Brasher meets my eyes silently. I stare right back. He's a tall man to be wearing that particular sweater vest. Before he sits down, I notice it isn't quite long enough. His hairy belly isn't something I particularly wanted to see, but I imagine he spends all day staring at people he'd rather not. I guess we all do junk we don't want to.

He looks down at a file sitting on his desk, and I follow his gaze to a photo of me and Hope, both of us smiling on a blanket on the beach. It's torn down the middle, and taped back together. I know who taped it. And I know she's gone now, never to return. Like a pencil in a wood chipper, irreparably damaged.

All my fault.

I gulp and sit down on the hard wooden chair across from Dr. Brasher's desk. My eyes veer away from the photo and right into a pink notebook. Hope wouldn't use a black and white speckled composition book, no. She made mom buy her a special English journal, with sparkly bling and a splashing dolphin. Sometimes she acted like she was nine years old.

My heart stutters. Why does Dr. Brasher have Hope's stuff? Did the judge send it here? My fingers itch to reach for it, but nothing I do seems to go right, so I force my hands into fists at my side.

This has to go right.

"Ah, I see you've caught me," Dr. Brasher says. "I was just studying up on your case, a little last minute maybe."

I start to speak, but I can't quite get words past the frog lodged in my throat. I cough to clear it and then force myself to croak a few words. "Why do you have Hope's journal and that photo?"

"Please," he says. "Sit down."

I do, but I can't help another pointed glance at the journal.

"Does it bother you that I have it?"

I stomp down on the surge of emotion. I just have to survive the next hour. "No, I'm just curious."

"I see in the file that you're only eleven months older than her. Irish twins, as it were."

I've explained this so many times, the words fall out without thought. "Since I was born in early fall and she came along the very next year at summer's end, we started kindergarten the same year."

"That's awfully close in age. Did you mind having a sister when you were little? Were you ever jealous of her?"

I don't snort at him, or tell him to look at the photo. I

don't tell him that everyone was jealous of Hope. I don't tell him she ruined my life. I don't tell him I hated her sometimes. And I don't bother telling him I loved her, too. I loved her enough to keep giving and giving when all she did was take take take.

"Even if I was jealous, that's normal, right?" I ask. "Textbook, even. Half the kids in America are jealous of their new baby brother or sister."

He holds up the photo, one side of it flopping forward along the scotch tape fault line. "She looks a little different than you do."

Thank you Doctor Obvious. My brown curly hair looks nothing like Hope's long, blonde locks. Our eyes are the same shape, but different colors. My pale, lightly freckled arms and legs inspire vampire jokes galore. Her limbs are tanned and muscular from swimming. My angular face and bony body look even more gaunt when compared to her perfect curves.

I guess it's safe to say Hope didn't steal my looks, but she's taken most everything else I've wanted over the years, sometimes without even trying. When we were babies, she snatched pacifiers I wasn't ready to give up, my favorite stuffed animals, my snacks, and even my cutest clothing. As we grew, so too did the list in my head of stolen goods. I kept track of them all.

Not that I plan to confess that in an interrogation ordered by a judge.

"You're right. Only our face shapes look the same."

"Can you describe your relationship?"

I glance at the clock. "We've only got an hour, right?"

He smiles. "We have as long as you need, Angelica."

I shudder. "Don't call me that. My name is Lacy, okay?"

He makes a note on his yellow pad. It doesn't inspire confidence that he needs to write down my name, like he knows he won't remember it otherwise. Or maybe wanting to use a nickname tells him something about my brain. What does it tell him? I want to stand up and demand that he tell me. I want to know what's going to happen. I want to take everything back. Instead I clench my fists and try to school my face into a façade of calm.

I can't survive much more of this mock serenity. My head will explode. "For today we only have an hour, right?"

He nods. "I have another patient scheduled after you, but you can come back tomorrow and the next day, for as long as we need. We may be seeing each other a lot for the next few weeks."

My heart rate spikes. Weeks? I don't have that much time. Why would this take that long? I always finish tests in the first fifteen minutes. I write five page papers in half an hour. Why would it take that long to be evaluated?

Then it dawns on me. "Shrinks are all paid by the hour, right? So the more time it takes for you, the more money you make. Got to pay for that Porsche for the wife somehow, am I right?"

He shakes his head. "My wife drives a Subaru, and she paid for that herself. Would it interest you to know that psychiatrists are actually the worst paid doctors in America?"

I shrug. I don't really care much one way or another, but that might explain Melinda's dilemma.

"Speaking of," I say, and then stop. She asked me not to say anything, but maybe Dr. Brasher could do something about it. He might want to do something. It's not like I promised her I'd keep quiet. Things that can be fixed should be fixed. Before it's too late.

"Did you have something to tell me, Lacy?"

I look down at my feet and then back up to meet his eyes. "Do you like your secretary, Melinda?"

He raises just one eyebrow. "How is that related to psychiatrists being poorly paid?"

"I'll explain, but I need to know. Are you happy with her work?"

"Of course I am. I've been working with her for years. She's my secretary and also my office manager. She keeps things running."

"I get that you're not well paid, but she needs more money. She's got a son who's, well, I don't know exactly what his deal is, but if you don't give her that raise you can't afford, you might be looking for a new office manager."

Melinda's face had bleached white when we spoke earlier, but Dr. Brasher's doesn't grow pale. His cheeks flush crimson.

"Look, if it helps, you can write down that we spent as many hours as you want. I won't say a word." Happy shrink, better eval, right?

Dr. Brasher splutters. "I would never falsify my hours. And how could you know that Melinda needs money?"

I shrug. "I notice things." At least, now I do. "You only get one shot to get things right sometimes." Familiar tears well up in the back of my throat, my eyes misting. I take a big, ragged breath to head them off. "But whatever. You're the one with the fancy degrees, so I'm sure you know better than I do."

He steeples his hands in front of him and studies me. "Now you've gone all teenager on me, but you don't need to. I have an MD, yes, but I still appreciate insightful advice from any quadrant. Your file says you're in line to be Valedictorian, and I can see why. I feel as though I should set the record straight. For court-ordered evaluations, I'm paid on a flat fee basis."

Great, and my suggestion that he pad his bill makes me

look like an idiotic teenager at best, a chronic liar at worst. Another spastic misstep. Heat floods my chest and spreads up to my cheeks. "That sucks for you, but it means you want to wrap this up as fast as you can, right? I'm on board with that."

"It takes as long as it takes," he practically growls. This could definitely be going better. He breathes in and out a few times before saying, "How did you feel about your little sister when you were growing up?"

"I loved her, of course. Everyone loves Hope. I'm pretty sure it's involuntary, like pupil dilation, or breathing."

Dr. Brasher scoffs. "Pupil dilation?"

I shrug. "I got tired of being the smart one sometimes, okay? It sucks, being the plain one, the boring one, but it's not like I could do much about it. If I bleached my hair and tried to swim or something, I'd have looked like a pathetic wannabe, a disappointing, washed-out clone. So I focused on my strengths and just tried to love her for hers."

"Did you ever like the same guys?"

My hands start to sweat. I didn't expect him to have her journal. I have no idea what it says in there. I don't like unknowns in mathematics, and I despise them in real life.

"Hope was on homecoming court, okay? She's swim team captain, so she meets a lot of jocks. The kind of guy who likes her is usually good looking, funny, smart, athletic, or popular."

Basically, anyone who's breathing.

"And what about you, Lacy? What kinds of guys like you?"

"Up until this year, the closest I got to having a guy's undivided attention was when I read Hemingway or Chaucer."

"What changed this year?" He steeples his hands again.

It's starting to annoy me. "I bet you've already read all about it."

"I don't know your side of things," Dr. Brasher says. "That's why you're here."

"If I walk you through what happened and you write your report, then we'll be done, right?"

He nods.

"Where should I start?"

"Where do you think it all started to go wrong?"

He already knows what happened and he's got Hope's journal, so he's probably figured out that it's all my fault. Things went about as wrong as they could have gone. Fights. Missed school. Police. Drugs. Juvie. Possible expulsion. And the one bad thing no one ever seems to want to talk about.

I can barely breathe and I look away. Sniff and wipe my eyes.

She died.

The rest of the stuff doesn't even matter compared to that.

But looking back on all that mess, in the cluster my life has become, no one's asked for my side of the story. Not the judge, not a single teacher, not my best friend Drew, no one. It's like they're all afraid of the answer.

And maybe they should be.

It all started the day I met Mason. Is it ironic that the first truly great day of my life was probably also the very thing that set in motion the events leading up to the worst? Or does life always work like that? Mom lost Dad right after Hope was born. Maybe bad always nips at good's heels like a moronic, overeager puppy, shredding everything and peeing in the corner.

Dr. Brasher still stares at me expectantly and I realize I haven't spoken a word. "I guess it all started with Mason."

Dr. Brasher rifles through a pile of papers on his desk and then he looks back up at me. "Mason Montcellier?"

I nod my head, impressed when he pronounces the difficult last name correctly. "Yep."

"Why don't you tell me about him."

I bite my lip. I don't want to talk about Mason. It hurts. Not crippling pain, like when I think about her, but thinking about Mason hurts in a different way. Plus, I honestly don't even know how I feel anymore. I cared for Mason more than I thought possible, and now I have no idea how to feel about him. Do I love him? Do I blame him? Do I feel anything at all?

I clear my throat. "It was your typical story, I guess. Outrageously attractive boy meets nerdy girl. It was the 'happily ever after part' where things started to break down."

* * *

IF YOU ENJOYED THIS SAMPLE, please check out the full book here.

ACKNOWLEDGMENTS

My husband has been my most stalwart supporter for thirteen years. I'm working on final edits now, in Costa Rica, on our no kids vacation and he hasn't complained once. Thank you for always believing in me, even on days when I don't believe in myself.

Thank you Eli and Dora for your words of encouragement, your enthusiasm and your understanding.

Thanks Shauna and Esther, and Donna and all my other writing friends. Your support means more than you can possibly know.

Thanks to Peter, the best editor in the world. Without him Ruby would have been a little less transformed. Without his help, these blurbs would have been horrible. Beyond horrible, really.

And thanks to my mother, whose excitement and support knows no bounds. I always assumed all mothers were this good, but really, I've discovered my mom surpasses them all. Thank you Mom, now and forever.

ABOUT THE AUTHOR

Bridget loves her husband (every day) and all five of her kids (most days). She's a lawyer, but does as little legal work as possible. She has a yappy dog, backyard chickens, and a fish. She makes cookies too often, and believes they should be their own food group. To keep from blowing up like a puffer fish, she kick boxes every day. So if you don't like her books, her kids, or her cookies, maybe don't tell her in person.

43369162R00201

Made in the USA
Middletown, DE
23 April 2019